THE KING'S DAUGHTER

STEPHANIE CHURCHILL

September, 2017

ISBN-13:978-1548306007
ISBN-10:1548306002

*For my mother
(who has two daughters),*

*And my sister
(who is one of them).*

SOMEWHERE ON THE EASTERN COAST OF PANIA

IT SEEMS ODD THAT I would notice the birds. Of all the things my eyes could have focused on, it was the birds circling lazily overhead, as if the pattern of their flight was more significant than the knife at my throat, that caught my attention.

"Your miserable life isn't worth my spit," the man hissed toward Casmir. "But your woman here..." He licked his lips and tightened his hold around my waist.

I felt a rush of horror sweep over me, fearing what would happen next. Casmir lay face-first on the ground, heaving for air, blood and spit mingling then dripping in viscous streams to the grass. He could do nothing for me. Another savage kick connected with his stomach and he curled into himself. I screamed out and strained against the arm holding me.

The kick didn't have the desired effect. After a moment Casmir drew from a well deep within himself and pushed up onto all fours, slowly standing fully, making his way toward me. My captor sniffed and spun me, pushing me backwards, still holding the knife and grinning wickedly. I staggered backwards but caught myself, fighting for purchase on the crumbling edge of the cliff's face. I dared not break my eyes from the man with the knife, so I heard rather than saw pebbles and debris skitter over the edge behind me. Casmir stood at my side, took my hand in his. We would face our fate together.

"Alas, there is no time for sport, as much as I would have loved to make you watch."

The man with the knife sneered as he advanced forward a step, and his partner raised a sword, hefting it menacingly.

Death comes to us all, it is true, but for many death is seen coming from far off. They are ready when it arrives, have prepared themselves for the flight into the unknown. I never imagined that I would die this way, and I never saw it coming. Murdered at the hands of those we should have trusted.

But I get ahead of myself.

To continue my story from this point would be careless. Grievously careless. More background is required to truly understand the horror of our position.

~1~

BUTCHER'S ROW
IMPERIAL CITY OF CORIUM
EMPIRE OF MERCORIA

2 years earlier...

"WATCH OUT!!!"

The cry came just ahead of a torrent of offal-infused waste water tossed without care or concern over the top of a haphazard fence separating the butcher's yard and the street I walked. I leapt to my right, over a congealed puddle of mud and pig's intestines, only just avoiding a drenching by the foul addition to the already malodorous slop that ran down the middle of the street.

I had previously sworn never to come down Butcher's Row, but today I had much to do and was in a hurry to get my daily provision of bread. The road through the slaughter market was a shortcut. I cursed myself for my inattention as I brushed a thumbnail-sized piece of unidentifiable refuse from my newly washed skirt.

It was the first full day without my sister, and the first

day in my life I found myself utterly and completely alone in the city of my birth.

"The old forge is abandoned," she'd reminded me just two days ago as she made the final preparations for her journey. "I'll do the work and be home before you know it."

I thought her plan foolhardy, but she disagreed. Though we were sisters, two different creatures one would be loath to find. How could two people be born of the same parents yet view the world from such vastly different perspectives? I reminded her that our father left on a journey three years ago and failed to return. My heart thudded in my chest at the clear memory and wondered if she heard it.

The disappearance of our father had been hard on us both, coming only a handful of years after our mother died. I felt abandoned in those early days. Waves of darkness came over me first at night, and then when I couldn't control it any longer, during my days as well. I sat for many hours alone, staring at the walls of our home. Kassia chose to deal with her anger in different ways. She turned to the markets, and to thieving.

"Are you to do the same to me now?"

"Irisa, I am not our father," she huffed, securing the straps of the pack she would carry.

Her definite pronouncement reflected her determined spirit, independent and strong. With it, she had kept us fed these last three years. But it was her determination that propelled her to think ahead, to make a plan for our futures now that we had no father to do it for us.

Silent as a lump she had called Issak, the man she'd recently agreed to marry in order to free us from the constant worry over the rent owed our landlord Sveine, or Swine as Kassia referred to him. Originally intending to offer herself in marriage to Seva, Issak's father, she had returned home, somehow pledged to Seva's son instead. I'd met Issak once before upon a visit to his father's smithy. He was a tranquil young man with piercing eyes and corn-straw colored hair, and I couldn't comprehend the hardship Kassia anticipated in spending a lifetime warming Issak's bed.

"Here is rent money for that sack of donkey poo," Kassia said bitterly, giving me a handful of coins to pay our piggish landlord. "Once you pay him you should be fine. Just don't forget to pay him, Irisa. You know he threatened to whore us if you don't get him that money. Either that or he'll just send the soldiers to throw us both into the Black Tower."

"Kassia, I'll be fine," I assured her pleasantly, though my insides felt far from pleasant.

She ignored me. "I portioned this rent out from the gold coins."

Her tone suggested that I had already forgotten our recent good fortune and the reason she had made up her mind to spurn her recent betrothal to Issak. That good fortune had revealed itself as a strange customer come to hire Kassia. Though the man's personality had been as captivating as a mud brick, his payment more than made up for it. With his coin we could afford to pay our rent for a lifetime. Kassia however, had her sights set on something bigger, and she no longer had use for Issak. She wanted us to leave Corium, starting over somewhere new, and leaving behind the memories of our parents and our formerly happy days. Breaking faith with Issak was wrong, I told her, but her desire to be rid of this city of phantoms prevailed. Now she was bound for an abandoned mining camp tucked into the foothills of the Sidera Mountains outside Heywood, three days journey from Corium, to work on her new commission.

"The rest of it is tucked safely away. Get what you need to meet your needs, but don't take any more than that," she warned, eyeing me severely as if she suspected that the instant her back was turned I would take the small fortune and spend it all on provisions for those less fortunate than us.

But she was wrong. I wouldn't use it all. Just some of it.

"I've got plans for us when I return, and we'll need every ducat," she added with emphasis, knowing full-well my train of thought. "Assuming I find the last items I need in the market today, I'll leave at first light in the morning." A wicked smile dimpled her cheek, and as an afterthought she added, "See if you can learn a thing or two about sheep while I'm gone."

And with that, she headed for the market. I stared after her in mild confusion before returning to my day's work, though my focus continued to be interrupted by the imagined sounds of bleating sheep.

Now as I made my way out of Butcher's Row, I thought of my sister, wondered how her journey progressed, worried about her safe return, and wondered again how she thought we would ever care for sheep.

From Butcher's Row I turned onto Baker's Street and sought out Sigmus the Baker's shop. Kassia and I bought our bread here when we had money. Other times Sigmus would send his daughter Tess with a bag of unsold leftovers, to help him "clear the shelves" he'd tell us.

I greeted Sigmus then selected a nicely browned loaf. His daughter Tess scampered through, and I tousled her curls before turning to peer toward the doorway with the arrival of an acrid scent of smoke. The other customers did likewise.

"I wonder who it is this time," Sigmus mused concernedly, raising an eyebrow as he did his best to peer over the heads of the busy shoppers congesting the path just beyond his stall.

"This time? Is this a common occurrence on Baker Street?"

"Two last week alone. The poor miserables." He shook his head in resigned understanding. "All our ovens have been working to capacity since the Emperor started importing foreign wheat, the harvest being as miserly as it was last year. We can't keep up. It was only a matter of time before a spark took hold, and now it seems to happen frequently."

I paid then thanked him, making my way down the street toward the chaos, unable to resist going to see for myself what had happened.

Finding no trouble on Baker Street itself, I turned the corner near where Seva the Smith and his son Issak lived. It was there I saw it: remnants of their smithy now a blackened ruin, with only the stone built foundations left intact.

All dead... I heard people say. Soldiers came early this morning, set fire... no way out...

I pushed through the crowds to get a better look. Two imperial guards stood out front of the ruins, making eye contact with as many individuals in the passing crowd as they could, as if they looked for someone specific.

I surged to my right to avoid the soldiers, flustered by the intensity of their scrutiny, and bumped into the back of a milk maid carrying full pails of milk on a shoulder yoke. The tip of her yoke came up just under the kerchief covering my hair as I backed away, flipping it off my head and freeing my bound tresses. I grabbed at my kerchief, but not before one of the soldiers called out: "Hoy there, little maid! I bet you know how to make a man feel like royalty..."

His voice was edged with so much lusty confidence that my steps faltered, and I turned to look at him. He stood with his thumbs tucked into his sword belt, a vulgar smile spreading his lips thin as he leered at me.

"I'd ride into the night with that one," his friend laughed.

My face blazed bright red, and I spun, shoving my way through the oblivious crowd.

"Adonia, come back!" they called after me. "Let us worship you here rather than at your temple! You'd save us the trip!"

When I finally made it back home, I barred the door, pushing up a chair behind it as a bolster. Long into the night, I sat near the meager fire in our crumbling hearth, staring at the flames as Kassia often did when something bothered her. A stiff wind blew off the Bay of Bos, sending continual shudders through the derelict boards of our home. With each creak of the door hinges, I jumped, remembering both the work of the soldiers on that smoke-filled street and their brazen lewdness, imagining them coming for me next. That night I dreamed of smoke and fire.

The man was ugly. No delicate or flowery words, not even a string of poetic verses skillfully woven by the finest bard in all of Mercoria, could convince me otherwise. His carriage and attire, elegant and dignified, marked him as a nobleman rather than a thug; even so, the affect of his homely visage wasn't diminished. I smiled politely while consciously avoiding the instinctive flinch that threatened when I saw him standing just outside my door.

"Irisa Monastero," he began, not even bothering to introduce himself. "You will come with me."

With a twitch of his mustache, he looked hurriedly over his right shoulder and down the long, dark alley toward the main road. I followed his gaze. He was alone and clearly anxious about something. I turned back to study his face, not easily forgotten once seen. Our strange customer, the one with the sun pendant. He had the look of a troll, I decided.

"If you are here for my sister, she's away to work on your project. I expect that she'll be back soon," I offered, hoping the information would satisfy him and he'd go away.

He wasn't satisfied. Instead, he grabbed me by the upper arm, turned me and muscled me inside, closing the door behind him.

"Irisa, we have to go. Now." He spoke with an air of authority tinged with familiarity, as if he was my uncle and we had known each other all our lives.

But he wasn't, and we hadn't.

"I can't... You can't..." I began, but he ignored me.

When I made no move, he pushed past me. "Are these your father's things?" he asked, pointing at the table where my father used to work, the table which still held his parchments, quills, and ink pot.

"Yes, why?"

"I wish we had more time..." he muttered to himself. "That son and heir of a mongrel," he rumbled. I wasn't sure if he meant my father or someone else.

"Why are you here?" I asked.

But he continued to ignore me. Instead he began picking things up at random, stuffing them into a satchel. Satisfied that he'd retrieved enough, he whirled on me, thrusting the satchel into my arms.

"We go. Now. There isn't much time before they get here."

"Would it be impolite of me to ask where it is you think we're going?" I dropped the satchel at my feet with a thump and crossed my arms, doing my best to mimic the same sickly sweet tone and sassy attitude that Kassia used all the time when someone tried to make her do something she didn't want to.

He picked it up again and thrust it back into my arms. "There is no time to explain. It is enough for you to know that your life is in danger, and we must leave at once."

I had no reason to trust this man. I knew nothing of him except that he had paid Kassia a ridiculous sum of money to perform a task for which she wasn't qualified. Inferring from that knowledge he was likely mad. Yet despite the risk involved in going with a man I did not know, there was something about his demeanor, the conviction in his voice, which made his story seem unequivocally true.

When I still didn't move, he grabbed my arms again. With a shake of frustration, he rumbled, "Do you know Seva the Smith?"

"What?"

His unkempt eyebrows rolled toward the bridge of his nose into an unbroken line as he scowled in irritation. "Seva the Smith... do you know him?"

"Yes, of course," I replied uneasily.

"Finding Seva has led them to you, here. They are on their way now, and I only just managed to arrive ahead of them. If they find you... if they find me..." He paled and took a deep breath. "Unless you want to be here when they arrive, come with me now." Without another word, he spun and strode through the door and into the alley.

The leering faces, the lewd comments, Seva and Issak dead. My mother dead. My father disappeared. My sister gone. Taking a fleeting look back at my home, I clutched the satchel tightly to my breast and followed the stranger into the watery light of morning, trusting my fate into his hands.

We didn't get far before they came. In fact, we didn't even make it out of the alley.

"Irisa, here!" my new minder cried, pushing my head down as we dove behind a smelly pile of trash not more than a stone's throw from my door and crouched there, deep in shadow.

Three guardsmen wearing the livery of Emperor Ciasan stopped outside my door. One of them knocked heavily, and, when no one responded, kicked the door in.

In that moment my minder grabbed my hand and dragged me away in the opposite direction. I could hear the ransacking of my home as we dodged unidentifiable piles of refuse. But because of the stout profile of my rescuer, we didn't get far; soon a soldier called out after us. We had been spotted.

Knowing the city better than the man who tried to lead me, I pulled him from behind, directing him into an even tighter alley and then in through a door I knew would be unlocked. I closed it behind us just as the sound of running feet turned the corner to follow us. They kept going, and we both leaned against the darkened timbers of the abandoned hovel, our breaths ragged, our chests heaving.

Once my heart slowed to a less laborious pace, I sagged down onto a crate by the wall.

"Might I be so bold as to ask your name?" I whispered. "If we are to face danger together, it is more efficient to call you by a name rather than refer to you in the general sense."

I could see the man's face from the light that filtered in through the widely spaced slats of the door. He appraised me sidelong for a moment but did not crack the slightest smile. "Figor," he offered miserly, as if parting with the fragment of a family heirloom.

"Figor." I considered the name. "Who are you?"

He fingered the sun pendant hanging from a finely wrought chain over his robes. "I am adviser to King Bellek of Agrius."

"I don't know who that is," I admitted. "Why did you come for me?"

"I meant to retrieve both you and Kassia," he scowled. "Where is she?"

"Kassia?" He nodded at my question. "She went to Heywood to work on the project you hired her for."

He took in the news and turned, pacing into the darkness of the dingy room and back.

"This is not good. Complicates things."

"What does? Why?"

"Her disappearance. I never expected it. I didn't expect her to do the work, to be honest. I just needed a reasonable way to give you the money, to make initial contact without raising suspicion."

"We would have been happy to take a simple donation," I quipped with a smile. He didn't appear amused. He paced again, lost in concentration.

"First I need to get you away, and then I can worry about finding your sister. She can't return home."

"No, I suppose not," I agreed, thinking that there wouldn't be anything left to return to. "What does Ciasan want with me and Kassia?"

"Nothing."

I scrunched up my nose and considered his sun pendant, remembering that he'd said he was an adviser of King Bellek of Agrius. "So why does Bellek of Agrius want us?"

"He doesn't. He doesn't even know you exist."

"So what then? Figor, you're making this a challenge," I snapped.

"I am a friend of your father's," he stated finally, as if admitting the fact pained him.

"My father!?!" I shrieked, then quickly brought my hand up to cover my mouth. We both froze, fearing that someone might have overheard.

He offered a deep scowl at my breach. "We should move along. They may come back this way, and we need to get out of here."

He pushed the door open, peeked outside, and when he decided it was clear, nodded toward me to follow him. We crept away silently, continuing away from my home in the opposite direction from which we'd come.

My heart pounded, and my head pulsed in time with it, with each step I took. I couldn't form a single question in my mind. In fact, I couldn't think at all. If my mind had been the wheel at a riverside mill, someone had thrown a log into it, clogging the mechanism.

We pushed our way into the heart of the nearby market, and Figor breathed a sigh of relief, for there were no soldiers, and the early morning market was in full swing. We could blend into the crowd and make our way to wherever it was he planned to take me.

I pulled up next to him and grabbed his arm. "Is my father still alive?" He looked down at me but said nothing. "Figor," I started again, feeling my frustration rise. "Is my father alive?"

I'd said it too loudly. Several heads turned to search out the source of the outburst. Figor stopped abruptly and leaned in toward me. "This is not the place to discuss it." He looked around to see if anyone still watched us. "I'm taking you somewhere you'll be safe." He straightened and brushed off his robes. "We aren't safe here," he added, indicating the busy market.

Steadily we climbed out of the poorer district of Corium and into the wealthier suburbs. We passed along several more streets then turned off the road, entering a yard through a small gate. An immaculate townhouse nestling back from the street rose like an elegant sentinel over a small garden. We made our way to the door, Figor knocked, and we waited.

And waited. Awkwardly, or so it seemed to me.

"Your landlord is named Sveine, yes?" His words broke the silence like a tangible force. He didn't look at me when he asked, stared instead at the wood grain of the door.

A bee buzzed curiously near my ear, and I resisted the urge to swat at it. "Sveine of Vlandre he is called. Why?"

"Because I need to consider all my options," he replied cryptically.

I wanted to ask more about this, but just then the thick wooden door opened to reveal a middle-aged woman who, upon recognizing Figor, ushered us inside, closing the door quickly behind us. Bright sunlight spilled into the room through the thick glass panes of the front window, revealing bolts of fabric, lengths of ribbon, and other costly goods piled neatly about the room.

I took all of it in with a single breath.

"As promised, this is Irisa," Figor said to the woman who stood smiling before us. "Irisa," Figor said to me, "you will stay here until I return for you. The next leg of your journey requires a bit more... arranging..."

"The next leg of my journey... Figor, where..." I started, but Figor cut me off.

"Irisa, I want to explain it all to you, but it will have to wait. For now, trust me. You will be safe here. These people are friends. It's complicated, and I have many things to work out. You won't be safe here long, and I need to find Kassia. When Rolbert, the master of this house, returns home, he will get you out of Corium." He eyed the woman over my shoulder, and she must have assured him with a look, for Figor relaxed a little.

Before I could pepper him with more questions he wouldn't answer, another knock sounded on the door. The woman opened the door to a young man who looked to be a young clerk.

"Bergen, what is it?" Figor asked him. What I could see of his face behind his thick brows and unkempt beard wrinkled with concern.

The boy crossed to Figor and whispered something. The color drained from Figor's face as he listened. In a moment he recovered then bowed to the woman, saying, "I am being asked after. I must return to Casmir," and turned to leave with the young man.

Apparently I uttered a small cry, for Figor turned back to me again. His face softened of the pinched concern he had just shown. Taking my hands, he looked deeply into my eyes then said gently, "Irisa, you are safe. Wait for my return. I will find Kassia."

"But I don't even know where I am, and you never explained about my father. Figor..." I stuttered as he turned and exited, leaving me alone with my new minder.

Strong, warm hands came to rest gently on my shoulders. "Come, let's find you something restorative to drink."

I lacked the will to contradict my new minder so allowed her to lead me into a hall just off the vestibule. She sat me down in a soft chair, and while even more opulent than the first room, this time I didn't even bother to examine my surroundings. In a moment she pressed a cup into my hands, and without knowing what I did, I took a sip of a warm liquid, allowing it to slide down my throat. It did make me feel better. She pulled another chair closer so that our knees touched when she sat.

"Now then," she began, leaning low so I would look up to meet her eyes. "We have not been properly introduced. My name is Miarka."

~*2*~

"*GO ON, DAUGHTER, TOUCH it.*"

My father released my hand and gave me a gentle nudge toward the table laden with bolts of fabric. I stood staring, wide-eyed yet unmoving, my arms hanging heavily at my sides. I glanced up at my father and he smiled down on me, encouraging with the warmth of his expression. I looked back at the fabric then up at the merchant who looked on, his face a neutral canvas of indifference.

"*My daughter, it will not bite. I promise.*"

I continued to stand unmoving, until I shook my head slowly from side to side. I did not want to touch the fabric for fear that it would melt away like a delicate wafer on the tongue. My father sighed and picked up my hand. We moved on.

Kassia was ill again, as she often had been this year. Common childhood illnesses caught most children at some point, but Kassia had been unusually unlucky and seemed to contract them all. She was particularly bad just now, and mother stayed near her continually to nurse her along with her friend Jeah. Though they never said it when they thought I could overhear, I knew that both my mother and father worried for her survival. In order to escape the confining walls of our small home, my father thought it best to get me away. He brought me here, to the market, to teach me what no book could teach, he'd said.

The lesson of the fabric, even if I would not touch it, accomplished one thing: as time moved on, seeing that shining bolt of fabric had created a longing in me for better things, things that my parents could not provide, things that our impoverished state would never allow. From that time on, I took in what I could of the lords and ladies, their hair, their clothing, their carriage. I memorized it all, internalized it. Though I was invisible to them, I saw them, and I remembered.

Cool like a pool of sparkling water, gentle like the whisper of a meadow's breeze, as light as the gossamer of a spider's web... Silk. I had never touched it before, and it was delicious. Closing my eyes, I allowed myself the brief luxury of pretending to be draped in it from head to toe as it fell over my frame with lithesome ease. No good would come from such a lapse, I reminded myself. I sighed sadly then placed the sample back on the table. It was a lovely dream, though one I would never realize. Not someone as poor as I was. I shook the dark thoughts from my mind.

Regardless of the mysteries of my future, I would take each day with my usual practicality and level-headedness, finding equilibrium amidst the chaos any way possible. My thoughts turned again to Kassia, and I wondered where she was now, hoped she would do the same.

"The color suits you." I turned at the words, and Miarka crossed the room, a smile on her round face.

I felt caught out. "I'm sorry for disappearing... my lady..." I began uncertainly. I didn't know what to call her, and using her proper name seemed too familiar. "When you left me to go speak to your cook, I felt restless, came back out here to...."

She made a clicking sound with her tongue then waved

her hand as if it was nothing. "I told you to make yourself at home. You have done no wrong." She stepped to the table beside me. "And please, call me Miarka."

Her warmth and kindness melted any remaining unease I felt at being found here.

"It complements your milky white skin." She brushed her palm over the blue silk I had just examined. "And your hair..." She lifted a strand that had escaped the confines of my kerchief. She let the strand cascade off her palm slowly, and it caught in a beam of sunlight as gleaming, spun-gold. "We will make your first gown of this, I think. For now..." She paused as if considering. "I have no daughters, but one of my old gowns will do."

She led me upstairs to rummage through a storage chest. Finding what she was after, she pulled out a folded bundle, saying "This will be more suitable for you, for now at least." Shaking out the folds, she spread a moss green kirtle across the back of a chest before helping me undress.

"My husband is away right now, in Agrius of all places, can you believe it?" She winked as she said this, as though I should understand a deeper meaning behind the words. I didn't. "Trade has been busy there, despite everything, though he should be home soon."

I gave her a look, though she seemed to misunderstand it. "Apologies, my dear. How insensitive of me to bring it up."

Once she'd snugged tight the laces with a final flourish, she spun me around to face her. "Perfect!" She clapped her hands together in acclaim.

"Now for your hair. It's been many a long year since I've seen its like."

At her mention of it, I reached up and touched the sides of the kerchief covering my hair, an instinctive habit I'd formed over time as a way to reassure myself that no one would see it.

"Irisa, please? Let me?" Gently, as if wooing a skittish foal, Miarka removed the linen scrap and freed my locks. Her eyes widened in revelation. "You are Adonia herself!" she gasped.

Adonia was the goddess of desire, and the comparison troubled me, for it was this very resemblance which compelled me to downplay my features as much as possible. My parents had always encouraged me to do so, explaining that I would be safer that way. The leering guards outside Seva's ruined smithy had proved the wisdom of their concern. It was for this reason I found what others might call a benefit to be more troublesome than it was worth. With the kerchief in place, the comparison to Adonia was less obvious.

"This resemblance makes you uncomfortable?" She arched a carefully manicured brow at me, and I nodded. "Irisa, I can understand why your father would have encouraged you to hide your beauty growing up. Men are not generally to be trusted around Adonia." She scowled at the thought. "That's why we have the temple."

Relieved that she understood my predicament but uncomfortable with her mention of Adonia and the temple, I exhaled a shaky breath. Satisfied, she sat me down, picked up a brush, and worked it through my tangled locks.

"Your father didn't have the means to protect you while you were growing up, so the kerchief was wise, but he does now. You needn't be ashamed of what the gods deemed fit to give you."

"What do you mean he does now? Miarka, is my father alive?" I twisted around on my stool to face her. "Figor never answered me, and I must know."

"Of course your father is alive! Good heavens, child, you

didn't know?" she clucked, as if my ignorance was absurd. I shook my head, too dumbstruck to speak. "Here, you look to be in need of more of this." She poured me another glass of wine, and I took the proffered cup, drinking greedily. "Figor sent me word late last night that you would arrive this morning. Why he wouldn't bother to inform you about your father I'll never know. Men," she huffed. "Now, what else has Figor neglected to tell you..." She tapped the palm of her hand with the wooden comb. "Come, let's go sit somewhere more comfortable and sort this out."

She lifted me from my stool and we moved across the room to a pair of elaborately carved chairs situated near the window. I clung to my cup as I would a lifeline, taking slow sips as I waited for the next hammer to fall.

"I don't know what is happening to me," I breathed shakily. "Figor just showed up this morning and made me come with him. Soldiers nearly caught us, but we got away."

Miarka's face paled. "Oh, my dear child!" she exclaimed. "I will clear everything up for you. So Figor never told you that my husband will take you and your sister to Caelnor Palace in Brekkell to meet up with your father?" Then she reconsidered. "No, he wouldn't have told you that since he didn't tell you your father was alive."

"Brekkell? Why ever would he do that?" I quavered.

"To wed you to Prince Isary, of course!"

She appeared genuinely surprised that I wouldn't have come to that conclusion on my own. I stared at her, my mouth agape in utter disbelief. The woman was mad. There was no other explanation for it. Everything that had happened so far was one giant mistake: Figor hiring Kassia, giving us the money, his arrival this morning to rescue me from soldiers... none of it real. How could it be? Figor was mad, and so was Miarka.

My eyes flicked about the room, seeking an escape. I had to leave this raving woman and find my own safety. Figor could go to *Myrkra* for all I cared.

"Oh dear," she muttered, seemingly oblivious to my internal war. As if attempting to clear up my confusion, she continued, "With you as wife, the prince will finance your father's rebid for the throne of Agrius."

I felt faint and must have looked about to be sick, for she grew pale with the dawning of realization.

"Oh dear, oh dear," she repeated softly, her eyes wide. "I have assumed too much." She brought her hand up to her throat. "Then you'll not be knowing that your father is Prince Bedic Sajen of Agrius," she ventured feebly, "the true heir to the throne?"

With that, I jumped up from my chair, allowing the cup to tumble from my hands, and ran from the room. Miarka followed at my heels as soon as she could react, but I had already made it downstairs, reaching a small chapel just beyond the hall rather than the front vestibule I had hoped to find before she caught up with me.

"Irisa, my dear," she gentled, taking my shoulders gently between her hands and turning me to face her.

The clear features of her face blurred as tears began to stream from my eyes. "It's not true, any of it! How could it be? How could my father be a king when he is only a scribe?" I wanted to sink to the floor, but Miarka supported me so that I would not fall.

"Irisa, my dear girl," she whispered, taking me into her arms, "but it is true. All of it. I'm so sorry for telling you like this. Had I known..."

I melted into her, letting my tears fall freely, my world shattered, my mind muddled, my relationships confused. In an instant, Miarka had turned everything I thought I knew on its head. Everything I thought I understood was wrong. Nothing was as it seemed and never would be again.

She held me there, smoothing my hair, allowing me to empty my eyes of every last tear before she lifted my chin to meet her compassionate gaze. "I think you need a lie down. Will you let me take you upstairs?"

I nodded, sniffling, and she handed me a strip of cloth to wipe my nose before leading me upstairs to a room of my own. Once she had gone, I sat down on the soft bed, clinging to the bed curtains as the only thing of substance left in the world.

I slept the next full day, disturbed only by Miarka's chamber maid bringing me food which I left untouched. Miarka peeked in on me a few times, but I ignored her, and she didn't seem bothered, content to let me sort my feelings and find my own peace.

The morning of the second day however, she knocked and came in to find me sitting near the window, staring out at the back garden.

"Why would he never have told me?" I asked without breaking my gaze from the view. "Such a secret to keep from us, he and mother both." I turned pleading eyes toward her, hoping she would cave in and tell me she had made it all up.

Miarka swept across the room and stopped just behind my shoulder. Reaching out her hand as if to touch me, she let it hover before finally resting it lightly on my arm. When I didn't flinch or recoil, she relaxed.

"I'm sure they thought you would be safer not knowing. It's hard to betray a secret you don't know."

I considered this and agreed that it was possible, even if

it didn't do much to ease the sting of it.

"Tell me everything. I need to know it all."

She sat next to me and told me everything: the identity of my mother and about her marriage to my father before Bellek came with Ildor Veris at the head of his army, to take the throne. Figor, the man who had brought me here, had been an adviser to my father but now served King Bellek and spied for my father. She blamed Bellek for the loss of their trade and the reason she and Rolbert had come to live in Corium.

"Bellek's son, Prince Casmir, is in Corium right now, meeting with Emperor Ciasan. It's why Figor is here, and the reason he contacted you." I thought she would choke when she said Prince Casmir. "But it's also why it's so dangerous for you. If you are caught..." She trailed off as if the end of her sentence was obvious.

And it was. If I was caught, I was a threat to Bellek's throne, as the heir of my father. This is why Figor had come for me — because he knew who I was and could get me to my father — and why Rolbert would take me to Elbra once Kassia came. With his daughters safe, our father could pursue his throne without fearing for us.

"He wants his daughters back, Irisa."

The shriek was mine, though I refused to be held responsible for it.

Even at such an early hour, the day threatened oppressive heat despite the breeze blowing off the Bay of Bos, for it did not penetrate the inner reaches of the house despite the wide-open shutters and breezy-wide corridors. According to Miarka, a storm blew far out at sea, explaining the unusually heavy rains over the last two weeks as well as the savage thunderstorms terrorizing livestock and children alike. Miarka worried constantly about Rolbert, daily watching the sky with wrinkled eyes.

This particular morning found me helping Miarka's maid Helena shell peas when a storm of another sort erupted inside the house.

"Ilex, get back here, you ungrateful lump!" came the shout from somewhere beyond the kitchen.

Helena gave me an uneasy glance then stood to investigate, upending the bowl of peas in her haste. I shooed her away with a promise to take care of the mess. I dropped the last handful of sweet green pods back into the bowl when the attack happened — a flurry of writhing, furious energy in the form of a nearly weightless ball of fluff. Ilex, I presumed.

"Ilex, you disgraceful lump of cotton, get off the Lady Irisa!"

Strong arms lifted the little dog, holding her aloft over the chaos, while the attack's cessation left me sitting askew on the floor, covered in white fur and pea pods. The writhing Ilex appeared unhappy with her new situation and showed it by repeatedly nipping at the hands of the stranger. He ignored the dog, plucking a piece of fluff off his jacket before offering to help me up.

"My lady, I apologize for this, truly."

I brushed away the remnants of detritus from my skirts and was about to reply when Miarka burst into the room, a look of dark fury hot on her face. The sight of my disheveled state erupted her: "Rolbert, get that thing out of my house this instant! I will not have the heir of Bedic Sajen assaulted in my own kitchen whilst under my protection!" She turned her fury on little Ilex, who for the first time stopped squirming.

"Oh!" I exclaimed, surprised and delighted at the fluffy

ball of cotton. "The poor thing! Look, she is scared to death of you!" I peeled the little dog out of Rolbert's arms and cuddled her close against me, making soft shushing noises. Miarka kept silent, for what could she do? I was both her guest and the heir of Bedic Sajen, the highest of accolades in her book.

Doing her best to conceal her disdain for the small creature in my arms, Miarka changed the subject. "Irisa, may I present my husband, Rolbert?"

Rolbert had conceded his prize into my arms, but rather than feeling sorry for his loss, his expression was triumphant. Ilex nuzzled her way into the crook of my arm and rested her head on my forearm, content in the security of my protection.

"My lady." Rolbert bent at the waist, dignified even as he winked at me.

"Where did you find this beast, and why is it in my house?" Miarka demanded of Rolbert.

"The poor little pup was all tangled in a bush of ilex. I could hardly leave her there now, could I? Alone and defenseless, to die a most grisly death?" Miarka appeared to want to dispute this notion, but for my sake she kept silent. "She was just outside Prille, near the docks. She traveled with us all the way home, and it's a good thing too! She brought us luck as we passed through that squall on the sea."

Rolbert seemed to be a good-natured type, light of temperament and big of heart. Charm effused from every part of him, and I liked him immediately.

"Let's let Helena finish up here while we get you changed. Rolbert, take that thing out of here," Miarka demanded.

Rolbert reached over to take Ilex out of my arms, but the little dog would have none of it, not even from the man who had been her savior.

"She's taken with you, my lady," Rolbert pronounced happily. "It appears as though the heir of Sajen has a ward." He laughed at his homegrown humor.

Miarka glared at the dog yet kept her mouth shut, taking my arm instead, and led me upstairs to change.

Later that night we sat around an overly abundant table, a welcome meal meant to celebrate Rolbert's return home. Rather than invite their sons as was their usual custom, Miarka had put them off, citing an illness. They wanted to keep my identity a secret.

"So my wife has filled you in on the dastardly truth of that scoundrel on Prille's throne then?" Rolbert speared a section of parsnip, popped it into his mouth, and chewed as he glowered at the image he'd conjured in his mind's eye.

I nodded, stating that she had, but before I could say more, Ilex perked up and dashed to the door, barking furiously. We had a visitor.

"I shall make an offering to the gods for your speedy recovery, Mama. It truly is a miracle." The newcomer leaned casually against the door frame, arms crossed and eyes narrowed with lancet focus. Miarka's son appeared clearly irked by the healthy condition of his mother. "I got word from Helry to join him for a meal because you had the plague. You seem to have recovered. It's a good thing Molle sent me over with this," he lifted a small bundle, "else I may not have heard about the miraculous goings on in this house."

His gaze shifted to me, his brows arching in a question until he noticed the little dog pawing at his lower leg.

"Jahn," Miarka began, pausing to consider how best to explain the situation. Ilex took matters into her control and barked up at Jahn. "Rolbert, would you take that beast away?"

Rolbert rose grudgingly, but Ilex would have none of it

and instead scampered around Jahn's feet, refusing to be caught.

"I'll get her," I offered, seeing an opportunity to make my escape, allowing the family time to sort their issues in private. Jahn remained where he was as I bent near him to retrieve my ball of fur, but instead of coming easily into my arms, Ilex flopped over onto her back, exposing her snowy white belly for a good rub.

Jahn crouched down next to me and reached out a hand to accommodate Ilex's wishes, his earlier look of displeasure replaced with a look I knew all too well, had seen on the faces of men all my life.

Miarka saw too and moved in to intervene. "Jahn, may I present Irisa?"

Her unadorned introduction made it blatantly obvious that she hid something, but Jahn let it go. He knew his mother too well. Instead he picked up Ilex whose agreeable submission smacked of contrivance, and we stood.

"Irisa, this is my youngest son, Jahn," Miarka added, completing the otherwise insufficient introduction.

Dusty-blond hair cut to enhance his narrow face and strong jaw swept back from eyes which only moments before revealed deep suspicion but now appeared light and dancing. I noticed that they were the same frost-blue color as my favorite silk from his mother's shop.

"Lady," he said, keeping his eyes fixed on my own as he bobbed his chin, a smile quirking at the side of his mouth. Without breaking his gaze from me, he asked his mother, "Mama, since when do you and father keep a lapdog?"

"Ilex is mine," I whispered.

"Then I should return him to you." He handed Ilex over to me, and as he did so, our hands brushed overlong.

"Bellek's spies have been busy these last few days," he

intoned, turning to his mother. "You wouldn't know anything about that, would you?" Jahn returned his gaze to me, and I lowered my eyes. "In fact, some of Ciasan's soldiers have been conscripted into the work. Some poor sot's smithy was burned to the ground only a few days ago. They have been visiting the homes of notable Agrians today asking questions."

"Indeed?" Miarka replied weakly.

"If you'll excuse me," I broke in, "I should let you catch up." No one seemed to notice, so I brushed past them and fled upstairs to my room.

As the night was still quite warm, I left the bed curtains and the window open. Leaning back against the frame and propping up a pillow at my back, I surveyed the scene just beyond the window. Bright points of starlight pricked through the deep velvet sky at intervals, suggesting the haphazard ways of the gods. It was said that the various shapes of the stars, if interpreted correctly, could give guidance about the future. I didn't believe it for a minute, but the idea intrigued me in the moment. My future was uncertain, but I knew I was not powerless to influence it.

I wasn't prone to nightmares like Kassia was. Many nights in our youth she would awaken me by her screams, shrieking from whatever terror held her in steel bands of cold dread. After our mother died, I alone comforted her until her tremors passed. This night the terrors were my own, but there was no one to comfort me.

In my dream, I toured Corium on the arm of Jahn, taking in the sights as a woman of position rather than a poor beggar child. We were met with well-wishes and nods of admiration for the lovely couple that we undoubtedly appeared... until Captain Ildor Veris found us. With a flick of his wrist he called the guards who immediately arrested us. They whisked us away to meet up with the evil Prince Casmir, the "brat of a boy" Miarka continually called him. In my dream he stood before me a reedy twelve-year-old, ordering me chained and gagged, thrown into a dungeon for all eternity. The sentence had just been handed down, and I cried out in anguish when Ilex awakened me with wet kisses.

It took me a long moment to focus my eyes on the solidity of my timbered bed and the crisp cotton curtains starched starkly white, of the bright morning announced by the cascade of sunlight streaming through the slit in the shutters I had closed the night before. Once my breathing calmed, I rose from the bed, somehow silently summoning Miarka's young chamber maid who helped me dress. Still somewhat shaken from the memories of my dream, I made my way downstairs, thinking of the danger I felt I'd brought on this family.

Miarka took note of my pallor, and I briefly explained my dreams and concerns regarding them. She clucked her tongue, muttering that matters were going horribly wrong. I assumed that she was referring to last night's scene with her son, but there was no time to ask her before she breezed out of the room.

Rain had passed over the city while we slept, and as a result the morning's air was much cooler, lighter. I stepped out into the brightness of the sunshine and made my way through the kitchen garden. The flagged path glistened, bees flit about from bloom to bloom with industrious effort. I closed my eyes, inhaling the sharp scent of rosemary.

"I would hear it from your own mouth." The voice pierced the peace that had only just begun to trickle over me, and I spun to locate the speaker. Jahn sat hunched on a turf bench just behind me, staring at the dirt, his chin resting in his hands. I stared at him blankly until finally he looked up and repeated himself. "I would hear it from your own mouth. That you are daughter of Bedic Sajen, that you are his heir."

"So your mother tells me," I replied quietly, hurt by his accusatory tone.

He stood and paced away from me, clearly agitated, and I wondered what impact the fact of my identity had on him, why it had brought him back to his mother's house so early this morning, and in such a state of agitation.

"You don't approve of the Sajens?"

He looked up at me and saw the threatened indignation and quickly clarified, "No, it's not what you think." He waved a hand in dismissal. "My parents have served your father faithfully ever since they fled here to Corium from their home in Lyseby, after they lost their trade with the coming of Bellek."

"Were they in the cloth trade there as well?"

His eyes reflected a queer light at the question, but I couldn't decipher it. Rather than answer, he changed the subject. "Who else knows you are here? Who else knows who you are?"

"Helena," I answered, then also listed the chamber maid. "Aside from that, no one else."

"Did you really not know who your father was prior to coming here?"

I nodded that this was so.

"How could it be? How could you be raised to womanhood and not know who you truly are?"

How indeed! Does any of us know who we truly are? He didn't seem inclined toward existential questions, so I bit my lip to hold back the sarcasm.

"My mother made a mistake in telling you," he

proclaimed. "She should have left that to Figor or to your father."

"But why? Don't you think I have a right to know?"

"You do, but it wasn't her place. Your father should have told you himself," he replied dourly. "I will make her promise never to do it again."

"Because she is regularly in the habit of harboring the children of long-lost heirs to usurped thrones?" I asked with a crooked grin, thinking it amusing under the circumstances. Under my breath, I added, "unless Figor does indeed bring my sister here."

"You have a sister?" Jahn's head whipped around at this revelation.

"Yes, Kassia, though I don't know where she is," I said sadly. "After Figor found us, she left Corium to visit a small mining town — Heywood — to complete the work he'd paid us to do. Figor is looking for her, though I think it is difficult for him."

"Yes, Figor must be careful. Casmir's spies have been active enough since you disappeared. He walks a difficult road, being planted in the Agrian court." His brows furrowed. "I know of Heywood. A group of Agrian exiles lives near there, and they might be of more use than Figor. If I could make contact with them, perhaps they might know of a way to get you to your father."

At that moment Ilex burst into the garden several paces ahead of Helena who strode just ahead of Rolbert.

"My lady," Rolbert cried, "you must come quickly! Now!" Neither Jahn or I moved. "Come!" he added frantically.

Jahn leapt to his feet and took me by the hand, pulling me toward the house. "What is it, father?"

"Ciasan's men. They are here to search the house. We

must get her inside."

Jahn all but picked me up in his haste. "Where can we hide her?"

"I'll show you. Just get to the buttery!"

We pushed through the house, and when we passed the door separating the hall from our passageway, I heard Miarka's placating voice. Though she bought us time, she couldn't hold them off for long. My heart leapt into my mouth, and I bit my tongue to contain my frantic fear.

We had only just slipped into the buttery when the sound of heavy footfall came from the passageway we'd just left.

"Jahn, help me lift the top of this barrel," Rolbert whispered hoarsely. Once the lid came off, they lifted out a separate interior casket filled with barley. This container only went half-way down the full size of the barrel. "Irisa, get in, girl. If they open the lid to check inside, they'll just see a barrel of barley." He winked at me.

I looked at the tiny space then back at Rolbert, wondering how I would fit. He urged me with his eyes, pleading that there was no time to argue. The two men lifted me up and over the side, and I hunched down as far as I could.

"It's a good deal you're such a petite little thing," one of them said, though I couldn't tell who, for they had already replaced the false top and lid, snuffing out all sound.

Utter darkness nestled all around me, and I blinked to clear dust from my eyes. The air felt stale with an overpowering scent of barley, and I wondered how I would breathe for long. No sooner had the question formed in my head than one of the men plucked out a cork from near the center iron ring. A single stream of light flooded in, bringing with it a wisp of fresh air.

"Stay silent and don't move," I heard a voice say, and then all fell quiet once more.

I forced myself to breathe slowly and deeply, disciplining my mind not to envision being caught. I didn't truly know what would happen if the soldiers found me, and it was best not to allow my imagination to run wild.

It didn't take long for my imagination to ignore my instructions.

Did they have orders to take me to Ciasan? Would Prince Casmir take me back to Agrius, or would he order my execution?

Breathe, Irisa. Think of Kassia.

I pictured her long auburn hair, unkempt and blowing in the wind, just as it did all those times we hunted for wild berries in the meadow beyond the city.

"I bet you know how to make a man feel like royalty..."

"I'd ride into the night with that one..."

The voices of the guards near Seva's burned out smithy echoed in my head, distracting me so much that the heavy footfall of someone entering the buttery rattled me. I inhaled a sharp breath and clenched my teeth.

The intruder lifted the lid of the barrel, and soon a hand reached down inside and began to sift through the contents. How long before knuckles scraped the bottom which should have been lower than it was? I dared not move, for even the slightest shifting of fabric could betray my existence.

"Kenon, where did you get to?" a far off voice called.

The hand stopped digging.

"Searching the buttery," he called back.

"Because you think she got thirsty? Get out here, you dullard!"

The lid dropped back into place, and steps retreated. I sank back as much as I could and exhaled my held breath, closing my eyes.

Later that night, Miarka, Rolbert, and I sat around the table in the great hall, picking at our food. No one spoke much, and I wondered if each of them wrestled with the thought constantly invading my mind: how long could I stay here undetected?

Several more uncomfortable weeks passed. While Jahn reported that Ciasan's soldiers still kept an eye out for me, no one returned to the house to search again. Slowly life settled into a new sort of normal. No word came from Figor, and Kassia did not appear at the door.

Miarka saw to it that a chest slowly filled with new clothing for me to take to Elbra, and she taught me what she could of court etiquette.

"You mustn't act as if you were raised in a back alley once you meet Prince Isary."

It was easy to develop a false sense that I was a daughter of Miarka and Rolbert, and that Figor would never return for me. The truth felt rhetorically insubstantial.

Until it didn't.

A brilliant blue sky arced overhead and songbirds perched on the spreading branches of an almond tree whose shade I enjoyed as I worked on small mending projects for Miarka. The day was too pristine, I decided, to waste indoors. I had just tied off a knot when the familiar form of a man navigated the path from the house toward me. I stood to greet him.

"Irisa, it's time to go."

It was Figor.

~*3*~

"*SHOULDN'T YOU CALL ME* Your Highness or something?"

Though it might have been wishful thinking, I thought I detected a slight falter in his steps after my uncharacteristically audacious question. After giving me a look of wry amusement, he recovered quickly then tightened his grip on the lead of the mare carrying my things and continued on as before. I smiled back even though I wasn't satisfied with the indifference my prodding had produced.

"Since I know who I am now, there is no sense in us pretending otherwise," I pressed as if he hadn't ignored me.

"I would have told you soon enough," he replied dryly.

I took a deep breath to hide my frustration then tilted my face upwards toward the sky. It was the first week of August, and the blue sky stretched unashamedly naked overhead, lacking even the simplest puff of cloud to give its expanse a single point of interest. The sun baked down relentlessly, heating the muck-infused puddles last night's rains had left behind.

"If I wasn't so hot, I would stop right here and force you to tell me everything," I glowered. "Everything." I narrowed my eyes at him. "Luckily for you, I just want to get to my new hideaway with the hope it's cooler than these streets."

The heavy air, unusual for Corium this time of year, made breathing difficult. "Thick like pea pottage," Miarka had called it that morning. "It will settle again as the day wears on, mark me! Then the rains will come," She tucked a renegade strand of my hair behind my ear before giving me a quick hug at my departure.

"I do have one piece of news for you," Figor acquiesced finally. "Something that should make all of this easier to bear. Your sister has been located."

I squealed then quickly clamped my hand over my mouth when several passersby eyed me curiously. "Jahn said he'd look for her!" I whispered feverishly. "Did he find her? Where is she? When can I see her?"

"She is... recovering from injuries."

The news hit me like a physical blow, sucking away the very life of me, leaving my emotions destitute. *I am not our father*, Kassia had promised.

Figor noticed and added quickly, "But she is fine, Irisa. She is being tended to, and very soon she can travel. I will bring her to you and then you will depart for Brekkell together."

I flicked a glance at him then looked away. I didn't want to focus on, couldn't concentrate on, the news I'd just learned. Instead I whispered, "Did Jahn find her? He promised he would."

"No," he replied tartly. "I found her." He held up his hand to forestall any more questions. "Jahn will collect Kassia when the time comes and will bring her to you."

"He did keep his promise to help..." I whispered, smiling to myself.

"Indeed," Figor hissed before muttering "meddler" under his breath.

Very soon we arrived at our destination, a nicely kept house on a notable street, though not nearly as affluent as Miarka's had been, and smaller. Before we approached the door, Figor pulled me aside.

"You must not let on about your identity while you are here. Your patron knows who you are, but not his wife or daughters."

"Why am I here, exactly? Why couldn't I stay with Miarka?" I had been safe enough since the time the soldiers searched the house, so I didn't see any reason not to proceed with Figor's original plan.

"Let's just say that I was encouraged to find you a different way to Elbra," he spat sourly.

His peevish tone surprised me, and I wondered who in Miarka's household had pushed him to it. Could Jahn have been more concerned about the threat to his parents my presence brought than he let on?

"Your father's informants are being closely watched, and this man has no connection to Agrius. I admit that he isn't my first choice, or my second or third for that matter, but it was the best I could do under the circumstances." This last part did little to reassure me. "To his credit, his business will enable him to get you and Kassia out of town. And because he is a bit... unscrupulous... it was easy enough to persuade him to do exactly as he was told." I cast him a questioning look, and he added, "One word to the magistrate's court liaison about his unorthodox ways..." I caught his meaning, though it didn't much assure me of my safety. We moved to the door. "I should also warn you that you won't be too happy with me after this."

He knocked on the door. A maid opened it and escorted us into the home's hall. Seated at a large table near the vast hearth sat Sveine of Vlandre.

Swine.

"This is your grand scheme to get me out of Corium? I'm to go with Swine, of all people?" I rasped in a harsh whisper as Swine made his way toward us, his repugnant yellow smile fixed firmly in place.

"I told you you wouldn't be happy," he whispered out of the side of his mouth.

"My lady," Swine said as he bent over to kiss my hand. My skin slithered where he touched it, but I kept my face composed and smiled banally at him, focusing my attention on the coolness of the flagstones at my feet and the wriggling dog in the crook of my right elbow. "You be welcome most in my home, as honored guest."

"Irisa, this is Sveine of Vlandre," Figor introduced, as if we'd never met. "He has agreed to take you to your next destination once your sister arrives."

"Figor man most persuasive," Swine added with a scowl.

"And Sveine knows that failure will be costly for him. Very costly," Figor growled in return.

Swine moved away to beckon a servant to fetch my things. Figor leaned toward me. "It shouldn't be long. Remember everything I told you."

And with that he left me.

Again.

My father was a scribe. I was a scribe's daughter. The certainty of this knowledge rested on all I had been told, all I had experienced in my nineteen years of life. Until Figor arrived that fateful afternoon, until Miarka broke the news that had devastated my perception of the world: I was not a scribe's daughter; I was a king's daughter.

As my mind wrestled anew with this twist, I lay in a cocoon of night's darkness, staring at one of the many rough, timbered beams of the long, low roof running from front to back of the home of my former landlord. The loft in which I, along with the rest of the family, slept was the uppermost story with two other levels containing the private, domestic rooms just below this, then the public rooms beneath at ground level.

Immediately after Figor left me with my landlord for safekeeping, Swine's wife Orsilla arrived home, a happenstance for which I was grateful at first. I hadn't welcomed the idea of whiling away the afternoon with that pig of a man. I would quickly come to find out however, that Orsilla's presence did not improve matters.

She was a tall woman, standing almost a head above her husband. Her sharp, pinched features put me in mind of a bird of prey, always watching, always waiting for the right moment to act out some primal act of carnage. Upon seeing me, Orsilla cast her husband an accusatory look, and he visibly wilted. Pulling her aside so their daughters would not overhear, he quietly explained the situation, and something shifted. Her bearing changed, and I could only hope that she reacted to the surfeit of coin Figor had paid them rather than because Swine had just told her who I was. Once again I found myself questioning Figor's wisdom in bringing me here.

"Come, my dear," Orsilla invited as she approached me with outstretched arms and a smile which thinned and stretched her lips from cheek to cheek. "Your things have been stashed above, and our house is your home as long as you have need." Swallowing my insecurity, I took her hand and accepted her offer of hospitality.

Swine went off to attend to his affairs, but Orsilla insisted that her daughters sit down with their new guest to become better acquainted. Each of them eyed the other but accepted their mother's command.

After a time of stilted conversation, Orsilla excused them. "Darya, Alla, to your duties," she instructed.

The girls stood, giving her a brisk curtsy. "Da, Maika," they said and disappeared.

Orsilla turned next to Kalyn and Miramne. "Master Pjer will be here soon for your lessons.

The youngest of her brood stood and curtsied as Darya and Alla had done. "Hvala vam, Maika," they replied before leaving me alone with Orsilla.

The robust afternoon was by now a feeble thing, frail and brittle and full of shadows that had crept from hiding to take up permanent residence in places of prominence. Like a mouse caught in a corner, frozen and transfixed by the baleful stare of a cat, I sat across from Orsilla as she appraised me. I resisted the urge to fidget.

"You are the daughter of a business associate, or so my husband tells me?" It was the story Figor and I had concocted before coming, and I nodded. "Your father must be in a dangerous trade, to bring you this far but not be able to take you farther?"

I shrugged and smiled blankly, giving away nothing and hoping she assumed I hadn't a clue about my so-called father's business. Either that or she assumed that I was as empty-headed as a barrel of whiskey on a Kavador trading cog, an assumption which suited me equally as well, for either of these would prevent her from pressing me too closely.

She must have assumed the latter. "My daughters," she began as she nodded in the direction they had all exited to attend to their duties, "are being taught figures and sums, reading and writing. Darya and Alla have gone off to help their father." I spotted a glint of pride in her eyes in her attempt to impress me. She had no reason to suspect the level of my own unusual education, but I wasn't about to let on about it.

She moved through several more banal pleasantries before our interview was finished. It was soon time for the evening meal, and I welcomed the respite, thankful that none of the daughters engaged me in conversation and that Swine appeared too caught up in his own affairs to pay me any mind.

Now as I lay on my borrowed bed, listening to the gentle sounds of slumber and cuddling Ilex close, I forced my mind to calm itself, to stop wondering how long I would have to pass time under this roof. Escaping to Elbra seemed far preferable to continuing under the scrutiny of the carrion bird Orsilla.

My mother would sometimes take Kassia and me outside Corium, to a place where a copse of trees secluded a gentle stream. Kassia and I spent delightful hours picking flowers while my mother sat on a blanket, distant, sad, and lost in her private world. I saw glimpses of this side of her at home, but it came out most actively in this peaceful place, as if it reminded her of something from her past, a past that she never spoke of. When the time came for us to return home, she'd gather our blooms in a basket. At home she filled every empty receptacle with fragrant and effusive color, bringing joy to her eyes even if only for a short time. Those were the memories of my mother I liked to keep closest to me, for in those memories her smile was like the first ray of sun after a storm.

Orsilla was not a woman to enjoy such pleasures. She ruled her house with an iron will, efficient and severe in all she did. Her daughters gave her obedience, but I saw little love warm their eyes. They certainly had no love for their father either, and they treated him with the same coldness as their mother. Between Swine and Orsilla as a couple, there seemed to be nothing more than the rudiments of transactional communication — business partners in practice, married couple in name. All of this left the house feeling gloomy, the company dismal.

Except for one person.

"So where did you get the dog?"

It was Kalyn, the second to youngest of Swine's herd. While his youngest daughter, Miramne had refused to pay me any attention as payback for my taking her bed, Kalyn had shown me an honest and sincere regard, being yet too young to have developed the haughty pride of her older sisters. I returned Kalyn's question with a warm smile, encouraging her friendliness. "A friend of my father's brought her back from a foreign land. She was his gift to me."

Kalyn's eyes widened. "Oh?" she wondered excitedly. "Which land?"

I hesitated then admitted the truth.

"Oh, Agrius! My mother is from Haern, a small island just off the coast. Her family still lives there, but I've never met them. I have cousins there. Do you have cousins? I wonder what it would be like to know them. Mother writes letters and keeps in touch with all her family constantly, but I have never met any of them."

"Your mother doesn't seem to like it here," I observed, curious to see how the girl would respond to my prompting.

She shrugged. "Mama inherited businesses from her father when she was young, but they were struggling. When Papa and Mama got married, they moved here to fix things, and

Papa took over the running of them. She hasn't been happy since." Kalyn continued to ruffle Ilex's soft fur while Ilex herself chewed on one of Darya's slippers. Kalyn quirked a satisfactory smile even while allowing the destruction.

Midday was as good as full, and Kalyn would soon have to join Miramne for lessons with Master Pjer. The rest of the girls were away, while Orsilla, as she did most days, busied herself by overseeing Swine tending to his affairs. The rest of the house was peaceful, and I closed my eyes to revel in the quiet. Thusly entranced, I felt rather than saw a shadow darken the tiny garden gate as Swine entered.

"Papa!" Kalyn squealed as she ran to her father, flinging her arms around him. He scooped her up, and she embraced his neck as he swung her in a circle. They whispered to one another, Kalyn's expression one of rapturous delight, and I fought back against the scene, not wanting to see Swine as a doting father but rather a slimy landlord and questionable businessman. It didn't match the Swine I knew, the piggish landlord who had nearly conscripted my little sister into becoming a whore as substitute for payment of rent.

The two chatted happily and cozily as they made their way up the narrow path toward the house. When Swine spied me, he stopped, and a smile of a different kind spread his lips. "No word come yet from Figor man?"

I shook my head. Kalyn watched on, oblivious of the undercurrents that surged between us. Swine stepped closer. "You can hope he come back else home of old will be returned. Same rules." The confident pig was back.

He looked like he had more to say, but just as he took a breath to speak, Kalyn wriggled from his grasp and dropped to the ground. Swine's eyes hooded over in so instinctive a way that I knew Orsilla had joined us outside. Kalyn wordlessly went in search of Master Pjer.

That night, late, after the household was asleep, I felt sorry for myself. A quiet peace lay draped over the house and the city like a well-used blanket, so I slipped out of bed, scooped up Ilex, and crept down to the kitchen garden in the yard behind the house.

The sky shone with millions of stars, though rather than the comfort of familiarity, the sight made me feel small. "Ilex," I began in a quiet whisper, afraid to disturb the calm, "what will become of me?" Ilex had no answer. I rubbed her ears between my thumb and forefinger and she forgave my rudeness in awakening her from her sleep. "Do you think I'll ever see father again? Or Kassia?" Kassia must see the same stars as me, I thought, and this did more to comfort me than anything else. It was a connection, even if an imagined one.

My sister and I were so unlike one other, but I felt responsible for her. Her reckless nature was surety that she needed constant looking after. Despite Figor's assurance that he would bring her here, I was less than settled about her. Figor played a deadly game of survival himself, with one foot in the viper's den and the other lodged in my father's court.

The stars felt more distant now, unreachable.

"Ilex, I feel lost. The world is changed now. I was raised the daughter of a scribe. But now?" I picked up the little dog under her front legs and raised her to look into her face. She stared back at me with liquid eyes full of innocent love. "Now I am the daughter of a king. How is one to come to terms with that?" Ilex sneezed. "The daughter of a king, Ilex. Bedic Sajen of Agrius..." The name tasted foreign on my tongue, no matter how many times I said it. Would I ever grow used to the idea?

"Sajen," I repeated again, tasting the sound of it. The crickets sang a night song and my words blended with their chorus. "You can keep my secret, can't you, Ilex? Of course you can, dear one."

Time passed and still there was no word from Figor or Kassia. Orsilla grew ever more anxious, casting me sideways glances when I wasn't looking. The oldest girls remained occupied with their own concerns, ignoring me in their usual way. Swine turned more and more fearful.

One morning over a simple breakfast of porridge, the arrival of a messenger from Haern broke the tedium. Orsilla took the missive and read it quickly, scanning the contents as a small, private smile curved the edges of her lips. Finished, she rose and excused herself, saying nothing.

Later that afternoon Swine came to find me.

"You pack. Tomorrow we leave."

When I plied him with questions about the timing, about why Figor hadn't come, about the method of travel, he didn't reply. I would have to wait to have my questions answered.

A new day dawned, hot, sticky, and unpleasant. A gusty wind blowing off the Bay of Bos brought the co-mingled scents of salt, fish, and seaweed — a refreshing change from the other more insidious odors of refuse and dung coming from the poorer districts farther up the bank away from the bay.

I looked out over the street below from a window just under the eaves. Servants strapped bundles of my belongings to a mare who would carry them from here to an awaiting ship bound for Brekkell, and to my father and a prince of Elbra.

The urgency of our departure surprised me. Other than the missive Orsilla received yesterday, no other messengers had arrived, and certainly not Figor himself. I scanned the scene on the street below but didn't see Kassia. If we were to leave soon, where was she? Telling myself to remain calm, I turned away to survey the room, looking for anything I might have missed in my hurry to pack. Spying a knot of twisted rope which had served as a chew toy for Ilex, I snatched it up then made my way downstairs.

Just as I entered the hall, Swine entered from the street. Dressed for travel, he wore a light gray robe of linen held tightly against his bulging midsection by a belt of braided cord. To protect his balding head from the intensity of the sun, he wore a felt cap that draped his pate like a limp lettuce leaf.

"Time to go and mounting on horse to do," he announced as he scanned the room, lost in thought and not really seeing me.

"Has Kassia arrived?" I ventured as a jolt of excitement raced through me.

"No sister. We go anyway. Too much time wasted."

"But why? Figor said we must wait..." I began.

"Messenger arrive. Now be time of going." Swine seemed irritated, distracted by matters.

"You mean you got a message from Figor? Why didn't you tell me?" I swallowed my exasperation, doing my best to remain calm.

"No messenger from Figor. Ship is ready and we go," he replied with an edge of irritation.

"But we can't leave without Kassia," I reminded him.

"Sister be at the docks," he returned, absent-mindedly. Immediately he turned and went back out to the street.

With no way to counter him, I smoothed out my skirts and followed him, turning back only to look over the room one last time. I wouldn't miss this house or any of its gloomy company, Orsilla in particular. At least if I had to travel to Brekkell with my porcine landlord, I wouldn't have to lay eyes again on his prey-eyed wife. She had been unusually absent that morning at breakfast and hadn't returned since. I was grateful, for it meant that I wouldn't have to offer awkward thanks for her begrudging generosities during my stay.

Plumes of smoke rose from cook fires burning in houses all along the quiet streets as we passed through the city. My eyes followed the plumes as they merged far overhead into a hazy white canopy that drifted inland and away from the coast, dissolving into blue where the jagged peaks of the Sidera Mountains pierced the sky.

Once past the Palace of Coria, we turned our horses down a narrow lane descending at a steep angle toward the Bay of Bos. As the shimmering water of the bay came into view, the reality of my situation hit: I was leaving Corium. Likely for good. Gripping the front of the saddle, I squeezed until my fingers blanched of color before forcing my chin up. I took a deep breath and calmed myself. I was on a path that could not be reversed. There was no sense fighting it.

We finally came to a stop along a long line of ships moored closely together, prows to dock, and a groom helped me dismount. Swine called out to the stevedores, and I wondered if Kassia was somewhere here waiting, though perhaps she was already aboard the ship.

As I watched the last of my belongings being unloaded from my mare, my eyes caught the familiar form of Orsilla pressing through the crowd. She stopped and stared at Swine as he worked through the meaning of seeing his wife where he didn't expect her. Startled gape turned to confusion, and his mouth opened to speak then closed again. All the while, light didn't touch Orsilla's eyes. She smiled, though the smile was as brittle as the edge of the morning's heat.

Just then, a man whom I'd never seen before stepped out of the crowd, moving to stand across from Orsilla. He was older, with closely cropped hair graying at the temples. His straight patrician nose descended in a straight line between sharp eyes focused like lancets on Swine. Bearing erect and meticulous in grooming, the man announced in every detail his high nobility. I pressed into the side of my mare, sensing that something had gone very, very wrong for Swine. How it would impact me I had yet to determine.

The man accepted a packet of papers from a clerk behind his shoulder and held it before Orsilla. Heavy parchment, tied and sealed in wax in the way of scribes, told me they were legal documents. He swiveled his head, and seeing me for the first time, nodded before returning his attention to Orsilla.

"Your cousin was most helpful, as you hoped he would be. Everything is in your name alone now, as we agreed — deeds, titles, transfer of ownership, etc."

Orsilla reached out with eager yet delicate fingers and carefully took the packet, holding it in front of her as a precious thing, placing one hand on top while stroking the seal lovingly.

"What be this about?" Swine interjected, blotches of red color rising on his cheeks.

"Your wife has requested my assistance with the return of what belongs to her. You won't be needing these any longer," the newcomer replied gently, as if he was a schoolmaster speaking to a slow-witted student.

"Of course I be needing papers and ownership! Ship to delivery make," he spewed as he glanced my way. The newcomer didn't follow his gaze. "Must care to take of daughters!"

"Care for your daughters, Sveine?" Orsilla pressed forward toward her husband. "You don't care for them the way you should. You took everything, leaving us with nothing! What good is your pitiful love when ownership of the business is more profitable? You will be out of the way now." Orsilla gripped her newly won prize, shaking the pile in front of Swine as a diabolical sneer spread her thin lips. "And precious Kalyn will never be influenced by you again."

She nodded and several armed men stepped forward. With shock I spied Figor amongst them. I willed him to make eye contact with me, but he would not. His eyes remained fixed on Swine, his face a chiseled stone statue.

I didn't have much use for Orsilla, but even this seemed extreme for her. Swine's face slackened as this last and perhaps most brutal revelation sank in: He would never see his most beloved daughter again. I looked away. That he loved the little girl was no surprise, but I didn't want to feel sorry for him. By the gods, he had earned his share of agony. That his surly wife was paymaster for that agony didn't even necessarily move me. Watching made it hard to escape the truth of his humanity, in the tragedy it forecast for little Kalyn, an innocent in that house of villains. For however misguided it was, she truly loved her father.

"How you pay?" Swine asked, his voice a mere squeak in the midst of the raucous noises of the bay side. It was obvious he already knew the answer, for as he spoke, he looked in my direction. Orsilla confirmed it with a nod.

A knife gutted my insides. Swine's problems had now become my own, for Figor's plan had obviously failed.

"We will talk about how Irisa Sajen came into your hands

at another time, but for now... gentlemen?" The armed men moved to grasp Swine by the arms, and as they did so, Figor made brief eye contact with me. It was a mere flicker, yet it communicated that he knew full well the difficulties we now both faced.

Without another word, Swine turned on his heel and went with the men willingly. Orsilla watched him go then turned toward me, arching a brow. There was no malice in her expression, only completion. It wasn't about me, she communicated by her look, only her daughters, only her right to rule her own roost in her own way. I was only an accessory to her scheme and of no consequence. She held my gaze for a moment, then clutching her new life to her breast, she walked away, the back of her receding into the brightness of the full morning.

Once she was gone, the newcomer turned his attention to me. "Allow me to introduce myself to you, Lady Irisa." His expression was neutral except for a slight quiver at the corner of his mouth. "My name is Ildor Veris."

He offered his arm upon his introduction, but I didn't take it. I froze instead.

"Ah, so you have heard of me," he added, a light smile touching his lips.

The Defiler of Prille, Miarka had called Bellek. Ildor Veris was his trained hound, the strategist behind the attack on Prille in the days of my father and grandfather. Now he held the reins of the Agrian king's military forces, meting out his version of justice however he saw fit, the king himself a mere puppet. Miarka called him brutal and single-minded, a tenacious man who would stop at nothing to achieve his ends. The tales she told of him only supported her claim.

And now he had me, a rival claimant to the throne he

served, in his power.

"Of course I have heard of you," I said, doing my best to keep my voice steady when in reality my hands shook with fear. I clasped my hands together under my cloak lest he see. "You had my grandfather killed."

"Yes," he replied, not bothering to deny it.

There were more armed men just behind him, and I knew I had no other option but to go with him. Figor had departed with Swine, so I couldn't even look to him for help, but if he had been concerned about my immediate safety, he would have stayed. In that moment I chose my course and took his arm, stepping in next to him. If he was surprised by my immediate acquiescence, he did not let on. With the gallantry of a trained courtier he turned me and we walked, following in the direction that Swine had taken.

Stevedores called out as they loaded and unloaded, birds screeched and wheeled overhead, men went about their business — yet in all the cacophony, the sound that stood out to me most was the thumping of Veris' heavy boots as each foot struck the wooden planks of the dock as we walked.

"Where are you taking me?"

"How much do you know about your family? About the Sajens?"

"Not much," I admitted. "Only what I learned from…" I bit my lower lip, realizing I had been about to give away Miarka's involvement. I had no idea what this man knew of my recent situation, but if Miarka's family was to be compromised, it wouldn't be by me. "…from a friend," I finished instead, hoping he wouldn't notice my hesitation.

He smiled as if I'd given him the best possible news. "If this friend of yours is a lifelong supporter of your family, it's likely that he or she left out some rather important details. It's time you learned more about your family." He paused mid-stride and looked at me, earnestly searching my eyes. "Perhaps this same friend is the one who deposited you with Sveine for safekeeping?" I may have paled but did my best to hold steady. His face softened. "Never mind. I will talk with him personally about that later. Irisa, I am taking you to the land of your father. We are setting sail for Agrius."

"But I was going to..." I began then stopped, horrified over what I'd been about to say.

"To see your father? In Brekkell?" I nodded, fearful, yet still relieved that I hadn't told him something he didn't already know. He patted my hand. "Irisa, there is no need to worry. I mean you no harm."

"How did you find me?"

"Sveine's wife was most helpful. When she learned your identity, she sent word to me..."

"How did she learn who I was? Did Swine... Sveine... tell her?" I asked him, unable to hide my alarm.

"She didn't say," he replied, a smile curving his lips to demonstrate his amusement. "She was not aware she was entertaining a royal guest initially, but when she put the pieces together she contacted her cousin, Taibel Rebane, in Haern. Rebane is a friend of mine, and both of them knew I would be interested, of course. In the end, this is the best possible scenario for everyone, you'll see."

He flashed me a smile, but rather than evil intent, I found only a warm regard, a simple delight that was somehow reassuring despite everything I had been told about him. He steadied me by the elbow as he assisted me aboard his vessel.

"How would sailing to Agrius rather than to my father be the best for me?" I asked him, confused by this man who was supposed to be a monster.

"You, Irisa Sajen, are the means by which we stop a war."

ANYONE WHO OBSERVED US for any length of time would not have guessed that Kassia and I were sisters. We were different both inside and out. To my bright blonde, her hair was deeply burnished copper. My features were open, and though quiet, I maintained a ready smile. Kassia's mien appeared perennially taciturn, her lips down-turned, her face closed. While I welcomed it not at all, I had been told often enough that I was beautiful and understood this. Kassia bristled at any suggestion that she was, despite the evidence of her beauty.

Kassia had kept us fed these last three years since my father disappeared. Each of us had come to rely on the other, and I missed her dearly. Therefore it was with dismay that I discovered Kassia was not on board the Árvök as Swine had said she would be. It had been a ruse, a lie uttered to cause Swine to act upon his instructions, forcing him to think he obeyed what he had been told to do precisely. And now I knew it had been Orsilla pulling the strings behind the scenes. Kassia was left behind in Corium, I would not be reunited with my father in Elbra, and Swine moldered away, locked in the hold of the ship. Assuming Swine didn't betray him, what could Figor possibly do for me now?

Everything seemed futile now as we rounded the jut of land making up the entrance into the Bay of Bos from the Mercor Ocean. Nothing had happened to make me think I was a prisoner in the strictest sense of the word. I had not been clapped in irons or locked into my stateroom. Freedom to roam the ship was mine. Even so, I remained wary.

I stood now on the upper deck as the ship's captain piloted the Árvök into deeper waters against the incoming tide. The bosun shouted commands at the crew which in turn responded with exacting precision, their movements honed through years of experience. We hugged the coastline as the ship navigated southward past the city of my birth, and as the outline of the city's many buildings faded into obscurity, I wondered if I would ever see it again.

If anyone had been observant enough, if they had cared enough to ask me how I felt in that moment, what would I say? I didn't even know. My stomach fluttered like a spring meadow full of butterflies. My heart rose up into my mouth, skipping every third beat. I was determined, yet I missed my sister. I questioned my sanity and the choices I had made to acquiesce so easily, yet upon reflection there seemed to be little else I could have done. If I had chosen to run rather than give in, what would have happened to me? Should I have fought back?

Truly none of it mattered. Here I was, and I would never know the 'what could have been.' I fought hard against the cloud of despondency that threatened to descend and cling to my spirit like an unwanted caller.

According to Captain Ildor Veris, we were bound for the 'land of my father', as if the phrase should draw out a pining to connect to the nostalgic past I had long nursed from childhood. But I could not pine for something I knew nothing about, because there had been no stories about Agrius in my childhood.

How was I to connect to a past and its history of which I knew nothing about? Miarka and Rolbert had told me little enough, and even that bit hadn't had time to settle into my imagination long enough to form a mythos of my memories.

The longer I dwelt on my lack of knowledge, the more a heat burned, turning into the fire of a longing to know, to understand, to connect with people and events long lost to me. In Agrius I saw not an unwelcome future, but an opportunity to learn the truth. Yes, Captain Veris was correct, though for reasons he hadn't intended: going to Agrius was the best course for me. For only in Agrius would I find the answers I sought.

"I trust that you found your accommodations suitable?" Veris' pleasant question broke my reverie, and I turned to him. Flawless in manner, smooth and charming in speech, it was difficult not to like him.

"Yes," I replied, matching his pleasant tone. "They are most suitable."

In fact they were more than suitable. Upon arrival, the ship's steward had informed me that the cabin I occupied was Veris' own, underscoring the oddity of the situation by way of a raised eyebrow.

"King Bellek will be pleased to know it. He would be most displeased to hear your voyage was an uncomfortable one."

I must have made a face, because he recognized the underlying fear.

"You have nothing to fear from King Bellek..." he began, then with a sideways slant, added, "or from me."

A viper suggesting I not be afraid of its fangs? Charming though he may be, I still did not trust the man.

"Walk with me," he continued. Taking my hand and placing it along with his other hand on top of his arm, we began to stroll along the rolling deck. "Irisa, you will find that much you have been told in your life is, at its heart, more complicated than you realize."

"Since I was told nothing about any of this in my life, you are correct," I admitted.

He cast appraising eyes on me for my frankness and continued. "King Bellek sits the throne of Agrius quite securely, and has done so for twenty-five years now. His son, Prince Casmir, will ascend after him. The land has been at peace all this time." He looked at me to gauge my reaction, then added, "Your father wants to end that peace."

I watched a pair of sea birds circle the ship high overhead, considering all he'd just told me. Irritation rose to the surface, and I blurted out, "So by kidnapping me, you hope to spoil his plans, is that it? If you had just killed him when you killed my grandfather, you wouldn't be in trouble now, would you?"

I surprised myself with the outburst, biting my lip and cursing my lapse.

A somber smile curled the corner of his lips. "Irisa, would it surprise you to know that King Bellek has a stronger claim to the throne than your father? If one considers the current laws of succession, that is."

The assertion did surprise me, but it did not tamp down my irritation. "And this was reason enough to overthrow my grandfather? To kill him?"

His rejoinder was swift, his passion matching the heat of my irritation. "You do know why sometimes hard things must be done to secure a throne, don't you? Why some must be sacrificed for the sake of a kingdom?"

"The needs of the many outweigh the needs of the few?" I offered, hiding my skepticism. He seemed surprised by my quick mind, raising an eyebrow at my unexpected answer, so I added, "Yes, I've read the philosophers, despite the conditions of my upbringing."

He took my pessimism in good humor, countering easily, "Of course you have, dear girl. But I refer to threats, Irisa. Threats. Threats to power and security."

"I don't know what you mean."

He smiled, as if my confusion pleased him. "Not all threats are as the poets would make them out to be. Some are subtle." He stopped and turned to face me directly, searching my eyes earnestly. "You aren't a threat to King Bellek or Prince Casmir, are you?"

He appeared to be in earnest, not teasing me. Thoughts of Figor, of my father's plan to invade Agrius, of all the things I knew or thought I knew flit across my consciousness. I shook my head by way of response, the irritation I had felt only a moment before gone, evaporated like a puff of smoke in the wind.

"Good, good," he replied, seemingly relieved. I wondered if he'd expected defiance from me. Kassia would have given him as much, and I was suddenly glad that she wasn't here.

He patted my hand again and we turned to walk on.

"You see, King Bellek believes that you should not be held responsible for the misdeeds of your grandfather." Then almost as if to himself he added, "I have big plans for you, and you will be glad of the day I came for you."

By now we had made a full lap around the ship's main deck so stopped. His gaze drifted to my neckline, his scrutiny resting on my bennu necklace. Kassia and I had been given them as young children. While my father had intended that we keep them hidden, I figured it didn't matter any longer so wore it openly. It was only in this moment it occurred to me that this decision might have been a mistake. Perhaps the bennu represented something beyond what I had guessed, that its symbolism implied a danger I knew nothing about?

He made no mention of the bennu, but instead took my hand and kissed the back of it. "Make yourself as comfortable as possible. We will be at sea for some time. My apologies for not having a maid to see to your needs. While your participation on this return voyage is welcomed, it was not anticipated. We will try to rectify the situation as soon as is practical." And with that, he walked away.

I stayed where I was, wishing I could flatten the fluttering butterflies flitting about once more in the pit of my stomach. His answers had been thoroughly unsatisfying, and I felt more confused than ever. His attempt to clarify my situation only added more questions. He would keep me safe he'd said, but from what? I had nothing to fear from him or King Bellek, so from Prince Casmir perhaps? And what of the misdeeds of my grandfather? I was pleased not to be held responsible for them, but the nature of those misdeeds remained elusive.

As I pondered, I made my way toward the stern, looking to the sky as I went, hoping the answers to all my troubles might be found there. But the sky had no revelations for me this day. Clear and blue, it spread overhead as a fathomless celestial bowl. I turned to make my way forward, and as I did so noticed a small cloud on the horizon just over my left shoulder. Was it a storm cloud, and did it move toward us or away from us? *"You will find that much you have been told in your life is more complicated than you realize..."* he had said. Perception, like that cloud, could mislead, and without a guide to help me navigate, the evidence could be misinterpreted. Having evaded the soldiers seeking me out in Corium, it was easy to think that now I'd simply jumped from the pot into the fire. Or had I? Like my orientation to those clouds, did I now race toward the storm or away from it?

I was certain I had entered a chimerical dreamland. After being at open sea for many days, this deep-water bay secluded from the deeper waters of the Anglera Sea on Mercoria's southern shore brought with it a welcome visual respite. The water of the bay mirrored the blue expanse overhead, sparkling cerulean and clear as crystal. Crouching along the far shore lay a ramshackle town with no obvious merits. Even so, I was mesmerized. Perhaps I had read too much poetry as a child, but everything about the scene put me in mind of magic, mythical beasts, and roving poets.

Built at the mouth of a river cutting into the heart of a steep-sided gorge, the town sat in the foreground, its backdrop a canopy of mist produced by cascading waterfalls flowing over the gorge's edge. Rainbows lit by the bright sun danced around the waterfalls, spilling in arcs to the river below, generating an aura of light and color that conjured up my sense of fanciful magic. Even the knowledge that we had come here to meet up with Prince Casmir who had left Corium ahead of us couldn't shake the fanciful mood in which I found myself.

"Lynchport, my lady."

Never mind Casmir. The name jarred enough.

"What did you say?" I asked, unable to hide my astonishment.

Figor stood next to me at the railing, his smile suggesting both amusement at my reaction to the name and an appreciation for the view. That he'd taken the liberty to stand next to me considering the distance he had kept from me since boarding was surprise enough.

"Lynchport. Home to generations of pirates and other ne'er-do-wells from time immemorial."

"So did they ever actually..."

"...hang people?" he finished for me. "Oh, yes. Regularly, though it's an act long out of use."

We fell into silence as I watched the ship move toward the shore.

"What are you going to do about Swine?" I asked after a time. "He knows who you are, what you did."

I thought he might get angry that I'd risked asking him aloud. To my surprise, he showed no sign of irritation. "I have made certain he can't talk. He's been... shall we say, a bit too sleepy. Seasickness can do that to a person."

"That can't be sustainable forever, surely."

"Leave it to me," he said, patting my hand in an attempt to be reassuring.

"Because you did so well taking care of things the last time?" I asked before chiding myself. It was not in my nature to be openly snarky, like Kassia, but her absence was telling in this case. Without her to make the rapid-fire quips, the responsibility fell to me.

He didn't take this remark with the same good grace as he had done so many times before.

"Irisa," he glowered, "nothing I do requires your approval." His tone was harsh, rasping, like the grit under the boot of a passing workman. "Up until now you have lived your life safely tucked away from all harm..." I made to break in, to contradict his notion of safety, when he held up a finger to silence me. "You do not understand the intricacies of court, the subtleties of shifting loyalties, and of half-truths. In short, you do not understand the situation you find yourself in."

"Then you must enlighten me," I responded, a waspish

edge to my words. "For if you do not, I will do my best to figure things out on my own, no matter what I find upon our arrival."

"Ah, yes. And in so doing, you will learn many things, will be told many things. But who to trust? In the end, it won't matter." He paused and looked over his shoulder to make sure no one was close enough to overhear. He had already been speaking softly, but now he lowered his voice to just below a whisper. "Your father will retake his throne, and then none of it will matter. But we need to get you out of Agrius before he can do that."

"You still plan to try to get me out?"

He lifted his eyes and flicked his gaze toward Ildor Veris. "Yes. It is time for change, but your father wants you safe before that can happen." He paused. "There is no other way," he added then moved away to talk to a member of the crew as the Árvök anchored.

I watched him as he went, noticing his precise carriage, his erect chin, as if his every movement was choreographed, planned out in detail, this man who worked for House Vitus but served House Sajen.

My attention turned toward the smaller tenders setting out from shore to meet us. Once alongside, the port procurator climbed the ladder to board. Our ship's captain gave him greeting, soon joined by Ildor Veris. The men exchanged pleasantries, and after a few moments, Veris pulled the procurator to the side for a private word. The mood changed. The procurator blanched of color, took a step back, and stared in horror. Veris said nothing more, watching the procurator as if strengthening his position by look alone. After a moment, it appeared as if the procurator capitulated, for he nodded. With a gesture of invitation, the procurator waved Veris to follow him then climbed down to his tender for the return trip to

Lynchport. I found the entire exchange curious.

Late into the evening, I found it difficult to keep anxious thoughts from overwhelming me. Try as I might, the onslaught continued at a ferocious pace. Fear over what awaited me in Agrius fought against my desire to find answers. Insecurities defeated my confidence. The shadows filling my stateroom had no answers for me, and I decided that strength and conviction are easier to find in the daylight hours, while darkness ushers in the echoes of doubt as the piquancy of day fades.

Then there was the matter of the procurator and Veris' business in Lynchport.

It wasn't any of my business.

I still wanted to know.

Sleep. Just sleep, Irisa.

But I couldn't. The lure of the question was too powerful. I allowed another hour or so to pass before deciding the passageways would be clear, then slipping out of my cabin, I crept toward the main deck. Veris had taken a berth with the captain, and finding the corridor outside it empty, I crouched low in a shadowed corner.

Pressing my ear to the wall, I listened intently.

"For what reason? He says he doesn't know who hired him."

"Or won't say."

"Just...one more mouth to feed... rid ourselves..."

"...have to answer too many awkward questions in Prille..."

Most of the voices were pitched too low to hear, so I missed large portions of the back and forth. I identified Veris' voice, and likely the captain, but I sensed there were others present as well.

"Hanging. We're in Lynchport after all."

I held back a gasp, bringing my hand up to cover my mouth. It seemed that Lynchport was about to reclaim its reputation. Echoes of Figor's assurances earlier in the day rang in my ears, and an icy finger worked its way down my spine.

After more unintelligible conversation, the room erupted into laughter. I vowed never to eavesdrop again and fled back to my cabin, though sleep came with great difficulty. The face of Kalyn danced in my memory as I remembered her smile, her innocence, and the love she had for her undeserving father. I would not cry for Swine. The tears wetting my cheeks now were for Kalyn.

Sea gulls screamed somewhere out beyond my window, and I rolled over, rubbing my eyes to peer at the morning light. Gentle waves lapped against the side of the ship still anchored in Lynchport's calm bay. My head felt fuzzy from a poor night's sleep, so it was with resignation that I swung my legs over the side of the bed. I quickly dressed and made my way onto the deck. I had slept later than I'd intended to.

Whispered segments of last night's overheard conversation haunted me. I wanted to pretend I'd misheard, or that I'd dreamed the whole thing. Evidence of the cold, hard reality however, was found in the small boat piloting its way to shore with a handful of armed men and one disconsolate looking former landlord.

I had no love for the man. He was a treacherous lout at best, but for the sake of his daughter, I felt a stab of pain in my heart. Swine's separation from Kalyn was divisive enough, but death would finalize it beyond repair, and she would never understand why it had happened. Loss was something I felt a keen acquaintance with, for my own father had been taken from me, and this after my mother. A tear threatened to break loose, and I swiped the back of my hand across my eyes as I turned away.

Hours passed before I saw Ildor Veris again. It was early afternoon, and he stood on the main deck listening to a sergeant who stood before him, relating news with vigorous intensity. The man illustrated his message with wild gestures, his face a contortion of rage pulling down the corners of his mouth. Occasionally he made a point by pointing toward the shore. As I walked toward them, I noticed a patch of dried blood staining his shirt. A blood-caked bandage wrapped the hand he cradled against his chest.

It was the blood that made me check my step.

"The old beggar told me he saw the necklace, and no mistake. So I knows it was her," I heard the sergeant say. "Can't be no one else."

Veris' back was to me, so I couldn't make out his response, but in return the sergeant muttered something about the necessity of haste. He brushed past Veris, making his way toward me to get to the ladder to board the return tender to shore.

"She's a tart that one, and she'll rue the day she pulled that blade on me, she will."

This last comment was intended for me, I realized, as his smile curved upwards in a wicked arc when he met my eyes. His look hinted at a depth of evil that made me shudder, and I stepped aside to let him pass. I hoped just then that whoever the man intended to find would run and hide, for no good could come from the devilry he intended for her. I shook the thought from my mind and turned my focus to Veris.

He half turned toward me, his face pensive as he fingered the jeweled pommel of the dagger he kept at his belt. It was some long moments before he acknowledged me.

"Ah, Irisa," he began slowly, breaking from his internal deliberation. His eyes lightened as he raised my hand to his lips. I appreciated the courteousness of his gesture, but the weight of Swine's impending doom weighed too heavily on me to match his mood. "I just received word that King Bellek has taken ill. We were to meet Prince Casmir here and then sail for Prille together, but he left word that he has gone directly home to Prille. We must be off soon, so will depart shortly." When I didn't respond, he noted it. "Is something amiss?"

"Why are they going to hang Swine? What did he do?" I had no patience for tact.

He seemed genuinely taken aback by my question, surprised by my vehemence, though he recovered quickly enough. "Whatever gave you the idea that he was going to be hanged?"

"I overheard you, last night with the captain."

I thought I caught a hint of fire flash behind his eyes, a minuscule twitch of the muscle under his left eye, but it was gone as quickly as it had come. His smile remained, though I sensed that he looked at me now with a revised opinion.

"Irisa, you mustn't take all you heard to heart. We were merely talking, sharing a tankard amongst us. Sveine will be staying in Lynchport, it is true. He fell ill as you might know, and it would be better for him to recover ashore rather than aboard ship where we cannot hope to properly care for him." This matched what Figor had told me about the sleeping draught. Perhaps Veris was telling the truth, and they only meant to leave him here. The reasons needn't be nefarious, did they? "He isn't your concern, so you must not think on it a moment longer. All will be well, I promise."

I wanted to believe him. It matched my recreated image

of him, an image opposing the view that Miarka had fostered in me. "I have some skill with herbs and healing, if you would only let me..."

"Irisa, you need not worry about matters that are not your concern." His face communicated the sincerity I needed. "Oh, and before I forget..." He opened his coat and pulled out a parcel wrapped in silk and tied with a golden cord. "Seeing your necklace yesterday reminded me that I have a gift for you." I took the gift but didn't open it. "Now if you'll excuse me, I must see the captain. We must leave for Agrius as soon as we can be underway."

When he had gone, I slipped the silk parcel into the purse at my waist then turned to watch the tender carrying Swine reach shore. My porcine landlord trundled onto solid ground, was led into the crowd, and I saw no more of him. I paced the deck for some time afterward. Later I somehow managed to eat the small meal offered me late in the day. I returned to my cabin where I sat worrying about many things: Swine's fate, my future, and Kassia.

After allowing myself time to wallow, I decided enough was enough. I chided my undisciplined mind and pulled myself back to the present, remembering that I'd never opened the gift Veris had given me earlier in the day.

Removing the golden cord and outer silk wrapping, I uncovered a slim silver box inlaid with small jewels. Nestled inside on a small cushion I found a pendant about the size of my bennu, hanging from a finely wrought silver chain. I pulled the chain from the box and let the pendant dangle. The silver disk featured a blazing sun like the one Figor wore, like the one on Veris' dagger. I placed it gently back into the box and closed the lid, thinking that I wasn't yet ready to be won over. If Veris thought it was as simple as giving me a gift, he had another think coming.

The coming of night brought calm seas, and since our voyage so far had acclimated me to a swifter current, the placidity unnerved me. I slipped away from my cabin to the deck above and stood along the rail, looking for the shore off the port side. A deluge of stars exploded across the sky, and a sliver of moon hung just over the edge of land in the distance. Gentle waves licked the ship's hull. The whisper of a breeze moved loose strands of my hair against my cheek, and every intake of breath filled my lungs with a taste of the sea.

The noise was so faint that if it hadn't been such a still night I wouldn't have heard it. I turned and noticed a man leaning casually against the mizzen mast on the quarter deck. Something caused my feet to move, and I found myself climbing the stairs to reach him.

"I told you I would take care of it."

It was Figor.

"Veris assured me that he would not be harmed. That's true, is it not?"

He made no reply. I approached him carefully, and as I neared him, a powerful aroma washed over me, oily and sweet yet pungent, thick with complexity, and wholly indescribable. In his hand he cupped a tiny object with a long stick that reached up to his mouth. He pulled the stick from his mouth and exhaled a puff of smoke.

"Nothing is as simple as it seems, Irisa."

"So people keep telling me."

"You would do well to remember it." He took another draw and blew more smoke, nearly translucent against the rising moon. "Especially once we reach Prille."

"So what about Swine?"

"Sometimes sacrifices must be made."

I didn't want to believe what he implied. "And he is yours, Figor? Your sacrifice?"

He barked a mirthless laugh. "You know nothing of my sacrifices!" The ferocity of his reply cowed me, but he didn't seem bothered by my recoil. He puffed a few more times then tapped the bowl of the object against the mast before tucking it into his coat. "Irisa, you know I can't afford even the hint of suspicion," he said finally, just above a whisper.

"At the cost of a man's life?"

"What do you think?"

I had no words. Everything he had just said, everything he had just implied, was repugnant. Figor was worse than Orsilla who had merely sold her husband. Figor had him killed. No, I had that wrong. They were both complicit. They were both to blame.

Then I considered my father... he planned to wage a war on Prille. How many lives would be lost in his pursuit? If Veris intended to use me to stop a war, didn't that make him the hero?

Later as I lay in my bunk, I fingered the bennu around my neck, considering the vagaries of life and death. While there were certainly answers to be found in Agrius, the benefits would come at the cost of playing the game. Figor had played it all his life, it seemed. Whether or not I was a worthy competitor remained to be seen.

~5~

"IRISA, YOUR FATHER GAVE you an admirable education considering the conditions of your upbringing," Ildor Veris offered lightly, his mood bright like the narrow stream of yellow morning sunshine splashing onto the surface of the tiny table in the captain's quarters where we took our breakfast.

"Indeed?" I asked, placing a delicate slice of rich, white bread on my plate. I kept my eyes focused on the dish of butter close at hand so I wouldn't have to make eye contact with him.

"Yes, quite remarkable," he mused as he sipped his watered wine. "As such, you know how kings and queens sometimes form peace agreements?" He eyed me as if my understanding was a given.

I raised an eyebrow, reaching for a bowl of dried figs. "That all depends on the circumstances, of course," I answered carefully. He'd asked innocuously enough, but the breeziness of his tone suggested a hint of calculation that spurred on my caution.

"Oh, undoubtedly!" He slapped the table with the flat of his hand good-naturedly. I resisted the urge to startle. "Very astute, of course. But what if, in this case, it involves disputes over what the Romanii call *continuitatis lege?*"

"I'm not sure, my lord," I replied slowly. I hated to show that I wasn't keeping up with him, but I honestly had no idea what he meant or where he was going with the conversation. I did not know of this *continuitatis lege*, for I knew little of the Romanii, a race of people on the far side of the world, and I did not speak their foreign tongue.

"Marriage, Irisa. Marriage." He looked triumphant. "When there is a dispute over the continuity of rule, you mend it with marriage. You, my dear, are to be a peace offering, remember?"

My eyes widened. "You intend me to wed?" The notion shouldn't have been shocking. Alliance by marriage was the way of the world. Certainly my father had intended for me to marry Prince Isary of Elbra. Miarka had told me as much. But coming from him in such a way, before I had satiated my morning hunger with even the smallest bite of food, caught me off guard. I deflected my unease by shifting the contents of my plate in a partial circle.

He smiled broadly, unaware of my discomfort. "Of course!" His exclaim punctuated his enthusiasm. "I will explain everything fully once we reach Prille, and after I have arranged a few details. I simply wanted you to warm to the idea before we arrive." He wiped a delicate silk cloth across the forearm of his sleeve to remove the ruby-red droplet of wine that had spilled in his exuberance. "Until then..." He stood from his seat. "We are about to drop anchor in Haern to fetch you a maid and to restock. Soon enough you will meet your intended. A little more patience, Irisa, and then all will be made clear."

And with that enigmatic hint, he breezed away before I could press him any further.

True to his word, later that day we arrived in Haern, a large island off the southern coast of Agrius. Too nervous to take in much of our host's manor, my overnight in Ildor Veris' domain passed by in a blur. We left again, early the next morning, the final leg of the journey to my future.

There are times when a person makes a choice that, in the abstract, seems full of wisdom and maturity. It is only when faced with the consequences of that choice that the abstract becomes tangible, and the choice made on a theory, feels less than wise. This was one of those times for me.

Even though no one had held a knife to my throat to bring me to my present circumstance, it had in fact, come about by a kind of coercion, Figor and Ildor Veris each perpetrators of that coercion in his own way. Even so, I had chosen to accept my fate, persuading myself that despite the disruption of my life, it was for the best. Now as the lines of Prille's buildings came into better focus, the bastion that was my previously flawless reasoning came crashing down around me. The very act of standing took every ounce of energy I possessed. Being brave is easier when one bases such bravery on the theoretical rather than the tangible.

From high on the forecastle of the Árvök, a stiff wind snapped the sails sharply overhead. The rise and fall of buildings, one merging into the next, created a haphazard line against the blue sky. In the far distance, purple smudges hinted at the existence of the mountains dominating the island's heart. Prille had its origins as a timbered fortress perched atop a rocky outcropping on the far side of a deep water sound, guarding access to the interior of the island from the Eastmor Ocean. Over time my ancestors expanded and developed Prille so that now it spilled down from the heights toward shore to become the largest port on the island and home to the kings of Agrius.

From my vantage point, Prille's architecture appeared vastly different from Corium's. Tall, narrow structures of polished, pale stone fit with steeply pitched roofs lined the streets at the city's height. Clay brick and timber replaced those more exotic ones as the city descended down the cliff side. Such an exotic view should have captivated me, but my mind could not shake the distraction caused by the suggestion of a memory that was not my own.

How much of the city looked the same to my mother when she arrived here all those years ago, to marry the heir to the throne of Agrius, before the day Bellek came with fire and terror? I tried to imagine dark smudges of smoke billowing from burning, charred ruins, the streets as they overran with armed men, killing and ravaging as they went. I closed my eyes to listen for the cries rising from the throats of a people savaged, the communal grieving and groaning over the destruction of homes and places of work. But I could not do it. The day was too bright and beautiful, the visible Prille too real, too near, to see it in any other way.

"My lady, isn't it beautiful?"

The question felt like an intrusion into my private grieving, and I inhaled a slow, quiet breath at the question, doing my best to cover the rawness of my emotions.

When Veris had informed me that he would acquire a maid for me in Haern, to see to my needs and help me with my attire and other ablutions, my spirits immediately rose. The voyage had been a lonely one, and I looked forward to the companionship. This surge of hope was dashed however, when the prospect of Raisa and the reality of Raisa contrasted quite dramatically.

A middle-aged woman who had served as a nursemaid to noble children all her life, Raisa cared for little beyond the nursery doors. While she would be useful to me as a tutor of courtly manners, she would not be a good companion, for she was as interesting as tepid dishwater. Since I felt no immediate affinity for Raisa, and Raisa saw me merely as another charge, I felt no urge now to confide in her the conflicting emotions I felt upon my first sight of Prille. Trust had to be earned.

"My lady?" Raisa repeated, looking at me curiously for my lack of response.

"Yes, indeed it is beautiful," I replied blandly, hiding a deep sigh as her bovine eyes blinked in return.

A strange curtained carriage without wheels and carried by a handful of stout men awaited us just off the ship. I could not spot Veris anywhere among those filing off the ship as we disembarked, but fortunately Figor greeted us on the dock, escorting me to the carriage as Raisa followed behind. I held Ilex in one arm, and Figor took the other as we walked, pulling me close to whisper, "Obviously matters have taken a different course than I originally planned. I encouraged Veris to keep your presence and identity obscure for the time being, and he agreed. Your life should be quiet for a while, giving me time to think of a new way to get you to your father."

Before I could respond, he bowed and pulled back, allowing Raisa to board our conveyance ahead of me. A liveried groom stepped up to take my arm, helping me in before closing the curtain meant to protect the vehicle's occupants from outside observation.

The air in Prille exhibited traits similar to those of Corium's — rotted fish, salt, and refuse — which, when combined with my anxiety, worked to create a stifling atmosphere under the heavy layers of silk curtains. A surge of nausea threatened to overwhelm me with each step of the carriers, drawing me ever closer to my awaiting fate. When finally the men lowered our carriage to the ground, I felt I had a decent control over my emotions. I emerged from the close air of the traveling compartment into a private cobbled courtyard surrounded by a low garden wall.

"My lady?" Raisa placed a hand under my elbow in support when she thought I would collapse. "Are you well?"

I did not feel well, but before I could admit as much, we were greeted by an elderly man who introduced himself as Perijan. Taking note of my pallor, he offered a deep obeisance before asking, "My lady, how may I serve you? Shall I call for a physician?"

I shook my head, wanting nothing more than to find a place to rest, to find a way to regain a sense of harmony. Remembering my new station, I straightened my back pretending not to be off-balance, and with my chin held high asked him to take me to my rooms instead. A look of respect passed over his features before he bowed formally and turned, leading us through a long, narrow building and out into another courtyard around which sat more interconnected buildings, courtyards and passageways.

Finally he opened a large door at the end of a covered arcade alongside a quiet quadrangle. The room felt cavernous, with other rooms behind closed doors. Multi-paned windows of costly glass ran along the far wall, making the place feel bright and airy. Raisa scurried in behind me, immediately beginning the process of unpacking and making the place our home.

"These rooms are for your use as long as you have need of them, my lady," Perijan told me. "You will be assigned a steward to oversee your needs as soon as it can be arranged. In the meantime, you may call for me as needed."

"Thank you, Perijan," I replied courteously. He inclined his head as if my thanks were not necessary.

"You will be left alone now to recover from your journey. Someone will retrieve you later."

And with that, he left us to fend for ourselves. Though the door moved on well-greased hinges and closed with only the faintest click of the latch, the sound reverberated in my brain like the boom of a thousand-ton weight striking the earth. I turned and slumped back against the door, closing my eyes, drawing fresh, cool air into my lungs. I heard rather than saw Raisa about her work and focused on the sound hoping to clear my mind. It didn't work. Eventually I opened my eyes to take in the details of my new home, and the sumptuousness took my breath away.

Finely woven tapestries draped intricately carved marble walls from floor to ceiling. Lavish furnishings covered in silk and damask, along with articles detailed with gilding and precious stones, dotted the floor, tables and chests. Everything seemed too fine to touch.

And then the panic truly set in. What kind of world had I stepped into? Was I truly meant to exist in such a place? Any of the etiquette or customs Miarka had taught me felt suddenly and woefully inadequate.

Perijan said someone would retrieve me later. Was I to dine in the great hall with the king and his court? And what was I to do in the meantime? Recover from my journey, he'd said, but I was too full of anxiety to truly rest. I had no idea what was expected of me, knew nothing about how my presence would be explained, what my duties were, if any.

This room which had only moments ago felt cavernous began to close in around me, and a sense of entrapment stole through my being. A wide door opening onto a porch beckoned, and after checking to make sure Raisa remained busily occupied, and noting that Ilex distracted herself rummaging behind the wall hangings, I slipped out.

The porch overlooked a small garden hemmed in by cunningly designed hedges and vining plants in front of a stone wall. Two broad trees on either side provided ample shade, spreading branches over a wide set of stairs leading down to the immaculate lawn. Birdsong filled the air, insects flit about, and a strong scent of growing things all worked together to create a languorous ambiance. Away from the waterfront, the air was fresher here, and I inhaled a deep breath scented with late summer's flowers. After a time, I descended to the green lawn, traversed around a tiny fountain in an efficiently cobbled courtyard, then wound my way around shrubs and flowering plants to the back hedge. Grabbing a handful of twining vines, I eased myself up and over the wall. My sister Kassia wasn't the only one who knew such tricks.

I dropped lightly to the other side and found myself in another garden. The thought occurred to me that if I wandered far from where I was now, likely I'd not find my way back, though at the moment I didn't care. Because I imagined my appearance to be less than lady-like, bedraggled and travel-weary as I was, anyone I happened to meet in my explorations might take me for an intruder rather than a guest of Ildor Veris. Even so, I brushed debris from my skirts and tidied the loose strands of hair that had dislodged in the vines I'd just climbed. I set off. Equilibrium did not come to the timid.

The stones making up the path had darkened to a deep green from years of moisture and algae, and they felt delightfully cool to my weary feet. I closed my eyes and inhaled deeply again, happy to be free of the sea air, thinking the damp air suffused with a hint of age a better replacement. Moving on in silence, I made my way along the side of the wall until I emerged into yet another courtyard where my delightful solitude came to an end.

The pair, a man and a woman, stood in an embrace near the center of the courtyard. The woman laughed while the man's husky voice encouraged her. My arrival had been nearly silent; still, I was found out. Two pairs of eyes rotated toward me. The woman seemed unconcerned by my appearance and considered me with benign eyes full of amusement. After a moment, she lowered her gaze and hid a giggle under her hand.

The man appeared even less concerned, maintaining his hold on the woman even as he studied me, seemingly unsurprised by my sudden appearance. One hand continued to clamp itself around her backside while his other hand hid from view somewhere under the bodice of her gown. Immediately uncomfortable, I wanted to turn and flee, but it would have been pointless. I couldn't be unseen, nor could I unsee what was before me. A fierce blush blazed across my cheeks.

His mouth twitched at the sight of me as he studied me from head to toe, taking in my untidy appearance and neglected locks. I must have been a sight. Turning back to the woman, he pulled his hand free of her disheveled garment, slapped her on the backside, and motioned his head toward a bench as he leaned in to whisper something in her ear. The woman smiled knowingly and did as he bade.

The man seemed determined to engage me in conversation so walked toward me, his pronounced swagger a sign of the exorbitant confidence he placed in his own value and status. His wore an expensively cut coat trimmed with the finest stitching, announcing a bearing of wealth, prestige and noble birth. He was shorter than average, had a balding pate, and ears that stuck out slightly more than average. His plump lips surrounded a generously wide mouth, and as it opened now to speak, I dreaded what would come out of it.

"Adonia..." he said, using the name of the goddess whose comparable visage troubled me. He lifted my hand to plant a kiss on my fingers, and I checked my desire to recoil.

"I wander, I wander,
the road all alone.
Unaware and ragged, I haunt the desolate places
until your beauty I find,
restoring my lost exuberance
in the fatal world that was my misery."

I had never heard such nonsense, even in all the years I consumed books of literature and poetry. I glanced over at the woman on the bench, simultaneously embarrassed for myself and for the man who had only moments before embraced her. She made no indication of concern.

I returned my gaze to the man who had finally finished spouting off his poetry. "You must have me confused with someone else, good sir," I replied as lightly as I could, trying to sound less flustered than I was even while considering how to extricate my hand from his.

"My Adonia, the fowler's snare can never match the trap you..."

He continued on again even though I showed no sign of encouragement. The man had a sort of charm, though misguided, and as he prattled on, it seemed to me as though he considered himself irresistible. Perhaps his charm could not be resisted, though for other reasons, and he knew it? Instantly a cold finger of dread wiggled up my spine. What if this was the man Ildor Veris intended me to wed? Even worse, what if this was Prince Casmir? My salvation arrived before I had time to reach any conclusions.

"Ah, my lord! They told me you were practicing at the pell." It was Ildor Veris, and he strode purposefully toward us. "I bring you a wife, as promised."

My heart dropped like a cold lump of stone. As Veris closed the distance between us I perceived that his gaze was fixed, not on the balding limpet clinging to my hand as I'd originally thought, but rather on someone beyond us, in the middle distance. I followed his look and noticed for the first time another man in the shadows, leaning casually against a column, his arms folded as he took in the scene.

Now that he had been addressed, he straightened and stepped into the dappled sunlight where I could take in more of his measure. His considerable height was matched by a slender build and topped with a full head of dark brown hair touched with bronze, putting me in mind of my father when I was a child. His jaw boasted the ghost of facial hair along his jaw and chin, as if he hadn't tended to his grooming that morning. He wore a generous linen tunic, damp from obvious exertion, over silken hose encased by soft leather boots running up to mid-calf. A practice sword hung at his hip, evidencing his recent visit to the pell as Veris had suggested.

Veris stopped at my shoulder surprisingly untroubled by my presence when he likely expected me to be in my chambers and opened his mouth as if to speak again. But in that moment, he took first notice of the poet-postulant still holding my hand. Scowling, he offered, "Wigstan," in greeting, a curt bob of his chin punctuating his displeasure. It was enough of a distraction for me to finally pull my hand free.

Wigstan returned the scowl, muttering, "I prefer Wolf."

"Of course you do," Veris returned dryly, his nose crinkling with distaste.

With a sniff of disdain, Veris turned his attention back to

the newcomer who broke in with his own question. "Cousin Ildor, what is this about?" The man was obviously intrigued as his gaze switched between me and Veris, clearly surprised by the news. He hadn't expected this. I resisted the urge to smooth my hair, recalling my rumpled appearance and vine-tousled tresses. "I don't recall mention of a wife, and so soon upon your return from Mercoria. You've only just arrived, have you not?"

"I sent word that I had a surprise, did I not?" Veris called out.

"Well, yes, but I thought maybe it was a new courser. A wife is something altogether different."

Veris waved his hand impatiently. "This is the Lady Irisa." He indicated me. "I will explain everything later. My man has returned from Haern, and I must be off," adding a "Wigstan" and a nod as an afterthought.

"I prefer Wolf," Wolf repeated irritably.

I did my best to hide a laugh. "Wolf?" I asked him, my brow arched in amusement.

He smiled impishly, indicating the woman behind him, and with a helpless shrug, laughed.

"He is named Wigstan after the god of virtue..." the newcomer offered as he closed the distance between us, "...when he should be named Cyrdric after the god of depravity!"

Both men laughed heartily at the private joke, slapping each other on the back.

My soon-to-be husband studied me closely, his smile sportive. He seemed to be enjoying my discomfort. "I suppose I should have pressed Cousin Ildor more intently to learn what brought about this change in my fortune, but I was too taken aback. Would you care to enlighten me how this came about?"

"I am afraid that is a bit of a long story, sir," I replied quietly, feeling at a disadvantage for many reasons.

"Lady Irisa..." he mulled, testing the sound of my name as he considered it. "You are not from here, are you? Mercoria, perhaps? The accent is telling."

"Yes," I answered, breaking my gaze from his, hoping he wouldn't press me too closely for answers I couldn't give.

He nodded, triumphant at his accurate guess. "I suppose Cousin Ildor retrieved you while in Corium." He studied me up and down for a moment, as if assessing livestock for purchase. "Do you know when it is we are to be wed?"

His tone was engaging, light, and encouraging, though I couldn't match his congenial mood considering the circumstances. "No, sir, I'm sorry. He told me nothing more."

"Who is your father, Irisa, your family, if I might be so bold to ask?"

There was no sense lying, and no getting around the truth. "Sajen, sir. Bedic Sajen." I dropped my gaze to the ground, cursing Veris under my breath for his lack of sensitivity and candor, either with me or with my partner in this surprise.

Both men startled at my response. "Bedic Sajen? Are you certain?" His eyes widened, and he looked as if he might need to sit down. I nodded. "I had no idea Bedic Sajen survived long enough to have a daughter!"

They looked at me as if I would supply the answers to the mystery, but when I said nothing, they eyed each other.

"Irisa," my husband-to-be began carefully, his voice even and measured, "do you have any idea who I am?"

I raised my eyes to look at him, to see if he was teasing or if he was in earnest. He had asked kindly, though with a certain amount of disbelief. "I must confess that I do not," I answered, adding a hesitant "my lord" just in case.

Wolf stared at me, his mouth agape. After regaining his composure, he rearranged his expression back into one of casual politeness. "Dear lady," he coughed, "this is Prince Casmir."

"I'm to wed Prince Casmir..." The phrase stuck in my head, repeating over and over like a jackdaw in the last two hours since I'd returned to my rooms on the arm of the very man who was to be my husband. Prince Casmir. Of House Vitus. The enemy of my family... "Of course I'm to wed him. Why did I not see it coming? *How* did I not see it coming?" I turned haunted eyes to Raisa who brushed out my hair for bed. Her lips thinned into a straight line, but she wisely kept her opinion to herself.

After I'd disappeared over the garden hedge and Raisa couldn't find me, she'd paced with worry, simultaneously wondering if she should search for me on her own or call a guard in alarm. When I returned, she greeted me with exasperation at first until she realized that it was Prince Casmir who accompanied me. Her words turned bumbling and incoherent as she thanked him. My own reaction to his identity had been considerably different. Shock induced generalized numbness, and I remained silent as Casmir led me through the corridors to my door. Misreading my reticence as illness, Casmir suggested that I dine privately here tonight rather than in the hall if I preferred it. I nodded that I did. "Tomorrow, if you are up to it, I will take you on a tour of the city. Perhaps we can become better acquainted, and you can tell me the 'long story' of how matters came to be as they are." This time he took my silence as acquiescence. Saying his goodbyes, he offered a gracious bow and turned to leave.

I watched him in an odd, detached way until Raisa took me under the elbow to lead me to the bath she had prepared and which now stood lukewarm. As I explained to her that

Prince Casmir was to be my husband, her eyes bulged, and she uttered a gasp. After a light meal left mostly untouched, I fled to the porch to gaze at the night sky, to search out the comfort of the stars, and ponder the life ahead of me. "I'm to marry Prince Casmir," I said again. I was alone, and no one could hear me, but somehow saying it aloud made it seem more real. Ilex leapt onto my lap, and I stroked her soft fur.

Miarka had called him a "brat of a boy", though he was no boy. He was a man older than me by several years. At least he wasn't Wolf, I reassured myself in consolation. And yet...how was I to know he wasn't just like Wolf? Perhaps he too was a libertine, earning a nickname of his own in description of questionable aspects of his character. There was no way to know yet, though as had been the case with Veris, I'd found Casmir to be nothing like the description Miarka had given me. He was courteous and attentive. Other than being awkward, our first meeting hadn't horrified me, it had intrigued me. At least it did now that I could look back on it, the initial shock having worn off.

"Ilex, what do you think?" The little dog did not respond of course. Her little pink tongue flicked out of her mouth as she stretched a back leg to nibble an itch. I ruffled her fur and gazed back at the night sky.

On our voyage to Agrius Veris had been quick to assure me of my own innocence. I was not guilty of my grandfather's misdeeds — whatever they had been — he had said. If I listened to Miarka, to Figor or my father, Prince Casmir was my direct rival. It was at that moment that the genius of Ildor Veris' plan struck me.

I was a peace offering, he'd said. I was to prevent a war. My father's war. Marriage to Casmir would unite our houses, ending the rivalry. He needed me to marry Prince Casmir before my father married me off to the prince of Elbra, satisfying those who still wished a Sajen on the throne. If I married Casmir, both sides would have their way. He was the genius, and I the sacrifice. The question I had yet to answer was whether or not it would be an honorable one.

~6~

WE STOOD IN THE back of the crowd, near the Petulant Gate on the northern side of the city nearest the palace. Crowds pressed us in on all sides, and my father held my hand tightly so I would not get lost. We had come alone, my father and I, to watch a parade of nobles descend upon the palace for a great assembly. My father explained to me the reason for the visit of so many glittering men in bright jewel-encrusted clothing, but his exact words meant little to me. I only understood that it was a yearly oath-giving, and something that was really important to these men. Important enough that they dressed like frivolous peacocks in a holiday pageant.

"What will they do in the palace, father?" I asked him, peering up at his towering height.

He squatted down to eye-level so I could hear him over the roar of the crowds. "They will meet with Emperor Ciasan, daughter. Every year these men, these nobles, must visit and renew their vows of loyalty and fealty to the Emperor, as is their duty. They come from all over Mercoria."

I scrunched up my nose, not caring about duty. "But what will they DO," I emphasized.

My father considered before replying. "They will assemble in a great hall, a large... no, a cavernous room filled with glittering gold and *gleaming marble. One by one they will approach the Emperor as he sits upon a great throne. They will kneel, kiss his hand, and repeat a vow."*

"Will there be feasting and dancing?"

My father laughed. "Of course, yes."

"It must be a wondrous thing to see." My father seemed pleased with my questions until I added, "I would not want to be a part of it."

"Why not, child?" His face turned grave again.

"Because to be around such men, such a spectacle, would fill me with dread. They are not like me."

"Irisa," my father began, taking my hand in his own and straightening up, "there is nothing about those men or their ceremonies which should inject dread into your heart. They are mere mortals, my daughter, just like me." He patted my hand and turned to watch the tail end of the magnificent display of wealth and splendor while I considered his words, still not convinced that I had anything in common with the men on display.

"My lady," the woman said as she dropped a knee.

I sat in the morning light filtering through the open doorway, creating a dappled patch of warmth on the deep, rich brown skin of the striking woman before me. Her black hair cascaded down her back in oiled ringlets under a sheer veil dotted with tiny jewels around the face edge. Her slender build reminded me of a willowy reed of grass, her silk gown tailored to emphasize her gracefulness. Despite the coolness of the early autumn morning, her arms were bare to the shoulders. Delicate tattoos laced her right upper arm, spiraling in whorls under gold bands all the way down to her elbow.

Thick, dark lashes fringed brown eyes under precisely plucked eyebrows. A slender nose, full lips painted the color of a rose, and high cheekbones all worked together to make her the most exotically beautiful woman I had ever seen, and I couldn't help but stare. When she lifted her gaze to my face, she caught out my bad manners and smiled a smile of wry amusement. Ilex however, was not impressed. She yapped away, making a furious noise.

"My name is Addis," she purred, her velvet tone thick with an accent I couldn't place, "wife to Wigstan of Bauladu, and I bring you greeting. Le'ul Casmir thought you might appreciate some company."

"You are Wolf's wife?" I squeaked as I tried to edge Ilex away with my foot, immediately regretting my thoughtless remark. The sobriquet could hardly be endearing to her. She acknowledged the truth with a graceful incline of her head, ignoring my slip altogether. Everything about Addis screamed a refined noble upbringing, and I was suddenly and fiercely curious about her and the story of how she came to be married to the wolf Wigstan. I also felt slightly intimidated by her.

Before I could continue in my fumbling ways, servants brought in trays of curiously shaped pots, setting them in a circle around a single low stool. Remembering my manners, I signaled to Raisa to take Ilex away then welcomed Addis more formally, and we sat.

"In my country, it is customary to honor friends with kopi. I will make it for you."

I had no idea what kopi was, but I was willing to find out.

Addis picked up a round-bottomed, black clay pot and set it on a dish of hot coals. With an open saucer-like pan in one hand, she scooped out a measure of small, green beans from a small sack at her feet then emptied them into the pan which she held over the bed of coals. As she constantly shook the beans around, they slowly roasted to a golden brown. A powerful aroma wafted from the beans, its potency reminding me of burned lemon grass, toasted nuts, barley, old wood and leather. When the beans were roasted to her satisfaction, she dumped them into a heavy wooden bowl and proceeded to crush them with a heavy wooden cylinder, blunted on one end, until the mixture resembled course sand.

The water in the black clay pot had come to a boil by this time, so Addis poured the crushed beans into it, swirling the mixture for just a moment before removing it from the heat. She set it gently aside and we waited.

After a few minutes, Addis picked up the steeping bean mixture and immediately a waiting servant placed a new tray on her lap. Several small, thick, glass cups huddled together in the middle of the tray, and into these cups she poured the concoction in a single stream.

She lifted the tray to offer me a cup, and with a small nod said, "Buena tutu."

I took one and drank.

Then I spat.

This time she laughed, and I was relieved to see that she took no open offense at my reaction. I hadn't intended to insult her, but the kopi tasted exactly like the roasting beans had smelled: like wood, leather and burnt lemon grass.

"That is a common first reaction." Her eyes lit when she smiled. Waving her hand toward me for the cup, she added a dash of thick cream before returning it to me. "Try this," she offered. I sipped more delicately, and while the hot liquid still tasted of leather and nuts, some of the bitter edge was gone. It was sweeter, richer. I took another careful sip. This time when the hot liquid snapped on the back of my tongue, I winced but also wanted more.

We each drank three of these cups of kopi, and then servants took away the cups, trays and pots. Addis and I were left alone again.

"Thank you for the kopi, Addis. It was very kind of you to think of me in this way."

She acknowledged my thanks with a slight head tilt.

In fact, the kindness meant more to me than I could adequately explain to her. I had slept poorly the night before, dreaming of the wicked Prince Casmir from Miarka's stories. No matter his graciousness last evening, fear still pervaded my thoughts and feelings as I anticipated spending time with him touring the city later in the day. His thoughtfulness in sending Addis to visit me helped ease my anxiety, even if only a little.

Uncertain about what was expected of me next, I invited her to walk in my back garden, thinking she would enjoy the same languorous ambiance I had discovered there last night. She agreed, so I led her along a graveled path, doing my best to appear less awkward than I felt. My mind spun thinking of topics that might interest her when all I really wanted to do was ask her questions about my family. Considering that I knew little about her or her feelings toward the Sajens, I resisted the urge.

"I thank you for your visit today. Everything here is rather... new," I began, but Addis waved away my worry with a flick of her hand.

"You need not worry. Captain Veris explained matters to Le'ul Casmir. This is why he thought my visit would comfort you, for you know no one, are... new, as you say... to all of this."

Just how much Veris had explained to Casmir wasn't clear, and her assurances did little to ease my mind. I didn't know much about royalty, but I did understand that royalty did not generally wed the impoverished. Addis must have sensed my tension concerning Casmir.

"Le'elt Irisa, you truly do not need to be concerned." She

patted my hand. "You are among friends." She looked me full in the face and smiled gently. "Do you like books?"

Her question descended like a ray of sunshine breaking through the clouds. "Yes," I replied eagerly and found delight reflected back in her eyes.

"Good!" she exclaimed. "I hoped as much! Come with me," and with an artful flourish she swept her hand through my arm and pulled me along with her.

As we went, Addis pointed out places of interest. When we passed by a small building emanating warmth and humid air, she laughed at my fascination. I wanted to tarry longer, but she informed me we could visit the *balneae*, or a bathhouse in the Romanii style, later. "Le'elt Irisa," she continued, "you will see it all in good time! Now come, or the day will waste away before you ever see the Bibliotheca!"

Finally we entered a cobbled yard appearing to be the central square of the palace complex. Without pause, Addis struck out directly through the bustle of people. Clerks scurried about, servants hurried on errands, and a stream of people stood in a loose line waiting for access to an official hall. *Petitioners of the court*, Addis called them. "King Bellek hears them when he can be bothered. Otherwise members of King's Council sit in for him, sometimes even Ildor Veris, though mostly Le'ul Casmir takes on his father's duties." And then as if divulging a secret, she added quietly, "Though he doesn't much fancy the task."

"Why not?" It seemed odd that a man bred to take his father's place would not relish the notion of taking on the responsibility early.

She didn't answer, instead turned and pulled me along in her wake, angling toward a tall building with a brightly tiled dome roof. A broad staircase swept us upward toward an oversized door nearly as wide as the stairs had been. As we passed under the lintel, I looked up and noticed that the door was as thick as the walls of Corium and as tall as an oak. Once closed, I had no doubt the doors could withstand a tsunami.

A great colonnaded foyer greeted us just inside. All was quiet as a tomb except for the slap of Addis' sandals on the cool marble floor. A man dressed in the white robes of a scrivener greeted Addis with "Le'elt Addis Nega" and a deferential bob as we passed by, approaching another set of double doors. While the entry hall had been cold, silent and empty, the new room was anything but. Lushly woven carpets spread underfoot down the length of the central aisle. Tables sporting candle trees dotted along the central aisle which was long and narrow, standing three stories tall, and capped with a great dome inlaid with gold and intricate carvings. Either side of the central aisle housed aisles of shelves which branched off into shadow. It smelled of dust and candle wax.

Addis stopped in front of a white robed figure who greeted us. "Grand Master Lito, may I present Le'elt Irisa Sajen?" I bobbed my chin in a manner I hoped mimicked the way Addis had done earlier. The man was elderly and round, with a face as pale as the winter's moon. His eyes and nostrils flared in equal proportion at Addis' introduction, but he quickly recovered. "I thought I would show her around so that when she feels the need, she can read at leisure. Perhaps she can learn a thing or two under your tutelage."

"Yes, of course, Le'elt Addis. I would be happy to be of assistance to you," he began, turning beneficent eyes toward me, "or to the Lady Irisa, in any way. You need only ask for me."

"Irisa, Grand Master Lito is Grand Scriptstóri of the Bibliotheca," Addis offered by way of explanation.

"A scriptstóri?"

"You would know them as scribes, or scriveners."

Of course. My father was a market scribe in Corium. This was how he had managed to educate us, through the network of those he worked with and for. It had depended upon whatever books my father could borrow from those other scribes or the clerks he came across in his trade. He had managed to collect a few of his own over time as well, though he would never tell me how he had come about them.

Addis beamed at me then grabbed my hand. "But come now, and I will show you more of the palace."

As we walked, she told me about her home in Aksum. "My father is Negus. There is little trade between Aksum and Agrius, and my father thought that my marriage to an Agrian lord would increase commerce between our peoples." I was not familiar with the term Negus and said as much. "You would call him king," she explained.

"Your father is a king?"

"Yes, though I am only first daughter to his second wife," and she shrugged as if hers was a common existence not worth mentioning. "That is why they called me 'Le'elt'. It means king's daughter in your tongue. It is why I call you Le'elt, for you are also daughter of a king. Or at least a man who wants to be king." She said this last part though half-closed eyes, a subtle smile playing at her lips.

"Veris couldn't have told you all of that, surely?" I asked suspiciously.

"Irisa, it is the duty of all within the palace walls to know the business of all others within the palace walls. Do you know nothing of *salay*, of intrigue?"

I confessed as much by shaking my head, and she pondered for a moment before murmuring, *Curious*, without really answering my question. When the mood passed, she continued as if I'd never spoken. "Now come, and I will show you the balneae, or Romanii bathhouse, before it is time for you to meet Le'ul Casmir." She gave me a knowing smile, revealing a row of perfect teeth showing brilliantly white against her rich, kopi-colored skin.

The carriage without wheels, like the one that had transported me to the palace from the Árvök yesterday, was more or less a wide, cushioned chair with raised sides all around. The seat centered on a platform supported by two stout poles carried on the shoulders of six burley men. This time there was no curtained top, all the better to view the city as we progressed through it.

"I will take you first down the main avenue toward the Temple of Zinon and then past the Seat of Kings," Casmir said as he helped me into the litter. He settled himself next to me and nodded to his groom. "You might like to see the place where the kings and queens of Agrius have been crowned going back centuries."

The men lifted the chair, placing it stably onto their shoulders before trotting off as though their passengers weighed no more than a sack of grain. While I expected to be jostled around like a bouncing river otter, I was surprised instead by the gentle side to side roll, almost as if we floated down a gentle meadow stream.

Casmir noticed my mute wonderment. "These men are palandiers, and this is a palanquin. I often forget that Mercoria does not have them," he said gently. "Much of the interior of our land is highlands and very rocky. The earliest kings found that it was the most efficient and comfortable way to travel in the days before there were roads or much settlement. As you will see, it works just as well on the crowded streets of Prille." He smiled at me pleasantly, and I did my best to return his smile, as if riding in a palanquin next to a prince was something I'd done every day of my life. Never mind that this prince belonged to a family who had all but extinguished my own.

An armed guard saluted as we left, but none joined ranks behind us as escort. Any citizenry who even deigned to notice watched our passing with nonchalance, as if seeing their future king was an everyday occurrence. Perhaps it was. In fact, most were far more curious of me than him. A subjugated people were not normally a curious people. Miarka had told me that the people feared King Bellek, so why would they not also fear Bellek's son? If anything, they appeared indifferent, leaving me bewildered.

Now as we rode in the palanquin through the narrow, cobbled streets of Prille, I pondered the unconventional prince next to me, this man who would be king, my husband-to-be. From all appearances, he seemed to be good-natured, intelligent, and easy to converse with. That he knew his worth and position was evidenced in his bearing, confidence, and the way he assumed the deference of those we encountered. Even so, there was a distinct lack of arrogance in his demeanor. He was not humble exactly, but neither was he haughty or imperious. If anything, he seemed utterly unaware of himself at all, as if he knew who he was, was content, and that was the end of it.

All of this applied to his dress as well. Unlike Veris or even Figor, his attire was casual: a light, loose tunic over trousers tucked into calf-high leather boots, and while impeccably and expensively tailored, he wore no jewels or other ostentatious adornment. Like the day before, his jaw boasted the shadow of a beard, as if grooming was something he hadn't bothered with.

Even so, his hands and nails were clean and trimmed, and his hair tidied back.

I also noticed he wore no sword or other weaponry. So I asked him about it. After raising a brief eyebrow, he shrugged his shoulders as if to ask why would I?

"Wolf tells me you like books, and that Addis took you to the Bibliotheca. Did you enjoy it?" I flashed him a brilliant smile and answered that yes, I had enjoyed it very much. "Grand Master Lito is a brilliant man, very useful, a good teacher," he replied. "I will have to show you my favorite collection sometime."

"You like to read too?" I was a bit surprised that such a man would find pleasure in a quiet pursuit of the mind. Considering his sword practice the day before, I had taken him to be more of a man of action.

"Of course! It's a useful thing to know a verse or two at the right moment." He cocked me a crooked grin.

We moved on to other subjects, and I found Casmir to be well-rounded in his knowledge of all we discussed. He finished with a brief history of his upbringing and education at court which included book knowledge as well as use of arms and military strategy.

"All good young men of the court know how to use a sword, though some of us are better than others. Poor Wigstan of Bauladu was sent to Prille by his father, to be fostered here, calling on an old favor my father owed him. He came at the age of ten, a young whelp of a boy. He never took well to his education. His tastes ranged in other directions." He laughed, and I could tell it was a good-natured barb from a friend who regarded the subject of his banter very highly.

"Your friend Wigstan... he and Addis... they are unusual together..." I wrung my hands in nervousness, not sure how to ask my question without offense.

I had observed the interactions between Wolf and Addis for the first time just before our tour began. Wolf had been sent to retrieve me not long after Addis and I returned from exploring the palace. Wolf greeted me with a twinkling eye and a murmured "Adonia" before taking my arm and guiding me to a broad portico overlooking the sea beyond where Casmir and Addis waited for us.

Wolf deposited me next to Casmir who uttered a nearly inaudible *Adonia indeed* under his breath. Addis seemed to pay no mind to Wolf who mutually ignored her. When we parted ways, Wolf and Addis barely acknowledged one another, going their separate ways, each oblivious of the other. Now, in the relative privacy of the palanquin, I thought I could ask Casmir about it.

He let out a snort of laughter. "He is one lucky lout, isn't he?" I stared at him. "Wigstan of Bauladu," he said formally, "is sole heir to the great house of Argifu. It's mostly a moth-eaten inheritance on the rocky cliffs of Fyrgdun's southern face, but it's an old family, wealthy, historically anyway, though their fortunes have long-since waned.

"Addis is the daughter of the Negus' second wife," he continued, "so not worth much politically to him beyond the wealth of her father. Her father saw her as dispensable, more interested in increasing trade between Agrius and Aksum. But to Wolf, she was the means to reclaiming glory and wealth for his house."

"Did it work? Reclaiming glory and wealth for his house, I mean?"

Casmir looked at me askance. "Not really, no. Wolf's father faces problems that money alone cannot fix, regardless of who his son and heir espoused.

"They have no particular attachment to one another, but that is not unusual for noble marriages, Irisa. Addis seems happy to have escaped Aksum, because here she has more freedom than she could ever have imagined at home. It keeps her from caring too much about Wolf's inclinations. They both give each other freedom to stay satisfied by whatever means they so choose."

I tried my best not to scowl, knowing first hand Wolf's inclinations and what it likely took to keep him satisfied. If Casmir thought this was a good arrangement for his own personal affairs, he had another think coming. Perhaps Miarka was right about one thing at least: maybe Casmir was the rake Wolf was. A character flaw not unusual for a prince, I decided.

I cast him a sideways look, and asked, "And what keeps Addis satisfied?"

Casmir gave me an appraising look before answering thoughtfully, "Addis is a diplomat. Her first loyalty is to herself and then to her homeland." The answer wasn't what I expected, and my face must have given me away, for he smiled. "This surprises you?"

"I admit that your answer was more candid than I anticipated."

"The Negus of Aksum has a gem in his daughter, though I'm not sure he fully appreciates it. She is very skilled in the art. I won't pretend to understand her motives, for her father doesn't recognize her contributions. One day I have no doubt that she will surprise him. But enough about Wolf and Addis. If we are to be married, I would know about you."

Well, I'm the granddaughter of the man your father killed. I was raised in poverty while you grew up in wealth and privilege — my inheritance. I was forcibly removed from my home then captured by Ildor Veris and brought here against my will. How did one put all that tactfully into words? Instead, I asked him, "You seem pretty accepting of the choice Captain Veris made on your behalf regarding me."

"It has never been about my choice, Irisa."

I nodded then stared down at my skirts, uncomfortable with his casual approach to something as weighty as marriage. I twisted the fabric between my fingers. "What do you want to know?" I asked instead, looking up at him finally. It still seemed hard to believe that this prince would consent to wed a girl raised in poverty, despite her bloodline. "I don't know how much Captain Veris told you already."

"I know that you were raised in obscurity, oblivious of your true identity. I know that all of this is very new to you, and that you were brought here against your will." Then with a mischievous glint in his eye, he added, "and as such, you seem fairly accepting of the choice Cousin Ildor made on your behalf regarding me."

"As you've said yourself, I was brought here against my will. There seems to be little point in protesting what I have no power to control." I looked him straight in the eye, surprised at my own boldness.

The muscle at the side of his mouth quirked, and he dipped his chin in acknowledgment, amused by my straightforward answer rather than affronted.

"My father earned his living as a scribe for hire in the market," I began, getting back to his original question about my life. "It didn't pay well, and he often went days with no work." I frowned at the memory. "He refused to be taken into service within the household of any noblemen. I don't think he wanted to be enslaved by service to one person." I looked around at the market we had entered, noticing for the first time a row of people chained to posts like livestock for sale. Slavery had been abolished long ago in Mercoria, so the sight startled me. "Like them," I said, pointing at the poor miserables and scowling as I tried to hide the shudder that raced through my frame. "How horrible for them," I added in a whisper. "How absolutely abhorrent."

Casmir saw the direction I had pointed but said nothing. We rode on in silence for some time, and I inhaled the scents of the cook shops, realizing I'd not eaten anything since breakfast. Casmir must have had the same idea, for he flagged a merchant who ran over to our conveyance bearing a small basket of pastries and a flagon of something to drink.

We moved on, munching on our snack, and Casmir prodded me. "You were telling me about your father," he reminded gently.

I went on to explain my father's secret tutelage of his daughters then described the poverty and deprivation we knew on a daily basis, and the fear that pervaded our home life. "As a child I couldn't put it into words, for it's just how life was. Yet it was nearly palpable, enough to make our lives seem different even from those who lived near us, those just as poor as us. I had no idea who my parents truly were or what they had lived through. Yet now I understand their fear, how real it was. They lived with the fear of discovery every day."

I stopped suddenly, biting my tongue. I had spoken without regard to the identity of my companion, having no real knowledge of his feelings or opinions on the matter, only those things Miarka had tried to impart regarding Casmir's character. What was safe and what wasn't when it came to the history between our two families? For Casmir's part, he gave nothing away as I spoke. He either graciously ignored my awkwardness or was authentically oblivious to it. His face maintained a neutral expression as he listened intently to all I had to say.

Rather than put me at ease however, it only served to unnerve me further.

I finished artlessly with, "And that is the bulk of my life for the most part." I didn't offer up any information about my father's disappearance shortly after my mother's death, and neither did I mention the arrival of Figor, our flight through the streets of Corium in an attempt to escape Ciasan's soldiers, or Veris' subsequent acquisition of me.

We sat in silence, and I wondered what sort of indictment this prince would give me now that I'd told him the things Veris likely hadn't bothered to. Perhaps he would choose to send me off by boat to the distant shores of Romanus to work in a mine, or maybe he would simply set me to work in the palace kitchens, scrubbing pots. I predicted the latter. It was probably cheaper for the royal purse.

After a time he spoke. "But your parents loved you. In this you have the advantage over any of my wealth or power."

The assertion disturbed me, for it suggested an undercurrent I couldn't fathom. I wasn't even certain he'd actually spoken, that maybe I'd only imagined it, so quiet were his words and barely discernible from the din of street noise.

"Yes," I ventured by way of response, "they did."

"You asked me how I could be so accepting of the selection Cousin Ildor made for me," he continued, his voice level, his tone even. "It's because he is more father to me than my own ever was. He took special interest in my education, in my sword skills, in my... future... than either my mother or my father ever did." He turned impenetrable eyes on me. "So yes, I trust him with my life, and if he says that marriage to you is best for me, for the kingdom, then that is all I need to know."

He looked away, suddenly interested in a shabby shop on his other side, and the moment was gone. Whatever this intimacy had been, it was over. His solitary reverie shifted, and his aspect regained its customary courtier's mask as he directed the palanquin to return to the palace.

But we didn't get far.

"Kassia!" I nearly jumped out of my seat before Casmir restrained me with a hand, calling an immediate stop to the palandier. It took no more than an intake of breath to realize my mistake. As I climbed from the palanquin I saw that aside from the feral look in her eye and shabby dress, the girl looked nothing like my sister. In fact, it was almost laughable that I'd initially thought she was Kassia. She had hair black as night, olive-toned skin, and almond-shaped eyes. A small tattoo on her wrist identified her as a *hemu*, a Kavadorian slave.

Casmir followed me from the palanquin and stood patiently beside me. The slave girl clearly knew who he was, for her eyes bore into him as he approached, her look focused, more intense than it had been toward me. Despite the practiced nonchalance of Casmir's exterior, I sensed a profoundly different man on the inside. Muscles taut, he seemed like a cat waiting to pounce on a mouse. When he leaned toward me, I felt the pommel of a knife tucked into his waistband. He wasn't unarmed after all.

Shadows crept from hiding as the afternoon grew old. The market itself took on a deeper chill, hinting at the coming of evening. As the sun shifted in its arc, a beam appeared and slanted its way through a crack in the rooftop across the road, highlighting the far end of the slave girl's table, striking a stone, and catching my attention: a ring made from twisted wire, a polished blue agate the size of one of Addis' kopi beans nestled at its center.

I had always been captured by beauty. Kassia called it one of my failings, for she didn't understand it. Casmir noticed however, and much to my surprise picked up the ring and slid it onto my finger with a wink. He paid the girl a silver penny, clearly many times the ring's value. Then several things happened at once. I felt a slight tug at the pouch around my waist. Immediately Casmir reacted with the instincts of a striking snake, grabbing the girl's wrist, twisting it backwards savagely. She didn't resist, merely looked up with a peculiar smile even while her nostrils flared from the pain.

It was a clumsy move on her part, and I wondered what she thought she would accomplish. The penalty for a theft of this nature was amputation, and she'd had no hope of escape even if she'd been successful in her theft. To try it within reach of a magistrate would have been one thing, but Prince Casmir was no mere magistrate.

True to the law, Casmir pulled his knife from his belt. He intended to mete out justice here and now it seemed, and I cried out in alarm. The reasoning side of my brain understood the law, but my compassionate mind rebelled against it.

Casmir seemed to have no such conflict.

He kept hold of the girl's wrist, but rather than cut off her hand as the law required, he bent over and severed the rope connecting her ankle to a peg driven into the ground.

"What's your name," he asked harshly.

The girl's eyes lit with fire, blazing a bizarre triumph. "Chloe," she answered, her voice steady and even in her boldness.

A single palace guard materialized out of nowhere, and without breaking his gaze from Chloe, Casmir commanded, "Luca, bring her."

~7~

EXPECTATIONS ARE LIKE WILD horses: beasts of power, unknown, risky, and full of potential.

I had escaped the previous night's meal in the great hall based on a misunderstanding. Not wanting to correct Casmir's assumption that I was ill from the long journey to Prille, I hadn't been required to meet King Bellek or any other courtiers. This night was different, and I was terrified.

My expectations for the evening cavorted all over the realm of possibilities. I could walk up to King Bellek and be put to death on the spot. He had killed my grandfather and would have killed my father if he'd found him; why not me? Or I could meet him and find out he wasn't a bad fellow and get on like old friends. This didn't seem likely. The most reasonable prospect would land somewhere between the two extremes.

"There you are!" Raisa huffed as she rushed over toward me. For a woman I'd only ever known to be cool as an eel fresh from the river, she was positively enraged. In her defense, I had kept myself hidden in this corner of the back garden for the last hour since returning from my tour of Prille, and she'd likely been worried about her charge. If for no other reason than because she'd considered her own skin if something happened to me. "We need to prepare you for the meal, and there isn't much time left!" she whined.

The tour with Casmir had dredged up many of my insecurities, and upon my return to the palace, I managed to settle many of them secluded under the sheltering boughs of a young olive tree. I resisted the urge to tell Raisa that she was lucky I hadn't fled the palace and boarded a ship bound for Jungolara or Mazi Mari disguised as a juggler or a barrel salesman in my anxiety.

She shivved me inside with a sharp finger then set about washing and redressing me. I was too desultory to pay much attention to my surroundings, but when she pulled too hard on an errant strand of unwieldy hair, my head snapped up and I shrieked, fully awakened from my reverie. It was as I did so that I saw them: a pair of familiar eyes, connected to a certain market slave, a girl I'd all but forgotten in my repine.

"Why are you here?" I blurted, half-rising from my seat, pulling my hair from Raisa's grip. It fell into dishevelment, and Raisa cried out in frustration, the pins she held in her mouth falling to the floor. I crossed the room toward Chloe, stopping just short of her. She sat on the floor, chin dipped, peering up at me through the long, limp hair hanging in her face. Her posture hinted at her tension, caught like a cornered animal.

"Why are you here?" I asked again, staring uncomprehendingly.

"My lady, she is a gift to you... from the prince," Raisa interjected, not concerned in the least that there was a slave in my quarters, only that she needed to piece together my hair once again.

I swung on her. "A slave? A gift? What kind of a gift is that?" Fury radiated from me, and my hands shook.

Raisa eyed me dully as if I was a dolt who knew nothing.

"Come, we have little time." She looked tired, like a mother who'd spent the day hovering over her uncooperative toddler.

With a backward glance at Chloe I acquiesced then brooded while Raisa finished her work. What was I to do with a slave? I thought I had made my feelings on the subject perfectly clear.

When Raisa finished, she raised me up to see the results of her work. She had done well. Too well. For a girl used to keeping her looks unremarkable, it was a shock to look at myself now. Never before had I seen myself the way Raisa had arranged me, my clothing and hair elegant and beautiful. If men thought I looked like Adonia at home in Corium, dressed in a dull kirtle with my hair hiding under a kerchief, what would they think tonight? At least I would be on the arm of Prince Casmir, under his protection, even if I couldn't control their libidinous thoughts.

It was a tradition in Agrius for all of the highborn visitors to be formally introduced to the king prior to any evening meal, so that in a ceremonial way, he only dined with friends. I didn't know how I fit into the description of friend, but I was to marry the king's son; he could hardly kill me on the spot, could he?

Casmir waited in a small corridor outside the great hall along with a handful of other guests awaiting their own introductions. If I thought my own appearance shocking, Casmir's was no less than my own. Gone was the man with whom I'd spent the afternoon — the casually dressed, nonchalant nobleman who made easy conversation. In his place stood a regal exemplar, an exacting, sophisticated prince draped in rich silks. A light cloak slung across his shoulders, hanging down to the tops of his soft leather boots and pinned at the neck with a brooch boasting an immense ruby. He was exquisite, even if he remained unshaven.

At sight of me, he inhaled a sharp breath. "My lady," he murmured as he bent over my hand, kissing it in greeting before turning me to walk to our places at the door to the hall. "Ready?"

"Not really. Do these people even know who I am?"

"It's hard to say what sort of gossip spreads, though if they know anything, it's not from me." My face must have betrayed my worry, for he added, "You will be at my side, so no one will press you too closely."

His assurance should have eased my worry, but I was about to enter the den of wolves, and I felt like prey. Swallowing back the bile threatening to rise in my throat, I offered him a weak smile.

Bright torches blazed all along the inner gallery of the colonnaded hall while vibrantly colored tapestries hung against the outer walls. Fashionably dressed women watched with unreadable expressions; men gazed in open adoration. Casmir snugged my wrist against his arm, and we stepped out, a path opening up for us as we went.

Without a doubt we made a striking match, and I knew full-well that Casmir knew it too, for as I cast a sidelong glance at him, I noticed his mouth quirked to one side in satisfaction. Princes were nothing if not confident.

I did my best to keep my face neutral, pretending to be comfortable with the attention as we walked, one step firmly after the next, up the long hall toward a raised dais at the other end. Inside my bones felt as if they were made of nothing more substantial than smoke and wind, swirling like a maelstrom of chaos. I kept my eyes forward, focusing on breathing, on the next step, on remaining upright. Even so I could not help but notice people stare. Most dropped their gaze, but others had no such good grace, and their judgment weighed on me. Clearly they guessed who I was, but did they know the whole story, or only a carefully crafted version?

The longer we walked, other, darker thoughts threatened to invade. Images of my mother and father, of my grandfather, aunts, uncles, cousins...

No, not now, I told myself. Another time. I inhaled a slow, steady breath through my nose.

Casmir squeezed my hand as we neared the dais, and I turned my attention to the man on the throne. I couldn't have been less impressed.

King Bellek sat his throne like a lump. His face was round and scarred, his hair bushy, his beard scruffy. Nothing about him, including his rumpled clothing, indicated that he was a king or that he had led a successful coup against my grandfather.

"When I was a very young lad, I remember my father being fit and vigorous," Casmir had told me that afternoon.

Circumstances had turned Bellek into a man exhibiting the characteristics of one used to the excesses of food and drink.

Next to him a petite woman sat on an ornate chair, smaller and less esteemed than the one Bellek sat. At first I was tempted to compare her to Orsilla, Swine's wife, for she was dark and hawk-like, but then I looked more closely and found keen intelligence without the calculation in her sharp gaze. She watched me with Casmir, her expression devoid of any clear emotion, though if I had to guess, she appeared sad. Casmir's mother, I thought.

Behind Bellek stood Ildor Veris, dressed elegantly and proudly. His face maintained a carefully arranged formality of deference to his royal cousin, though I detected a peculiar light in his eyes as he took in the sight of me on the arm of Casmir — a marker along the road of his plan.

Figor stood below the dais, to Bellek's right. Unlike the deference Veris portrayed, Figor appeared disturbed. This slip in his facade surprised me, for usually he kept a tight rein on his emotional appearance. While the match between Casmir and me worked to further Veris' goals, it opposed those of Figor, for he wanted my father on the throne instead.

Casmir stopped just short of the stairs to the dais and knelt on one knee before his father. I did the same, my hand still on his arm. I forced myself to calm the inner turmoil raging inside by focusing my mind on the feel of the wool of his sleeve, the cool pavers under my thin-soled slippers. The room stilled, became as quiet as a tomb.

And we waited.

I dared not lift my eyes to ascertain his mood.

When finally the silence turned uncomfortable, King Bellek spoke.

"So," he began, his words billowing from his cheeks like smoke from the end of a burned willow reed, "you are the daughter of that cockalorum Sajen sop, eh? What rock have you been hiding under all this time?" My chin rose in alarm, my eyes widening in horror. I felt Casmir tense beside me. "Come to beg a scrap have you?" Willow reed indeed. The man looked at me as a dog would its fleas. He had kept his voice quiet, making it unlikely that anyone in the room had heard him. For that, at least, I was grateful. "Has my son here impressed you with the size of his generous... hospitality?" He hacked a cough, and Casmir stood stiffly, raising me up gently with him. Bellek looked me up and down appreciatively, taking in all aspects of my appearance with hungry scrutiny. "He is generous you know. Though I'm sure I don't need to tell you," he added with a lusty leer and a wink. Casmir remained steadfast, but I felt the muscle of his forearm tense through the fabric of his sleeve.

Ildor Veris leaned over to whisper something in Bellek's ear, and he scowled. Veris kept talking and Bellek calmed, nodded, then sat up a little straighter. His narrowed eyes considered me sharply. He waved us up the stairs to stand before him.

Casmir stood in a wide stance, feet apart, facing his father as a calm, placid sea, guarded and practiced. He had not learned his poise from his father, that much was clear. From the corner of my eye I observed Casmir's mother. She hadn't so much as twitched an eyelash since I had first set eyes on her. She watched silently, her eyes hooded, and her thoughts hidden behind a carefully arranged mask. Just like Casmir.

Lowering his voice even more than he had done previously, Bellek continued. "Cousin Ildor says you're to wed my son, is that right?" I didn't know how to reply to that so didn't. He stared at me a moment longer, considering. "Chin up, girl. Casmir, tell me what this is about!" His scrutiny switched to his son.

"Your Grace," Ildor Veris broke in, "the Lady Irisa is eldest daughter and heir of Bedic Sajen. Her marriage to Prince Casmir would unite our two houses, Sajen and Vitus, ending any remaining hostilities." He was a master diplomat I decided, beguiling and firm all at once, able to whisper honeyed words while communicating a sharp truth.

Bellek harrumphed. "I didn't ask you." Veris straightened but didn't look flustered. If anything, he looked affirmed. Bellek flicked his eyes back to Casmir. "Well, what do you say, my son?"

"It is as Cousin Ildor says, Father," Casmir replied tonelessly.

Veris smiled at Casmir with approval, and Bellek closed his mouth. Casmir's mother's eyes caught mine, but I couldn't make out the meaning, for her face remained placid.

After a few moments, Bellek pushed himself to standing. "Well, if Cousin Ildor says it, then it must be true." He waved his hands dismissively at Casmir. "We're done here. Let's eat." He took a ponderous step and moved himself off, thus ending any further introductions before the meal.

It was an odd introduction and not one I'd expected, having such significant political underpinnings as it did. King Bellek seemed almost indifferent to the unification of our two houses. All my life I'd imagined that a king held the ropes of power, pulling them to steer the vehicle of government and administration under a watchful, thoughtful eye. Perhaps I had been wrong about kingship, naive even. Perhaps Bellek was indifferent. Veris caught my eye and smiled.

Guests broke from their neat rows throughout the hall, ignorant of the conversation that had just taken place upon the dais, and moved to mingle as servants hurried from the fringes of the room to prepare the tables for the meal, setting out platters of food, flagons of drink. Casmir guided me away from those appearing most eager to engage us in conversation, expertly moving through the crowd. When I thought he might offer up some sort of explanation for what had just happened, he offered instead, "Let's find a drink," the conversation with his father seemingly forgotten. I followed a pace behind, and he flagged a passing man carrying a pair of goblets, handing me one.

He leaned in toward me as if to divulge a secret, but then something else caught his attention.

"Ah, Figor, just the man I wanted to see..." he said, grabbing the robe of Figor as he passed.

Figor looked startled, the look he gave me communicating that he'd rather be anywhere but here, talking to the prince and the Sajen daughter. "Yes, my prince?" he inquired courteously.

"This dear lady is new to Prille, and I imagine you can understand she is a bit... overwhelmed... by matters here. She has a maid to teach her the manners of court, yes?" He looked to me for confirmation before continuing. "But I would like her to have someone a bit more senior to take charge of her education, and to make himself available as needed."

"My lord, there are..."

"Figor," Casmir laughed good-naturedly, "I choose you. End of story. Say yes."

"Yes."

"Right then, it's settled."

Figor moved off stiffly, looking to be in need of a drink. Casmir watched him go.

"That man is brilliant, but he is a little stiff and needs to get away from his dusty records and law books from time to time. Perhaps some time with a beautiful young woman such as yourself will loosen him up a bit." Casmir winked a knowing eye, raising my hand to his lips to kiss my knuckles, and I felt a flush of heat race across my cheeks.

I was kept from needing to make a reply by the arrival of Wolf who slapped Casmir on the back. "Casmir, you wastrel. Can't you allow the poor girl to adjust to her surroundings before you try to overwhelm her with your pathetic charm?" Dressed as finely as a peacock, he stood a full head shorter than Casmir.

Casmir returned Wolf's jab in kind, and the two took up bantering with one another. I found it difficult to follow along but was rescued from the necessity by a mild tug on my skirt and a pair of wide eyes staring up at me. "Do you like kittens?" asked the owner of the wide eyes.

I smiled and lowered myself down to the level of the young girl. She was younger than Kalyn, Swine's daughter. Remembering my heartbreak, I took in the features of this new girl, looking for any differences between them that would keep me from comparing the two. Her long brown hair curled about her shoulders, framing her oval face. She clutched a small calico kitten to her breast as she waited for my reply, her face serious for one so young.

"I do," I replied warmly, reaching out a hand to pet her kitten. "Do you like dogs?"

"Oh, yes!"

"Then you should come meet Ilex sometime. She is like a little puff of cotton, and she could use some cheer. We are new here, you know."

The girl nodded sagely. "Yes, I know. My name is Kathel. Casmir is my brother. I have sisters, but they are all older and don't live here anymore. Sometimes I need cheer too."

Before I could say anything more, Casmir's mother stepped in next to Kathel, putting her arm around the girl's shoulder. "Kathel, it is time for you to find your seat, though you cannot stay late enough for the entertainment tonight."

"Yes, Mama," Kathel replied obediently.

The arrival of Casmir's mother had alerted him, and he turned to introduce us. "Irisa, this is my mother, Evet." The light in his eyes shifted, though his mood toward his mother was still unreadable.

"My lady," I said as I dropped my chin, lowered my eyes, and bent my knee.

"You are welcome here, Irisa," she said softly, taking my hand in her own and raising me up. I met her eyes, but rather than finding any hint of meaning I'd noticed earlier, I found stiff cordiality. "We will do all we can to see that you have what you need to make this your home." She broke her gaze from me, scanned the room quickly, as if looking for someone.

"Thank you... Lady Evet." Did I call her Lady Evet or something else? I felt utterly out of my element, a fish ashore. "I would love to speak with you some time, to get to know you," I added, deciding it was true only as the words tumbled from my mouth.

She smiled at my awkwardness and replied, "Of course, my dear." Offering no more than that, she murmured a pleasant parting and dismissed herself, out of the hall rather than to the high table to sit by her husband as was her right.

"We should find our places," Casmir whispered. He placed his hand at the small of my back and led me to the dais where we sat at the farthest end of the high table. Casmir offered me the end seat while he took the one next to an elderly man on his left.

The meal washed over me in numbing waves. I felt as if in a waking dream, with each bite of food, each nod of greeting, each polite smile requiring a force of effort on a very conscious level. By the time the dishes were cleared away and a troupe of musicians entered, my body felt marinated in fatigue down to every muscle and sinew.

I was reminded once again of the fact that Casmir had been bred to this and I hadn't. He seemed to enjoy himself, partaking of the rich food and wine through each course of the meal. He also had an ability to be one man in one setting and an altogether different one in the next. A man of two faces, perhaps? Perhaps this was how one survived at court. Veris, Figor, Casmir, Evet... each of them managed the art as if without effort. With such a practice commonplace at court, how did one come to know who was true and who was false?

My mind wandered this internal path so deeply that it took me a moment to recognize that Casmir had turned to ask me a question.

"You found the gift I left for you, I trust?" he asked again once he knew he had my attention. The effects of the rich, red wine left him relaxed, his features open and convivial.

It took me a moment to decipher which gift he meant, and I frowned. "You mean my slave," I rumbled. The effort to stay present at the long meal had pushed all thoughts of Chloe from my mind. Waves of indignation threatened to overtake me now that he'd reminded me of her.

His mouth twitched at the scarcely suppressed bitterness of my reply. "Of course," he responded mildly, narrowing his eyes as if seeing me for the first time. "She is yours to do with as you will," he attempted lightly.

Did he think that taking power over an individual's very life then handing it to another was a thing of no consequence? "Indeed," I muttered darkly. "And I will."

He nodded slowly. "As I intended." And then without missing a beat, he lowered his voice, leaned in, and murmured, "Irisa, I thought you would be pleased." Confusion pitted his words as his eyes searched my own.

I said nothing, too infuriated to speak, and he gave up. Taking a deep drink, he turned to his other seat mate and started up a conversation about the downside of hunting wild boar on foot rather than horseback.

I slumped into my seat, feeling more exhausted by that single exchange than by anything else that had occurred the entire evening. I considered the full wine goblet at my right hand, thinking of the welcome release quaffing its contents in one gulp would bring before deciding against it as not in my nature. Why I felt so miserable confused me as much as it had deflated me.

"You look upset," said a voice from behind me.

I stood wearily and turned to greet Addis.

"I am tired," I deflected rather than verify the truth of her observation.

She didn't believe me, but took me at my word rather than contradict me. Taking my arm, we strolled away from the half empty table to a corner where we could observe the boisterous assembly.

"You will get used to it, you'll see. People will keep you at arm's length for now. They don't know what to make of you."

I was grateful for her kindness, for her immediate and accepting friendship. I knew I was in over my head, and she seemed to acknowledge my need for a steadying hand.

"It's not that. If anything, I welcome the distance from others. I'm not like them." She accepted this and I moved on. "I have encountered two Casmirs this day, it seems: the man and the prince. If only I knew which one was the real one."

"Irisa, let me share something with you. If you understand this, it will all go the more easily for you." She turned and faced me, putting her hands on each of my shoulders. "No person is ever as simple as you to want them to be. Not Casmir, for certain. He can't afford to be."

"What do you mean?"

"Every person wears a different mask to fit the need of the moment. Princes perhaps are the worst offenders, for they live in a constantly shifting world of friends and enemies." We walked on, and I considered her words as I studied the flickering shadows created by the rush lights along the wall. "The one thing you must remember is that solidity is only as good as the view you have. Just be sure to study everything from another angle, because perception differs from person to person, from one season to the next, depending on the circumstances."

I took in her words, considering them to see how Casmir fit, the afternoon Casmir and the evening Casmir. "So a day prince and an evening prince?"

"Yes, I suppose you could say that," she said cryptically, her smile taking on a queer light. "If I were you, I would remember your own wisdom in this very thing: the day prince and the evening one. Everyone is someone different behind closed doors. You would do well to remember. And perhaps stay safer by doing so."

"So I can never trust anyone?"

She smiled knowingly.

"My pardon, ladies..."

We turned as one to find Wolf, standing on a stone bench behind us where a niche had been cut into the wall. He leaned against the wall, one ankle crossed over the other jauntily, cup in hand. He saluted us with it and took a sip.

"A lovely feast," he offered, his toothy grin wide as he looked down on us, his scrutiny aimed a little lower than necessary.

"Undoubtedly," I replied simply.

"Oh, what a feast indeed..." he croaked before jumping to the floor, sidling in between Addis and me. "Delicacies of all varieties, a little to please everyone, I'd say." He took both our arms and began to walk us along the far wall shadowed within the protection of the hall's support columns. "I pity the celibates. It would be a hard thing..." he winked at me, "to attend a feast and not eat."

I gulped back an uncomfortable gasp as his innuendo became clear. Addis however, laughed heartily at her husband's double meaning.

"How do you find a princess?" he continued, clearly

warming up to his audience.

I had no idea and admitted as much.

"You follow the foot prince."

Again Addis laughed, but this time I did too. I couldn't help it.

"You know, if the harp sounds too good to be true, it's probably a lyre."

He may have been drunk and a shameless flirt, but he was charming, and I quite liked him.

Most of the guests had departed by the time I made my way back to my rooms, my mood lightened by Wolf. Raisa greeted me in her usual somber way, helping me out of my gown and into a light shift of unadorned soft cotton. She brushed out my long hair, but I would not let her braid it this time, preferring the freedom of it to the feeling of bondage that braids ultimately gave.

After she saw me tucked into my bed, she dismissed herself to her own rest. I lay awake for a long time but couldn't get rid of the notion that Chloe sat on a straw pallet on the far side of the room. I had no idea whether she slept or was awake. When finally I knew I wouldn't find rest until I talked to her, I got up, thankful that Raisa had left a night candle burning on the table.

Chloe eyed me from her place near the hearth as I crossed the room toward her. The feral look I had seen in her eyes that afternoon was still there, but to my relief I found no hate, only curious regard.

I pulled up a stool and sat near her.

"Why did you do it?" I asked simply. There was no need to explain what "it" meant. She said nothing, kept staring at me with her wide, fathomless eyes. "Prince Casmir had every right to cut off your hand," I continued, "then have you beaten within an inch of your life. But you did it anyway, and so clumsily, too. Why?"

At this last bit the corner of her mouth turned up into a cat smile, and she tilted her head to the side. "You think stealing from you was my purpose?"

Her eyes narrowed at me as if she had won a contest I knew nothing about. I was at a loss to understand where she was leading. Unless... "You mean you wanted to be caught?" The realization struck me like a physical blow.

Now she grinned openly. "You think I couldn't have stolen without being caught? I could have taken your purse without notice if I'd wanted to." She held up her fist and opened her fingers to reveal the agate ring Casmir had purchased from her.

My eyes widened into orbs at the sight of it. My head swiveled back toward the box where I'd left it locked away securely before the meal. I snatched it out of her hand and she laughed, not bitterly, but out of pure amusement as I put it back on my finger and clutched at my night dress, feeling a sudden chill.

"So why then?" I prodded.

She shrugged as if the answer should be obvious. "My master used me for far more than selling his worthless jewelry. I needed to get away from him, one way or the other."

"But you risked everything when you stole from me, when Prince Casmir caught you. Didn't you know that?"

She scowled. "If you think so, then you know nothing about him."

I rocked back on my stool, overwhelmed by what she implied.

I had misjudged Casmir. Badly.

The hour was very late, well into the wee hours of morning, but I had to know. On impulse I grabbed a light cloak from its peg, threw it around my shoulders, and went in search of Casmir. It never occurred to me to wonder if he was still awake at this hour. Instinct told me he was.

As I had no idea where to find him, I conscripted a passing duty guard from the corridor. He hesitated while giving me a curious appraisal, but ended up doing as I bade him.

When we reached Casmir's suite, the guard knocked heavily then backed away, peering down at the flagged floor of the corridor, avoiding my eyes. Immediately I wondered if I'd made a mistake in coming.

After a few moments, the door flew open, and rather than a servant, it was Casmir himself holding the door. A blast of hot air and intoxicating fumes hit me like a wall. He swayed a bit as he took a moment to focus and work out who I was. Once he recognized me, his eyes bore into the guard menacingly before he stepped aside to let me in. In the background I could hear Wolf call out, "Did she bring a friend?" Both men were clearly drunk.

A red flush spread over Casmir's face, and he swallowed hard as I brushed past him, his desire poorly restrained by intoxication. I wished now that I'd done more than simply throw a cloak over my night dress, that I'd pulled back my hair into a simple plait. As it was, it fell about my shoulders in unseemly disarray, and I chided myself for not thinking through my actions, reminded once again that I existed in a world foreign to all I'd ever known. Perhaps this was the reason behind the guard's discomfort. Well brought up ladies didn't do such things.

Now I was a lamb among the wolves, so to speak, and I

had to trust the prince's good character. *Everyone is someone different behind closed doors,* Addis had said. Now her words took on a deeper significance.

Once fully in the room, I saw that the men had no intention of retiring any time soon. A fire blazed in the deep hearth, creating the nearly intolerable heat. Torches lit the walls around the room, disguising the deep night, and the table was laid out with food and drink. Wolf sprawled across a bench, cup in hand, and when he recognized me, his eyes widened and he sat up.

Careful to keep a bit of distance between us, Casmir crossed his arms and watched me from behind hooded eyes. His breath came fast and shallow. "You shouldn't have come. It's late."

I thought he might be right. But I was here now and couldn't undo my coming. I pressed on. "Chloe knew you wouldn't hurt her. Why?"

This caught him by surprise. He raised an eyebrow then shrugged. I didn't buy his attempt to brush the matter aside and stepped closer to read his eyes, to see the tension in the corded muscles of his neck and the vein that pulsed just beneath his skin.

"Why," I whispered again, turning my face up toward his to study him more closely.

A muscle worked in his jaw as he clenched his teeth, his breath ragged. He lifted an unsteady cup to his lips, drank deeply, then set it on the table behind him. He moved closer so that his face hovered just over mine. I could feel his hot breath on my forehead. I wanted to step back, uncomfortable with his nearness, but I didn't want to back down now. I needed his answer.

He searched my eyes. "She is a slave. Bought and sold

legally," he said quietly, fighting to steady his voice, "and her owner is free to use her as he pleases." His eyes flit over my face and neck. A war raged behind his eyes, and he seemed on the precipice of making a decision. "But..." he inhaled, "she deserves better treatment, not as a plaything for a man who would use her for sport."

And the spell was broken. Casmir pulled back, picked up his wine cup again, and quaffed the rest in one shaky swallow. I found that I had been holding my breath so let it out calmly so he wouldn't hear.

I didn't know what else to say, stood staring between Casmir and Wolf who had been sitting on the edge of his bench wide-eyed as our conversation unfolded. He looked clearly relieved while Casmir appeared utterly exhausted.

"I'll see you back to your room," Casmir whispered finally. The fog which had enveloped him upon my arrival seemed to have evaporated, our conversation having forced his lucidity.

We passed down long, dark corridors, neither of us speaking, until we reached my suite. Before I could open the door to escape, he reached for the door handle, holding it shut. With a soft rumble he said, "Don't ever come to me like that again." He searched my eyes to see that I understood, and I nodded, my heart thudding in my chest.

When he turned to leave, I stopped him with a light hand on his arm. "I plan to release her, you know," I whispered.

"I know," he replied, lifting my hand gently and noticing for the first time the agate ring on my finger. He turned it to study the blue stone then kissed my fingers tenderly, whispering in return, "I counted on it," before turning and walking away.

I stood in the doorway watching him go until I could no longer make out his form as it became fully enveloped in night shadow.

Immediately I went to cut Chloe's bonds. She watched me passively as I did this, as if she'd fully expected it to happen all along. I knew now that she had.

I pulled off my cloak and dropped it where I stood then climbed into bed. Ilex lay curled up near my pillow, but she only lifted her head to see that it was me before closing her eyes again. I was just about to blow out the candle near the bedside when Chloe called out, "I'll most likely be gone in the morning."

I said nothing, simply puffed out the flame, plunging the room into darkness.

DAWN CAME EARLIER THAN usual, just to spite me. Perhaps if I kept my eyes closed my eyelids would serve as a sluice gate, keeping at bay the overwhelming anxiety I knew I would feel once I allowed myself to land fully back into wakefulness. That I would feel that way was certain, and I questioned whether I was strong enough to handle it.

Since the moment Miarka let slip my true identity, I had worked hard to come to terms with it, and most days I accepted it. I knew time was my ally, helping me grow into my new life, my new role, and the future ahead of me. And then there were days I felt weak and powerless, caught up in a strange surge of tides beyond my control.

After successfully keeping my head buried under my pillow for longer than I should have, I could no longer ignore the morning light streaming through the windows. I sat up, regretting the choice immediately. My head pounded out a beat consistent with a battle-ax beating a tabor. Never mind that I had consumed little wine the night before; intoxication had sources older and more primal than fermented drink it seemed.

I took a shaky breath, remembering the war I'd seen rage behind Casmir's eyes, a decision poised on the edge of a knife before him as his face hovered just over mine.

I pressed the heels of my hands against my eyes and held them there, willing my heart to settle. I felt ridiculous. Casmir was a Vitus, I a Sajen. We were from rival houses, and Figor actively worked to make plans to get me out of Prille, away from Casmir and away from any plans to wed us. War would come, and my father would retake the throne that rightfully belonged to him. I sighed. Why then, did I feel so unsettled?

Eventually I threw my legs over the side of the bed and stood, hoping that the bite from the cold floor against the soles of my bare feet would bring me out of my fanciful imaginings. I thought of Addis' kopi drink, wondering how it would taste first thing in the morning.

Very soon Raisa realized I was awake and retrieved my clothes, setting to work dressing me then pinning up my hair, her mouth turned down at the corners all the while. At first I thought she was upset with me, as if she knew I had escaped my room late last night after she'd gone to bed. I felt guilty at first until I stepped into the outer room, finally understanding her vexation.

Chloe. She hadn't left as she said she would, and Raisa appeared to take it personally.

"There are dividing lines between our kinds, or there should be..." she muttered. I ignored her.

"You're still here," I accused, walking toward the place she sat on a cushion near the door to the porch. She bent over a lyre twisting at the strings in adjustment.

The closer I drew, the more her efforts distracted me, and for the moment the lyre, more than her continued presence, intrigued me.

"Where did you get that?" My father had taught me what he could of music, but it had been many years ago, and I'd forgotten most of it. She lifted her head and pointed with her chin toward a small chest. "Do you play?" I pressed.

She placed the instrument between her knees and with deft fingers plucked out a melody, exotic and haunting in its simplicity. I watched and listened for a few more moments, entranced by the beauty of the melody, before coming back to the more immediate question.

"Why are you still here?" I asked again.

"Where would I go?"

Thoughts of Casmir, of our late night encounter, had so preoccupied me that all thoughts of Chloe had fled my mind. A pang of guilt tugged at the corner of my heart. I had freed her, and for that I owed her something more.

"Well, if you are to be my maid, you may as well look the part," I said, not concerning myself with what might happen to her after Figor found a way to get me out of Prille and back to my father.

She stopped playing and made a face, but I could tell by her eyes that she was pleased. Raisa however, was another matter. When I asked her to find something suitable for Chloe to wear, she obeyed, not wanting to contradict me, but she did not bother to look happy about it.

"And Raisa," I added, "can you arrange an audience with the Queen?"

"She is simply called Lady, my lady. She was never made queen, and no other titles were given her. I will contact her steward, Perijan, to arrange something."

"Thank you. I am taking Chloe to the Bibliotheca."

Raisa drew in a breath. "But... My lady... you can't..."

"I am not a prisoner, Raisa. I have my freedoms, do I not?"

"Yes, but you can't..." she waved at Chloe, "...it is expected that you..."

"Expected? Raisa, no one expected me at all. Now Chloe and I are going, and I hope to have word from Perijan upon my return," I commanded, attempting to sound imperious.

"Yes, my lady," Raisa muttered. She still looked doubtful, but she went about her other duties.

I had no idea what the unofficial wife-to-be of the heir apparent was expected to do, had no idea what Raisa's objections had been about, and for the moment, I didn't care. I wanted to explore my father's home, to see if there was anything left of his or my grandfather's legacy within the perimeter of stone, courtyards, and towers.

Chloe and I struck out for the central square across from the Bibliotheca. Even at such an hour, clerks scurried about their duties, and a line of petitioners formed, waiting for the opportunity to plead for justice from their king. I wondered if Bellek would choose to do his duties today, or if someone else would sit in for him.

Streaks of clouds lined the sky from east to west, as if an artist had taken his brush and drawn lines of white across his canvas of blue. The morning sun set fire to the clouds, painting them with hues of bright orange and pink. It was too pristine to be inside, I decided, so I chose to descend the steep cobbled causeway and through the gateway into the lower ward rather than go immediately to the Bibliotheca as I'd originally intended.

Raisa had dressed me in muted colors, in fabrics and with a cut that would not draw attention as I'd asked her. Now as we walked through the crowds of the palace tradesmen going about their morning business, no one paid us any mind as I'd hoped. Likely word hadn't reached the lower orders about my identity, and I was happy to let it stay that way. I hoped they assumed I was simply a ladies' maid.

A mini-city in its own right, the lower ward contained barns, stables, granaries, baker's huts, smithies, and numerous kitchen gardens all of which were peopled by the same kind of working-class servants I used to encounter in my daily life rather than the scribes and courtiers of the upper class from the upper ward. Everyone we met greeted us courteously and in a plain-speaking manner. Except that the architecture was vastly different, I felt like I could have been on a street in Corium.

We wandered as far as the outer curtain walls where I found a set of stairs nestled against a circular tower. We climbed, Chloe a tentative step behind me. Each of the stairs was hewn from a single large stone, worn in the middle from the countless numbers of feet which had traversed them over the centuries.

Once we reached the top, several duty guards eyed us curiously, but they left us alone. I found a space between the crenels to view the city on the other side of the wall, and the view was spectacular.

The city of Prille spread out all around, down toward the water and out on either side. Behind us on the horizon, and just visible over all the buildings, hung a dark purple smudge evidencing the mountain peaks making up the heart of the island. One of these peaks, Fyrgdun, sheltered the lands of the Argifu family — Bauladu, home to Casmir's friend Wigstan, or Wolf, as he preferred to be known.

I wondered in that moment about Wolf and his family — their history and loyalties. Had they supported King Nikolas when war came to this island, forgiven of treason afterwards as a form of appeasement to bolster support for a new, unknown king? How many other nobles found themselves in a similar position, and were these the ones to still bear a grudge, throwing in their lot with my father's current bid for the throne?

Perhaps Grand Master Lito could shed some light on the matter if I was careful how I went about asking my questions. My mind made up, I turned to call for Chloe.

"Chloe, let's go..."

The walkway behind me was deserted. I scanned farther along, thinking that maybe she explored down the length, but still there was no sign of her. The tower which sheltered the stairs we'd climbed to get to the walkway was just behind me. I stepped into its dark interior and began to descend the narrow stairs. Just as I reached half way, I heard the scuffle and the voices.

"Come on now, you know lots of ways probably... teach us some things..."

The voices coaxed, eager in their urging, though they remained light and amused, which was a good thing. I hurried my steps. And then something shifted; the voices turned angry.

When I reached the last step, the lower room came into view. Chloe stood in the middle of a circle of men, knife held threateningly as she rotated. Her feral eyes blazed, and she snarled as she lunged out at one man, connecting with his arm and tearing his sleeve. A crimson blotch appeared where she'd struck. He yelped and jumped back, blood dripping from the cut. She waggled the blade again, but another one lunged at her from behind and by chance grabbed a fistful of her hair. He yanked it savagely while another grabbed the knife from her hand.

"Stop this instant!" I yelled as I emerged into the light.

Five pairs of eyes spun on me in surprise. Most faces were blank with surprise, but one of them registered recognition.

"Lady Irisa!" he gasped. I remembered him as Luca, the

man who had materialized yesterday in the market, the one Casmir ordered to seize Chloe.

"Let her go." I growled as I stepped fully into the center of the group.

Nobody moved.

"I said, let her go!"

Luca nodded, and the man who had Chloe by the hair let her go, though with a look that indicated he wasn't happy about it.

Chloe let loose a vicious blow to the man who'd held her, and he doubled over in pain. He moved to react, but Luca put out a hand to stop him.

"What's this about?" I asked angrily.

Luca shrugged. "She's a slave. We only wanted a bit of fun. You of all people should understand that."

I gave him an odd look, confused by his meaning. "She is no longer a slave," I hissed. "Casmir gave her to me, and I have freed her."

"My apologies, my lady." Luca looked more surprised than apologetic, but he complied, a new light shifting behind his eyes.

"You should see to that," Luca said, eyeing Chloe's slave tattoo, before he turned and signaled the men to follow him out.

Once we were certain they had left, I took Chloe's hand, and we walked quickly away. Chloe kept her eyes downcast, but I could tell a fire smoldered there. She kept one hand over her slave tattoo as we went. Slaves were rarely freed, an aspect of her situation I hadn't considered. Once a Kavadorian slave, always a slave. No one ever freed them. Where was the profit in that? She had thrown the dice for freedom and won the day she encountered her prince, but would she ever be truly free as long as she had her tattoo?

Upon our return, Raisa took in Chloe's down-turned, shamed expression and must have guessed what happened, for her usual censorious mien softened, and rather than the *I told you so* quip I expected, she kept her mouth shut, turning almost maternal toward Chloe. Perhaps this was what she'd meant to warn me of earlier.

It was true that I didn't know what was expected of the unofficial wife-to-be of the heir apparent, but until I found out, I would choose my own method of influence. I had not chosen my position or situation; it had been flung at me. It was time to use it.

After inquiring after Casmir, I was told that Bellek's rebound into good health had been short lived. He had returned to his sickbed, and today Casmir heard the pleas of the court in his father's place. I hoped I might catch him during a break between sessions, delighted when this notion proved itself out into reality.

Casmir sat alone on the edge of a trickling fountain in the courtyard outside the chambers, his eyes closed as if in sleep. Crystalline water poured from a central spout, its pattering providing a melodic backdrop for birdsong. I hesitated as I advanced toward him, remembering our encounter the night before. He sat here now as Casmir the Prince, not as Casmir the man, and I hated to disturb the serenity of his peaceful moment.

Just as I made up my mind to return at a later time, he spoke.

"You have no idea the balm the sight of you is." He hadn't so much as twitched an eyelash.

I smiled. "My lord, you're not even looking at me."

He opened his eyes, patting the lip of the fountain next to him. Evidence of his previous night's carousel showed in his hollow, shadowed eyes, smudged as with charcoal.

"I find the peace of this courtyard soothing after listening to the prattling of men who can't even find their way out of a sack of grain without help."

My resolve faltered, and I wondered if this might not be the best time to bring up Chloe's issues. He'd seemingly heard enough of them already.

"My minders will be back for me soon, to begin another round. You wanted something?" His face wore a mask of polite awareness but not of invitation. He was tired, was humoring me. I could feel the weight of it even if he tried to hide it.

I hesitated only a moment before charging in. "Chloe, the slave girl I freed... she was harassed by the wall guards this morning. I told them she was free now, no longer a slave. They obeyed me and left us, but I fear for her, that the same thing will happen again."

"I will speak to Cousin Ildor, will have him talk to the men. She will not be bothered again." He paused, and I thought he might say more, so I waited. "Is there anything else?" he asked finally.

"I was also wondering," I began cautiously then stopped. He eyed me warily, in the way I imagined he eyed most petitioners. Doubt flickered, and I wondered if I dared continue. "Why didn't you free Chloe yourself? Why have me do it?"

He inhaled slowly and deeply. "Because I knew that you considered slavery abhorrent. You said you could never own a slave. I believe those were your words."

"And you don't think those things too? You told me last night that she didn't deserve to be a plaything."

"Slavery just is, Irisa."

I opened my mouth to protest, to tell him that it didn't have to be so, that it didn't exist in Mercoria and why couldn't it be the same in Agrius, but he broke in before I could.

"It only matters that you think it abhorrent. She is free now... either way." He shrugged.

His indifference surprised me. He had seemed more moved by compassion yesterday afternoon in the market. Two princes, I thought, remembering Addis' words of wisdom.

Before I could continue, Figor arrived to summon Casmir. "My prince," he offered with a practiced half bow. "We are ready to continue."

Casmir sighed deeply, then pulling himself to standing, he kissed my hand as if I was any other lady at court and entered the Council chambers, leaving me more confused than I had previously been. Figor gave me a cryptic look then turned to follow.

"Figor, wait," I called after him.

He checked his step and turned warily back toward me.

"Remind me again why my father must regain his throne?"

His expression turned horror-stricken, and his eyes darted around the courtyard to make sure we were alone. He closed the distance between us in several rapid steps and hissed, "You must never, ever talk about this. Not ever. Do you understand?"

I nodded a shaky head as he turned angrily and stalked back into the Council chambers.

I sat immobile for a long moment. My hand burned where Casmir had kissed it, and I thought again of the man as I'd discovered him last night. We'd walked a hair-breadth path, the abyss on either side fraught with all kinds of unknown dangers, and I felt heat rise to my cheeks at the memory.

As matters stood now, I was to wed him. Why could I not be the Sajen to rule rather than my father, even if it meant ruling on the arm of a Vitus? Not for the first time I questioned Figor's resolve to steal me away to my father. Convincing myself there had to be more to the story, I rose and walked slowly back to my rooms.

"Did you talk to Perijan?"

I strode across the room toward the place Raisa worked, clearing my throat and doing my best to pretend my encounter with Casmir and then Figor hadn't affected me as deeply as it had.

Raisa looked abashed. "Yes, my lady, but he said it was not possible."

"What do you mean, not possible?"

"He said it isn't done, that the Lady Evet must first send for you. It is not seemly for you to initiate an audience." She shrugged. Usually Raisa could be relied upon to know the customs of court, generally speaking, but this time her lack of knowledge held us at a disadvantage. As if reading my mind, she admitted, "It is unusual."

I had to wait, it seemed, until the Lady Evet sent for me. No one wanted to make things simple for me, it seemed.

"What am I supposed to do while I am here?"

Pretending Figor hadn't chided me the last time I saw him, I spoke out boldly. Time for the evening meal approached, and I found him sitting in an open arcade just outside the great hall. He tensed, uncomfortable with my closeness and still unused to being seen with me.

"Nothing."

"I can't do nothing, Figor."

"Yes, you can. It's simple. You simply do nothing."

"It's not in my nature."

He folded the parchments in his hand, tucking them into a scrip at his waist. "Irisa, let me make one thing perfectly clear to you." He lowered his voice and leaned in. "You are not meant to be here. Not yet, at least." He searched out the long corridors to the left and right of us. "Not without your father. I am doing what I can to make a plan to get you out, but there are difficulties, and it will take some time."

"And if I don't want to go?"

"It's not up to you."

I didn't know what to say to that. It wasn't any more in my nature to be contrary than it was to do nothing. Kassia was the contrary one, but Kassia wasn't here.

"Irisa, your only job is to keep quiet and wait."

"I can't keep quiet, Figor. There are things I need to figure out. And I want to enjoy myself while I'm at it."

His eyes narrowed. "I've seen you with Casmir. Don't get attached."'

I decided that the folds of my skirts were suddenly fascinating and began to fiddle with them, knowing that if I looked at him now I'd give away my secret thoughts. Wanting to change the subject, I asked, "I want to speak with Evet, but her steward won't allow it."

Figor waved his hand. "It doesn't matter. Just leave it alone, Irisa."

"But what if your plan doesn't work, and I stay?"

"We will deal with that if it happens, which it won't." He stood in dismissal of me. "Now if you'll excuse me, I have matters to attend."

"Surely it is alright if I help Chloe?"

A look of irritation flit across his face as he scrunched up his nose trying to decipher what I'd just said. "Chloe?"

"Yes, she's the slave that Casmir gifted me, and I freed her. Surely I can help her while I wait for you to save me?" I'd said this last part a bit more sardonically than I'd intended, but he was too distracted to notice.

"Yes, yes, fine..." He waved his hands and turned to leave. "Help your slaves," he threw back as he went.

I smiled a cat smile at his retreating back.

Later that night as I prepared for bed, I specifically asked Chloe to assist me rather than Raisa. I wanted to take her measure, to assess whether she still felt shaken after her encounter in the tower. She assured me that she was fine, a spark firing her eyes as she waved away my concern. After questioning her closely, I concluded that she was telling the truth. How she could have put it behind her so easily amazed me, but apparently I hadn't counted on her resiliency. All the experiences throughout her life had likely hardened her, lining her spine with steel.

Long into the hours of the night, however, I found out the truth. A continuous low, whimpering moan woke me. Confused by its source, I slipped out of bed to investigate. Most of the room wore the dark cloak of night. Even so the far corner glowed with eerie light. As I approached, the shadows took on a diabolical look, dancing as a result of a fire which burned in a small brazier, highlighting the figure of Chloe sitting hunched near it.

I tiptoed toward her, not wanting to disturb her even

while remaining steadfast in my concern. I knelt down carefully, instantly realizing the horror of the situation: a band of metal glowed red in the fire. Once Chloe deemed it hot enough, she pressed it to her wrist, burning the skin of her tattoo, sobs of agony wracking her body each time.

I grabbed at her hands as she made to pull the heated metal from the deepest coals for another attempt. After prying the bar out of her grasp, I pulled her into my arms. Her pain-wracked body shook, and sweat beaded up along her forehead. I smoothed her hair to her head as I rocked her back and forth.

Peering over her head, I studied the result of her midnight work: the skin of her wrist puckered and blistered where she had burned it. Some of the tattoo remained, but the rest was mutilated skin.

"I will get some salve," I whispered after a time. "We will bandage it well. And tomorrow I will talk to Addis about how to fix this tattoo of yours. You will not continue to bear the mark of your abuse. You are free now."

Very early the next morning, before Raisa awoke, before Chloe, even before Ilex could be bothered to get up, I rose, dressed myself simply, and slipped away to the Bibliotheca. The early morning air smelled of baking bread, birdsong the only noise to pierce the peace of the central square as I crossed toward the repository. I smiled, remembering the early morning sessions of tutelage with my father and sister. Kassia had never warmed to the pursuit of knowledge. She learned what was required of her, but beyond that her curiosity ended. For me, what was necessary wasn't enough. If I learned a little about a thing, it only piqued my curiosity, and I wanted to learn more. Here in Prille, in this Bibliotheca, I could indulge my curiosity as much as I wanted. And because of my newfound position, I could do just that.

Thinking to learn what I could of Kavador and the slave trade, I crossed the cavernous main room and progressed up and down the aisles, looking for anything that might help. Perhaps a history of trade or economics would help. The scriptstórii of the Bibliotheca had worked long and hard throughout the centuries, producing a useful index system to find materials. Once I figured out how topics were arranged, it was a simple matter to find a manuscript about Kavador.

I decided to take my book to a small back room, wanting to be out of the way and unobserved as the scriptstórii trickled into the repository to begin their day's work. Pulling up a stool, I moved aside a smattering of loose parchments and sat down at the large table in the middle of the room.

The binding on the book I'd selected had been poorly maintained, and almost immediately a loose page fell to the floor. When I bent to retrieve it, I saw another loose page under the table. It wasn't one I'd dropped.

Tattered and yellow with age, I smoothed the surface and scanned it quickly, thinking to leave it for a scriptstóri to find later. Maybe whoever dropped it would be back for it. The script was hastily written, as would be a private missive rather than the formal script of a court scribe. It was the signature at the bottom which stopped me up short: Nikolas Sajen.

"Oh, my pardon, lady!" The interruption elicited a squeak from me, and I felt caught out even though I had done nothing wrong. "I didn't expect anyone in here." It was a younger scriptstóri, and he looked around the room nervously. "Can I help you with something?"

Yes, you can leave, I thought. "No, I have everything I need, thank you," I said instead, moving my hand over my newfound prize lest he see it and want to take it away from me. He nodded and was just turning to leave when I reconsidered. "Wait, please. Actually yes, there is something you can help me with."

The man didn't appear to have recognized me, so perhaps I could get information from him that wouldn't be tainted by knowledge of my identity. I surreptitiously lifted the book about Kavador and slid my prize further underneath it. "What can you tell me about Nikolas Sajen?"

His lip curled in derision. "Nikolas Sajen was a fool," he growled.

A bristle of fury rose at his assertion, but I checked myself. Instead I schooled my face into a calm, casual regard to encourage him to keep talking. "Why do you say that?" I asked as innocently as I could.

He eyed me with suspicion, apparently wondering why anyone would question the notion. Anyone ought to have known what sort of man my grandfather was. Thankfully he seemed inclined enough to want to share his knowledge and display his superiority, so he kept talking.

"Because he was a depraved tyrant, of course!"

"Of course," I added with a nod to show him I was on his side, to encourage more information from him. My heart pounded.

"The lavish life at the cost of the kingdom, the baitings and blood sport... all of it. He was a depraved man with a taste for things that weren't always natural." He leaned in, clearly relishing his gossip. "Everyone knows that."

I offered him a weak smile and nod to let him know I agreed even though I had no idea what he was talking about. What could he mean by baitings and blood sport, I wondered. A taste for things that weren't always natural. A cold finger of unease traced a line up my spine.

"All of those merchants who traded in flesh... They benefited mightily from that monster. Thank the gods we rid our shores of him and the rest of his lot with the coming of Bellek."

"But Agrius has slaves today, yes? Surely the trade still happens. They can't all have gone."

He choked off a snort that was likely meant to be a laugh. "Indeed," he replied, eyeing me in a new light. "Slavery has been around for generations. But that's not the part I'm referring to. Slavery's not so bad such as it is. That wasn't enough for Nikolas though. He took it all to a new level, a much more depraved one. The savagery he supported and encouraged..." He shook his head. "Agrius was a different place then, from what I hear." His cheeks reddened as he realized he was admitting his youth, his pride prickling at the idea. "We've purged most the records already, but I think there are a few trade records left, if you'd like to read them?"

I nodded, not wanting to turn down his assistance, and he left me momentarily, returning with a small volume in his hand.

"It's not much, but it explains some of what I meant."

"Thank you," I said. I felt sick.

"And to beggar a kingdom to do it too..." he whispered to himself. Before he could say anything more, someone called his name. He startled and realized the neglect of his duties, stood tall, and excused himself without another word.

Inwardly I cringed, having no love for the man's hate of my family. He was young and only knew what he had been told by those who had come before him. What was harder for me to dismiss was his tale. If even a fraction was true, it was disturbing at best. Was this the inheritance my father would have received?

It didn't follow along with my knowledge of him. Now I turned my attention to the discovered missive hiding under the book.

I took it up and read, though it did nothing but add to my confusion.

Personal missive, indeed. My father, Figor, Miarka – everyone had told me a version of their truth. But what if none of it was true after all? If this scroll was legitimate, Nikolas Sajen, my grandfather, had agreed to accept my mother, Naria of Pania, as wife for my father in marriage in exchange for his silence. For what, the scrap did not say. What did he want Aleksandar of Pania to stay quiet about, thus agreeing to the marriage between the daughter of Pania's king and his own heir? Did either of my parents know about this, and was it yet another secret they had kept from me?

I fingered my bennu necklace then tucked the yellowed parchment into my waistband. I returned the book on Kavador then decided I should return to my apartments to prepare for the day. Raisa likely wondered where I'd gone, and I didn't want her to raise the palace guards on my behalf, thinking I'd gone missing. Grand Master Lito entered just as I strode across the room, a question on his face as he saw me pass.

~*9*~

"*WHERE DID YOU LEARN* to fight like that, in the guard tower that day?"

Two days had passed since Chloe's incident in the tower. Now that we were distanced from it a bit, I felt emboldened to ask her about her remarkable ability to defend herself. Her physical scars were healing, and Addis had done her best to alter what little remained of the slave tattoo. Ildor Veris had ordered the men regarding her, and I was certain that no more abuse would come her way in the meantime. Even so, she'd remained withdrawn despite her assurances that she was fine.

She sat silently strumming her lyre, shrugging as an answer to my question.

I took a deep breath and searched the sky, as if patience could be found overhead. It was a bright afternoon, and for once the wind remained calm. A wisp of cloud resembling a frothy ocean wave undulated in the upper heights of the heavens, and I settled back against my hands to watch it.

We had escaped the confines of the palace for a brief picnic in a broad meadow just outside Prille. The break had been selfish, for my sake primarily, but I had also hoped that the calm would entice Chloe to open up. Eventually she gave in.

"No one wants to have to know how to do those things." She cocked an eyebrow at me. "You learn things for survival. When life is never a guarantee from one day to the next, you do what you must."

I understood survival, but not in the way Chloe understood it. Kassia and I had scraped out a living after our father disappeared, but we had never truly been in physical danger. Our means had been meager, but at least we'd had a place in society. We always lived on the edge of it, but within that realm we had always been relatively safe.

"You unarmed one of the guards, and they are blade trained men. That's not something casually learned."

Chloe eyed me warily, but I smiled and begged one of the guards to stand and face Chloe.

The man I'd chosen was Luca, the guard involved in the assault on Chloe. I'd purposely sought him out, befriended him, thinking it might be a good way to help Chloe regain the power she felt she'd lost, and to show her she had nothing to fear from the men any longer. He'd responded well to my efforts, displaying a genuine show of remorse for what had happened. He seemed genuinely pleased when I'd asked him to accompany us this afternoon.

Now as I explained that I wanted him to fight Chloe, he backed away wide-eyed, fearing the ramifications of disobeying Veris' order to leave her alone. Amused by this, Chloe laughed and insulted him, hoping to draw him into a fight. He bristled by way of response, soliciting a wicked grin from Chloe. She drew him in with a wave.

The contest didn't last long. Within moments Luca found himself on the ground with Chloe standing just beyond his head, his knife in her other hand. The other two guards whooped with laughter, and Luca muttered darkly as he pushed himself to standing, warning that neither of his peers could do better. The challenge only encouraged them. In turn, each tried, and each failed.

By the end, Chloe heaved with effort, triumphant in her success. Beads of sweat snaked down her face, and she gulped down air as she leaned over, hands pressed into her thighs.

"It's my turn. Teach me?" I urged her. "I want to learn."

After a bit more coaxing, she eventually gave in.

Standing in the same circle as before, she demonstrated a few basics. My attempts to mimic her fell woefully short, and we all fell into fits of laughter, the guards included. It was in this compromised state of hilarity that Casmir and Wolf found us.

Peering up from within a heap of crumpled silk, my hair falling around my ears, I sobered when I saw Casmir looking down on me from high atop his horse. His mood was unreadable as he issued curt orders for the servants to clean up and for the guards to return to watchful attention.

Once finished with these matters, Casmir approached, and I swallowed hard, uncertain if he would reprimand me for my unladylike behavior. I stood, smoothing my skirts and brushing away the dirt as best I could, eyeing the guards and Chloe sidelong as I did so. None of them would meet my look.

"Irisa," he began as he raised a finger to wipe away a smudge of dirt from my nose. "Your elbows," he continued, his voice firm, "are too far from your body." He adjusted my arms. "They should be like so."

"Yes, my lord," I replied soberly. "I shall do better next time." I did my best to appear duly reprimanded.

"Next time?" He arched a brow.

"Yes, my lord. I intend to learn to defend myself."

"From whom do you need to protect yourself?" He snatched the blade from my hand and stepped closer. "Do you think?"

I pretended to think then looked up at him in earnest. "Highwaymen." I nodded toward the road. "Ravishers." I nodded at Wolf. "That sort of thing."

He dipped his chin, and his face hovered just over mine. "Then perhaps I should teach you myself?" He picked a leaf from my hair.

"My lord, if I may," Wolf interrupted, pressing himself into the narrow space separating us. "I will teach her... So you don't know all her tricks, so you have to stay on your toes..."

"Why would you think she'd need to use her skills on me?"

Wolf grinned wickedly, and I blushed, clearly out of my element.

Casmir laughed. "Then I must concede. Teach her all you know. But let's keep it professional, shall we?"

The afternoon lengthened, and what was meant to be a brief picnic turned into a dalliance as other young lords and ladies joined us from the palace. The majority of the gathered group stood together in a wide circle as many of the young men engaged in a spontaneous wrestling match.

I had joined in on the fun for a while, but the gentle breeze and warmth of sun whispered languorous ideas about a possible nap, so Chloe and I pulled away to watch from the sidelines.

Now as we lounged in the brightness, I spoke. "You have been with me for only a few days now, but we haven't had much of a chance to talk in private. Since you are to be my maid, I would know more about you."

"There is nothing to tell, my lady," she answered,

avoiding my eyes.

"Of course there is. Everyone has something to tell." I smiled at her warmly, doing my best to encourage her disclosure. "You know I was not raised to this." I waved my hand toward the circle of finely dressed lords and ladies. "You and I are not so terribly different, are we?"

She considered the matter for some time. "That villain at the rubbish shop where you found me acquired me from traders after my parents died a couple of years ago. Up to that point we had been owned by a horse dealer in the wide plains north of Prille. That's where I was born. We had a relatively good life there, considering we were slaves."

"You worked with the horses then? Groomed them, fed them?"

She eyed me with amusement. "No, I broke them for riding. My family before me knew the trade going back many generations."

"How did you all become slaves?"

"My parents were slaves, as were their parents before them. It runs in the family, you know." She quirked a smile at the irony of our two relative inheritances. "They were just about to buy their freedom. You could do that in those days, you know. But they never got the chance. That's when everything changed."

"What changed?"

"Your grandfather."

"What did he do?" I asked warily.

She cocked her head to the side, as if surprised I wouldn't have already known. "He took management of the slave trade under the crown. It wasn't enough that the slave trade thrived in Agrius. He needed slaves to feed his taste for sport, and the profit supported everything else in his court."

She turned almost accusatory eyes on me, then remembered herself. "He was a fool."

This was the second time someone had called my grandfather a fool. I had questioned the reliability of the scriptstóri from the Bibliotheca, but Chloe's account supported it. Why then had Miarka described the Sajens as saviors, mightier than fabled warriors?

"So I have heard," I said pensively. "A family in Corium helped me try to escape. This was just before Ildor Veris found me." I wasn't certain how much of my story, if any, Chloe knew, but I continued as if she did. I trusted her, and it felt good to talk to someone. "Unlike you, they spoke of my grandfather as if he was a hero of old. I wonder why?"

"Hard to say, isn't it?" She picked the reedy stem of grass and put it between her lips to chew. "Maybe they were involved in the blood sport in some way. It was those people who lost out most when Bellek came."

While I had ceased to be surprised by the things I was learning about my family, her suggestion regarding Rolbert and Miarka felt like a punch in the stomach. I compared the picture of my memory of Miarka, the woman who had offered me such kindness and support, with that of a trader in flesh, someone who bought and sold humans to be used in blood sport. Jahn had avoided answering me when I'd asked him what his parents' business in Agrius had been before their move to Corium, so it all made sense even if I didn't want to believe it.

Everyone can be someone else behind closed doors, Addis had said. I pushed the thought aside.

"And the people of Agrius supported the... the blood sport?" I asked.

"Some did. Some didn't. It was a cause for significant unrest among many factions, but Nikolas kept the dissenters quiet. Those he couldn't quiet, those with money and power... those were the ones who caused the trouble for him. They had a conscience even if he did not. The controversy simply made things easier for Bellek when he came."

"But slavery still exists in Agrius," I prodded. "Bellek didn't do away with all of it."

"It does. But the blood sport does not."

I studied the grass as I thought over her words, examining a particular rock near my foot. A small beetle cut a laborious path across it.

"You knew Casmir wouldn't harm you," I ventured. She tilted her head in confusion over my abrupt change of subject. "That day I met you, in the market. You expected to be freed after he caught you trying to steal my purse, which is why you did it. How did you know?" She shook her head and acted as if she would not reply. "Chloe, you said I knew nothing that night, and it's true, I don't. But I want to learn and I need you to help me understand. If I am to be successful in my role as wife to Casmir, I need help. Would you help me?"

Chloe eyed the meadow, her former feral look returned, as if dark memories swirled in her mind's eye, mocking her with dredged up hurts, poking at deep scars she wanted to forget.

"Please," I begged softly. "Let's walk," I suggested, thinking the exercise and movement might free up her tongue, "where no one can overhear."

She nodded, and we choose a loose path around the meadow just inside a growth of trees where we could be seen but not heard.

"When I was a girl about the age of five," she began quietly, "I used to dream about being a princess. I imagined that life as I knew it was all a mistake, that I was not really the daughter of two slaves." She studied her hands, recalling her past in the scarred lines that crisscrossed her palms. "I imagined instead that I had been born into a royal family – into Bellek's family. I thought they were beautiful people. Wealthy. I had absolutely no idea what their lives were like, but I imagined it must have been perfect."

She leapt up onto a fallen log and walked the length of it, balancing with outstretched arms. When she reached the end, she made her way back and squatted down next to me, picking at the bark at her feet. "Then I grew up. I learned things. Experienced things." She knew what I was thinking, so added with a shrug, "I was a slave, was required to do whatever I was told. That didn't always involve riding horses." She eyed me meaningfully.

"One day Prince Casmir came to view my master's horses. I resigned myself to what would likely happen. Buyers rarely bought their horse and left directly. I assumed he would be no different than any other noble who frequented my master's trade. I demonstrated the beast for him, and when I finished, my master inquired if he wished anything else." She said this last part so softly and so matter-of-factly that I had to listen closely. "But Casmir did something unexpected. He laughed at my master. 'I force myself on no one, slave or otherwise,' he said. Unwilling to lose the extra coin it would bring, my master pressed him harder, and Casmir turned on him, furious. 'Ask me that one more time and I will take her from you, free her,' he fumed. I don't remember what they said after that. I was too shocked at my reprieve."

Somehow I wasn't surprised by her story. Miarka had intended me to think certain things about Casmir, and yet the Casmir I had come to know did not reflect Miarka's stories.

Chloe continued, "It has been said that as a young man Prince Casmir didn't act like his friends, and unlike so many others, his revelries were not public affairs. It was like he was too serious-minded to run wild."

I looked sharply at her at this, for a serious-minded Casmir did not line up with the reluctant ruler I'd judged him to be. Addis said he didn't fancy sitting in for his father to hear the pleas of the court, and I remembered the look of resignation on his face when Figor called him back into the Council chambers.

"It is also known that he never enacts summary judgment on thieves as the law decrees. This is why I vowed I would find a way to use that knowledge to gain my freedom."

I contemplated the many facets of Prince Casmir as I knew them in the quiet spaces throughout the rest of the day, even through the evening meal. Later that night I lifted out the sun medallion that had been a gift from Ildor Veris and held it up, allowing it to dangle. The bright metal rotated slowly, the firelight striking against it so that it glinted along the etchings making up the sun on its face. I took off my own bennu and lay both side by side on the table next to each other, studying them in contrast.

The bennu belonged to my father, the sun to Casmir. After a time I returned both necklaces to the small box in which I kept them and locked it.

That night I dreamed of a bennu flying toward the sun.

Another day brought one more experience to add to the novelty my life had become. Casmir invited me to join him that afternoon on a hunting expedition, and the notion both terrified and thrilled me — terror from my lack of ability with horses and thrill from spending time with a man who intrigued me.

In the meantime I wanted to talk to Grand Master Lito.

"Lady Irisa, how may I help you today?" The Grand

Scriptstóri spread his arms wide, his sleeves swinging from the voluminous cut and drape.

A younger scriptstóri sat near Grand Master Lito, and at his greeting the man startled. I recognized him as the one who had shared his gossip with me concerning my grandfather. His eyes went wide, and he stood, nearly knocking over an ink pot at his right hand. "Lady Irisa?" he squeaked.

"Yes," Grand Master Lito confirmed, "Lady Irisa Sajen."

The young man jumped back, knocking over his stool in his haste. "My pardon, Lady," he screeched as he bowed, then hurried away, his face pale and waxy. Grand Master Lito watched him go, confusion pitting his face as he muttered something about young people under his breath.

Knowing how I'd purposely misled him, I hid my mischievous smile from Grand Master Lito and pulled out my bennu necklace, holding it up for him to see.

"I am curious if you know what this is."

Grand Master Lito took the silver medallion and fingered the twists and turns of the engraved lines with a single finger. "Come with me," he said, handing back the necklace and gesturing for me to follow him. He led me to the back room and cleared away a pile of books and parchments then invited me to sit.

A single window punctuated a spot high up in the wall facing east, allowing a shaft of sunlight to filter down toward the center of the room. Dust motes danced within the light, animating the air over our heads. I watched him as he paced.

"The bennu is an interesting bird," Grand Master Lito began, assuming the tone of a tutor teaching a student.

"What do you mean?"

"The bennu has come to symbolize rebirth. It is an ancient, fabled bird, and if it ever once existed, there is now no trace of it left in the world." He followed a narrow path around piles of books and parchments, his hands clasped behind his back. "The bird is said to live a long life. When it dies, it dies in flame and combustion. Its progeny is born by rising up out of the ashes of its predecessor."

The story hit me like a memory of something I couldn't quite grasp. Perhaps it was a story one of my parents told me in the cradle, one which barely filtered through the threads of my awareness as sleep tugged at the edges of my mind during its telling.

"Why do you want to know about this bird?"

"Because my father gave it to me, and I don't know why. Do you know why he would have done so?"

"You don't understand its significance?"

I laughed a mirthless laugh. "It's significance? Hardly! I was only seven or eight years old when he gave it to me, and he never explained what it was or what it was for. Only that I should wear it always and never show it to anyone. Since you are Grand Scriptstóri, I thought you might understand why it mattered to my father."

Grand Master Lito glanced at the door then pushed it gently closed. He came back to the table and leaned against it, tenting his fingers in thought.

"Your father was a rash young fool when I knew him."

Even though his words communicated censure, his smile belied the sentiment.

"You knew my father?

I had naturally assumed that anyone who served the Sajens had been conveniently removed or replaced.

"Of course!" He replied, surprised that I would think otherwise. "I have worked in this place," he spread his hands wide, "since before I even existed I think. Certainly well before the coming of House Vitus. I taught your father. I was his tutor. In fact I taught all Nikolas' children: Bedic, his older brother, and his younger sisters."

"He had an older brother?"

Grand Master Lito's look turned speculative. "Yes, his name was Soren, though he died a young man."

Like most things regarding his past, my father had never spoken of his older brother, never told me he had sisters.

"His two sisters were sent away at a young age of course, to finish their education in the courts of their intended spouses." He tapped his fingers against his lips in thought. "But enough of that. You are here for the bennu..." He scoured an alcove for a flagon and poured us something to drink, pausing to cough as he did so.

"A prince is expected to commission a badge for his house before he is wed. This one is likely your father's, though no one ever received them."

He needn't have explained the reason for this, for I understood it all too well. Bellek's forces attacked Prille during the wedding ceremony itself. There was no celebratory feast, and therefore no time to hand out badges.

"Most people assumed your father would choose the maul, the same sigil used since his grandfather, Sajen." Grand Master Lito raised his eyes to study the sturdy beams of the ceiling. "Out with the old..." he whispered.

"What did you say?"

As if shaking cobwebs from a dusty old manuscript, he shook his head. "Never mind. Just a memory tickling at the back of my mind."

"So you never saw this before?" I broke in, touching my necklace with my hand.

"No." He shook his head. "They would have been

handed out after the wedding, naturally."

Grand Master Lito looked uncomfortable, awkward in the knowledge that chaos descended upon Prille during the wedding ceremony itself.

"Tell me about my father's family."

Grand Master Lito's eyes flicked to the closed door, but just as quickly returned to rest on my face, considering his words. "Has no one told you the history of the Sajens?"

"Parts, but I want to know it all. I don't know who to ask. It seems a dangerous subject of inquiry."

He nodded his understanding. "The first place to start is to explain that Sajen was illegitimate."

"Sajen was illegitimate," I repeated. The right of succession generally belonged to the firstborn with the requirement of legitimacy. "Then how did he get the throne?"

"To find the source of the problem we must go back to King Ancin."

Grand Master Lito dug through a dusty stack of parchments in the corner, pulling a book bound loosely with leather straps from the bottom of the pile. He opened the cover and paged through the heavy parchments until he found what he was looking for.

"He was an impatient man, brooding and dangerous. His reign was defined by war, for he spent most of it away from Agrius fighting his enemies. As a result, there was little opportunity to procure an heir. Oh, he had other children of course, but none legitimate. Sajen was his oldest," he said with significance, "born to Ela, daughter of one of Ancin's nobles on the north coast. His wife Thyra however, failed to provide him with a legitimate son, and the poor woman was running out of time."

I didn't need to hear the details of what would happen to

Thyra if her time ran out.

"One day Thyra found that she was with child, and Agrius celebrated the news. Everything progressed as it should, but as had always been the poor woman's fate, her good fortune turned against her. Not long after she gave birth to Vitus, the legitimate heir to the throne of Agrius, King Ancin died. No one expected it, and as you can imagine, chaos erupted in Agrius. Someone needed to wear the crown, and most people supported Vitus as prescribed by law. But because he was just a babe, he couldn't act for himself. Seeing his opportunity, Sajen snatched up his father's crown.

"Not wanting to fight a costly war to dethrone him, most in the kingdom looked the other way during his coronation. Kingdoms ruled by a queen regent raising an infant king are generally insecure ones. In the end, Thyra fled, fearing for Vitus' life, knowing he would be a threat to Sajen's security. She managed to remain obscure, and Vitus grew up. Bellek is his heir."

Ildor Veris had told me aboard the Árvök that Bellek had a better claim to the throne than my father. Now I understood what he meant. I had no reason not to believe what Grand Master Lito had just told me, and a chasm opened up at my feet, threatening to pitch me into its dark depths. My father had no right to the throne. His war was not a just one.

"Sajen's son Raullin succeeded him, and then Nikolas, your grandfather. Nikolas had a dark soul." Grand Master Lito's look clouded over. "In the months just before Bellek came, your father started to disagree bitterly with your grandfather. Bedic had never seemed to care much before, but something changed him in those last months."

"Do you know what changed him?"

"No," Grand Master Lito answered sadly. He shook his

head. "I may have been the royal tutor, but I wasn't privy to the inner sanctum of the family secrets."

"So could his disagreement with Nikolas be the reason he changed his sigil to the bennu?"

"Most likely, yes. I believe he made a vow to do things differently than his father. Out with the old, he told me once. This is probably why."

So my father hadn't been accepting of Nikolas' ways. Even if his line had been illegitimate, it spoke volumes about the kind of king he would have been.

"So if the factions in Agrius disagreed over Nikolas' depraved ways, my father would have been the agent of change. The bennu would make sense in light of this. Something new rising up out of the ashes." The idea intrigued me, and something inside shifted. "There was no need to overthrow Nikolas," I said wearily. "They needed only wait for my father to take the throne." How then had Bellek succeeded, I wondered?

"Very astute, just like your father was, even if he didn't think his old tutor noticed." Grand Master Lito tapped the side of his nose. "This book," he patted the leather bound journal, "is a collection of my observations about those days. I have always kept it hidden away here because most documents from Nikolas' reign have been purged. No one knows I have it, so you must keep the knowledge to yourself." He smiled gently, and I warmed to his concern. "But you, of all people, should know about it. There might be more insights you could glean from it about your father and mother."

"Did you know my mother too?"

"Oh, yes, but I've told you enough for now. I think you have enough to think on for the time being."

"Yes, thank you. I should be going anyway."

"Irisa, scriptstórii are to be politically neutral, and I would hate for anyone to be threatened by what you learned in these pages. That's why you must keep it secret."

"Isn't that a dangerous course to follow? To purge the records? His reign may have been driven by a dark soul on the throne, but those events happened. How else will we learn from our mistakes if we erase the history we don't like? What threat is there in the knowledge of the past?"

"There is more threat in the truth of history than you know, dear girl."

"Thank you for telling me these things, especially if you put yourself at risk for being political."

He looked pleased even while he waved away my concerns. "We are alone here. It is no matter."

We both stood and he ushered me toward the door; but before he opened it, he took my hand and patted it. "There is much of the good of your father in you. The good I knew existed when he gave me opportunity to see it. You will be good for Casmir. You two are much alike. There's so much potential in him if he could only but see it. Maybe you can help him." He patted my hands again.

He opened the door and we progressed back through the main room. He made his farewell, though as an afterthought pulled me close, pitching his voice low. "Be wary of those around him. There are currents around the throne, and those currents will seek to use you, to use Casmir."

"Grand Master Lito!" A middle-aged scriptstóri rushed toward us. "Grand Master Lito!" he called again.

Grand Master Lito ignored the man, looked intently at me instead. "The Council..."

"Grand Master Lito!" The scriptstóri was upon us, tugging at Grand Master Lito's sleeve with heightened agitation.

"What is it man!" He muttered angrily, turning on the man.

"That cat has done it again! Ink everywhere. It's pooling on the Beol Codex!"

"By the gods!" Grand Master Lito screeched, and the two were away, leaving me alone to wonder what he had been about to say.

Clouds moved across the endless expanse of sky like a billow of smoke from the fires of a smith's forge. Wind powered the movement as it swept down the island from the northern stronghold of Fyrgdun's peak to whip at the pennants dotting the courtyard. It would have been preferable to me by far if I could have spent the afternoon sprawled on a blanket in the green grass, studying the clouds for unique shapes. Instead, I stood shaking before the gentlest mare in all the king's stables. At least I had been assured she was the gentlest mare in the king's stables. As I had little experience with horses, I wouldn't have known the difference.

I eyed the beast sideways as Casmir drew up behind me, offering me his hand. I climbed to the top of the mounting block and reached over the horse's head for the pommel.

"Hold here instead," Casmir said, guiding my hand to the horse's mane. "You don't want to pull the saddle sideways."

The mare twitched her ears curiously, waiting for her nervous rider to mount. I whispered my apologies to the poor beast for any crimes I would inevitably commit against her.

Once settled, I sat motionless with fear. I had only just begun to register the baying of hounds, signaling our departure, when a hand covered my grip. "Irisa," Casmir said gently. I chanced a glance at him. "Unless you have a pocket full of snakes and choose to taunt this poor beast with them, you are safe enough. You can loosen your grip before you choke the life from that pommel." I took his advice and relaxed my grip, but only a little. "I will guide her. You just relax and enjoy yourself. We will get you riding lessons soon to match your knife skills... for when you take up life with the highwaymen," he added, his eyes twinkling a devilish delight.

I tried and failed to match his light mood, though I truly did my best to follow his advice. I relaxed back into the cantle and took in the scene as horses and riders made their way through the narrow streets of Prille, clearing the congested heart of Prille, and into the countryside with its wide, green spaces.

The farther we rode from Prille, the more Casmir relaxed too. The resigned, closed off prince he had been outside the Council chambers slowly disappeared, replaced instead with the casual, easy-going man he'd been that first day in the palanquin. Displaying a very congenial nature, he talked readily and easily on a variety of topics, his favorite being his love of horses. I laughed with him about my inexperience, and told him the story of Kassia's intent to buy a horse the morning of her departure from Corium on the last morning I'd seen her.

Casmir countered with a story of his own, recalling an encounter he'd had in Corium with a thieving horse purveyor who was trying to cheat a young girl intent on procuring a horse.

"I talked the man down to a pittance in exchange for not turning him into Ciasan's authority. But the thing that made my day was the look on his face when I paid for the horse myself rather than making the girl decrease her own clearly meager funds. The man's eyes nearly popped from his head when he realized it! It was so worth a few coins to see the merchant fume over his lost ill-gotten gains."

"What did the girl do?"

"I honestly don't know. It's unlikely she even knew what happened!"

He laughed again and his eyes danced with merriment. I silently stored away this new aspect of his character. The kindness he had shown Chloe had not merely been for my benefit, it seemed. The man had a vein of compassion running through him, even if he was loath to show it often.

"Why did you do it?" I asked carefully. I had the distinct impression he didn't often let his guard down, and I didn't want to scare it back up again.

"She looked to be in need of a kindness," he replied hastily.

Very soon the call rang out for us to stop. We had arrived in a beautiful meadow sheltered below a high bluff on one side and the wall of the forest's edge on the other. Pristine white tents dotted the middle of the meadow, and servants buzzed around tables laden with food and drink. While Raisa fussed over the arrangement of cushions around a fire, Chloe went to fetch refreshments.

Casmir gave me an adequate farewell, but he seemed eager to get to the activity at hand. I couldn't blame him, so gave him my best wishes on the hunt. I found a place on Raisa's expertly arrayed couch and took in the busy activity livening up the previously peaceful meadow. Young squires unloaded and set up their lords' hunting equipment while others bustled about getting food and refreshment to fuel their afternoon. Impatient hounds bayed and pulled at leads, awaiting their release. The fervor of excitement was nearly palpable, and I couldn't help but become caught up in it.

I surveyed the lords themselves, dressed casually and standing about in packs of half a dozen here and there. Casmir stood with one such group, and while I didn't know their names, their faces looked familiar. The men clearly deferred to his rank, yet they stood at ease with him in the way of old friends.

Something caused Casmir to break from his conversation, to turn away from the men and look back at me. He offered a fleeting smile before returning to the banter with the men.

It's never been about my choice, Irisa. If Veris says that marriage to you is best for me, for the kingdom, then that is all I need to know.

Casmir's casual, if unenthusiastic, acceptance of our intended marriage shouldn't have bothered me. I wouldn't be around long enough anyway, for Figor intended to steal me away long before. A lump of disappointment settled into the pit of my stomach just as Chloe returned with food and drink. I had only just helped myself when a shadow hovered, interrupting my reverie.

"My apologies, dear lady, for my neglect of you these last many weeks. It was not my intent, but matters have detained me to an extent that it could not be helped." It was Ildor Veris.

I inclined my head and indicated that he join me. Veris removed his gloves and held out his hands to the fire to warm himself. He noticed the direction I had been gazing.

"Casmir is a good boy. Always has been." He articulated his words with efficiency, succinctly clipped, though his tone was not unkind. "I've known the lad since he was born. Couldn't love him more if he had been my own child."

"Casmir feels the same about you."

He twitched a smile but said nothing. We sat for a time watching a new log take to flame. After some moments he continued. "My big plan for you, Irisa, daughter of House Sajen, is that you wed the prince, uniting the houses of Vitus and Sajen at long last."

"Of course, my lord," I replied courteously. He'd made this known quite clearly long before.

"The substance of your role is quite simple, Irisa: marry the man, give him children, make him happy."

While I didn't disagree with his words, it seemed odd to emphasize it in such a way. I gave him a curious look. "Of course, my lord," I said again. "It is also what I want. Why would I not? I will help him in every way that I can. My father prepared me for such a role, though obviously I had no idea at the time. I will rule alongside him to the best of my ability."

He snapped his eagle eyes to attention over his patrician nose. "Irisa, Casmir is surrounded by advisers. The same men who have helped his father will help him also."

In other words, his list of my duties had been purposefully narrow in scope. My eyes narrowed imperceptibly, but he didn't seem to notice. "So you want me to marry him, give him children, and make him happy."

"Exactly." His face shone with the same pride a teacher shows when his pupil grasps a concept. "Simple, no?" He nibbled on a few more bites of food, then washed it down with the remnants of his cup. "I am so happy that you understand. Casmir is just what Agrius needs. With the fidelity of your commitment to him, he cannot fail."

What he meant rather, was that with my Sajen blood tied to his Vitus blood, conflict would be avoided, keeping the throne secure. Rather than point this out, I chose acquiescence and said instead, "I will do my best to be the wife and consort he deserves, my lord." Whether or not he understood the truth I meant to relay in those words was another issue. I would indeed, be the wife and consort he deserved. I couldn't go along with Figor's plans. I needed to stay in Agrius.

"The announcement of your betrothal will be made

soon." He rose. "The wedding will take place in late winter." He straightened his coat and adjusted his belt. "There is nothing you need to worry about, Irisa. Take your ease and fulfill your role." He offered an elegant bow then cast a glance at me as I watched Casmir. "It doesn't appear as if that will be too big a hardship for you." And he strode off.

The piercing blast of a hunting horn sounded then, and I watched Casmir lead a group of men on the chase, eager in his search for the glory that came from blood. The day would come to prove that he was indeed a good leader of the hunt, but only time would tell if he would be a good leader of men.

~10~

"A BIRD FLIES ON unseen powers, floating, flitting, soaring and diving on a current that no human eye can see. But the bird knows it is there. In fact, it seeks out the best conduit for its aim, achieving feats of acrobatics that only it understands. To those of us on the ground, it seems a miracle. We who are earth-bound could never hope to achieve such a feat."

My father lifted a perfectly manicured finger, pointing at a flock of blackbirds passing overhead. I watched them, though I didn't see any particular magic in their flight. They were simply birds, and not terribly beautiful ones at that.

"You must remember, my daughter, that when a being is in the place it belongs, like a bird, what is magic to another creature is merely a natural habitat. You will thrive, my daughter, when you assume your rightful place."

I scrunched my nose up at him, wondering where my rightful place was in the world. We lived in a dusty market, among those who bought and sold wares to survive, who daily haggled over prices, whose lean frames ached with hunger. It seemed a hopeless world to imagine anything being right. Especially a future.

"Why does she hide like a fawn in a meadow? Is she so poorly disposed since my arrival that she cannot offer even the most basic of common courtesy?" I turned from the window and paced angrily across the room toward the door, resembling an agitated bumble bee more than a lady-in-training. Chloe and Raisa watched me, their expressions sympathetic even while they remained impotent to help.

I was admittedly crabby. The mellow autumnal weather had turned colder as winter's icy breath threatened from the strongholds of the northern lands. It was said that an unusually early storm had already capped Fyrgdun's highest peaks with snow. I hoped this event didn't presage the coming winter, for my thin Mercorian blood had enough adjusting to do without a worse-than-usual winter.

And if the upheaval I'd experienced already in the last several months of my life hadn't been enough, the continued silence of Lady Evet frustrated me too, perhaps even more than it should have. It was all I could do to keep from seeking her out myself.

I hadn't had much time. My days of late had been filled with the mundane, from sewing wedding clothes to continuing tutelage in court etiquette. In any time that remained, I did what I could for the city's poor. I hadn't even been able to return to the Bibliotheca to visit Grand Master Lito again.

For the umpteenth time I returned to my seat, picking up my stitching as I did so. Raisa muttered predictable platitudes about Evet, assuring me that her silence likely had perfectly justifiable reasons. Even Addis, a woman supposedly accomplished at intrigue, watched on with no help to offer.

"I think I shall try to get an audience with her again later," I said, dropping my work into my lap untouched before ever having begun.

Chloe stood slowly then crossed over to my chair and knelt down. "I urge you to caution," she whispered. "Your position is still precarious, despite this." She spread her hand over the fabric in my lap. "Perhaps wait to push matters until after the betrothal, when you have more claim to Casmir. It would be harder for him to cast you aside then, if you were to upset someone by your breach of etiquette."

I nodded. Her caution was probably wise, though the idea that Casmir would cast me aside seemed unlikely, for it wouldn't serve Ildor Veris' ends. Without thinking, I reached up and pulled my bennu necklace from inside my bodice and fingered the intricate maze of lines making up the design. I thought about what Grand Master Lito had told me about my father, that he was displeased with Nikolas' rule, but my ponderings were cut short when Saer, my door steward, interrupted.

"Yar Hátin, a boy from Figor is here to see you."

Giving the man a nod, I set aside my work to see what news Figor sent.

A young boy stood just inside my door. He had the look of a clerk, but highborn, as if he was a third or fourth son sent to school to learn and become a scribe. "I am Bergen. Master Figor has asked for you. Will you come?"

"Of course."

Bergen offered me his arm, and I took it, hiding a smile at the serious way he tended to his task.

We progressed silently, passing through a warren of corridors until finally we arrived in the courtyard outside the place where the King's Council met. Figor paced along the far wall, hands clasped behind his back. He looked up when he heard my feet scratch the graveled path and beckoned me to him. Bergen waited unobtrusively just out of earshot.

"Irisa, the Council is about to approve a request that concerns you, and I thought you should know." He lifted his eyes and bobbed his chin toward the Council chambers. "I must be back soon which is why I've asked you here." He indicated a bench, and we sat. "A question was posed this morning regarding the crown's authority to wed you to Casmir, independent of your father's authority."

"A question you posed, no doubt? I assumed that as a daughter of a deposed house there would be no issue?"

"That is what most would argue... in fact, have argued, most vehemently, yes."

The wind whipped a small pile of brown leaves in a whirling circle, sending them spinning then skittering across the cobbled yard. Bare branches overhead filtered a weak sun and scratched at the stones of the wall just behind us.

"But you know better..." I prodded.

"Your wedding to Casmir must be stopped, and questions are good things. Even if it only unbalances and buys us more time to..." He paused and made a habitual glance around the courtyard, "...make good on the plans for your escape."

I didn't feel it would serve any purpose to tell Figor that I'd decided my wedding to Casmir should not be stopped, so I said nothing.

"It is a legal technicality only," he continued, "this matter of authority over your fate."

"What do you mean?"

"When your grandfather was deposed, a writ of attainder should have been passed to disinherit your father, and subsequently his heirs, from any claims to the throne."

"And that was never done. How convenient." I knew that Figor had to have been the brains behind the oversight.

"Indeed."

As Bellek's prime legal counsel at the time, Figor knew such an act would have worked counter to his future goal, the one he was attempting to actuate now. Prudence had kept him quiet at the time. "So what do they plan to do?"

"It was suggested that we pass the writ of attainder ex post facto, or retroactively, to correct the delinquency." He smiled dryly before continuing. "But I reminded them that doing so would essentially negate the purpose of the marriage, for it would take away your claim to the throne, the claim they are relying on to oppose your father's planned rebid for the throne."

I pondered this for a moment, I was no legal scholar. My father's line was illegitimate, the basis for Bellek's throne-taking. Yet my grandfather, and thus my father and me, had never been tainted with the label of treason. Men's reasons for crowns and rule, the very nature of anyone's right to do it, was really a philosophical matter, was it not? More theoretical than practical. Figor, I had learned, was a masterful legal mind, and the reason the Council valued him so much. His intellectual acuity had been his salvation and the impetus behind his rise to royal favor for two kings.

"Someone else offered another technicality, one which I admit I did not foresee. The Council can make you a *vesaet* of Ildor Veris. This the Council can do on its own authority, without any other outside influences. Ildor Veris then, will be the legal authority to agree to your marriage to Prince Casmir."

"What is a *vesaet*?"

"It is similar to a ward, an orphan taken under protection, though a *vesaet* by definition is broader than that, giving more freedoms to the holder of the privilege."

"But I am not an orphan! My father is alive, and..."

"It doesn't matter, Irisa. As I said, the argument is a thin veil to begin with, so the solution need be nothing more either. What it does though, is put you under the direct, legal control of Ildor Veris."

"I'm not sure how that is much different than the practical power he had over me on board the Árvök," I said, gracing him with a wilting look intending to remind him of his inability to get me safely out of Corium as had been his original plan.

"Except that now he could marry you himself if he wanted to." He raised an eyebrow as the notion washed over me.

For a fleeting moment of panic, I wondered if perhaps this had been Veris' real plan all along, to bring me to Prille under the guise of intending me for Casmir when he intended to wed me himself after becoming my legal guardian. He would then control my inheritance — essentially the throne of Agrius, or at least a rival claim to it. He'd still have to wrest it from the hands of Casmir, but he seemed wily enough to be capable. Was his true intent to make a bid for the throne himself?

"Now I must get back into the chambers, for they will begin again soon." Several other men trickled past us, coming from wherever they had gone during the break. "Stick close to your rooms until you hear from me. And above all, be careful. At least until I can ascertain what Veris' real plan is."

"Figor," I said as I reached out to touch his sleeve tentatively, "how did you come to serve Bellek if you are faithful to my father? Was it not always the way of things?"

"It is not for your father I do these things."

And with that, he left me alone on the bench, leaves swirling at my feet like the vortex of intrigue that was the palace. Figor looked over both shoulders as he walked, even though the door was not far.

There is a man used to watching his back, I thought to myself. And rightly so after decades of living a double life. I had yet to make up my mind if his role was heroic or foolish. Once again I found myself contemplating the fact that nothing was as simple as it seemed.

The familiar scent of candle wax and aging parchments filled my nostrils as I strode past rows of studious scriptstórii at work. Grand Master Lito was not among them, so I turned my steps toward the back room.

And found it empty.

"My lady, may I be of service?" It was the same scriptstóri I'd embarrassed earlier.

"I am looking for Grand Master Lito."

"I am sorry, but he is not here now. Can I help you instead?"

"No, thank you. I was simply hoping to continue an old conversation. There was much more he had to tell me, but he was called away last time. I will come back later." I glanced quickly around the room, hoping to spot the book he had shown me, but I didn't see it among the other papers and collections piled haphazardly about.

"Is there something you need help finding?"

"It's nothing. There was a book Grand Master Lito showed me, but I don't see it now."

"Oh?" He looked concerned and stepped fully into the room. "Perhaps I know it and can direct you?"

"It was a history of..." I began, but then remembered Grand Master Lito's warning to tell no one. "It's no matter."

"I will make a point to ask Grand Master Lito about it

next time I see him."

"Thank you for your time."

He nodded in acceptance, and I made my way back to my rooms. Figor sent word late that afternoon that the Council had in fact made me Ildor Veris' vesaet, putting him in legal control of the entirety of my inheritance, such as it was. Though this news worried Figor, I wasn't as skeptical. Even so, something nagged at the back of my mind, likely caused in part by memories of Miarka's stories. At dinner that night, as I scanned the room hoping for sight of Grand Master Lito, Ildor Veris caught my eye. Lifting his wine cup toward me he smiled and nodded, and I wondered in that moment, if perhaps everything Miarka had warned me concerning him was in fact, true.

The next two days leading up to my betrothal passed with Figor's concerns of conspiracy unsubstantiated. I decided that perhaps he had lived too long in his world of intrigue and double dealing to see the honest truth for what it was. Maybe in this case, Ildor Veris' intentions were simple and straightforward. Figor had long grown used to watching his back so closely lest his secret be revealed that he saw conspiracy in everything.

The day of my betrothal dawned bright but crisp, the north wind breathing timidly yet persistently. The Autumnal sun angled over the rooftops, drenching the room with golden rays. A single ray highlighted my hair as I sat on a stool, providing Raisa a bright palate on which to work. She had just placed the last pin in my hair when a retainer from Ildor Veris arrived to escort me to the Great Hall to meet my new guardian.

I could well understand the temptation facing future

generations to jump to certain conclusions regarding my kidnapping and forced marriage into the house of my family's avowed enemy. However the truth was that I went into the arrangement willingly, even if the scribes' records could not accurately portray my personal thoughts on the matter. Clerks rarely bothered to capture the essence of the hearts of women.

To my surprise, both Figor and Ildor Veris met me at the thick oak doors to the Great Hall, Veris to escort me to the front, and Figor, no doubt, to make sure that he did, thinking a marriage to Veris more disastrous than one to Casmir.

Veris was all smiles, though I saw a bitter light in Figor's eyes even if no one else noticed. Veris extended his arm, attendants opened the massive doors, and we entered the cavernous hall with its ancient timbers and stout stone construction. How many royal betrothals had this hall witnessed? Certainly that of my parents those many years ago.

I had been told that the betrothal would be a simple affair, nothing more than the giving of consent and the signing of papers. Certainly nothing ceremonial, for that was the purpose of the wedding ceremony itself. Even so, no one warned me that so many people would attend this private affair. I supposed that when it came to princes, there was no such thing as private.

"It appears as though everyone wants to see the heir of Sajen," Veris whispered to me as we walked.

Rumors had abounded since my arrival, but never open talk. No doubt everyone had an opinion regarding who should take on the role of bride-to-be of the man in line for the crown. In fact, such speculation was likely a sport for nobility the world over. Royal marriages brought strengthened political alliances and fortunes, and most usually both together. That Casmir would wed the heir of Sajen had never entered anyone's mind.

How could it have? Prior to recent events, the general populous did not know my father still lived or that he had children.

Silence echoed deafeningly as we made our way through the throng to the front of the hall where King Bellek stood behind a small table at the foot of the dais, his Council flanking him. Figor circled the table to stand behind King Bellek. Pallid and depleted, his skin hung on his frame. Dark circles ringed his eyes, and his eyelids drooped. Even so, he stood tall, unaided, and appeared alert as Veris released my arm to join the other men at the table.

In much the same way, Casmir stood just outside the circle. Dressed in an unadorned coat of blue wool, there was nothing about his presentation which would have suggested he was the heir to the throne. Intending to elicit a response from me, he winked, and I quirked a smile then returned my gaze to the proceedings.

The gathered men made a show of deliberation, as if what was about to happen still required consideration, then Veris signed the document on the table. Bellek waved me forward along with Casmir, and Veris joined our hands and stepped away. Casmir bowed over my hand to kiss it, saying, "My lady, I offer you my heart if you would have it, to hold forever if you desire it." His words, spoken clearly with strength and purpose passed through the ranks of observers like a ripple of the ocean's current. "And any other body part for that matter," he added near my ear, barely above a whisper.

The whole thing took less time than it had taken Raisa to dress me that morning. We turned to face the hall, and Casmir replied to well wishes and greetings from those who desired the advantage of closeness to their future king.

I sought eye contact with Figor, mostly to vaunt the success of the betrothal and the failure of any imagined conspiracy. He met my look but remained unmoved. Veris on the other hand, appeared paternal, proud of what had just taken place.

It had all seemed pointless, Figor's worry. In that moment I decided that Figor truly found conspiracies where none existed. Veris offered us his congratulations, and I offered a smile, turning away from Figor.

Casmir and I worked our way through the crowd of individuals whose names I immediately forgot, when I caught a glimpse of Evet watching us closely from a side gallery. I tried to steer Casmir in her direction, but with each greeting given and taken, more well-wishers moved in, and the crowd around us thickened. In a moment of panic, I craned my neck over the crowd to find her. Our eyes caught and held. Briefly. And in as much time as a single intake of breath, she turned and left with her ladies in tow.

Later at the evening meal, word reached us that King Bellek's health had worsened even further, and he had taken to his bed once again. Somber faces lined the great hall from one end to the other. More tables than usual had been brought in to fit all those who had come to Prille to witness the betrothal, yet the expected din such a crowd would normally produce was absent. Instead, sedate conversations rose and fell like a fragile butterfly on a summer breeze. Casmir sat with a melancholy to match, yet I couldn't put my finger on why. For a man who so easily wore his court mask, he was ever hard to read.

"Would you like some company when you visit Evet?"

Her question came seemingly out of the blue. I lay my sewing in my lap and stared at her.

Recent days had passed in a blur as we tended never-ending duties, and to sewing for the upcoming wedding. Wolf's father had taken ill, and soon she and Wolf would be returning to Bauladu. The pressure threw our wedding preparations into a frenzy, for Addis was an accomplished seamstress and we would miss her contributions once she left.

In order to ease my melancholy over her early departure, Addis suggested I come along for part of the journey. I immediately agreed. When I raised the matter with Casmir, he briefly considered joining us, though the idea failed before it even got off the ground. No sooner had he begun to make arrangements than Figor found him and scolded him for even considering such a notion when his father's illness required him to stay in Prille to attend to the Council.

"Cousin Ildor is more than capable of tending to affairs," Casmir muttered. In the end he acquiesced, though he stalked off without a word.

This drama had so occupied my mind that Addis' question hung in the air incongruously. I hadn't even considered Evet since the betrothal.

Addis sat now with one eyebrow arched, waiting for my reply. Chloe had urged me to wait until after my legal attachment to Casmir lest I risk offense, but Casmir and I were now betrothed, so what did it matter now? I flopped the work onto the stool in front of me and stood.

Just as we neared Evet's door, I happened to look left across a garden and saw her approach a side door. She reached to open the latch but paused, glancing my way. She was too distant for me to read her expression, but she held my look long enough to know there was meaning there. Did she invite me to visit? Would I finally gain access?

I quickened my pace, running through the myriad of questions I wanted to ask her. Addis knocked on the aged wood of the outer door, but nothing happened. I knocked again, and after several long moments, the door finally opened, though the narrow space between door and frame remained blocked by Perijan who stared at us without greeting.

"I would like to speak with the Lady Evet, if I may?" I offered politely.

"The Lady Evet is not here."

"But I just saw her. I know she is inside just now. How can you say she is not here when I know she is?"

"You are mistaken," he replied, emphasizing each word as a single rap of a gavel on stone.

Not wanting to be deterred by the aged guardian, I pressed on. "I simply want to offer my condolences on the poor health of the King."

"I will pass along your wishes. Good day." And with that, he closed the door in my face.

I stood there blinking like a witless sheep. The ladies behind me shuffled their feet uncertainly. Was it me, or was it her? Had I misread her look?

Deep in thought, I turned to retrace my steps back to my rooms, though almost immediately I reconsidered. Turning my feet instead toward the Bibliotheca, I thought to seek out Grand Master Lito, hoping he could provide the answers to the matter of Evet's evasion.

No sooner had I arrived at the Bibliotheca than another door, this one figurative, was slammed in my face. The Grand Master was nowhere about. Thinking to search out the book he'd shown me that last time we talked, I made for the small back room to look for it.

"Excuse me." It was the junior scriptstóri who hated the Sajens. Once he realized who had disturbed the silence of the small back room, his expression soured. "Grand Master Lito is

Stephanie Churchill

not here," he accused, as if I was to blame.

"I see that," I replied pleasantly, hiding my irritation. I grew suddenly tired of being brushed aside so easily, yet I thought first to persuade him with a pleasant demeanor. "May I know where he is? I must speak with him."

"Grand Master Lito has taken ill. Quite ill, I'm afraid."

"Oh, I am sorry to hear this! I have some skill with herbs. I would be happy to visit him, offer help..."

"There is no need," he clipped. "A physician attends him."

One of my ladies stepped forward haltingly. "Yar Hátin is good with herbs, she could..."

"I bid you good day." He interrupted, holding the door for us as an invitation to leave.

He stood sentinel at the door to the back room as we passed, watching as we crossed the hall toward the main door. It was only at the last minute I veered off course, deciding I didn't want to be thwarted so easily. I would not run and hide, defeated in my attempts to find answers.

"Addis," I told her, "I am not going to flee just because a junior scriptstóri looks sidelong at me. Stay if you wish, or go, but I want to seek comfort from the books. It may not further my agenda, but it will be a small victory even if an insignificant one."

She smiled slowly and nodded, dismissing the other ladies back to work. I made for a side aisle while she took up a position not far away.

I inhaled the familiar scent of aged parchments and rested my head back against the far wall, focusing on the rise and fall of my chest with each breath of air. Bright afternoon sunlight poured in through the large windows overhead, and I closed my eyes to let the golden rays warm my skin. Very soon a debilitating weariness overcame me, and I questioned my decision to stay.

It was for this reason that I sensed rather than saw someone draw near. I opened my eyes to find Casmir watching me. His gladness turned instantly to concern, for my face must have betrayed my weariness.

"I will have a word with your maids, for they seem to be overworking you." He walked toward me, and I tried to put on a smile for his sake, but my effort fell flat. "I will never be known as a man who can read a woman's thoughts at a glance, but perhaps I could persuade you to confide in me? My Adonia has been tossed to the winds of late, and I would help if I could."

His words struck me as sincere, but I found that I didn't know how to reply. I could hardly explain the entirety of my predicament to him.

He correctly read my overlong consideration as restraint. With a single finger, he lifted a stray wisp of hair from over the front of my left shoulder, stroking the bright gold under his thumb. "Your sister... Does she have your coloring?"

"No, she has hair like," I paused, considering how best to describe it, "beams of an autumnal sunset slanting through a forest of oak, deep waves of amber, or a nocturnal wood ablaze with fire."

"How else are you different," he coaxed, his smile encouraging a returned smile from me as well as a lightened heart. Initially I hadn't welcomed the interruption, but now I was glad he had come.

"For one thing she doesn't much care for these," I returned, running my hand along the spines of the books of poetry on the shelf before us.

He cocked a smile. "I can't blame her."

"You do not care for poetry?"

His lowered his chin as if to share a secret.

> *"The fair Adonis, turned to a flower*
> *A work of rare device and wondrous wit.*
> *First did it show the bitter baleful stir*
> *Which her assayed with many a fervent fit*
> *When first her tender heart was with his beauty smite;*
>
> *Then with what sleights and sweet allurements she*
> *Enticed the boy (as well that art she knew),*
> *And wooed him her paramour to be -*
> *Now making garlands of each flower that grew,*
> *To crown his golden locks with honor due;*
> *Now leading him into a secret shade*
> *From his beauperes and from bright heaven's view*
> *Where him to sleep she gently would persuade,*
> *Or bathe him in a fountain by some covert glade.*
>
> *And whilst he slept she over him would spread*
> *Her mantle, colored like the starry skies,*
> *And her soft arm lay underneath his head,*
> *And with ambrosial kisses bathe his eyes.*
> *And whilst he bathed, with her two crafty spies*
> *She secretly would search each dainty limb,*
> *And throw into the well sweet rosemaries,*
> *And fragrant violets and pansies trim,*
> *And ever with sweet nectar she did sprinkle him.*
>
> *So did she steal his heedless heart away,*
> *And joyed his love in secret unespied."*

Without realizing I had done it, I stared at him as I listened, entranced. His voice dripped with the dewy nuance of a sultry summer night, and I found that I'd been holding my breath. "That was beautiful," I whispered, still caught up in the spell his words had woven.

"It's pure frippery of course." His eyes laughed now, and

the spell broke into thousands of shards, the pieces tinkling with music as they fell around us.

My mouth thinned into a straight line. "For someone who places no value on poetry, you certainly know some choice lines."

His face took on a wolfish look. "Poetry has a few timely uses, I admit." He picked up the strands of my hair again. "Beyond poetry, what else do you read?"

I pulled away from him and turned toward the shelves, running a hand along the neat piles. I had chosen this aisle at random so had no idea what was even to be found. Casmir watched with curiosity as I perused, but I hadn't gone far when I stopped and removed a tome of philosophy to show him. "Do you know it?" I asked, unable to hide my eagerness.

"I have likely read it, yes, but..."

"And what do you think of it?" I broke in, unable to hide my enthusiasm.

He pulled the bound work from my hand and replaced it. "It seems as though my Adonia has her head turned by philosophy before the poets..."

I didn't let him finish, had already brushed past him to continue my search. "There is another treatise on governance..." Feeling suddenly self-conscious, I glanced over my shoulder and found him watching me with an expression I could not read. "What is it? Why do you look at me so?"

"I am trying to imagine one of my sisters speaking about such matters the way you just did. You could almost rival Grand Master Lito for your passion."

"You mean they don't share a similar enthusiasm?"

I had been so used to a scholar's way of life from my father that I never realized our tutelage had been unconventional. It never occurred to me to consider that other noble ladies wouldn't have had my same experience.

"Oh, they were fully educated, as was expected, but..." He looked suddenly uncomfortable, almost embarrassed. "Let's just say I am not accustomed to the women in my family having such interests for their own sake."

"So they did not enjoy learning?"

He shook his head. "No."

Just one more factor to separate me from the rest of my peers, it seemed. The chasm of awkwardness I'd felt upon my arrival in the palace had just grown exponentially wider. How could I ever hope to fit in?

I looked down, studying my hands. "Casmir," I began slowly, "my father taught me so that I could someday wear a crown. I understand that now, even if I didn't when I was young." I ventured to look up at him and found him paying close attention. "If I am to wed you, I will do my duty by you. I will also be your strongest advocate. But I won't stand by and simply watch as you rule. I will rule with you. Didn't your mother do the same?"

There it was again, the court mask. There was no way to fathom what he thought.

"No," he said, giving nothing away.

"No, as in she wasn't your father's advocate, or no, as in she didn't stand beside your father as he ruled?"

"No, as in he never sought her advice. Irisa..." he said, taking my arm and turning me to leave, "we will find something for you to do, something to keep you busy."

He entwined his fingers in my own then pulled me closer. I got the impression that he meant to distract me by way of seduction. His fingers brushed against my palm and I felt a tingle of expectation.

"Busy? I don't want to be busy, I want to do something

that matters. I don't want to wear a crown yet have no purpose."

He stopped again then turned to face me, pulling me toward him. "I have certain things in mind to keep you busy," he murmured. "They will have to wait a bit yet, but..."

"Casmir, I'm serious!" I tried to push him away, but he resisted.

"Oh, I've never been more serious." His breath blew the tiny hairs near my face, creating a tickling sensation, but I remained adamant and gave him a doubtful look. He sighed resignedly. "There is charitable work you could do, for example. The poor and sick are always in need of comfort."

He lifted my hand to his lips and kissed the inside of my palm. His breath was warm, and his rough-shaved chin scratched like a hemp sack; even so, my heart skittered like a drunken rabbit as his fingers worked their way up the inside of my wrist, pulling up the sleeve higher as they went.

"Yes, that is something I would be glad to do," I exhaled, my words losing force.

"We will discuss that later. I came to find you for another reason." He pulled my sleeve back down, becoming suddenly thoughtful. "What would you think if I accompanied you to Bauladu with Wolf and Addis after all?"

It was a swing so sudden that I couldn't find an answer for him. Instead all I could think to say was, "Figor won't be pleased. He wants you to stay here. Why neglect your duty when Figor speaks sense?"

"Because Figor doesn't want me to go." I pulled back and gave him a doubtful look, unaware of any rancor between Casmir and Figor, but he continued his persuasion. "Cousin Ildor is here, doing what he's always done. My presence will not make a stitch of difference one way or the other."

"But the rule is your inheritance, not his. And with your

father ill..."

"My father is the least of my concern at the moment..."

He nuzzled in closer, and all thoughts of Figor and of Evet evaporated. I gave up and nodded my agreement. Casmir looked triumphantly pleased. It was strategically and purposefully done, but I found I didn't care.

~11~

I WATCHED A BOY chase a silken flag as it wafted in the breeze just steps ahead of him. Over and over he tried to capture the elusive streamer, weaving in and out and around the legs of servants and retainers, oblivious to the mutters and irritated looks cast by those around him. His mother called after him, chiding him for his recklessness, catching him just before he dodged under a palanquin hoisted on blocks. The silken flag escaped his grasp, and he broke into a wail of utter misery.

I could not blame the boy. Not so many months ago I would have been tempted to help him race after his prize had I still lived on the streets of Corium. So much had changed since then, and even the atmosphere of festivity infusing the entirety of the upper courtyard did not pull me from my protected perch under an overhanging awning just outside the family's private apartments. My indoctrination into the ways of the upper echelon of royalty, combined with my natural inclination toward blending in had motivated me to be an exemplary student each day in my lessons. For this reason I stayed where I was, taking in the atmosphere as an observer rather than a participant.

It was an odd scene for something as unremarkable as

preparing a train of palanquins for a journey. Perhaps wedding fever had caught and spread throughout the palace. Perhaps it was the anticipation of the New Year only weeks away. Regardless of the reason, a normally tedious chore had assumed a merry mien; and this despite the weather, for the day had awakened blustery and overcast.

Sight of a white breasted eagle soaring overhead drew my eyes skyward. He flew against the wind, making headway despite the clouds blowing furiously in the opposite direction. What invisible forces drove him I wondered, remembering my father's lesson about birds. What looked like magic to the earth bound was something only natural for the eagle, for he flew in his rightful place, using the gifts and skills natively his own.

"Le'elt Irisa..." It was one of Addis' young maids. "Le'elt Addis wishes you to have these for the journey."

She handed me a pair of kidskin gloves, tanned to an exquisite softness and stitched so delicately that I'd have been hard pressed to know the glove had not been formed this way in nature. I instructed the girl to give Addis my thanks then watched her thread her way back through the throng.

It was then I saw Casmir and his grooms arrive. I smiled, content in the knowledge that my obscure location guaranteed no one could observe my delight in seeing him, delight evidenced by the light blush coloring my cheeks.

"I warned you not to get attached to him."

Figor's voice cut into my happy examination like a bucket of water dumped on a bed of hot coals. Feeling caught out, I jumped then tried to cover my reaction with defensiveness. "What makes you think I am attached?"

"Irisa, I am old, not blind." He scowled at me, but I avoided looking at him, pretending I didn't notice. "I am sending Bergen with you," he continued, waving his arm toward the boy. "He will watch out for you and direct you regarding what you are to do."

"Watch out for me, direct me, Figor he can't be more than twelve, maybe thirteen," I protested. "How can he possibly watch out for me? Besides, we have guards," I indicated the dozen mounted men patiently awaiting our departure. "And Casmir will be at my side," I added, neglecting to keep my face passive.

Figor scowled again at my obvious pleasure. "His duty is here, with the Council."

"Yet he has chosen to go along, despite your displeasure." I set my face, determined to defend Casmir's choice when all along I agreed with Figor, thinking duty truly did require him to stay. "Let him have some fun. Once Bellek is... well... gone... He will have plenty of time to..."

Figor snapped me a look. He had no desire that Casmir have time to do anything, for if my father succeeded in his rebid for the throne, Casmir would never sit upon it. It would be my father's and then mine alone. I decided not to pursue my argument and was saved making any reply with the single blast of a trumpet signaling our imminent departure.

"Stay vigilant and watch," he instructed as he turned to leave. "Oh, and Irisa, remember what I said about attachment."

Our journey from Prille to Bauladu would take no more than a week, if that, for the road to Bauladu was wide and well maintained. Casmir and I could not stay long once arrived, for another week's journey home would use up much of the time left before the New Year's celebration. Our return couldn't come soon enough for those unhappy with our departure, thinking it foolish for the heir apparent and his soon-to-be-bride. Although from my perspective, what may have seemed like a waste of time served me as an excellent opportunity to see more of Agrius.

Our first day out, despite the blustery wind, progressed pleasantly. I found the countryside outside Prille rejuvenating and could not help but wonder just how much of this countryside would have been familiar to my father as he grew up. He had spent more years living here than I had yet been alive.

We stopped several times to refresh ourselves and the palandiers, who, most remarkably, appeared little fatigued by their labor. At the end of the day, I welcomed the rest and the stillness that came along with it. I sat with my legs curled under me, ensconced on a thick woolen blanket awaiting the evening meal. A crew of skilled workers set up the tents in which we would sleep that night. Constructed from thick woolen layers with a waterproofed outer layer, they would protect us well from any inclement weather.

Casmir and Wolf sat across from me, bantering with one another, their spirits high, like young calves kicking up their heels after entering the meadow, freed from the drudgery of the paddock. Addis sat next to me, and we both watched the men. Amusement showed clearly on her face, but I was tired and found it difficult to join in.

Very soon after eating our simple evening meal, I gave up on the day and decided to retire for the night. Finding my tent prepared, I made to stoop under the entrance flap. Before I did however, something caused me to stop and turn around.

"Do the palandiers have a tent?" I asked to no one in particular.

Nothing obviously evident had caused me to stop and ask the question. Yet my query had been justified. As I gazed across our assemblage of travelers, there on the outer rim of camp lounged our palandiers, the men who had carried us on their shoulders for the entire day. And sure enough, there appeared to be no tent for them, only sleep sacks.

No one answered me, and I turned to see if Casmir, Addis, or Wolf had overheard. Only Casmir appeared to.

"Irisa, it's how it's always done." His voice betrayed his surprise that I would ask such a question.

"But that doesn't make it right," I countered before ducking inside my tent to retrieve extra blankets. I appropriated more from Wolf and Addis' tent. After brushing aside a startled page, I entered Casmir's tent to do it again.

"Irisa, why are you bothering?" Casmir asked, close on my heels.

"They are flesh and blood, are they not?" I returned, breezing past him when he tried to step in front of me.

I spied another blanket under his camp bed and snatched it up from around Casmir's legs. When he could find no argument to counter me, he bowed out of my way, allowing me to take my armful of blankets to the palandiers who received them with effusive thanks, though true to Casmir's word, the gesture left them mystified by why I would bother. After that night, a tent was set up for the men who bore our weight on the journey.

The next few days progressed in similar fashion. With each passing mile, the force of my recent and familiar cares faded — worries about Ildor Veris, all the secrets and intrigue of palace life, the mysteries of my family's past. I had all but forgotten Figor's intention to get me away from Prille and back to my father, had forgotten to wonder about the presence of Bergen.

Along with a lightened heart, the passing days also

brought a changing landscape. We had progressed over halfway to Bauladu, had entered the foothills of the island's interior mountain fortress. With eagerness, I anticipated seeing the seat of the great house of Argifu. I heard that the city perched on Fyrgdun's southern face, having been built straight out of the rock of Fyrgdun itself. Sprawling vertically from bottom to top, its streets wove back and forth across the mountain face as they climbed. When I expressed wonder at the idea of it, Addis only made a bitter face, giving me the impression that she did not relish the notion of dwelling at her husband's family seat. As my heart lightened with increased distance from Prille, Addis' seemed to grow heavier.

We made camp that night in a clearing nestled inside a thick wood adjoining a lush river. The winds had picked up over the course of the afternoon, and as we settled in around our camp for the night, fat flakes of snow began to drift down in a thick curtain, creating instant drifts in the dips and hollows of land. And it delighted me unlike anything I'd ever seen before.

"I have never seen the like!" I exclaimed, twirling in a circle, my cloak billowing around me like the seed of a thistle floating on the breeze. I tilted my face toward the sky, allowing the snow to land on my face, hair, and eyelashes and leaving a tingling sensation.

"Yar Hátin, you must come sit before you catch your death of a cold!" One of the maids responsible for preparing our camp tents bustled toward me to pull me out of the flurry, but I spun out of her grasp, laughing like a child. Soon Chloe joined me, then Addis and a few other women, and our small group flit about like dancing fairies, our laughter echoing in the dark wood. Casmir watched from the warmth of the fire, a cup of mulled wine in hand. With a disgusted huff the maid gave up, returning to her work. I caught Casmir's eye, and he gave me a slow smile.

After a time I returned to a place on a blanket near the fire, out of breath but happy. I made no protest when Casmir settled in next to me, pulling me toward him and drawing my hands into his to rub warmth back into them.

The flickering flames cast a red glow upon Wolf and Addis who sat across from us. I watched as Wolf drew Addis into a similar embrace to warm her hands as Casmir did mine. Casmir had caught the motion too.

"That vulgarian," Casmir murmured next to my ear, nodding to Wolf, "has a beast of a problem awaiting him when he gets home."

He referred to the trouble that Wolf would inherit from his father — the crumbling family fortunes and a collapsing city, a description suitable to far more than simply the palpable architecture of Bauladu. Many families were leaving the fortress that was Fyrgdun's mighty slopes, and heading to the lusher environs of the coasts. Without the substantial rents and payment of tributes that those families would have brought to the Argifu coffers, the entire fabric of the lord-to-vassal world would disintegrate.

"Addis does not seem pleased to be returning," I observed.

Casmir nodded his agreement. "She loves life at court, near the intrigue and power. She breathes it like air."

I had come to realize this very thing about Addis as well. She had become my friend in a way, yet there was also something just below the surface, something wild about her, something untamable, as if friendship was hers to bestow or remove on a whim, depending on how it suited her.

Before I had long to ruminate on this, a voice cut into the intimacy I was enjoying with Casmir. "Yar Hátin, will you come with me?"

Bergen beckoned from just outside the edge of firelight. With a curious glance at Casmir who simply shrugged, I pulled myself to standing and ventured toward the boy, grabbing a heavy fur-lined cloak as I went.

"What is it, Bergen?" I asked, doing my best to hide my annoyance at his intrusion.

Bergen eyed Casmir, a glint of suspicion pulling down the corners of his mouth. "There is something just over here that I would like to show you. Herbs. I thought you would know what they are?"

Snow blustered around us, piling in drifts around tree trunks and in hollows. How any herbs could grow this time of year, never mind how Bergen had managed to find them in this weather, I couldn't say. It had to be an excuse to talk with me in private, so I went along with him, glancing first at Casmir to see if he had reason to be suspicious, but he had already turned away and laughed with Wolf over something. Bergen called again, more urgently this time, and I turned my steps toward the outer ring of camp. He kept walking, and I followed. We neared a watchman who made to challenge us.

"It's okay, Marc. We won't go far." The man relaxed his stance. "Bergen has something to show me. We won't be long."

We walked by the light of the small oil pot Bergen waved from left to right in front of him as we went. The moon hid behind the clouds which had brought the snow, though patches of star-washed sky peeked through in places as the winds blew the snow higher up the slope. The forest felt deeply cold, and this far from the noise of camp, the wintry conditions took on a sentient feel. I threw the fur cloak around my shoulders, clutching it together at my throat as I trudged after Bergen, the crunching of fresh snow underfoot the only sound of our progression.

Trees filled in behind us, and soon I could not see the camp behind us. Bergen stopped finally, and turning to look about him, he scanned the trees as if gauging his location. The lamp he carried did little to light the area around us, proving my suspicion to be true. He had not brought me out here to show me anything. We couldn't have seen anything if he had.

I shifted my weight between my feet, uneasy. "Bergen, what is it? Why did you bring me out here? We can't be long or someone will grow suspicious."

Still he said nothing. A coil of fear snaked its way through my gut, and I was just about to suggest that we turn back when I heard the sound of heavy footfall surround us followed by an eruption of chaos in the direction of camp.

Before I could turn and run, a handful of men stepped just inside the circle of weak light. A heavy grip latched onto my wrist, and an arm snaked around my waist. I tried to pull away, but my efforts proved fruitless. A hand clamped over my mouth, pulling me hard against the chest of a beefy man wearing a boiled leather cuirass.

From our left a voice called out: "Lady Irisa!" A lone figure appeared. It was Marc, the watchman. Bergen called out, trying to stop him, but Marc misread his attempt and raised his sword to strike out instead. Bergen crumpled into a heap, his blood coloring the pristine snow with a gruesome hue. Despite my horror, I couldn't scream, couldn't move, for the man holding me tugged me backwards. My focus changed from the attack on Bergen to maintaining my footing.

Fortunately my captor kept his attention on the action. I fumbled in the folds of my cloak for the hilt of the small knife I kept hidden there. Numb fingers felt the smooth bone handle, and finally I fought it free of the fur. Slashing over my head, the blade made contact with flesh. The force of my release sent me reeling forward, and I nearly fell to my knees. Swinging back on the man, I found him doubled over in pain, his hands covering his face, blood gushing between his fingers.

Thinking no more of him, I turned to where Bergen lay crumpled, his eyes wide and staring yet unseeing, his oil pot somehow still burning where he'd dropped it. I stared for only a moment then snatched up the light and fled back in the direction of camp.

A struggle still ensued on the farther edge, and I paused, wondering which direction to go. Before I had time to make up my mind, a horseman drew rein just ahead of me, his mount snorting, eyes wide with fear. I jumped back, thrusting my knife in the face of the frantic beast.

"Irisa, it's me, Casmir!" the rider called out. He held his arm toward me, urging. "Come, we must leave this place now!"

"Casmir! It's Bergen, he is hurt!" I cried, remembering the sight of Bergen and suddenly feeling responsible. "We have to help him!"

"There is no time, we must get out of here NOW!" He spun his mount, waiting for me to come hook my arm in his so he could swing me up.

"But what about everyone else, we need to help..."

"Irisa, no. Come now!"

I paused for only a heartbeat and moved toward him. Fear propelled me over the horse's neck, and Casmir wheeled the horse, racing away before I had time to secure my seat.

We careened into the night, though how Casmir discerned which way to go I could not say. Eventually he turned us off the broader path onto a narrow game path, slowing our pace. We trekked in absolute silence for what felt like hours, until darkness fully descended and it became too dangerous to continue. He reined in the puffing mount, and we sat there in silence, listening for sounds of pursuit. Hearing nothing, Casmir leapt from the saddle, cautioning me to stay where I was. He tossed the reins to me and dissolved into blackness.

The horse released her breath in heavy snorts, reminding me of a blacksmith's bellows. An owl hooted in a far off tree, his call reminding me of our absolute aloneness amongst the other inhabitants of such a black night. I focused on the sound rather than allow my mind to chase after fears conjured in such close confines. Weak with fear and exhaustion, I slumped in my seat, wishing for nothing more than the safety of numbers back at the camp we'd just fled.

It seemed like an eternity before Casmir returned. When he spoke, his voice came from a disembodied void, his outline appearing as nothing more than a smudge against a backdrop of deeper emptiness.

"Stay up there for now," he whispered. "There is a small clearing only a little way ahead, and I will lead you."

True to his word, we stopped within moments and he lifted me down into an immediate embrace.

"Irisa, are you alright? Are you hurt? Did they touch you?" His fingers probed along my face and neck, searching for injury.

I assured him of my soundness, and finally he released me.

"Who attacked us?" I asked, not bothering to hide the slight quaver in my voice.

He pulled me toward him again. "Hard to say. They were well enough equipped and well-trained. A group of brigands perhaps, though they lacked purpose."

"What do you mean?"

"Brigands would be after money, equipment of worth.

They didn't do more than cause trouble, dodging in and out rather than commit to a direct assault. It was as if they simply meant to distract us from something rather than cause any real damage."

I thought of Bergen's crumpled form in the snow. "Perhaps they second-guessed themselves once they realized we were a royal party?"

"It's possible," he conceded, though he still seemed doubtful.

"How did you know where I went?"

He brushed the hair from my face in the darkness. "I knew the direction Bergen led you so set out in that direction. He had fortunate timing, this Bergen."

I imagined pursed lips as he added the last part so said nothing in reply.

The snow had fallen less substantially here, suggesting an easier night of it than we might otherwise have expected. Without tent or blankets, we would sleep exposed to the elements. I remembered the palandiers who now had tents, hoping they had survived the ambush to enjoy a safe, warm night even if we could not.

"It's too dangerous to light a fire. We have no idea if they are looking for us. We will have to abide as best we can without."

I felt around and found the carcass of a fallen tree. Decaying wood created a notch in its side, and it was here I threw down Casmir's cloak for our bed. At least the wind would be kept at bay.

Casmir pulled the horse down to lie against his back, then gentled me down in front of him, tucked up against his chest, my head just under his chin. We used the wide wool saddle blanket to cover ourselves.

"Irisa, what did Bergen want of you?"

I remembered Bergen's furtive looks, his worry over whether or not Casmir would stop me, if he would follow. I thought of Figor's warning, of his continued assurances that he worked on a plan to get me out of Prille and back to my father. Had Bergen just paid for another of Figor's failed plans? How many more lives would be sacrificed for my sake, for my father's sake?

I blinked back tears against the image of Bergen and the rivulets of blood streaming from the wide, deep gash across his neck then swallowed back a sob. Casmir tightened his grip, and I clutched at his arm just under my ribs.

"Irisa, what's the matter?"

"I can't help but see him fall there in the forest when I think of him."

Casmir pulled me in even more closely. "Don't think on it. There was nothing you could have done. You are safe, and that's all that matters."

We fell silent, and I considered his original question, what Bergen had wanted of me. How much of my suspicion did I want to reveal? "He wanted to show me something. Herbs, he said." I could only wonder at Casmir's reaction, but I imagined cynicism. "He was so young," I continued, shivering at the memory again. "Everything about it was odd."

"Indeed," he replied, an odd edge to his voice.

We fell into our own thoughts, and soon Casmir's breathing turned deep and even in the rhythm of sleep. I marveled at the ease of his slumber while I could do no more than breathe in the pungent scent of horse, taking in the sounds of the forest night while imagining echoes of clashing of steel.

"Irisa..." I cracked open an eye then rolled over to find Casmir up and about, the horse saddled and ready to go. "We need to get moving."

It was still before dawn, though a faint light made the outlines of trees visible overhead. Frost covered the ground, and a few drifts of snow filled small hollows where the wind hadn't taken it away. Thick undergrowth surrounded us on all sides with nothing more than a game track coming from the direction we had come and going on again in the opposite direction.

I rubbed the sleep from my eyes. We couldn't have slept more than a couple of hours. "How will we find our way?"

Gone were the soft lines of concern I'd imagined on his face last night, replaced instead with a hardened determination. He lifted me to the back of the horse then tightened a few straps before setting out. He led the horse afoot.

"The Wyr River is just south of us. If we head in that general direction we should come to it eventually."

After several hours of progress, Casmir called a halt. Consenting to a fire for warmth, we ate from the meager provisions left in the pack found on the horse's saddle.

"Could it have been brigands, back at the ambush?"

We hadn't conversed much so far that morning. Both of us were tired and disinclined to speech. He took in my question and chewed slowly, studying his food as if it would provide inspiration for his opinion.

"It is not an uncommon occurrence I'll warrant, and with winter upon us there are those who become more desperate as the lean times threaten." My face must have shown my doubt, for Casmir's eyes narrowed. "Do you doubt it was brigands?"

I dropped my gaze, trying to decide how best to tell him my concerns without giving away Figor's secret. It was a tough line to tread, but if I was determined to be Casmir's wife, truth would serve me best in the long run. He suspected the truth already, and if so, I wanted to show him that I wasn't blind to what might be going on.

"It did occur to me that maybe supporters of my father..."

"You think your father was behind it?"

He searched my face to see if I knew more than I was telling, and I grew instantly wary that maybe I shouldn't have suggested it.

"I don't know," I offered, avoiding his eyes while trying to sound sincere.

It was then the mask appeared, effortlessly donned as would a mummer in a play. Gone was Casmir the man, his place taken instead by Prince Casmir.

"This is why we left the rest of the party to head back to Prille alone. If those men were after us, after you, we need to get back to Prille as quickly as possible, but with care. We can travel undetected more easily alone." He threw off the crumbs from his lap and doused the fire. "We should keep moving."

Our travel settled into a routine, each day starting and ending much like the one before it. Most days we had food thanks to the small game we encountered, while other days we went hungry. Our travel alternated between walking and riding the horse. In this way the forest soon left its mark on us. While expensively woven and finely tailored, our clothing bore the fingerprints of the realm we traversed. Dirt smudged our cheeks, and I had long since given up trying to tame my hair.

Any lightness I'd felt on our outbound journey retreated,

replaced instead with a heaviness I couldn't name. I tried not to let Casmir see, but I sensed that he dealt with his own concerns so as not to notice mine. It was because of this state of internal reverie that I nearly didn't see the man-made mound of earth looming ahead when the horse shied.

"Tis only a charcoal kiln, you beast..." Casmir muttered darkly as he checked the animal, rubbing its nose as it tried to sidle away. "Where there is a kiln, there is a charcoal burner."

I studied the mound as we passed it, noting the thick, gray smoke billowing from the sides. "How do you know he is near?"

"The process takes several weeks, and they have to keep a close eye on the kiln. Too hot and the wood burns up, but neither can he let it go out. See those patches?" I nodded that I did. "That's where he pokes holes to regulate the temperatures, allowing it to cool for a time if it gets too hot. This one is still somewhat fresh," he said, hovering a hand near to feel the heat. "The burner can't be far."

His words presaged our discovery of a ramshackle hut just over the next rise.

"Hello?" Casmir called out. We stopped and surveyed the clearing. What little snow had fallen the other day now lay trampled in the tiny yard around the hut, turning it into a muddy mess. Everything was quiet. "Hello?" he called again. When no one answered, he motioned for me to wait with the horse. Going over to the hut, he raised the flap of leather covering the entrance and poked his head in.

"It smells of fresh smoke, so someone definitely lives here."

"We need a warmer place to lay our heads tonight. We've encountered no better options and it's unlikely we'll do so." I fingered the edges of my cloak, casting my gaze about the settlement, if it could even be called such a thing, for the hut was the only structure, and there was no indication that whoever lived here even had any animals. "We should wait a bit and ask for shelter."

Casmir looked as if he would argue with me, but he was interrupted before he could.

"Who is it? What do you here?"

A man padded through the patchy snow cover, his feet wrapped in fur laced all the way up to his thighs. Fur covered his head, and his cloak was also made of fur. He walked with the aid of a thick stave, likely part tool, part weapon.

"Peace, good sir. We mean you no harm!" Casmir called as the man approached the clearing, stopping short at the edge.

The man eyed Casmir with a long, hard stare, then took in our horse and me standing next to it. It was difficult to read thoughts from the chiseled face hiding under a bushy beard, though I imagined he wondered how it was that a fine lord and lady found his ramshackle abode so deep in the forest. If the man ever had visitors, it certainly wasn't anyone of substance. There was no way he could begin to guess at the identity of his unannounced visitors.

"We need shelter for the night," I said. "We were set upon by brigands back there," I pointed, "and we would appreciate the hospitality of your... roof." *Such as it is*, I added in my head.

The man stood still for an uncomfortable amount of time, and I wondered if he would ever move, much less speak.

"We will pay," I added, thinking that even one night could very easily cost him provision he couldn't afford. Casmir shot me a look but did not counter me.

"There be room enough for your lady, but you will have to sleep on the floor," the man pronounced finally.

"We accept," I agreed quickly, before Casmir could refuse. The man nodded.

"Irisa..." Casmir warned, his voice a low rumble.

"Casmir, it will be fine. Why would he do us harm? He has no reason to. It's obvious that we have little enough of value." Casmir looked about to protest again, but I cut in. "I will be safe enough. I survived the ambush. And I still have my knife," I added, patting the sleeve where my steel hid safely away. "Wolf has been an excellent teacher. Hunt with the man, find us meat. I will do what I can to tidy things up here while you are gone."

Casmir went away reluctantly, but I was confident that soon they would return with food. Once we had filled bellies and slept a full night under the protection of a roof, he would realize it had been a good decision.

I unbanked the small fire and found more fuel to keep it burning. Soon the men returned with two rabbits on a pole, skinned and ready for the spit. Darkness fell earlier in the woods, so we hurried to prepare the meal and eat it while we could still see. Our host seemed disinclined to ask questions, so we ate in silence, not wanting to invite his inquiry while respecting his privacy in return.

When we finished and cleaned up, the man led us inside. A pile of pelts made up a single bed in the corner. The man offered it to me, slinking out the door and into the night to find sleep somewhere else. I couldn't imagine where he'd gone.

"I will be right here on the floor next to you," Casmir assured me.

As I lay awake, staring at shadows, I wondered at the silence and complete lack of night scavengers. Every home had mice. And then I realized that this poor charcoal burner had no store of grain, so even the mice left him alone.

"Irisa?" Casmir's soft call pierced the deathly silence of the night.

"Yes?"

"I have thought on what you said about your father. Is there nothing else you would tell me of the ambush?"

His question caught me off guard. He'd said nothing more of it since the first day after the ambush, but clearly he had not dismissed the notion. If anything, it seemed to weigh more heavily on his mind the closer we got to Prille.

"No."

After a time, he replied, "Sleep well."

A taste of salt tinged each intake of breath, and this was how I knew we neared Prille. The landscape had smoothed and flattened considerably, with farmsteads appearing more and more frequently. Just as we came over a rise, the wide, smooth surface of the king's highway came into view. It was here we encountered the outriders, sentries who scouted the outskirts of the city.

The journey and lack of fodder had taken its toll on our horse, and she was weary; too weary to be carrying two riders. Even so, as the outriders approached us, Ada pricked up her ears and snorted, recognizing the horses from the stables.

"Hoy!" the riders called. One of them appeared to recognize Casmir, even in his bedraggled state, as they raced toward us. "My prince, we had no news of you! Are you harmed?"

"Peace, Captain," Casmir assured him. "We are unharmed. Send word to Ildor Veris that we have important news. I will find him straightaway."

The man signaled to his companion who spun in a tight

circle and galloped away at full speed.

"How are things in Prille?" Casmir asked the man.

"Captain Veris has been a very bear. Your disappearance made him furious, though I think it was the loss of your lady that really caused his ire. He has done nothing but pace and fume, and no one dares look at him crosswise lest he do something rash." Casmir's face darkened, his lips thinning. "Here," the captain said as he jumped off his own mount, "take mine. You will get back faster. Your need is greater."

We obliged him, dropping from Ada's back. Casmir flicked me a glance, and I wondered if he considered leaving me with the sentry, freeing him to return with more haste. However, once Casmir climbed into the saddle, he pulled me up behind him. He lashed out with his heels, and the beast leapt into action.

Once at the stables, a boy ran to meet us, taking the horse as Casmir jumped from its back. He immediately turned and helped me down, but he did so woodenly, his thoughts elsewhere.

"I must see Cousin Ildor immediately, must see what I can do to stem his tirade. Men should be sent back immediately to investigate what happened to us back there."

"Casmir," I said, placing a gentle hand on his arm. He looked back at me, his face grim. "Does it matter? What's done is done, and we are safe."

For the first time since meeting him, an obvious shadow crossed his features, hinting at a change that seemed somehow directed at me. "If there is a conspiracy, I would know about it." He turned to leave, but I grabbed his arm again. He turned and eyed my hand with a dark look that left me hollow, so I removed it and let him go.

I watched him walk, my heart aching, and wondered if

my easy introduction into his world, the idyll of our first days, was over.

~*12*~

HOW DESPERATELY I LONGED for news. Casmir and I had returned to Prille on our overburdened and depleted mount barely two weeks ago. Early the following day after our return, men were sent back to investigate the scene of the ambush and they hadn't yet returned. In the meantime, Veris insisted that a closer watch be placed on me, placing extra guards near my door and windows, and shadows to follow me everywhere I went, even within the palace itself. He'd said it was for my safety, to protect against any other kidnap attempts. I could not say whether or not he thought I was complicit, for we never crossed paths outside the great hall at meal times, and in such public places he kept his thoughts concealed as well as Casmir had ever done.

Regardless of whether Veris suspected me or not, word must have spread, and suspicion was rife throughout the palace. Thinned lips and curt nods, the wide berth that was given me as I passed in corridors and in the great hall — all of these borne of misgivings regarding my loyalty to their prince, to Agrius itself. I hadn't felt ostracized after the initial announcement of my identity, at my betrothal to Casmir, though perhaps the murmurs had simply remained covert. The ambush had merely served to confirm those speculations, giving people permission to display their distrust outright.

I couldn't blame them. Not really. Who would have guessed that I would choose, of my own free will, the rival house over loyalty to my own father? The denizens of this world had no way of knowing the truth as I had come to understand it: that my grandfather had preyed upon those he was meant to rule, that the ones most in need of his protection, his justice, had instead been the focus of his depravity. How could they know what I'd come to learn about kingship and the fidelity a ruler must keep, to justice and the intent to rule wisely? Perhaps it was too high a philosophical conviction for most. Perhaps no one else viewed it as I did. But that didn't make it any less true in my heart.

"Men have returned, Yar Hátin. They just entered the outer ward."

I turned away from the window where I stood watching a small bird hop a circle around a stone finial decorating a ridgepole just visible beyond my own garden wall. Chloe bent her knee to the floor as she spoke, keeping her eyes downcast.

"Thank you for your swiftness in telling me, Chloe."

I smiled down at her as I lifted her to standing, though my smile held more sorrow than cheer. She had survived the ambush and returned to the palace unharmed, and that was news good enough to ease a little of the sting of coldness I'd felt from Casmir these last many days. My plunge into despair had been hard and fast, and it felt more often than not as if I trod a thin line navigating the edge of an abyss. On one side was the strength forged in me since the days of my father's disappearance, and on the other hopelessness.

I grabbed a cloak and swept out the door in search of Casmir, hoping to arrive ahead of the news, hoping that the breach between us would soon be mended, that matters would return to the way they had been.

I found him alone.

"Casmir," I breathed, stepping quietly into the room and making my way toward him, "I heard that your men have returned."

"If I find that it was men from your father..." He hadn't looked up from his work, remained hunched over a pile of parchments when he spoke. He shuffled a few things around before finally looking up, his eyes smoldering. Lines of tension spidered out from the corners of his eyes, others rimmed his mouth.

I checked my step, taken aback by the heat in his words, like the blast of a smith's furnace.

"And if it was?" I chanced. "What does that have to do with me? I am to wed you, Casmir. I have chosen you of my own accord. What my father may or may not have done has nothing to do with me." *Never mind the fact that Figor is to blame*, I thought.

"Irisa, your father has spies at court. That is a fact. Maybe you were complicit, maybe you were not. The timing of your attempted abduction was rather convenient though, wasn't it? Perhaps I should have wondered why you were so eager to leave Prille so near the time of our wedding?" He stood from his work and pushed his chair away. "Irisa, loyalty to your father is understandable even if it is foolish." He walked around the table and settled back against it to study me. I felt an ignorant street urchin under his aristocratic scrutiny. His mood was black, and I wilted visibly. "If I find that you had anything to do with what happened..."

I gasped and stared at him. "Casmir, how could you think..."

"You are the one who urged me to stay home. Figor would be upset, remember?"

I rushed toward him, stopping just short of taking his hand, and looked up, my eyes pleading. "I only relayed the instructions Figor had already given you. And besides, even your own *dear Cousin Ildor* didn't want you to go! Casmir, how could you accuse me? I know what my family did, the horrible things they perpetrated. How could you think I would choose my house over yours knowing this?"

Before he could answer, a side door opened and a group of travel-weary men entered with Ildor Veris leading them. They stopped just inside the door and stood patiently, waiting to be acknowledged.

The scouts.

Casmir didn't even feign to notice them. Instead he stood like a cold, stone statue, immovable, imperious. "If these men bear ill news, any evidence that implicates you, it must be considered. The spy among us will be found out and punished." He shot a glance at Ildor Veris, taking in the sight of the newcomers as if noticing them for the first time, and then returned his focus to me. "I will still wed you," he continued, "because either way it serves Agrius. It will secure the crown, and that is enough."

"What have I ever done to make you doubt me?" I whispered. After all we had experienced together, I thought that perhaps we had reached the point where our union would be more than purely political.

Casmir didn't see the tears rimming my eyes, had already retreated around his table again to stare out the window behind it. Because he faced the other direction I nearly didn't hear him mutter "...expected too much from the beggarly-born."

I didn't know if he'd meant for me to hear his words, but

I had, and the wound was deeper than I thought possible. No one in Prille had ever given me reason to feel shame because of the conditions of my upbringing, least of all Casmir. But to have him utter such a thing now...

I glanced at Veris. He had to have overheard as well, had to have seen my reaction. Yet his face betrayed nothing of his feelings.

"I am tired," Casmir said finally and more loudly, wiping a hand over his eyes. "You should go."

I had wanted to hear the news the scouts brought firsthand, but in my weakness, I fled.

The parapet of the outer curtain wall gave an undisturbed view of Prille. I had come here on one of those earliest days with Chloe. I stood here again now, after so many changes, after I'd learned so much, gazing vaguely at everything and nothing simultaneously. Even the bright sun shining, the blinding rays reflecting back its brilliance as millions of shards off the waters of the bay, did not move me. A biting cold wind blew down from the north, snatching at my gown and whipping my hair into a frenzy. I had no cloak, and while gallantry might have otherwise moved one of the guards to offer me one of theirs, they kept their distance. Either my mood was clearly evident, or else they thought me a traitor like everyone else and did not want to bother with me.

It was after an interminable time that I broke my gaze from the vagueness and turned my attention to the streets of Prille far below. Lines of carters hauling loads of grain, the last of autumn's apples, or other items of produce waited for entrance just outside the palace's main gate. Dogs, chickens, and children wandered aimlessly through the lines. Goodwives and clerks, merchants and thieves... each went about various duties, oblivious to the drama playing out this very moment in the halls of their prince.

My eyes followed the sounds of commotion, settling on a raucous group of people arguing near a pile of overturned barrels. Salted herring lay spilled over a narrow alley between two streets. The owner of the barrels shouted at the herder of the errant cow who had knocked into the barrels. Men held back the furious man by his arms, keeping him from throwing a blow at the head of the cow herder.

The people of Prille, the common, the ordinary, my people. They were like me, whether they knew it or not. Though I had done it in Corium rather than here, I had walked the streets, breathed the air, just like them. I was one of them. I knew them well, and because of this, I knew I could be a just ruler. I hadn't asked for the job I'd been given. Fate had doled it out to me. Yet here I was, and while I had the power to do so, I would survive to make their lives better.

I will wed you, Casmir had said, as if I was now a burden to be borne. I swallowed back the throbbing ache of his wounding words. Regardless of my involvement in the scheme, they still needed me to unite Vitus and Sajen. Even if I entered a disharmonious marriage, I would be safe.

But what of Figor? I knew they could not implicate me, for I'd had nothing to do with it. But Figor...

Hiding up here served no purpose. I decided to seek out Figor, to warn him.

As expected, I found him in his private chambers, sitting at an expansive desk near the bright light of an eastward facing window. Clerks scuttled around, busy as bees at various tasks of daily tedium.

Part of me wanted to protect Figor's secrets, but I was too

upset with him to care. In a way, everything was his fault.

"You are under suspicion," I declared blankly.

Figor sat unmoving, as if I wasn't there, as if I'd not spoken. He scribbled more notes on his tablet, slowly, carefully creating the proper loops in tidy, rounded perfection. "I am made of willow, Irisa, not oak," he said after a time. "I have survived in this place for all these years because I am careful, and because I can cover my tracks. Mostly though, because I can bend when necessary." Laying aside the quill, he lifted his chin and made eye contact with me. "I have not built a house of straw." He tented his fingers under a disapproving gaze.

I felt instantly foolish, like a young girl instructing her tutor about the nature of the world.

"And you have happily served Bellek too, it seems," I accused bitterly. "You made a tidy life for yourself here while my family struggled to survive." It was a petulant, ridiculous thing to say, but Casmir's churlishness had rubbed off on me.

Figor stood and signaled to a passing scribe who retrieved his cloak and threw it around his shoulders.

"Walk with me," he commanded.

We left the warmth of the workroom and made our way out onto a flagged porch overlooking the sea far below. The wind blew briskly here, and sea birds shrieked overhead making it difficult to hold a conversation. It also meant we were less likely to be overheard.

"You will come to find that in kings there is rarely found a purity of black or white, evil or good. Subtle shades of each are found in every man." He gazed at the birds overhead, his hands clasped behind his back. "Would it surprise you to learn that I have no reason for animus against Bellek the man?" He turned and arched a brow, expecting to find surprise on my face.

He was not disappointed. "Nor do I," I admitted, frowning, realizing the truth of my statement even as I made it. Figor returned his gaze to the birds, and I studied him. His face bore his habitually grizzled beard, unkempt and thin over a pointed chin. "And Casmir is a good man. You should support him. Help me support him."

"But he will not be king, Irisa."

"Why do you insist that he must be unseated? If you hold nothing against Bellek, and nothing against Casmir," I started, but Figor interrupted me with a raised finger.

"I am neutral toward Casmir. Indifferent."

"Indifferent. Whatever word you choose... Figor, if you have no reason for animus against House Vitus, why do you persist on this course? I will wed Casmir. Houses Vitus and Sajen are united, and everyone wins. Why fight it? I will do what my father wanted to do when he took the throne. He raised me, remember?"

"Irisa, this is not about your father. It's never been about him, not truly."

"You said that once before, and I didn't understand it then. I still don't. Who is this about then? Figor, you make no sense. I want to understand!"

Figor sighed deeply, and I thought his shoulders slumped a little. He turned away from the balustrade and made to head back indoors. I trailed him, still confused.

"Power does not necessarily reside in a crown, Irisa." He'd sidestepped my question, but he still looked to see if I understood. I thought I did and nodded. "And not all stories are mine to tell."

I entered the workroom just behind him. Immediately he took up his work again. Our conversation was over.

"My lord." I dropped into a deep curtsy before Casmir, nearly ramming my knee into the ceramic tiles of the hall floor as I did so. I had practiced the move for so long in the afternoon hours that it felt as if I'd done it all my life.

Casmir took my hand and lifted me gently, kissed my hand, and drew me toward his side in one practiced movement. As was his usual habit, his face revealed nothing of his thoughts. To all observers, he was his usual self, dignified and princely. Stuffing all manner of conscious thought deep within me, I copied his manner and composure, following along as he greeted those around him.

Decorations of bright fabrics and greenery hung from every conceivable place in the great hall, for the New Year's celebration was the biggest in Agrius. Guests from all over had arrived for the celebration with plans to stay through for the coming wedding in two weeks' time. The palace burst with an unusual number of guests and would for the foreseeable future.

The thought made me glance at Figor who stood near his seat watching the ebb and flow of the crowd. His hand rested on the back of a chair, and his eyes roamed throughout the hall. He made eye contact with me, and I smiled. He nodded in return, and I noted that he appeared festive this evening, a contrast to his usually dour countenance. Whatever news had come from the scouts must have freed him from suspicion, even if I still remained ignorant of the outcome.

King Bellek was unusually absent from this feast, his favorite of the year I'd been told. His health had steadily declined in recent weeks, to the point that his physicians worried for his survival. The hearts and minds of the ruling class had already shifted, and they looked to Casmir as their sovereign, even if his father still wore the crown.

Casmir led us to our seats, what would have been his father's place for such a feast, and signaled everyone else to do the same. The meal began, and I took the proffered dishes in turn, preferring the lighter fare to the fatty and heavily spiced. My stomach churned over the conflict between Casmir and me, and I wanted to settle things. Casmir had not called for me all day, and I still did not know where I stood in his graces.

He avoided intimate conversation through dinner, and I wondered if he intended to keep me in the dark permanently. It was only when the last performer of the night left, and the musicians entered, dancers forming lines down the center of the hall, that Casmir leaned toward me.

"You ate lightly this evening."

"Yes, my lord," I returned, doing my best to keep my voice even. I could not bring myself to look at him directly.

He arched a brow then wiped his mouth. "I have news to share."

I remained silent, expecting my voice to quiver, reflecting the clamorous anxiety I felt.

"My men say there was nothing to discover. Their investigation into the surrounding countryside was inconclusive, suggesting it was simply brigands after all."

A flood of relief settled over me. "Casmir, I am faithful to you," I ventured, my voice sounding hollow in my ears. He let my comment pass by him without reaction, so I freed the delicate silver chain from my neck and let dangle the sun medallion Ildor Veris had given me en route to Agrius. I lifted it for him to see, and he reached out a hand to study it.

"The sun of Vitus? This is your proof?"

I pulled out the bennu from a small pouch tucked into my skirts. "This was the crest of my father..." I said this last word carefully, slightly, as if to utter his name might hinder our conversation. "... the one he chose when he was about to wed my mother. He planned to replace the maul of his father."

Casmir took the bennu and studied it. "What is it?"

"Grand Master Lito told me that it is a mythical bird birthed out of the ashes of its predecessor. A symbol of rebirth."

Casmir fingered the bennu a little longer. "Why did your father choose it?"

"He wanted to undo all that his father had done to the realm. Likely if he'd ascended the throne, had your father not come.... If he'd ascended the throne after his father," I corrected myself, "he would have introduced severe reforms. He planned to change Agrius in much the same way your father did."

Casmir nodded, keeping his gaze fixed on the bennu.

"There is more he has to tell me, though I have been unable to meet with him again. He has a book, a history of those days, of our two houses before... before." I swallowed hard, tired of being careful with my words. "He said that scriptstórii are to be above politics, that it is a danger to have, so no one knows about it."

"So what does this have to do with me?"

"Because by becoming your wife, our houses are united! Any unrest, any hostility, any remaining ill-will between our houses, regarding who has the right of it, will come to an end! Were he to retake the throne, I would rule after him anyway, would I not? There is simply no need for bloodshed." He still looked doubtful. "Don't you see?" I grasped his hands in my own. "Our goals are the same. Why would I need to escape, Casmir? I am home."

Casmir turned over my hands, lifted one to his lips and kissed it softly. "It seems I have judged you over-harshly, my Adonia."

"As did I when I thought you gave Chloe to me. I

assumed you meant her as a slave when you really intended that I free her."

He twitched a smile at the memory. "Yes, you were in a state, as I recall. And your visit later that night... well, let's just say of your purpose in coming could have been easily misread had I not already taken your measure." He kissed my hand again and returned it to my lap. "I would make it up to you. What would you like? Name it."

I hadn't expected this. Even so I had no need of delayed thought. "Propose the eradication of slavery." I thought his jaw would smack the tile floor at his feet. "Or let me visit the Council myself, let me propose it if you will not."

"Irisa, I..."

"Casmir, please? The worst that can happen is that they say no. At least let me try?"

"Irisa..." he continued, though I could tell his objection was losing force.

"Please, my lord," I said, offering up a beguiling smile. I lowered my lashes and gazed at him through them. "I promise to make it up to you. In two weeks' time."

"Very well, my Adonia. I will think about it. But now I will dance with you since I can do no more than that... for two more weeks' time."

We rose from our places and turned to make our way to the middle of the room, happy in the renewed harmony between us. As we did so, I noticed Veris standing behind us, watching closely. When I looked his way he maintained eye contact, not breaking his gaze before I turned fully around, moving into step alongside Casmir for the dance. Casmir already seemed to shake the difficulties from his mind, taking up the dance with energy and exuberance. Every chance I got, I stole a glance toward Veris and found him still watching.

~*13*~

THE BELLS OF PROXENOS *Temple, the large temple with the crumbling porch just across from the well square at the end of the main road beyond our alley, had already rung. That meant it was long past my bedtime and I should have been sound asleep on the pallet I shared with my sister. Except I'd had a sore tooth all day, and now it ached like an alley cat picking a fight with a trespasser in its domain. I couldn't sleep.*

My mother had given me herbs from Jeah, but the concoction hadn't produced its usual respite. The throb urged me out of the comfort of my bed to go in search of comfort from my mother. Only I hadn't made it. Instead I huddled down in the shadows, hidden behind a large chest against the wall. And I listened.

A guest had come to visit my father. After only a very short time of eavesdropping I knew the meeting was a clandestine one. My parents rarely socialized, and whenever a neighbor or a client visited, it was usually in the daylight hours. This man had come after my sister and I went to our beds, after darkness fell and the street watch came out after curfew.

"Two more caught and tortured," the newcomer stated. There was a rustle of fabric, and while I couldn't see the visitor or either of my parents, I imagined one of them leaning in closer. "It has become a

dangerous game, and I fear they come ever closer. You must be wary."

There was more silence, and I strained my ears to hear what would come next. I was not immune to understanding danger. Our home was in a part of Corium that knew violence and the ways of rough men. My father always did well by us, keeping us safe even if he could not close our eyes to what went on, and I had never felt fear for my life. This man spoke of a new kind of danger.

"My girls know nothing, and I would keep it that way. For now we live in this... this hole for safety." My father barked a harsh laugh. "This haven of rubbish is safer than what that hound has in mind."

"But for how long?"

Silence.

"For as long as we must. Until Caelnor comes around. Until I promise a tie of blood through marriage."

My father sounded sad and his voice broke at his last comment. Something about his admission pained him.

I heard a stifled sob, and a stool skid across the flagged floor. I feared my mother might have risen from her seat. I fled back to my bed in case it was her. I did not know who this Caelnor was, or why we needed him, but I vowed never to eavesdrop again. Curling up against Kassia's sleeping form, I draped my arm over her shoulders. Her soft breathing evidenced the peace of her sleep, and I closed my eyes, willing the same for me. For a long time however, peace remained elusive.

Prille woke up to a light dusting of snow the next morning. Clouds bearing winter's icy blast had blown through in the night, leaving behind a coating on every surface. Now that those clouds had gone, the sun maintained a brilliant vigilance, lighting up the frost and making the otherwise barren trees sparkle as if dotted with gemstones.

I spent the first part of the morning content to sit on a pile of straw in the king's stable. Kathel had brought me here, insisting she be present for the birth of a litter of kittens. Had it been up to her nurses, she wouldn't have come. It wasn't proper for a princess they'd said, even for one so young. When I assured them that I would personally accompany Kathel, they had to agree. How could they turn down the woman who would someday be their queen?

The mother cat hid away safely, tucked into a niche under a missing floorboard in the far corner of the stables where the boys who took care of the stalls slept at night. While Kathel would have preferred to help the mother along, I encouraged her to simply observe, explaining that she needed to do the work herself.

We made light conversation as we waited. Kathel shared stories of Casmir, of the many times he acted nothing like a prince but rather a doting older brother. She truly adored him, and I encouraged her confidences. The light murmur of our voices seemed to calm the mother cat, for she remained content in her knowledge that the humans hovering overhead would not bother her.

After keeping vigil for the entirety of the morning, it was time to leave the stable for Kathel's lessons.

"Why do they not come?" She studied the mother cat closely once again then peered up at me with serious concern, her nose crinkled.

"They will be born in time. You cannot rush such things. Right now we must get you to Grand Master Lito or else you will be late and he will be irascible."

She huffed, but I assured her that we would return later in the day to check again. This seemed to satisfy her, so we rose and made our way back outside.

The sun had vanished again, and a strong wind blew across the yard as we crossed it. I balled my hands up against my mouth and blew, hoping to induce some warmth back into my fingers.

Finally our hastened steps brought us to the royal apartments and the room where Kathel would take her lessons. The solid wooden beamed door creaked open, and I followed Kathel inside, curious to see where generations of royal children had been educated.

Casmir had studied here as a boy. I could imagine him, in the earliest blossoming of his youth, bowing over the hand of one of the barons' young daughters, reciting a verse of poetry to coax a blush in the same way he had done to me that day back in the Bibliotheca. I smiled at the image.

A young man wearing the white robes of a scriptstóri stood on the far side of the room with his back toward us, leaning over a table. As my eyes adjusted to the dimmer light of the interior, I realized Grand Master Lito was not there.

"A substitute teacher," Kathel whispered when she saw the man.

He turned, and I saw that it was the young man from the Bibliotheca, the one who had told me tales of the hated Sajens. His eyes narrowed almost imperceptibly when he saw me.

"I will be your tutor today, Princess. Grand Master Lito has taken ill."

Kathel made a face, but her good humor returned quickly enough and she took her place.

"I hope his condition is not serious, Master..."

"Orioc, my Lady of Sajen," he said with his chin high and his lip curled. "And Grand Master Lito's health is nothing that need concern you. Good day." And with that he turned to attend Kathel.

His blunt dismissal did not bother my pride, but it had pricked my curiosity. Now I would most certainly check in on Grand Master Lito, never mind Master Orioc's admonition. Because of it.

I left Kathel in his care and progressed quickly along the outer corridor leading directly away from the classroom and the block of administrative rooms next to it, intending to find Grand Master Lito's quarters. I had only had a vague notion of where that might be, but imagined that if I made for the central square, I could simply ask for directions at the Bibliotheca.

Soon I came to an intersection and paused. This part of the palace complex was unfamiliar to me. After considering my options, I opted to cut across a courtyard that served as one of many small garden hideaways. It was not as pristine as most and felt older, less tended, as if it had been abandoned many long years ago. Shadows loomed deep, and the skeletons of thickly overgrown vines created a close canopy overhead, intertwined as they were over and around themselves.

As my eyes followed a trail of vines connecting the rafters to a side trellis, I misplaced a foot and stepped on a loose stone, turning my ankle slightly. With a yelp of pain, I sought out a bench.

And that's where I found her. She sat without a cloak despite the cold. And more importantly, she sat without a minder anywhere in sight.

"My pardon, Your Highness..." I sputtered, feeling more like a silly child than a grown woman. How was I meant to address her? Should I curtsy and keep my gaze averted, speak or keep quiet? My surprise was such that any lesson I'd ever been given on court etiquette flew from my head, dispersing like a scatter of pebbles dropped to the earth.

Evet flicked her hand as if swatting a fly.

"Sit. This is a private garden, and you are to be my daughter. Let us not trip over formalities."

Her gown was made of plain green wool, and she wore no other adornment, neither veil nor kirtle. Her hair had been plaited simply then pinned at the nape of her neck. Eyes of liquid brown sat between deeply wrinkled crow's feet, and she watched me from under precisely plucked eyebrows. Her gaze reflected the same intensity I often found in Casmir's eyes. Wrinkles disclosed her age, but her features hinted at a former allure. Likely she had been a striking woman in her youth, even if not a beautiful one.

My scrutiny was not as subtle as it should have been.

"Do you judge what you see and find it lacking?" she asked.

"What do you mean?" I felt caught out, embarrassed by my blunder.

She shook her head but didn't explain. "My son finds you pleasing," she said after a time.

I still didn't know what to say. I had no gauge of this woman, so I didn't know whether I stood on a battleground beside her or on the field against her.

"I can't blame him," she continued. "He is young, and he is a man." A fiery blush raced across my cheeks. "Though beyond that he says that your father raised you well, to follow in his steps, that you are learned in the ways of kingship, of queenship." A slow smile spread her lips, like a conspirator divulging a secret.

I found it surprising that she knew so much from Casmir. He had never given me any reason to think that he had such a relationship with his mother, that he would confide in her.

"Yes," I responded, "though I didn't know it at the time.

The knowledge of my identity is still very new to me, and I wonder if I will ever grow fully used to it."

"So he is considering allowing you to attend the Council. Perhaps I have some sway with him yet."

"My lady?"

She twisted a jeweled ring on her middle finger. "Casmir, in fact all my children... They are my joys. My only joys. Like you, I did not grow up expecting a crown. Not until he came."

"Your husband?"

She barked a harsh laugh. "No, my marriage was arranged at a very early age. I refer to dear Cousin Ildor. He urged my husband to make an attempt for the throne. Once done, he has been in charge ever since. He was wise to find you, you know. To unite the houses. It strengthens his position."

A sound came from a nearby doorway, and she startled, but when nothing more followed she calmed.

"I have not ignored you by choice, Irisa. My watchdog prevents it."

"Your watchdog?"

"Perijan. He is Ildor's man. Keeps me quiet as he has always done. Keeps me from talking to you, from telling you things." She glanced at the doorway again. "Irisa, if you are to be Queen beside my son, you must do all you can to thwart Ildor Veris. And you need to try to convince my son of this."

"Does Casmir not already understand these things?"

"Casmir sees what he wants to see. Veris has always been like a father to him. More like a father than his own father." She scowled at the thought, and I wondered what past pain hid behind the words. "He is a good son, but he trusts Veris beyond reason. The man can do no wrong in Casmir's eyes, and he won't hear otherwise. His life is comfortable, and he has never had reason not to be. Our land is at peace, and he is a prince."

She stared down at her lap as she talked. Her face wore conflicting emotions. On one hand she was a proud mother, and her son would someday be king. He was young, strong, and handsome, and everything a mother could want. Yet something about her description brought her deep pain.

"But he doesn't want to rule." She looked up at me then, searching my eyes. "He wants what every other young man wants: fun and adventure. Ruling a kingdom will curb his freedom." She stopped, her eyes willing me to understand this side of Casmir. But only for a moment. The scowl returned. "It's because of this Veris thinks he can keep Casmir leashed as he did Bellek. Except my husband had more deeply rooted desires, was easily led. That's why he kept me away from my husband. Not so Casmir. He is strong, has a mind of his own. He just needs the confidence to realize it about himself. So far Veris thinks you are biddable, like most women. But if you are the kind of girl I think you are..."

"I could make a difference, could build him up, rule beside him."

Suddenly her eyes lit up like a torch at midnight. She grabbed my hand and squeezed. "Yes. And you have made a good start. But that also means Veris will..."

"See me as a threat." I finished for her.

She patted my hand in understanding. "Just as he thought I would be."

"Would you have been? Did you try to influence your husband?"

"In my way, but I wasn't raised to it. Only the daughter of a minor noble, and not wealthy. But I had practical sense. You have both, it seems, and kindness. Kathel tells me."

"So Bellek is a puppet..."

"Yes, the sot. Women, drink, pleasure... He was handsome

once, when I married him. The lure of the throne was all it took to convince him to take it. It was an easy job for Veris in that regard. My husband was happy to have the pleasure of his new rank, leaving the work to Veris."

"And you?"

"I had my uses to my husband, and to Veris. I produced an heir. But when I'd done my duty, that was the end of it," she said sourly. "Veris has kept me on a short leash ever since. Be wary of him, Irisa. And you must make Casmir see. If you can't help him see the hound behind the throne, at least be a louder voice in his ear than Veris." She paused and smiled, taking in my hair and face. "As his wife, you will have other methods of influence. And if you use those methods well, they should have more power over my son, I think."

She smiled knowingly, but before I could become embarrassed by her directness, something else spooked her, for eyes widened like a frightened rabbit, and she rose.

"He will do all he can to keep you quiet, Irisa. Befriend him, but don't let him succeed. His only concern is for power, not for who sits the throne."

Another sound came from the doorway, and this time even I heard it.

"There is more I would tell you, but now you must go. Perijan comes, and it will not go well for you if he finds us together. Find Grand Master Lito. He can explain about your mother."

"My mother?" She spun me and gave me a little shove. "What about her?" I pressed her again.

"Go!"

I walked quickly for the corbelled arch leading to another arcade outside the garden, but I wasn't yet fully away when Perijan found Evet. I heard them talking, but because my back was turned, I couldn't be certain if he had seen me or not. I could only hold my breath and hope that he hadn't recognized me even if he'd seen my retreating figure.

"Ilex, that kitten may look like a toy, but I assure you it is not!" Kathel chastised my wriggling excuse for a dog in the same way a mother would scold an errant child. Poor Ilex had been badly neglected by me in the past many weeks. Events had become so busy that I'd had little time for the tiny dog. Most of the time I'd released her into Kathel's care, and the little girl couldn't have been more pleased with her newfound responsibility.

Kathel and I had returned later in the day to check on the mother cat, but it wasn't until the next day that we found her delivered of four kittens. They were too new for us to disturb, though Ilex had no such tact. Kathel held the dog securely in her arms, and so far the mother cat felt no threat from us.

"We should go," I explained to Kathel, "before the mother grows uncomfortable with our presence and decides to move her litter. We can check on them again tomorrow. It will take some time for them to grow before we handle them."

Her face fell. "How long?"

"Two weeks is best."

She sighed heavily but accepted my word as she snugged Ilex more securely into the crook of her arm. We turned to leave the stable and saw that Ildor Veris and several of his men had just entered. I took a deep breath, remembering Evet's encouragement to be friends with him.

"Cousin Ildor," I offered lightly, inclining my head in greeting.

His men moved to the side to examine a horse, but Veris

kept his focus on me.

"I was told there might be a problem with my mare. I wanted to see for myself."

I glanced over at the horse in question and found that they examined a gelding rather than a mare. Veris noticed the direction of my gaze and without missing a beat, added, "My apologies, lady, the horse is a gelding."

I smiled sweetly, pretending I had not caught his slip. At least now I understood that he had come intentionally to find me.

"We were just checking on Kathel's charge - a mother cat who has just birthed a new litter. All is well, and we are headed back to the palace now."

"Mother cats are amazing creatures, are they not?" He moved to block the doorway with a subtle shift of his feet. "As are all mothers, in fact. Watching over their brood with care." He smiled down at Kathel who returned an adoring look. Veris had taken all of Evet's children under his wing, it seemed.

"Yes, cousin!" Kathel replied. "Lady Irisa tells me that we must not disturb the litter for some time, not until they have grown a little."

"The Lady Irisa is as wise as she is beautiful." He inclined his head graciously. "It takes wisdom to know when to leave the brood alone. To do otherwise would damage the natural order of things." He didn't bother to look at Kathel this time. "Because she knows that interference can have unexpected consequences."

Ilex squirmed in Kathel's arms, nipping at her hands. With a shriek, Kathel released her hold, and Ilex jumped to the ground, ran out the door and around the corner. Kathel took off after her. Thankful for the distraction, I tried to step around Veris, to follow Kathel, but he took a step closer.

"Because she knows her duty," he continued, oblivious of the ensuing chase between child and dog behind him, "and that her position could be a precarious one, that unpleasant results come from missteps. She knows to do her simple duty and no more."

"We are talking about cats, are we not?" I replied sweetly, feigning ignorance at the implied meaning behind his words.

"Of course, my lady." His smile returned and his posture relaxed, the perfect courtier once more. "I am glad we understand one another."

"Of course. Now if you'll excuse me," I said as I made to step past them. "I should return to my ladies and to my sewing. I have a wedding to prepare for. So I can do my duty by my prince," I added sweetly.

He bowed out of my way.

I kept my steps measured and slow so he wouldn't think I was running, which in fact I was. His threat had been veiled, but only thinly so. He wanted me biddable as Evet said, and he wanted Casmir to be the pawn his father had been.

I had already made my choice to stand by Casmir. He would have my heart and whatever talents I possessed to help him rule well. But Ildor Veris frightened me. And now he knew I had talked to Evet.

Salay, intrigue... Everywhere I walked there were breathless whispers and warnings. I didn't have to see anything in particular to know that the shadows had eyes, that secrets were sought, produced, and shared there. Rather than good intentions behind the masks of every courtier, I found calculation and hopes for self-advancement.

Daydreams of palace life had been more idyllic when I

was a child. Even as a new arrival to Prille I had been naive. The quiet darkness of my porch at night, a place which had once served as a serene poultice to soothe frayed nerves, only unsettled me further. For if secrets hid in the shadows, nighttime was the storehouse, and my porch its stage. What I sought most now was the protection of my hearth, of lamps lit and the laughter of my ladies.

"I have news," came a voice from the darkness. I jumped even though it belonged to Figor.

I glanced over my shoulder to see if anyone else had noticed. Finding Raisa and Chloe occupied, I stepped into the darkness with my visitor.

"How did you get in here?" I whispered.

"I came in through a back gate."

"I shall make sure it is secured then," I replied acerbically. I had no way to know for sure, but I imagined him smiling at the very thought, knowing full well that no lock would keep him from getting where he wanted to go.

"Caelnor has turned against your father and our allies here in Agrius are content enough that you wed Casmir. It serves the same purpose they say, so they have given up their support. There will be no counter rebellion. Your father will not be king."

The news was exactly what I'd wanted to hear for a long time now. So why did I feel a prickle of disappointment? Even if I'd wanted no part in the bloodshed, my father would have made a good king. Perhaps it was the loss for his sake that I felt a tug at my emotions.

"There is more news for you to celebrate." He said this last part dryly, knowing that the source of his disappointment was merely cause for my celebration. "Your father and sister escaped Brekkell after the break with Caelnor. Prince Isary's men are searching for her, but so far they have found nothing. Presumably that means they are safe for now."

The disappointment I'd felt only moments before dissolved into feelings of relief. I had heard tales of Prince Isary, and as much as I'd wanted to discount his vile reputation, I knew that I could not. That my sister was free of him made all my worry for her dissipate even if her whereabouts were yet unknown.

"So you have no more need to plot my escape."

"No."

In the dim light overflowing from my apartments, I could barely discern that his mouth thinned into a line of restrained disapproval.

"And you will do what you can now to help me support Casmir?"

"He is Veris' puppet, just like his father," he cut in, waspish.

"So help me educate him."

"Casmir is blind when it comes to Veris. Always has been. I advise him just as I advise his father, and he trusts my counsel, but he trusts Ildor Veris the man."

"More so than your wise counsel?"

"Ildor Veris can do no wrong in Casmir's eyes. You will come to know this soon enough, Irisa."

I sensed a sadness in his voice, as if a large part of his very existence was now ended. He had lived a secret life of support to my father for so long that I wondered if he would be able to find a new purpose.

"What will you do now?"

"I will continue to serve the Council as I have always done. For as long as they find value in what I have to offer." And then even more softly, he breathed, "My debt will simply remain unpaid."

"What debt?"

He shook his head and said, "I told you not all stories are mine to tell." He stalked away into the blackness.

~14~

"YAR HÁTIN... YOU MUST wake..."

Hands shook my shoulder gently, insistently, though I fought the draw. A dream entwined its rooted tendrils so firmly into my slumber-confused awareness that it dampened my desire to leave that delusional land of fantasy. If I awakened, I knew it would usher in the harsh reality of a new day.

"Yar Hátin, please..." the voice continued.

I cracked open an eye to find a darkened room, cold and uninviting. "It's not morning. Go away," I croaked.

"Yar Hátin..." It was Raisa, and she never called me Yar Hátin. I opened both eyes fully to see her face hovering just over the top of the single finger of a lit candle, its light wavering and flickering enough to animate diabolical shadows across her features. "You must wake up. You must dress."

Something troubled her. I sat up. "What is it? Raisa, what's the matter?"

"The king is dead."

I have heard it said that death is no respecter of persons. It comes for us all, be we peasant or king, master or slave, male or female, Mercorian or Agrian. Death strips each person down, for a man comes into the world with nothing and takes nothing when he goes.

A single lamp burned at the head of a litter placed on a raised platform in the center of the room. The figure upon the litter had already been washed and redressed, his hair combed neatly, arms folded across his chest in peaceful repose despite the early hour. Bellek had been a gruff man the few times I had seen him. Now in death his face softened, appeared kinder, gentler. Gone was the kingly finery. Dressed in pure white cotton, his aspect was deliberately simple and plain.

Raisa nudged me inside, just a step beyond the door. A liveried servant closed the heavy oak with the gentlest of touches. Despite the disruption, no one paid our arrival any mind.

Members of the King's Council, including Figor and Ildor Veris, stood in a solemn line at the back of the room. At the forefront, immediately next to the platform, stood Casmir nearest Bellek's head, then Evet and Kathel. Casmir, as I'd come to expect, stood emotionless, his face a perfectly constructed mask. Evet appeared understandably tired, though I was surprised to find a hint of sadness. Whether it was sadness for her sake or for something else I could not tell.

I moved further into the room, to join Casmir, but Raisa held me back. "Yar Hátin, you must wait here," she whispered in my ear, barely loud enough for me to make out her words.

After we stood like statues for an interminable amount of time, Casmir, Evet and Kathel moved away from the bed as if on an invisible cue. They proceeded from the room silently, and once again I attempted to move to Casmir as he went past. And as she had done previously, Raisa stopped me.

When they had gone I swung on her. "Why did you do

that? I simply wanted to offer my condolences!"

"Now is not the time, my lady. Casmir is, for all practical purposes, king."

"And I am to be his wife!"

"But you are not yet, and he is king now. Now come. We will dress you more thoroughly for what the day will bring."

"If Casmir is king, and I am not yet his wife, as you have so helpfully pointed out, what could there be for me to do?" I did not mean to sharpen my claws on Raisa, but my fatigue overrode tact and spoke for me.

She took my bad mood in stride and ushered me down the dark corridor, drawing me in closely to speak softly so as not to be overheard or disturb the relative peace that still existed despite the significance of the morning.

"It is true, you are not his wife yet, nor are you queen, but there are still duties for you to perform. You are still a figurehead. You must present yourself, be available, exude peace and tranquility. Even if you do nothing, you must be seen. The turbulence brought on as a result of a crown-changing can be difficult." I gave her a look, and she had the decency to blush despite herself before continuing. "People need to see you, most of all, perhaps more than anyone else, display strength and continuity. They need to see that you support Casmir. No one must have any questions as to your loyalty. Much will be made of how you behave toward your prince this day and in the days that follow."

It was the most wisdom the woman had imparted to me in all the months I had known her, and I was grateful.

We returned to my apartments, and Raisa dressed me in a satin brocade gown covered with a red velvet overcoat trimmed in fur. She placed a necklace of silver pearls hung with a golden sun medallion around my neck, and once she finished plaiting and pinning my hair, we made our way to the great hall.

Full morning had arrived with splendor. Light poured in through the colored window panes all along the length of the hall, setting the tiled floor ablaze with patterns of jeweled color.

A cacophony of activity whirled about as harried servants rushed to set up tables for the inevitable feasting that would accompany the burial ceremonies. While Bellek's death had long been anticipated over the course of his lengthy illness, and plans were undoubtedly already in place, the timing of his death couldn't have been worse, being as close to the wedding as it was.

Casmir stood at the center of the room, tight in the middle of a group of men who pandered for his attention. I struck out across the room toward him, and he saw the commotion of people parting to make a path for me. He had just smiled in recognition when a tall man wearing the sash of a priest of Zinon approached and pulled him aside to whisper in his ear. Without a look in my direction, Casmir turned with him and they left.

Casmir had served in his father's stead nearly full time these last several months. While he'd felt the freedom to pick and choose which duties he preferred, giving over the rest to members of the Council and to Ildor Veris, his freedoms were now curtailed. The title owned him. Permanently.

"Yar Hátin." I turned to see Figor before me, his chin dipped in deference. I gave him a quizzical look, and he had the grace to blush at his first-ever acknowledgment of my rank. "Prince Casmir has much to attend to, but he wants you to know he will speak with you as soon as he can."

I nodded, appreciative of the small gesture. He left me alone, watching the maelstrom of activity swirling around the hall. A few servants paused in their step to bob a chin, but most passed me unnoticed.

I felt lost and uncertain what to do. I needed to be a figurehead, Raisa had said. Show my support for Casmir. Yet no one watched, no one seemed to notice my presence. I noticed several visiting barons and their wives standing on the far side of the hall. None seemed to pay me any mind, except for one. She continued to dart curious eyes my direction. I could go engage in conversation with them, I supposed. But I did not want to.

"I wish to visit the Bibliotheca, to see if Grand Master Lito's health has improved."

In a surprising display of acquiescence, Raisa nodded her approval.

Outside the great hall, matters appeared less frenzied. Aside from the bells which tolled, marking the passing of the Agrian king, it could have been any other day. I crossed the square quickly, thankful for the fresh air outside the stuffiness of the hall. Once inside the repository of wisdom, even the smells of ancient dust and moldering parchment seemed refreshing.

A middle-aged scriptstóri greeted me. He expressed his condolences regarding the king, and I thanked him politely.

"Has Grand Master Lito recovered?" I asked, trying to hide my anxiety. "I have been overly concerned so have come to inquire after him."

"You are most kind, considering the loss of our dear king. But Yar Hátin, if I might be so bold... have you not heard?" The scriptstóri paled visibly, and I wondered why the death of Bellek would have affected him so deeply.

"Heard what?" I asked. He hedged, avoiding my eyes, so I pressed him. "What news are you so reluctant to share?"

"Grand Master Lito passed out of this world this morning. About the same time as the king. News of his departure was likely eclipsed by the greater grief of the king's passing." The man bowed his head in obvious grief.

I glanced at Raisa, but she seemed as surprised as I was.

"How... how did he die?" I had never known what ailed him these last many weeks.

"He seemed to show signs of improvement. We thought he would be recovered in enough time to attend the wedding. But in the last two days he took a bad turn, began hallucinating and raving. This morning a servant found him..." A sob wracked his body, cutting off his last words.

"My Lady of Sajen..." another voice cut in. I turned to see Master Orioc bearing down on us. "I see that Master Tarn has told you the news?" Poorly disguised glee hid just under his words.

"He has." I did my best to hide the bitter edge of irritation from my voice. It was only insufferable smugness which prompted his continual use of Lady of Sajen. I found that I wished he had been the one to pass out of this world rather than Grand Master Lito. "Master Tarn has also told me of his symptoms. Hallucinations and raving? It does not sound like natural sickness to me."

Orioc threw back his shoulders, puffing out his chest. "What do you suggest it is then?"

"I would not like to presume, Master Orioc," I spit back.

"Indeed not, I should think. For a moment I feared you intended to accuse one of our dear brotherhood of using poison against our beloved Grand Master."

Master Tarn gasped then covered his mouth as his eyes brimmed over with tears. He fled away from us.

I arched a brow. "Poison, Master Orioc? Why would you think I would ever suggest such a thing?"

His look darkened, and I felt the fire of my indignation

cool, and as it did so, a steadily growing coil of unease took its place. Poison. The word had come quickly to Master Orioc's tongue.

"And who will be taking his place, if I might ask?"

"Of course you may ask. The honor has been given to me."

"You are rather young for such an esteemed position, are you not?"

"And you are rather young to be queen," he snapped. He looked at me now as if he'd just been fed rotting meat.

"Indeed," I replied in return, narrowing my eyes at him. "And yet queen I will be, for the Council, and more importantly, Prince Casmir, wills it. Now if you will excuse me, I need to retrieve something that belonged to Grand Master Lito."

"I'm afraid that will not be possible."

"And why not?" I sighed, growing tired of the man's churlish attitude.

"Because his things have already been cleared away and disposed of."

"You don't want me to see that book, do you?" I asked bluntly.

"I have no idea what you are talking about, my lady," he said. He hadn't bothered to hide his slippery smile. "Now if you will excuse me..."

As soon as he bowed out of my way, I strode to the back room where Grand Master Lito kept his private things, finding it empty as Orioc had said. If the book held secrets about my mother, or anything else for that matter, they were now lost to me. The room could not have been cleaned so thoroughly just this morning. Someone had anticipated Grand Master Lito's fate.

I left the Bibliotheca with a head of steam, keeping such

a furious pace that I lost Raisa in the bustle of the busy central square. Deciding I would inject myself into matters of state starting today, I headed to the Council chambers.

Just as I reached for the handle, the door opened inward, and Ildor Veris stepped out.

"Irisa, what a surprise!"

"Captain Veris," I said. I didn't bother to hide my displeasure at seeing him.

"I am afraid you cannot enter. The council is meeting at the moment, discussing the prince's coronation."

"You mean our coronation, of course."

He inclined his head but did not reply.

"Casmir has promised that I might visit the Council."

"So I have heard," he clipped, unable or unwilling to hide his irritation at the notion. And yet he did not move or make way. "And you have heard the news of Grand Master Lito, of course?"

"What does Grand Master Lito have to do with…" His mouth spread an inky smile, and I remembered his warning to me that day in the barn. My spine turned to ice and my eyes widened with a fear I could not hide.

He recognized the realization, and his smile turned into one of satisfaction.

"My lady, may I suggest you find your women and," he began before pausing to look over my shoulder, "return to your apartments? We are quite busy at the moment mourning our king and preparing to install the new one. I'm sure you have enough work in your bower to keep you busy."

He turned, a half-smile on his face, and opened the door, returning to the Council chambers and closing the door firmly behind him. I stared at the solid oak, noticing the cracks and grains of the ancient wood with a strangely heightened awareness. Its solidity as a barrier would not signify anything as it concerned my conviction to involve myself with the Council.

Any concerns I harbored regarding the fate of Grand Master Lito fled in the face of Bellek's funeral the next morning. All of Prille turned out for this rare opportunity to be close to a person of such high estate.

A single contingent of palace guards guided the litter bearing the remains of Bellek to the Temple of Zinon in the predawn darkness. At the rise of the sun, the doors swung wide to welcome the people of Prille, enabling them to pay their last respects to their king. For many this was the first, and the last, chance to be close enough to touch the man who had been their king. A long line wove its way up and down the narrow lanes as people waited their turn. Late in the afternoon, just after the weak winter sun disappeared over the horizon, the royal family and highest-ranking nobility processed from the palace to the temple on foot.

Black silk banners draped the crossbeams of houses and stretched from pole to pole along the main square. Flowers littered the streets, tossed along the procession route like snow drifts. Despite all the pageantry and ornamentation, the city wore a somber mantle, reflecting the purpose of the event.

Evet and Casmir led the way, with me and Kathel a pace behind, a plethora of distant cousins and other relations behind us going back halfway to the palace itself. I watched Casmir from behind as we walked. He held his mother's arm, keeping his chin lowered but not downcast.

The actual content of the ceremony felt a blur, and I remembered none of the details afterward. Priests spoke, incantations were given, incense burned... It passed in a daze, surreal to me as one witnessing the death of the man whose ascension changed the entire course of my life and that of my mother and my father.

A feast awaited our return to the palace. Somber guests lined simply adorned tables up and down the hall. As the meal progressed, and the wine and ale flowed freely, the atmosphere of the hall lightened. People began to relax, and I sensed that we had turned a corner. Even so, my eyes couldn't help but stray to where Ildor Veris sat, and I found, to my dismay, that he kept watching me as well.

"Irisa, I have had news from Wolf that he and Addis will be returning sooner than they had originally planned. With the coronation comes the homage-giving."

"The homage-giving?"

I had not seen Casmir since early the previous morning. Despite his busy schedule, I was surprised at how relaxed he appeared. Casmir finished chewing, took a sip of wine to wash it down, and worked at cutting up a new morsel before responding. "The homage-giving is when the nobles make their vows to me, their new king. It is a public act of loyalty and fealty-giving. The relationship between king and his people is a binding one. It is secured by oaths."

I considered this. "So the crown alone does not bind their loyalty," I mused, not really looking for an answer. He looked up at me then with a half-smile, not certain if he needed to explain matters more thoroughly. "Nor does it necessarily indicate true power," I added, turning once again to look for Ildor Veris who had engaged his seatmate in conversation.

Casmir followed the direction of my gaze. "It is supported with advice from trusted sources. That is the nature of ruling, Irisa. Listening to those with wisdom and experience, hearing out many opinions and then deciding the best course."

"Does that include me, Casmir?"

His lips twitched, and I thought I sensed a tightening of the muscles at the corner of his eyes. He popped a bite of partridge in his mouth and chewed slowly. "Irisa, I have already agreed to grant you access to the Council."

"I know that. And I am grateful." I put my hand on top of his and leaned toward him. "But does partnership with you go beyond words whispered behind the bed curtains at night?"

"Along with other things," he quipped, smiling broadly.

"Casmir, I am speaking of coronation."

He looked truly surprised by this question. "Was there any doubt?"

"Yes. It has been suggested by... some... that I will not wear a crown. Like your mother."

"Irisa, the goal of our marriage is the joining of Houses Vitus and Sajen, to end any remaining ill-will over ascension and the right to rule. Our houses will be united and our offspring will seal it. You must be crowned and sit next to me for that reason. Who told you there was any question about this?"

"Cousin Ildor suggested it," I said flatly.

"Then you mistook his meaning." And with that, he swigged down the dregs of his cup, signaling a passing servant for more.

We continued eating, and when I remained quiet, he took up my hand in his.

"I am sorry that I have been unavailable to you. But considering the circumstances..." He chewed another bite slowly, as if it was the first time in the last two days that he'd had a moment to do anything with consideration. "It must have been rather overwhelming for you these last two days. My father was not exactly beloved by you."

I appreciated his unusual candor and repaid him with a

grateful smile. "He wasn't so much beloved by you either, I think."

Casmir studied the ring on his finger as he gripped his wine with his right hand. "My father was a simple man driven by simple things." He paused again. "It's complicated." He took a big drink and then searched my face. "If it's not my father's funeral, what then?"

"You mean aside from the fact that I'm about to wed the heir of my father's avowed enemy?"

"Besides that, yes." A newfound levity relaxed the tightness around his eyes. I suspected that the last several days had been overwhelming for him as well, making his concern for me all the more meaningful. "Because wedding your avowed enemy should not overwhelm you in the slightest, considering what you are getting." He waggled his eyebrows, smiling suggestively and I couldn't help but laugh.

"Has it been hard for you?" I asked him, turning suddenly serious.

"Has what been hard for me?"

"These last several days. The idea of wearing the crown, of ruling. I know you have been filling in for your father, but you don't seem particularly interested in the duties."

"Irisa, I was born to this. I have known all my life, all my years would lead to this moment."

"But that doesn't mean you looked forward to it, doesn't mean it's not still overwhelming. Birth into a thing does not necessarily equip one for the life that comes with it."

"So you are suggesting I'm not equipped for the job?" He was smiling, but I sensed a hint from his eyes that a slight hurt lurked in the background, as if I'd accidentally prodded a deep dark secret he was loath to admit.

"On the contrary. I believe you are more than capable

and will make an excellent king. Which is why, despite the...
involuntary, shall we say... nature of my arrival in Prille, I enter
our marriage willingly." I looked down at my plate of food as if
it contained the courage I needed to continue, then added,
"eagerly even." I dared not meet his eyes, for I knew the
direction my last phrase would have sent his thoughts. He was a
man after all.

So I was surprised when he bypassed the remark and
turned the conversation back around full circle.

"You didn't answer my question."

"My lord?" I asked him, confused.

"About what is bothering you."

He was more perceptive than I gave him credit for.
"Surely you heard the news of Grand Master Lito?"

Once again he considered his wine, picked up the glass
and gave it a swirl. A servant hastened forward to fill it, but
Casmir waved him away. "I did. The Bibliotheca will be
somehow lessened because of his loss. I am sorry for it."

I took a deep breath, uncertain if I should press into my
suspicions, yet I was certain that if I did not, no one else would.
Casmir would be king, after all. What servant or nobleman who
cared enough would risk angering their king for the memory of
a scriptstóri even if he was beloved? "I believe his death was not
natural."

Casmir's head snapped up, and his eyes locked onto
mine. "Why do you think that?"

"Because of his symptoms before he died. I believe he
was poisoned."

"Irisa, are you a physician now? You can read his
symptoms and diagnose him?"

I couldn't tell if Casmir was upset, surprised, or afraid.
Maybe all, maybe none. "Casmir, I grew up learning these

things from a family friend. I have a fairly broad understanding of medicaments and how to prepare them. I believe that Grand Master Lito was poisoned, yes."

"But who would do such a thing? And why? He ran the Bibliotheca after all, was not a commander of armies! Scriptstórii aren't meant to be political."

"Someone who knew Grand Master Lito knew something about my mother, I think."

"Your mother? What is there to know about your mother that is worth a man's life?"

"I don't know," I confessed. "But whatever it was, I think it was written in Grand Master Lito's book, the one I told you about. And now it is gone. I believe I know who took it." He raised an eyebrow in question, so I continued. "Master Orioc, the one who has taken Grand Master Lito's place."

Casmir picked up bread from the remnants of the food on his plate, tore off a hunk, and popped it into his mouth, chewing as he thought. He swallowed heavily then replied, "I shall ask Cousin Ildor what he knows of this, ask him to look into it."

"But you don't understand," I began slowly. This was the point things could get uncomfortable, and I wasn't sure I wanted to wade so deeply into these waters with Casmir just yet. Once I accused Ildor Veris of anything, particularly with Casmir, there was no undoing it.

But before I could make up my mind, a trumpet blast sounded out, announcing the beginning of the evening's entertainment. Casmir stood to welcome the troupe of performers, and our conversation was over.

The day of mourning a dead king had suddenly, with the blast of a trumpet, ended. The Kingdom of Agrius had begun a new era, one that looked ahead to a new sovereign and a house united against old hostilities.

~15~

MY EYES TURNED HEAVENWARD, searching the patchy clouds for any discernible patterns. From the corner of my eye I spied a knobby patch of sullen gray cloud that reminded me of a bulbous mushroom. With my turn done, it was now Kassia's turn, but she wasn't here.

The game had been one of our favorites as children. On mild summer evenings when the sun's baking heat finally swept under the shadow of the closest tall building, we would climb the timbers on the back side of our home in Corium and sit upon the ridge pole, staring up at the evening sky and taking turns to see who could find the most obscure object in the billowing puffs of clouds overhead. Kassia usually claimed to win, but I questioned many of her winning discoveries for their inexplicably fantastical aspects. I missed her terribly now, sharp tongue and all.

I needed her strength this day, for hers was a personality never to be daunted by any challenge. Today I faced the biggest one yet. It was the day before my wedding and coronation, and I stood in the forecourt of the upper ward waiting for my processional train to depart. If my grandfather was as despised as everyone told me, then I was uncertain about the welcome I would receive from the people of Prille. Why would they welcome back a Sajen princess when no one seemed to know the intention of my father to alter the course his father had set?

"Yar Hátin, it is time." The constable nodded toward my awaiting palanquin, and I boarded, assisted by Ildor Veris who would lead the procession as the ceremonial captain of the guards.

I purposely made no eye contact with him, and he made no comment. Once mounted, he led his contingent of palace guards followed by the rest of the train down through the lower ward and out through the main gate.

Crowds lined the narrow streets of Prille as we processed toward the Temple of Zinon. It was mid-afternoon, and the cloth of gold covering my palanquin fluttered in the light breeze blowing down from the north. People turned out dressed in their finest, many carrying bouquets of flowers. Others waved homemade banners. The sight warmed me, and I waved at the people as I passed, all but forgetting about Ildor Veris.

The enthusiastic response of the crowd and their adulation relaxed my coiled nerves. Shouts of *Adonia!* rang out, but rather than be embarrassed by the comparison, this time I took it in good humor as was the intent. Ignoring the tight security, I ordered the palanquin to stop so I could get out and walk among the people. Many shouted out their good wishes, and I joked with others in reply to their good humor, accepting gifts of flowers from many as I walked along.

The air, fresh and clear, ferried a light drifting of snowflakes, catching on hair and eyelashes. A girl younger than Kathel stepped out from the line of people and performed her best deep-kneed curtsy. She raised up a handful of wilted herbs tied with a string but kept her eyes downcast as she did so. I stopped in front of her and lowered myself to her level. "Thank you, sweet maid," I began, taking the proffered corsage, "I think these are my favorite." I slipped a finger under her chin and lifted her eyes to meet mine. A broad, toothless grin spread her face, and she rose, stepping back into place alongside her mother who placed a proud arm around her shoulders.

If I had set out with intentionality to conquer the heart of the city, I couldn't have been more successful.

"Yar Hátin," broke in the constable from my escort, "would you now return to the litter?" He was a handsome man of middle age despite a thin white scar running across the bridge of his nose. Already tall and long of limb in a hardened leather cuirass over a crisp linen shirt, his tall, knee-high boots of supple leather made him look even taller. A bright crimson cloak boasting an underlining of bright yellow draped his shoulders, and he carried a brightly polished halberd in his right hand. "We need to move along." He swung his arm gracefully to the side, almost in a bow, to indicate the following palanquin.

I nodded to him then smiled and waved at the crowd as I turned to climb back into the cushioned palanquin. We progressed down the final stretch of winding streets toward the temple and turned into an open square where awaited a richly furnished stage holding a cohort of musicians and an assortment of magistrates waiting to greet me.

Liveried guards dotted throughout the crowds of people lining the square, with the wealthiest merchants in their rich furs and gold chains standing prominently toward the front. The entire square was decorated with wooden frames hanging damask and silk banners. Streamers and more flowers hung from windows which had been flung open wide for the people to hang out overhead, giving them a better view of the woman who would wed their prince, who would be their queen on the morrow.

A youth who looked to be about sixteen or seventeen offered a speech of welcome infused with many words about uniting the two houses of Vitus and Sajen. A finely dressed man, the leading merchant of the guilds and the teenager's father I was told later, gave another speech and offered me my bride gift from the city, a purse of crimson satin filled with gold. I took the purse and thanked him before being led into the temple where I would spend the eve of my wedding night in a cozy room behind the temple proper.

A bevy of maids stood ready to greet me when I entered, and Chloe offered up a warmed cup of mulled cider.

"Yar Hátin," she said, offering me the cup as she curtsied, a smile of pleasure curving her lips. I took the cup with both hands and gripped its warmth, holding it to my cheeks.

The sitting room had been decorated with evergreen boughs and ribbons, and I inhaled a deep breath of the comforting aroma. A blazing fire burned in an enormous fireplace against the far wall, and Chloe led me toward it. "Come, sit by the fire and rest with your feet up. A casual meal will be laid for us here shortly," she said, indicating a table on the other side of the room. She slipped off my fur-trimmed boots and replaced them with a pair of embroidered slippers, sliding a cushioned stool under my legs. "It will be a quiet evening. Only us," she said, waving an arm around the room, "and no other festivities. We will not be bothered."

I nodded, my stomach fluttering with the enormity of what was about to happen on the new day: At mid-morning, Casmir would leave the palace and process to the temple in much the same way as I had just done. And then, in a simple ceremony, I would become his wife. I sank into the plush cushions and closed my eyes, wriggling my toes in the soft slippers as the heat of the fire kissed them with warmth.

"Irisa, doubtless you are aware that more men will come asking to take you to wife?"

My father stood opposite me, leaning up against the table that held his writing materials. I nodded quietly. It was a fact of life that when a woman reached a certain age, she would have a suitable marriage arranged for her. At least if she was wealthy. We were not, so it seemed strange, even if not unheard of, that my father wanted to arrange something for me. What could he possibly offer a prospective husband? Most girls in our part of the market were free to marry for love. It was one of the few benefits of being poor.

The innkeeper's daughter down the street had just wed a plumer from several streets over. And I'd only just heard this morning that the pie-seller's daughter had started courting a lighterman, though how she had met him, living as far from the bay as we did, I never learned.

In truth, I had my sights set on the son of the fruit merchant who kept a cart near the well. I dared not mention this to my father, for I knew that I had no hope of convincing him. He had just turned down Seva the Smith, a prosperous enough man for one such as me to have considered a worthy match. I was the daughter of a scribe, not a mercer's daughter, and his refusal had shocked me.

Kassia stood in a dark corner, having overheard the entire exchange, and scowled. I wondered what my father had planned for his youngest daughter, the least biddable, least decorous girl one could chance to meet. My father somehow sensed the direction of my thoughts and eyed Kassia, smiling warmly for a moment.

His face turned serious again. "Very soon though, I will have something to share with you. Not yet, but soon. I have to travel again in the coming weeks, and when I return I hope to tell you my plans for your future." He paused and looked at me closely, as if he rethought his *hesitation, but after taking a breath as if to speak it out, he closed his mouth, shook his head, and rubbed his eyes with a swipe of his hand. "No, not yet. Not just yet. When I return."*

But he never did return.

Laughter rang out from the far side of the room as a cluster of maids carefully laid out the prodigious number of individual pieces of clothing necessary to dress me for the coronation. I heard them, but their words did not penetrate my inner haze.

I stood transfixed before a mirror, gazing at the contours of my flesh outlined under a thin silk chemise. I was told that only half a dozen of these mirrors existed in all of Agrius. One stood in the wardrobe of the king's chamber, this one in the Temple of Zinon, and the rest were scattered about in the homes of the wealthiest nobles. An outer layer of crystalline glass lay overtop a metallic foil, a relatively new invention from the distant shores near the lands of the Romanii. I possessed a small mirror of inferior quality meant to be held by the hand back in my rooms at the palace, but this mirror... this mirror stood as tall as a person, and I could see from the top of my head all the way down to my toes at once, and with such precise clarity that the reflection before me could easily have been a duplicate of myself down to the last detail.

"Come away, Yar Hátin, and let me dress you," Raisa murmured gently.

I allowed her to direct me back toward the crackling fire where she fitted me with a corset and two layers of petticoats. Once satisfied that everything fit well and I could still marginally breathe, she slipped a plain gown of white silk over my head. Thusly adorned, plainly and with no jewelry, my hair hanging long down my back and barefoot, I would process into the temple's hall where Casmir would meet me. Only once this ceremony was over, when I was the wife of the prince, would I then dress in the costly coronation robes for our procession to the rock just outside the temple forecourt, the place which had overseen the coronation of every king of Agrius — The Seat of Kings.

"Was my mother to be crowned too, do you think? When it was time for my father to be crowned king?" Chloe glanced at me as she brushed out my long tresses and shrugged. She was roughly my age so hadn't been alive at the time, and she had also been a slave all her life, not one to be privy to the inner workings of the royal family or King's Council. "Likely no one will tell me," I answered myself. "Not that I can blame them overly. It is painful to dwell on the past. People lost their lives and fortunes that day."

I thought now of my mother and father's wedding, the day Bellek arrived, the day Ildor Veris orchestrated his own power grab, to use Bellek as a puppet. And now he thought Casmir would be pliable, though I knew he already had doubts about me. We would cross that bridge when we came to it, as the Mercorian cavalrymen were known to say. Now was not the time to worry about Ildor Veris.

When the time came, Raisa led me from my chamber up a short, dark corridor to a slightly larger antechamber which led immediately into the hall of the temple. A priest awaited us there before a closed door. I stood facing it, then closed my eyes and did my best to calm my breathing, to take in a few last, quiet moments. Once the door opened and I processed into the great hall of the temple, everything would change.

In my mind's eye I imagined Casmir emerging from a door on the opposite side of the hall as he would soon do, walking toward the altar from his side as I would do from mine. We would meet in the middle and join hands, facing one another. A priest would mutter his words of ceremony and we would make our answers and vows, and it would be done. A simple thing.

"Yar Hátin," the priest whispered. "It is nearly time."

I did not open my eyes but nodded my understanding. I pressed my open palms to my stomach in a futile attempt to keep the flutters at bay.

In what felt like an instant, I felt a rush of fresh air on my face and opened my eyes to see the cavernous hall open before me. Casmir appeared on the far side opposite me, and we walked slowly toward one another, just as I'd imagined.

He wore a rich velvet garment of black, red, and gold with a flat hat. His face bore his usual court mask, but he could not hide the light shining behind his eyes. Around the altar stood a handful of people: Evet, Ildor Veris, Figor, and representatives of the highest-ranking families in Agrius.

A flurry of thoughts fought inside my head, some telling me that I was not worthy to wed this man, this prince of Agrius, while other thoughts fought for dominance, telling me that this man wasn't even owed the crown, that it should be mine and mine alone. I wrestled these thoughts into submission and quieted my mind.

The moment we met and clasped hands, time stopped. The ceremony proceeded, but I neither heard nor felt anything save for the pounding of my heart. The words spoken came automatically, as if it was someone inside me who had only borrowed my body and I could do nothing but watch on helplessly.

Casmir leaned in to kiss me chastely on the cheek, and we turned to face the small assembly, husband and wife.

"Yar Hátin, please stand on this stool."

Raisa shivved me gently toward the stand. There was only a short time for me to change out of the white silk and into my coronation gown before Casmir and I would progress from the hall and out to The Seat of Kings.

"I am married," I whispered to no one in particular.

"Yes, and hopefully will remain peacefully so for decades to come," Raisa replied irritably, her usually dour self returned. "Now please stand still." The sweetness of a wedding day was no match for her efficiency.

Made from silk which had been woven with strands of pure gold, the cloth for my gown had been hand embroidered with colored thread then decorated with diamonds, rubies, and sapphires. Because cloth of gold was reserved for members of the immediate royal family only, it was an eye-popping extravagance. No one else at court would be wearing anything of its like this day.

"Now I must draw together the front of the bodice with these hooks and eyes, and it may take some time."

I remembered the chill of the procession yesterday and was thankful that the skirt of my gown was fully lined in ermine. Ermine also lined the edges of the bodice center front, making some of it visible through the gathering that Raisa now fastened together. Ermine also lined the lower section of the sleeves so that when they were turned back into a cuff, the ermine showed. I would don a heavy cloak and matching ermine-lined leather gloves for the trip back to the palace which would host a celebratory feast. The great hall opened up to those closest to the crown, but the gates to the lower ward would be thrown open to the general population of Prille so that everyone could receive food and drink in celebration of their new king and queen. I marveled at the sheer size and expense of this single event, only beginning with the extravagance of my gown.

When I had asked the master dressmaker about the excessive cost when he first came to visit, to take my measurements and take in my coloring, he had looked at me askance. Though the look lasted only momentarily. "This gown is not for Irisa, it is for the queen." It was in that moment that I realized something vital: with the placing of the crown, I would cease to exist. My office, the duty placed upon me by tradition and the forbearance of the people, took priority over my personal desires, over my name, or even my comfort. Irisa would cease to exist. I would represent something bigger than myself. Is this how all royalty viewed themselves? I very much doubted that Bellek had. I had yet to discover Casmir's thoughts.

Once Raisa was satisfied that my clothing was perfectly arranged, my hair plaited and pinned, and a chain of rubies and pearls set about my neck, she affixed the circlet of a princess on my head. I emerged back into the hall and met Casmir, surrounded by his inner circle of trusted friends.

"My bride," said Casmir quietly as he bent over my hand and kissed it. When he looked up again his eyes shimmered, but immediately he arranged his face for the court, his thoughts hidden safely away, and we turned as one to proceed down the hall's aisle, past the Council, past his family, and to the doors where we were announced by a blare of trumpets. A host of knights, lords, and heralds-at-arms led the way, followed by the nobles, then the priests in their ornamental robes. Lastly Casmir and I stepped out.

We traversed across the forecourt and out from under the entrance arch into view of a large crowd who had gathered below the promontory that was the Seat of Kings. All of Prille had shown up, it seemed.

A carpet of deepest blue stretched from the arch toward a raised platform, parting the awaiting audience like a walkway on the sea. Taking Casmir's arm firmly in my own, we moved down the carpet as men and women alike bowed a knee and lowered their gaze at our passing. Two lords - one Vitus and one Sajen - conducted us onto the platform.

The crowd quieted, straining to hear what would happen next.

The high priest ascended the platform and raised his hands toward the sky. "Hear you people of Agrius!" he called, his voice strong and sure. He turned toward the north: "I here present to you your sovereigns, undoubted and true. All you who come this day to do your homage and service, are you willing to do the same?" An enthusiastic reply erupted from the people and a trumpet blast echoed out.

The high priest turned toward the south, then the east and west in succession, repeating his words and question again for each direction. After the final proclamation, the entirety of the crowd swelled into a frenzy of acclaim, growing in force until the very streets of the city seemed to shake with it. Everywhere I looked, people waved their banners, cheeks bright red from the cold and excitement.

Next we knelt where we stood, each of us swearing an oath before the priest as he touched our heads with anointing oil. Once anointed, we turned to be seated on the thrones behind us. One priest bestowed upon Casmir his father's sword and signet ring, while the other gave me a ring to match Casmir's along with a jewel encrusted book symbolizing the law of the land.

Next, the two priests retrieved our crowns. They

approached us, their heads bowed, and the high priest lifted his hands and raised his voice, saying: "These crowns crown the faithful! May our servants, upon whose heads this day we place them for a sign of royal majesty, be filled with abundant grace and all princely virtues!"

He paused several heartbeats, then lowered his hands, a signal for the two priests holding the crowns to lower them upon us. The moment the crowns rested on our heads, bells rang and the trumpets blew once more. I resisted the urge to turn and look at Casmir, knowing that his face would betray nothing of what he felt.

I felt the weight of the gold and precious gems nestled into the intricate weave of gold bands making up the crown, and thought of my father. How would he have felt if he'd been here this day? Would he have been proud that he had attained, at least in part, his goal? Even if the throne did not belong to him, it belonged to his heir. Certainly I shared rule with the son of his enemy, but in our uniting, we ended the threat of bloodshed. His goals were accomplished, and now I could take up his cause to reform the laws of the land.

My eyes swept over the crowds, and I realized these were now my people. They had welcomed me, given me their approval, cheered and supported me with enthusiasm. And now I owed them my life.

Movement beneath the platform caught my attention as a single line formed. One by one nobles came forward to pay homage, kneeling at our feet each in turn, then offering the kiss of peace. On and on they came, their faces blending together, names mostly forgotten until the one I anticipated most.

"I, Ildor Veris, son of Inor of Haern, do become your liege man of life and limb, and of earthly worship; and faith and truth I will bear unto you, to live and die, against all manner of folk."

His eyes looked into mine with steady confidence as he spoke, and if I did not know better, I would have believed him. I kept my face schooled into the court mask I had begun to perfect, but I could not, would not, hide my elation when he finally stood and backed away, resuming his place into the gathered assembly. I followed his progress and gave him a look he could not misinterpret. And then I smiled, though it did not reach my eyes.

"My Adonia, can you bear the rest of the day?" Casmir's gaze strayed to my crown as we loaded into our palanquin for the procession back to the palace and the long feast.

In truth the crown was heavy. Made of pure gold and studded with precious gems, it was heavier than I imagined it could be, and it only got heavier with the wearing. How heavy it would be by the end of the day, or even in the figurative sense as the days and weeks passed, remained to be seen. Even my gown was heavy, lined as it was with gold thread and jewels.

"I will see it through," I returned lightly, offering up a smile.

He patted my hand and signaled that we were ready to depart.

Our escorted palanquin followed the straight road from the Temple of Zinon to the city's central square. From there we followed several twists and turns toward the palace. No snow fell this day, and the sun shone brightly over the western sky as it made its late afternoon descent toward evening. The canopy over our palanquin had been constructed from a single bolt of silk borne by two knights on either side. It fluttered gently in the light breeze. I smiled at the people all along the route, and

Casmir, noticing the acclaim the people held for me, squeezed my hand.

Alongside our palanquin marched Casmir's household officers and footmen on foot, followed closely behind by my ladies of the household on snowy white palfreys. Leading up the rear came the King's Guard, three by three, led by the ceremonial captain of the guard and the master of the henchmen, Ildor Veris.

Once delivered to the door of the great hall, we emerged from the palanquin onto a velvet carpet leading inside. Hundreds of candles lit up the great hall as Casmir led me down the blue carpeted aisle toward the King's table upon the dais at the upper end. We passed by long boards laid lengthwise down the hall where our guests stood in their places waiting as we took our places in front of our chairs. Casmir sat, and everyone else took their cue to do the same.

A great train of servants arrived bearing dishes for our table, including roasted venison, swan, and a peacock which had been re-plumed after it had been cooked so that it looked like a live bird. Other dishes bearing vegetables and soft white breads, salads and sweets, filled in around the meats.

Casmir stood, and with his arms held wide to the side, invited his guests to dine.

The rattle of knife upon plate rang out, and I turned my attention to the platter before me when a voice broke in. "My queen." A courtier dressed in elegant velvet trimmed in sapphires bent a knee before the high table. He offered us wine, and when he had poured, Casmir waved him forward before he could depart.

"Irisa, this man is Eron, son of Amalia, wife of Nikolas, and I have invited him to be our cup bearer for the feast." My eyes opened wide in surprise, for I had no idea that any Sajens were left at court and said so. "That is because he is not a Sajen. He was born to Amalia's first husband, Arnald of Dremesk, and retained his father's name and titles after the succession. He was a friend to your father. Perhaps he can tell you stories of your father's youth?"

"Of course, my king, if it pleases you." It certainly pleased Eron, for as he backed away, he beamed like the lighthouse on the rock overlooking Tohm Sound.

I smiled openly at Casmir and leaned in to whisper, "Thank you for that."

He merely smiled over the rim of his wine cup before he sipped. "I only did it to persuade you to dance with me more than the other handsome rogues in this place. I see many of them eyeing you, sizing up their chances against me."

"It's a fair concern, my lord," I teased, pretending to consider my options. "It will be a close thing." I turned back toward him and lowered my lashes, taking a deep drink from my cup. The liquid warmth traveled all the way down to my toes.

When the meal finished, I quaffed the rest of my wine, and as the musicians set up to play, the guests rose from their tables so that they could be moved back for the dancing.

Casmir held my arm under my elbow, and we rose to standing. I felt a little unsteady, and Casmir noticed. "It's just the excitement," I said in answer to his unasked question, though in fact it was the wine. I knew I'd had too much and wondered if I would come to regret it.

"Of course," he murmured in my ear, his breath warm on my skin.

We moved down among the people and took up dancing as song after song rang out. Eager to greet their new queen and the new wife of the man who had been their beloved prince, I greeted one dance partner after another. With each new partner came a new glass of wine, and by the end of the night, I very much wished I had not been so indulgent.

My maids busied themselves around me, their chatter incessant, the tones of their speech rising and falling like a chorus of birds.

"Yar Hátin, are you well?" I cracked open an eye to see Chloe looking up at me with round eyes full of concern. "You have nothing to worry about tonight. Prince... er, King Casmir... I think he will be gentle with you."

I twitched a smile but closed my eyes again and took a deep breath, trying my best to slow the spinning of the room. I wondered if anyone else felt it, or if it was just me? Sweet Chloe couldn't know that any worry I may have harbored over the remainder of the events of the night ahead was the farthest thing from my mind right at the moment. I didn't care what happened so long as I was able to keep my churning stomach at bay, could keep from emptying its contents all over my marital bed before it got used.

"Here, take a sip of wine..."

Raisa held out a cup toward me, but I barked a harsh laugh. "That's the last thing I need," I said as clearly as I could between clenched teeth.

When my jewelry and outer gown were removed, the maids busied themselves by folding the costly garment neatly and storing it away in a chest on the far side of the room, the volume of their chatter easing as they put some distance between themselves and my pounding head.

Raisa moved behind me to lower my petticoats. I stepped out of them and she set them aside. I closed my eyes again and took another deep breath, and she began unlacing my corset. With each tug, each level of lacing loosened, I gulped in a breath of sweet air, easing my stomach enough that I felt the crisis pass.

"Whoever invented this blasted contraption should be found then hung, drawn, and quartered," I muttered. The unlacing paused momentarily and I took another deep breath, happy finally to be able to breathe. "Likely it was a man," I added, wobbling slightly as I did so. I giggled at my own wit.

"Perhaps it was only a man who anticipated his wedding night?" I spun on my heels. It was Casmir. "A man who would have the pleasure of helping his new wife undress?"

I regretted my impulse, for my quick turn sent the room spinning even more. Casmir still held the long, loose laces in his hand, and he cocked a crooked smile. I glanced around the room, finding no maids, only Casmir. He must have entered silently and dismissed them after Raisa removed my petticoats.

Casmir pulled the corset free of me then turned and placed it on the chest with my other clothing. I reached out a hand to steady myself, found a table's edge, and wobbled next to it, certain that if I let go I would fall to the floor. He then removed his doublet, hanging it on a peg nearby, and, finding a chair, he sat down and began to unlace his boots, one at a time, watching me all the while, a half smile still in place.

We were now in the king's lodgings, rooms that had once belonged to Bellek but which had been remade for their new owner. Preparations had made it a private and cozy retreat for the newly wed couple.

"There is wine here, if you are thirsty?" He arched a brow in query and I shook my head, unwilling to trust my voice or my rebelling stomach to behave.

Once his boots were removed, he stood and slowly

poured himself some wine, wearing only his shirt and hose. He watched me closely over the rim of his cup as he sipped. "Irisa, come sit with me. I would talk with you."

He patted a chair, and I smiled at him, appreciating his consideration and tender regard. I willed myself to maintain a normal mien despite the movement of the floor underfoot. Poor Casmir didn't deserve a bride green with malady on his wedding night. I regretted those cups of wine, but what could I have done? It would get better, if only I could keep him talking long enough. With one slow step at a time, each requiring a level of concentration I never knew would be necessary for a simple walk across the room, I found the chair and sat carefully.

The fire crackled in the background, the only sound in the room. If anyone was still at their revelry at this hour, they had taken it upon themselves to enjoy it far from our chambers at least.

"You did well this day, my Adonia."

His words seemed far off, as if they came from another room entirely. I wanted to shake my head to try to clear it but knew I might pass out if I did.

"Thank you," I said quietly, my voice unsteady. Taking another deep breath I steadied my voice and said more boldly, "as did you."

He smiled and sipped again. He had worn a flat bonnet all day, and now that it was removed, his hair fell about his ears unkempt, as it was the first day I met him after he had been training at the pell. My eyes took in his disheveled hair, his loose fitting shirt, and I became suddenly very aware of our intimate setting, all that was about to happen perfectly sanctioned, approved. I gripped the seat of my chair to keep myself from spinning off it.

Casmir picked up the decanter and poured a measure in

a cup then passed it to me. I stared at the cup, not wanting more of what had been the source of my illness, but unwilling to seem ungrateful. I picked up the cup slowly and pretended to sip, though in reality I let the wine pass my lips then back into the cup again.

"Irisa, are you unwell?" It seemed as though he had said something before this, but I missed it. I laughed for some reason, unable to control myself, and he gave me a quizzical look.

He said a few more things which I didn't catch then set his cup down on the table and came to stand behind me. With gentle fingers, he plucked the pins from my hair, one by one, and as he did so, a slow cascade of brilliant gold fell down around my shoulders. He lifted the strands and let them slide slowly off his palms.

"You have no idea how long I've wanted to do that." And then leaning over me from behind, he whispered "Irisa" in my ear. He placed his hands under my elbows and lifted me to standing, brushing the hair away from my neck and kissing me softly where the hair had been. He slid his hands down to my hips and turned me so that I faced him.

My heart thudded in my chest, and I wanted to give in to the warmth that suffused my body, but my head operated its own set of rhythms, and I had to close my eyes to keep my brain from charging out of my skull. Casmir read this as acquiescence and pulled me tightly against himself, kissing me gently as his hands roamed down my back.

"You have a debt owing me, I believe," he murmured, his voice warm and coaxing. "I would that you pay it now."

"I do?" I tried to focus, but the spinning room whirled faster. It took every ounce of awareness I had to stand.

"For agreeing about the Council, remember? At the time

you said you would repay me in two weeks' time." He kissed my neck, his voice husky. "It's been two weeks."

I had a vague sensation that he reached out for my chemise, and I raised my hands to place them on his chest, but rather than finding warm flesh, I felt nothing but a rush of air and a feeling of dizziness as I fell to the floor, darkness and oblivion overtaking me.

~16~

MY EYES SNAPPED OPEN and I bolted upright.

Casmir sat in a chair near the window, sipping from a cup while he read over a parchment pulled from a scattered pile on the table at his right hand. He wore nothing but a light robe around his shoulders to keep the chill at bay. The fireplace held only faint embers, barely enough to light the hearth never mind heat the room. I glanced at the windows to try and determine what time it was, but the lack of light gave me nothing to go by.

He glanced my way when he heard me stir.

"Casmir," I rasped, "I am so sorry."

He rose, came over to the bed, and slipped off his robe, sliding in next to me. Brushing my hair away from my face, he looked searchingly into my eyes with obvious concern. "It was not how I imagined spending my wedding night, I'll grant you. How do you feel this morning?"

"My head beats like a tabor, but I'll live." I leaned into him, and he drew his arm around me as I buried my face in his chest. "You deserved better than that."

"Don't worry. We'll make up for it when you are feeling better, that I can assure you. In fact, I think you owe me interest on that debt now."

I looked up at him and he smiled wolfishly, even if his eyes hinted at a tenderness of warm affection.

"Did you sleep here too?"

"Of course. Where else would I sleep?"

I didn't know what to say to that, so said instead, "And you put me to bed?"

"Of course."

In my mind's eye I imagined his look of shock and annoyance as his bride lay crumpled on the floor in a drunken stupor. Then in an incredible show of self-control and restraint, he picked me up and put me in our unused marriage bed, pulling the coverlets over me before slipping into bed alongside me, leaving me untouched.

A pang of guilt stabbed me. "I'm so sorry," I whispered again. "People kept offering me wine, and I couldn't turn them down. Everyone was so eager to dance with me."

"Can you blame them?" he asked, smiling again as he twirled a strand of my hair around his fingers.

"I can't say I've ever wanted to dance with Adonia, no," I returned peevishly. "But a handsome king, yes." I looked up at him with a half smile, considering his tousled hair and the shadow of a beard on his unshaven chin. I inhaled his warmth, smelling a mixture of unwashed bodies and bed linen to match the faint odor of stale smoke mixed with the wine on his breath. My head still pounded, but my stomach was remarkably calm. "What time is it?" I asked him.

He looked perplexed for a minute, then glanced toward the windows. "The light is barely awakened. Likely it's still early."

"How much time do you have today?"

"They shouldn't come looking for me before midday, I would imagine."

I nuzzled my head into his shoulder and began to trace a line down his chest with my finger, finding a faint scar on his ribs. "So enough time that we might be able to make a dent in that interest I owe?"

He rolled onto his side, facing me, and let his gaze take in all of my face, hair and neck, lingering where my chemise pulled tightly enough to reveal the gentle rounding underneath. "Perhaps. But you do owe a lot of interest."

"Then I think it's best we get started, don't you? Before the debt becomes more than I can repay?"

He paused, as if thinking it over. "A debt that large... You could be beholden to me for a long, long time, in other words." He rolled away from me, onto his back with his arms behind his head as if reconsidering his options.

"Yes, though what good is a debt if never repaid?" I nestled against him again, as closely as I could, and drew circles on his chest and stomach. "I could consult a lawyer, but I think there is a chance that an uncollected debt eventually loses its force, dissolves and becomes ineffective, impotent..."

"Never say it!" he cried as he flipped onto his side again then pushed himself up so that he rose over me, his face hovering just a hand breath over my own. "Have you forgotten who I am?"

I raised an eyebrow as if I had no idea what he meant.

His lips brushed my cheek. "I am king, and I expect a full remittance..."

You would have thought the little dog had never been shown affection in all of her short life by the way she carried on. Kathel rubbed the soft fur of Ilex's belly, and the lump of cotton showed her pleasure by wiggling around on her back in unmitigated delight, snorting and flailing her paws in the air.

"Ilex, I can't keep this up if you wiggle away from me!" Kathel grinned broadly, scooting along on the floor after Ilex's wriggling body.

The poor dog had suffered terribly, her life reduced to little more than lounging and receiving pampering from the maids. Of particular torture for her were Kathel's daily visits in between her lessons and other duties, and it was all Ilex could do to manage the play time and constant love from the little girl.

Winter had passed by in a fury of snow and biting cold, but eventually spring blew in on a southern wind, transforming the browns and grays of winter into a promise of color and warmth. Buds dotted trees, and new grass hinted under the residue that winter left behind.

The novelty of Prille's winter waned over time despite the distractions of a new husband. I had grown up used to Corium's mild climate which changed little over the course of the year, bringing only cooler temperatures and a rainy season as respite from its eternal summer. Prille's colorless frailty had bitten deep into my spirits as I grew weary of the dreary weather, but the coming of spring renewed my bright mood immensely.

So it was with some surprise and a slight return of my melancholy that I took in Kathel's news.

"My mother is preparing to leave for Rimehost, and I must help so can't stay long." She picked up the toys Ilex had left scattered around the room and returned them to a box in the corner.

I stared at her, stunned. "What do you mean your mother is leaving? Why is she leaving?"

"Rimehost is within her dower lands, and with father gone, she is free to make it her permanent home. It is small, but it is dear to her."

I considered Evet's choice and realized the sensible nature of her desire. She had never wanted a life at court. Like me, it had been forced upon her. So I could understand her desire to escape. Even so, I had much to learn from Evet, had planned to learn what I could from her despite her warnings about Cousin Ildor. I was queen now, after all. Why would Casmir not support me?

"Will you go too?"

Kathel understood the ramifications of her mother's going, for her face fell at my question. "Yes, I believe that I will. There are many years yet before I marry, and I will stay with mother until then."

It was a heavy statement for such a young child to make, but I shouldn't have been surprised. She was born and raised at court, and all the years of her young life had been spent preparing her to be the bride of a husband in a far off land. That was the way of the world. It was as my father had intended for me, for my sister. We had just never known it. I would miss this serious young girl.

"I shall miss you," I told her, and she nodded but said nothing.

Three days later, Evet sailed away, taking Kathel and her significantly dwindled household with her. I waved at them from the quayside as they went, blowing a kiss to Kathel as she leaned over the railing, flapping Ilex's paw at me in farewell.

I had sent the little ball of cotton off with Kathel, for she had taken to the pup and it seemed like a fitting parting gift. She would have something to remember me by this way.

"You will miss her?"

Casmir took my arm as we turned to make our way back to the waiting palanquin to return us to the palace. "Ilex, or

Kathel?" I laughed. "Yes, I think so."

The day was warm and we slowed our pace through silent and mutual agreement to take in the luxury of the sun's rays. I still wore the heavy velvets of winter but in deference to the stronger rays of the sun had chosen to neglect a cloak. The freedom this small choice brought with it, combined with our short stroll on the city street, produced a surprising nostalgia. If I closed my eyes, I thought I could transport myself back to Corium, a poverty-stricken orphan once again.

King Casmir required a closer guard than the prince had, but the day seemed to work its magic on our entire retinue, for both the guards and my ladies maintained a greater distance from us than usual as we walked. We skirted a pile of crates to be loaded on a waiting merchant ship and encountered an old beggar hunched upon a pile of rags in the shadows. I stopped and reached into my belt to free a silver coin. The man nodded and mumbled his thanks.

"Kathel is so much younger than you," I continued, letting the insinuation hang there.

"Yes," Casmir laughed. "Everyone was surprised by her arrival, my mother most of all, for she thought she was finally done with her requirement to produce heirs."

I had never met any of Casmir's other younger sisters, but I knew that Evet had birthed enough living children to satisfy anyone who might have reason to worry about the succession.

"What happened?" Casmir chuckled then smirked, and I rolled my eyes and shook my head in exasperation. "I mean, why another child?"

"My father happened," Casmir said, frowning. "It's true he had little use for my mother after she had done her duty by him. She lived in her separate apartments and seemed to find a quiet enjoyment in the peace." We walked on and I let him take his time telling the tale. "But now and then my father would take it into his head to visit her."

"That must have infuriated dear Cousin Ildor," I quipped, immediately wishing I'd held my tongue.

"What do you mean?"

He stopped and turned me to face him. I twisted the toe of my shoe into the cobbles at my feet, feverishly trying to think of a way to back out of the ill-considered comment I'd just made. I needed to confront him about Ildor Veris, but I wanted to choose my time well, when he would be most receptive to my thoughts on the matter.

"I only meant that your cousin likely thought it a distraction from the important matters." It was a lame response, though thankfully Casmir seemed to accept it. "Do you ever miss your father?"

He considered this for a moment. "My father and I were never close, as you know. I pursued my training and my interests, and he his."

"You mean ruling?"

He laughed. "My father had no more interest in ruling than in weaving. He loved the benefits of the crown of course, but he never wanted to be bothered by its weight." My thoughts returned to Ildor Veris, and in his uncanny way, Casmir followed my train of thought. "He had a true adviser in Cousin Ildor." Casmir eyed me as if daring me to say otherwise.

I changed tack again. "You call Ildor Veris cousin. How is he your cousin?"

"What do you know of Sajen and Vitus?"

"I know that Vitus was the legitimate son of King Ancin, but he was only a babe when his father died. His oldest half-brother Sajen took the throne instead. Illegitimate or not, the people welcomed him."

"Yes. And Vitus had two sons — Abderus and Paro. Abderus is my father's grandfather. Paro is cousin Ildor's grandfather."

"I see."

Somehow we had bypassed the awaiting palanquins completely and continued on to the palace on foot. Casmir seemed to welcome the break in the same way I did, for he made no move to guide us back to them.

"Why all this interest in Cousin Ildor?" he continued.

I considered how to put voice to the concerns niggling the back of my mind. I knew that Casmir loved the man, was probably closer to him than he had been to his own father. But I also knew that love had been cultivated with a purpose and wondered if Casmir's love for the man blinded him. Evet seemed to think so. Casmir was my husband, and if he was to have my loyalty, he should also have my full honesty.

"He worries me," I said pensively.

"How so?"

"I'm not sure how to explain it." Which was true. I did not know how to explain it in a way that would not anger him. Grand Master Lito had warned me about Veris, and so had Evet. I didn't think I wanted to be direct just yet, so tried a circuitous route, to test my footing, so to speak. "The way he looks at me sometimes, I don't know if I trust him."

Casmir chuckled out of dismissal. "My Adonia, if you knew how *all* men looked at you..." He took my hand then raised it to his lips and kissed it. "Even so you remain the least vain creature I have ever met. That was the first thing I noticed about you."

"Really?"

"Well, aside from your resemblance to Adonia, yes." He

winked at me and I felt color rush to my cheeks. "You were unlike any other lady paraded before me over all the years. One of the most beautiful, yet one of the most self-effacing."

He looked at me out of the corner of his eye as we passed under the arched gate into the palace precinct and made our way through the lower ward toward the upper one. Those we passed paused and paid us deference. Casmir seemed not to notice, but I acknowledged those I could as we continued on our way, offering smiles and well wishes to them all.

We entered our private apartments and Casmir's grooms moved to help him remove his outer garments, to change into something more practical for the day's duties.

"My wife will help me," he explained, shooing them out the door.

Casmir turned to face me and took my hands in his own. "Cousin Ildor was my father's strongest supporter from the beginning. He has always done what is best for Agrius. I have not known a more faithful servant of this house. His finding you was perhaps the best thing he's done in my recent memory. You said so yourself. It unites our houses and ends the ambitions of those who would use another war for their own advantage." He pulled me closer. "And besides, your father's bid for the throne would have ended in disaster for him as well as for you if Cousin Ildor had not brought you here." He drew a finger down my cheek as he spoke. "You would now be wife to Isary of Elbra, remember?"

"Yes, I don't deny any of what you say," I began, but Casmir cut me off.

"And it is common knowledge that Isary of Elbra is a darkly depraved man," he pressed, though his attention waned as he breathed in the scent of my hair and leaned in to kiss my ear, his fingers straying down my gown. "With darkly depraved tastes..."

I ignored his searching fingers while my thoughts flit briefly to Kassia and her close escape from marriage to Isary. "I am still uncomfortable with Ildor Veris."

"But he loves you, and you will get used to him." Casmir nuzzled my neck as he spoke. "Your concerns will change over time, you'll see."

"Casmir, it is only midmorning... And you have those names to consider for the Council. And the question of appointing a Chancellor..." I tried to push him away but he would not be swayed from his mission.

"So? There is plenty of time to look over that dusty list of names. I have until the Fiortha Court after harvest."

"But Roger Moucel will be leaving soon, and you should announce his replacement within a fortnight. Shouldn't you think on it soon?" I tried to twist away but couldn't.

His fingers caught at my hair pins. "Roger has never offered an original thought in his life. His tedious droning will not be missed, so any replacement will go unnoticed as a result."

I swatted his hand before finally spinning away from him, trying to think of some way to dissuade his amorous intentions, knowing we wouldn't have privacy for much longer. "Now that I've paid back that interest I owed you, don't you think it's time I visited a Council meeting?"

Casmir followed me across the room in the same way Ilex had done when she wanted something from me. I moved behind a table, keeping him at arm's length.

"How much interest you've paid is debatable."

I raised an eyebrow and he grinned, his look wolfish.

Just as he was about to feint a move around the table to renew his pursuit of me, a knock sounded on the door followed by the entry of a clerk who, upon seeing us, ducked his head, and with an averted gaze said, "My lord, I hate to disturb you, but Figor insisted you see this immediately."

Casmir broke off his chase, and I retreated to the relative safety of a window alcove while he read Figor's note. When he had finished, he joined me, though his amorous mood had chilled. He looked tired.

"There was a slave uprising in Dalery. A contingent of soldiers has been sent out to quell it."

I said nothing for a long while, and my silence unnerved him. He knew where my thoughts had gone.

"Irisa, Agrius struggles. The royal purse needs the boost."

"But what about the people?"

"What about them?"

I fought to keep my voice under control. "The people who have to live as slaves. Casmir, the treatment of them — the abuse and neglect. They are people, flesh and blood just like you and me. I know you care, Casmir. Why else free Chloe?" He looked away from me but I pressed him. "Casmir, you are king. What is the point of that unless you use the power you've been given to help your people?"

"It's not so simple," he puffed, pacing away from me and crossing the room.

"Why? Why is it not so simple?" I came out from the window alcove, emboldened by the passion of my plea. "Don't shirk your duty and let Veris wield the power that belongs to you. That's what he's really after." I said this last part quietly.

Casmir whirled around on me. "Irisa, that sounds childish coming from you." Anger infused his face, crinkling his eyes as they narrowed at me. He thrust his shoulders back and inflated his chest with a deep breath.

I had touched a nerve, and the passion of his response unnerved me, coming as if from nowhere. Even so, I pressed on, heedless of his mood. "He can't wear the crown, so he ruled through your father, wants to rule through you too."

"Ildor Veris is a loyal servant of this house, a man I wish to appoint as Chancellor." He spoke quietly, his voice steady though hard, his eyes granite. "You sully his name by suggesting such a thing of him and degrading my own influence, by questioning my commitment. What do you think I do with all of these?" His hands swept the pile of parchments off the table near the window. They fluttered to the floor like a cloud of butterflies in the wind. "If not rule?"

"Casmir, that's not my intention, I simply wanted to help you see..."

"If Veris rules," he held up a pointed finger, cutting me off, "it is for the benefit of the people, not for personal gain. Who filled your head with such nonsense?"

My heart pounded, and I struggled to find the words to explain the truth to him. I did not handle conflict well, and when faced with the force of his anger, my logical mind turned to mush. "Grand Master Lito and your mother..."

"Bah. Grand Master Lito was old, and my mother... she did not sit in the Council chambers, did she? How would either of them know who rules?"

"You told me yourself that your father..."

"I am not my father!" He strode toward me quickly, like a snarling hound toward a prey animal, and I backed up a step toward the wall, surprised and a bit shaken by the force of anger I never saw coming. I had found his insecurity.

Seemingly realizing the aggression of his actions, he stepped back. "We will not discuss this again."

And with that he turned and left the room, leaving the door open behind him. A maid entered just after he left, looking behind her at his departure. When she saw me still standing by the wall, my face pale with shock, she retreated, closing the door behind her.

That night at the evening meal I sat by Casmir in my usual place at the high table, and while he did his duty by me, his anger still burned, and I got the sense that his actions were only show. He talked and joked with me, but there was no light in his eyes.

Whether he knew it or not, I finally understood what worried Casmir so much, why he had always balked at his opportunity to rule: He did not want to be compared to Bellek Vitus.

Early the next morning it was decided that Casmir should ride out to Dalery to put down the rebellion himself. The leaders of the rebellion had holed up in the abandoned tower of an unused outpost near the sea. Rumor had it that they had planned this for some time as a remarkable amount of provisions had been laid up. Dislodging them had taken more time than anyone imagined, and the Council thought they would give up more quickly if the king himself took charge.

Casmir was gone for several weeks, and even when he returned he was consumed by work. At evening meals he dined quickly only to return immediately back to his work. At night he came to bed late, slipping in quietly and falling instantly asleep.

During all this time I poured my time into the people. Addis helped me arrange the gathering of supplies for distribution to the needy in the city. Loads went out day after day, but finally, after stifling the protests of my advisers, I personally visited a lazar house outside the city in the hill country beyond the northwest gate.

When Addis and I returned to the palace late that afternoon, I noticed Casmir and Veris standing together under an archway near the corridor leading to the Council chambers. Veris appeared to be unusually worked up over something, a stark contrast to Casmir's serene and reasonable look. I was nearly past them when Veris glanced up, noticing me. A look of vitriol washed over him, covering the distance between us in tangible waves. I did my best to remain outwardly unswayed despite my internal unease and looked away, continuing on toward my destination.

Casmir did not attend the evening meal, but later that night as I prepared for bed, he arrived, earlier than he'd been since his return home. Sensing an intensity of purpose, Raisa and Chloe dismissed themselves quickly, leaving the hairbrush they had been using in my hand as they departed.

He stood just inside the door and fumbled with his hands, all signs of the confident king I had known him to be, gone. He studied me for a time, then after some moments walked over to me and knelt before my chair. "I have not been settled since our quarrel." Taking my hands in his own, his eyes played over my face and hair for a moment before he looked down again to study my fingers. "Your ring, you still wear it?"

He referred to the blue agate he had purchased for me that day in the market, the day we found Chloe.

"Yes, it is very dear to me. This..." I said pointing at my wedding band, "...was given me by Prince Casmir. And this..." I said of the agate, "...by Casmir the man."

He continued to study the blue agate ring, an excuse to keep his eyes from mine while he searched for his next words. "I was upset that you would question my commitment."

"But that's not what I meant," I protested.

He stopped my interruption with a raised finger. "I

know. But you pricked my pride. That is my only defense. Now I come with humility to seek your forgiveness."

His contrition stunned me. Humility was not a trait I expected from a man of Casmir's status or position.

"I was wrong to disregard you. You are an anointed queen, after all." I lifted an eye in question. "Your request to sit in on the Council... It has never been done before, so we will have to ease into it. Your presence will make waves, but if you will simply attend and not speak..."

I made to argue, but he continued, "Only at first. Once your presence is accepted, we will see about letting you persuade them regarding your very heartfelt convictions. Maybe in time your attendance will feel natural and you will be fully welcomed."

"And you still intend to appoint Veris as Chancellor?"

He looked pained, but he did not anger. "I do."

I let my argument die. There was no point in arguing while he was so conciliatory. "What changed your mind about allowing me to participate in the Council?"

He considered for a moment. "The rebellion in Dalery. I visited the tower, spoke to witnesses." He looked at me, his eyes heavy with remembered pain. "You were right to remind me of my duty. If your presence would help push your cause, then so be it. There is no reason you should not be there."

"Does Cousin Ildor know?"

"I told him late today, yes. He was not happy, but as you said, I am king. Not him. And you are my queen, so why should you not sit on the Council? Agrius has never had a queen rule beside its king. At least not in recent history. It is a new era, and with it time for change. Will that be acceptable... my Adonia?"

He twisted my agate and twitched a smile, giving me a look that suggested his thoughts had moved on from the

Council chamber to the darker reaches of our personal chamber. He lifted me to stand before him, and I lowered my gaze in order to control my excitement. "Yes, my lord. And I do forgive you." No matter how decorous my eyes, my smile was nothing but mischievous.

"And Irisa? Can we not talk of Ildor Veris? I would prefer the man inhabit my Council chambers, not my bed chamber."

"I would prefer he stay away as well. Especially for the next ten minutes or so."

"Ha!" Casmir swooped me up in his arms and kissed me. "That is a challenge I accept." We walked toward the bed and he flopped me onto it before sobering. "And I don't just mean tonight. I mean always. I don't want to quarrel with you over Cousin Ildor." I opened my mouth to speak, but he continued hurriedly, "I ask you to honor me in this."

I swallowed heavily, uncertain how I would thwart Veris' plan when the one person who most needed to see the truth of him would not discuss it. I nodded even so. I would have to find another way.

"Very good. Ten minutes you say?"

~17~

THE OPEN COURTYARD OUTSIDE an old watch house overlooking a disused sea gate had become the site of my lessons from Wolf in the use of knife and dagger. It was just off a little-used side alley behind a series of out buildings, and no one ever came here. The buildings stood next to derelict, and somehow the place had been overlooked as an area to be redeveloped within the palace precinct. While my lessons had of necessity gone on hiatus while Wolf was away to Bauladu, his return to Prille brought with it the return of my lessons. Today brought a new twist to these lessons.

He handed me a wooden practice sword, and I eyed it as I would a snake. He ignored the look. "I suggest you hold it with two hands like so." He demonstrated and I moved my hands to match his. "As the fairer sex, and as one who has not trained from birth, your arm strength is not great enough to wield it one-handed. Granted, this is only a wooden practice sword. A real sword has greater weight, superior balance, a greater elegance, and you will find that steel is much more graceful. But for now..." I took a few practice swings and he watched on while doing his best to hide his amusement. "Push your hands more closely together, like so. Use your left hand more as a guide than a grip. When the time comes, you will be able to turn the sword more quickly if you apply pressure to the pommel."

"But the time will never come as I will never use it! I simply want to be able to defend myself with a small blade. I can't carry a sword around the palace." I imagined the scene I would create walking through the great hall with a longsword as accessory to my silks and jewels.

"Ah, my lady, you must trust me in this." He smiled his most beguiling smile, and I did as he asked. "I don't expect you to ever use a sword, for to use it with skill takes a lifetime of practice. It is not something anyone, man or woman, can pick up quickly and be effective. I simply want you to grasp its use at the most basic level, that you understand how lethal it is, to know why you never want to pick up a sword in a moment of panic, thinking to defend yourself with it." He made a few more adjustments to my hands. "Good, good. And remember your skirts as you move. To move, cut, parry, and recover while fighting against your skirts will impede you under the weight of heavy steel. May I suggest you kirtle them?"

The suggestion was outrageously unseemly, so I gave him a look that implied that I didn't take him seriously. He winked in response and bent down to demonstrate what he meant. I kept a hand on his shoulder for support as he worked, feeling the air blow against the bare skin of my scandalously free legs.

"You seem overly experienced helping a woman do this. You know my husband would kill you if he knew what you were doing?" I was only teasing him to lighten the awkwardness I felt, but I did wonder what Casmir would think, despite his friendship with Wolf.

"I kept my eyes closed the whole time," he said as he

stood, winking once more.

He had me practice this way for some time, keeping my skirts kirtled as I turned with the sword in my hand. When he was sufficiently satisfied that I knew how to hold it, he added, "I advise you to come down here whenever you can to practice with a steel one, even if just for a few minutes. To build your arm strength, hold out the sword at full length and make little circles with your hand. Do this until your arm gets tired, and when it does, extend it farther. Remember, extension is stronger than tension."

I tried this, and realized that what he said was true.

"That is enough for now." He took the wooden practice sword from my hand and set it aside. Thinking we were done, I turned to leave, freeing my skirts. "Not just yet, Irisa. Now we dance."

"What do you mean, we dance?"

"You can dance, can't you?" I stared at him with wide eyes. "My queen, I did see you dance with your husband at your wedding and coronation feast. I know you can do it. And your husband seemed most pleased with it as well, as I recall."

I looked around our mock practice yard, instinctively looking to see if anyone watched us before realizing that we were, as always, alone. "But what does dancing have to do with sword fighting?"

"Your hand, if you please?" He moved in and we began the slow, rhythmic steps of a volta. "Sword play, my queen, is akin to a dance. It is seductive, sweeping, subtle." We spun in a circle, meeting one another's eyes as we did so. "You remember dancing with your husband that night, yes? I saw the way you watched each other." A fiery flush rose to my cheeks at the memory. We paused, arms extended overhead, our palms held flat against each other. The corner of his lips drew up into a provocative smile. "This is how you approach sword play, my lady. It is a dance of lovers, with the same passion and tension."

I wanted to pull away, uncomfortable with his overt flirtation, but his hold remained firm. "Does this unnerve you?" He pulled me closer. "Don't worry about Casmir getting upset. Even if he objects and forces me to one-on-one combat," he maintained a serious mien though his eyes sparkled with laughter, "I can best him. I know his secret: he has a tendency to bend forward when he tires, slowing his reaction time and making him helpless against a quick counter attack. I've warned him about this countless times, but he never listens. Once I'm rid of him, I will simply take you to wife and become King of Agrius in his place." He lifted the fingers of my other hand and kissed them softly then spun me away with a gleeful laugh.

"Thank you, Wigstan," I said, sliding my hand from his grasp, "that will be enough for today." I pulled away from him, signaling I was done, and the moment broke.

A warm breeze blew up from the ocean, bringing with it the tangy bite of salt and the lush breath of green. It blew strands of hair around my face, and I brushed them away in irritation.

His face wrinkled into a smirk, satisfied that by my use of his given name, he'd successfully accomplished whatever it was he was trying to accomplish. We sat for a moment to rest.

"How are matters in Bauladu?" I asked, desperate to change the tone.

Wolf's face clouded over and his shoulders sank a little. He brushed a hand over his eyes. "My home is not as it was when I was a lad. Much work needs to be done. Not only the manor and lands, but also for the economy as a whole. The people struggle, so they leave."

"I'm sorry." I didn't know what else to say.

"And Addis has received dire news from home. Her sister has taken ill."

"Her father's heir, or another one?"

"Iteya, her father's heir. It doesn't seem likely she will survive."

"Is Addis close to her sister? I had the impression that she wasn't."

"It's not so much her sister personally as it is the politics of her home and what it could potentially mean to her." Wolf gave me a sardonic look that communicated a bibliotheca full of opinions regarding his wife's aspirations. Casmir had told me enough about Addis to know her priorities.

"Would she ever be considered a worthy candidate?"

"She is wed to a minor noble of Agrius. I don't see how anyone could take her claims seriously, no." He glanced at the sky as if gauging the time by the sun. "We should get back."

I threw a light cloak around my shoulders despite the day's warmth, mostly to hide the fact that I wore a shabby gown pulled from a pile of old clothing meant for donation to the city's poor. We parted ways near the kitchen gardens, on the other side of the out buildings behind the great hall. I had just rounded the corner of a small baker's hut when I encountered him.

"Irisa Sajen, daughter of an ousted house, born into poverty yet plucked away by my benevolent hands... Why do you continue to disregard my warnings?" He leaned casually against the stone wall as if it was a natural thing for him to be found in the kitchen gardens on a bright summer day.

"You say these things as if I should be grateful to you?" I made to walk past him, but he stepped into my path, blocking my way.

He smiled at me, his lips thinning and curving up at the

edges. I took a deep breath and resigned myself to the fact that we would have some sort of confrontation here and now.

"Do you mourn Grand Master Lito?"

"What?" The turn of conversation caught me off guard.

"It would be an unfortunate thing, no, a very sad thing," he pretended to look mournful, "if others were to succumb to the same illness. More to mourn." He picked up an immaculately manicured finger to pick at his teeth.

"Are you threatening me?"

He laughed, not taking my rising anger seriously, as if I was no threat to him in any way. I thought of the swords hidden in the niche by the sea gate but then chided myself for the ridiculous thought. Veris didn't carry a sword, but I was under no illusions that he could best me in any form of attack I might foolishly consider. And besides, I was a queen. The notion was absurd.

"I am a crowned sovereign of Agrius," I reminded him. "It is my right and duty to look out for the interests of my people."

His lips curled. "Your people? My dear girl..."

"I am interested in ridding this land of slavery," I began, but then considered a new tack. "For now, that is all I am after. Why do you try to thwart me? What can you possibly fear from a mere woman? Would you lock me away as you did Evet?"

"Casmir holds you too dear. You have done your work well, I must say. I can't blame him much, considering his good fortune in you." His look turned lewd, but I stood firm, not wanting to show him that he cowed me.

"Why do you care? What do you have to gain? Because you do gain from it, don't you cousin?"

I spat the last word and his face changed as fast as a swift moving thunderstorm. He stepped in close, his breath hot on my face. "Your father was going to be a nuisance. A fly in my ointment. He had ideas about actually ruling the kingdom."

"Imagine that," I countered dryly.

"That's why I found Bellek. Yes, yes, he's of the legitimate line and all that," he waved his hand as if it was a minor thing, "but only some people care about such quaint notions. It worked though, as I knew it would. Stroking the pride of those with a proclivity for the pedantic. There were many others who didn't care but who didn't like Nikolas." His eyes took on the look of a person remembering scenes and events with his mind's eye. Within a moment he came back to reality. "Thankfully they didn't know what your father intended. Something changed him in his later days, from the pleasure-seeking prince who was more interested in spending down the purse in the vein of his father into a man of conscience. Fortunately very few knew this. But I knew, and that's why I had to act before he became king."

"And you think you can use Casmir too, is that it? Just like you did Bellek?" I turned and put some distance between us, balling my fists in the folds of my cloak.

"Casmir will only remain king if I choose it." His tone was clipped, precise, cold.

The man was sure of himself, arrogant beyond reason. He considered himself a *Konungur Framleithandi*, a King-maker of legend. "What do you gain?" I asked again.

"My dear, if you have to ask such a question, you know nothing of power and its benefits, do you? I don't care a whit about slavery, except that it is rather lucrative." He stroked the luxurious weave of his coat.

"You crave power. That's enough."

"I encourage you, dear girl, to make your husband happy. Give him children. Work on it as much as he wants.

Keep him distracted. He is young, in many ways like your father was. You are... pretty. Do your duty by him, and do it often. Wear your crown and play at being queen if it makes you happy, but stay away from the politics of ruling." He flicked a glance at my waistline. "Does Casmir have an heir yet?"

My face glowed with the heat of embarrassment and fury.

"You know he is capable of ruling. You only want him distracted," I tossed at him, losing control of my temper. Inwardly I chided myself for it.

He smiled again. "Distracted kings are as useful as a distracted prince once was." He shrugged as if it was a basic rule of life. I cocked my head, clearly missing whatever it was that he implied. "You still don't know the truth about your mother, do you?" I felt a knife gut my insides. "Tragic, really. A sad, sad tale."

"What about my mother?"

"Perhaps I will tell you one day, if you press me to it." He spread a gleeful grin. The son of a whore enjoyed this. Overmuch. "Like mother like daughter, really." When a look of utter confusion crossed my face, he smiled even wider. "I'm referring to Kassia, not you."

"What do you mean? What do you know about Kassia? What happened to her?" I didn't care what my odds were now, if I'd had that practice sword I would have swung it at his head in an attempt to knock it from his shoulders.

"You mean no one told you about Kassia?"

"I knew that she had to recover from injuries in Corium, but no one told me more than that." I stepped closer to him, straightening my back in my best impersonation of imperial fury, but it had little effect. He swirled from me and strode off, his laughter echoing down the walkway like a malicious demon in a macabre dance.

The moment he was gone, my shoulders slumped and I leaned in against a timber frame supporting a row of beans. Just then a kitchen maid entered the garden and saw my pallor. She froze in fear, not used to seeing the highest ranking member of the house in the middle of the greens she had come to harvest. She made a tentative move to offer assistance, but I waved her away and made my way back to my apartment holding back my fury and my fear.

Masters of the Bibliotheca are never given funerals. The tradition started centuries ago, though no one could recall the exact reason. Likely the custom had some trivial origin, but as often happens with humans, the reason behind it was lost, and a ceremony-free burial became the way it was always done... because that was the way it was always done. A tradition etched in stone by the very practice of it across the span of years and therefore enshrined as if sacrosanct with no one thinking to reexamine the reasoning.

The weeks immediately following Grand Master Lito's death had been a frenzy of activity, from the coinciding death of King Bellek, to my wedding and coronation. I had been given little opportunity to mourn Grand Master Lito at the time of his death, and had all but forgotten him in the maelstrom of life that followed. Summer seemed to have settled into a comfortable routine, and finally I found the space in my day to take a walk out to the place he was buried.

The spot felt peaceful and quiet except for a single towhee singing a jaunty tune in a leafy tree just overhead. Other than my escort and a handful of ladies keeping a discreet distance, I felt the freedom of solitude for the first time in months. Finding a patch of springy green grass, I folded my legs underneath me and sat, reveling in both the moment and the golden rays of sun filtering down through the overhanging canopy of trees. A pair of wrens flit past in a flurry of wings, and as a sense of calm descended over me, I picked out the drone of a distant bee hive. I ran my hand lightly over the grass, allowing the tips to tickle my palms.

Grand Master Lito's grave marker was made of plain, white marble. A single sun emblem decorated the very top, and under that came his name and official title, "Grand Scriptstóri Bibliotheca Prille" with the dates of his service. That was it. Nothing to give evidence to the kind of man he had been, his likes or dislikes, the people he knew and loved, or the influence he had on those he worked with. The sun emblem and dates referenced the royal house he had served, but nothing more.

I thought about the poor grave my mother laid claim to back in Corium. There had been no money for a marker, only the flowers that Kassia and I placed there each year on the anniversary of her death. Now that we had both left Corium, there was no one left to know of her grave, no one to mark it with flowers or any other form of remembrance. In the course of time, I figured that even the plot of poor ground where she had been laid to rest would be converted into something more useful, the bodies committed to rest there ignored or forgotten underneath whatever new thing would be built there. Coming generations would never know that as they walked the new road or lived in the home built over top, they did so over the grave of a woman who had once lived and breathed, who loved, and who had dreamed and feared.

Because of the line of thought my mind had followed, it came as no surprise when Figor materialized seemingly out of nowhere and found a place on the grass next to me. I had seen little of him since my marriage to Casmir, and I might have wondered at his sudden appearance now except that it served my purposes perfectly.

"Did you know my mother well?"

"I knew her," he said carefully, averting his gaze as if in deflection. My eyes bore into him, willing him to elaborate. Getting information from this man was like trying to pull hen's teeth. After a few moments, he continued. "I was born in Pania, was the youngest son of a minor merchant. One day a man from the palace happened by my father's shop when he was away. It was an unusual purchase, and complicated, but I made quick work of the problem, and this caught the man by surprise. Very soon after I was brought into the palace to receive instruction from a palace tutor."

"So you were raised with my mother?" I could not hide my shock.

"Not exactly. We shared a teacher, so I saw her from time to time, albeit from afar."

"So how did you end up in Agrius. Did she bring you with her when she came to wed my father?"

He shook his head and fell into silence while gathering his thoughts. "Naria was originally to wed your father's older brother, Soren."

"What?" Grand Master Lito had neglected to tell me this fact.

"In the grand scheme of kings and kingdoms, the arrangement had been made when your mother was a babe. Soren was heir to the throne of Agrius, and as is the way of kings, needed a royal match worthy of his rank." The words flowed from him forcefully, as if he spoke them in an attempt to defend someone or something. Or maybe I misread his emotion.

I took a guess. "Was my mother a willing participant in the match, do you think?"

His eyes shifted. "She was a princess bred to a royal marriage. She knew her duty," he replied quietly. We fell to silence, and I digested what he had said and what he hadn't said, the latter sometimes being the most revealing. After a while he continued. "Soren was...a rash young man." Figor's eyes shifted again. "For this reason his father, Nikolas, sent him away for a time to be fostered in the house of Aleksandar of Pania. Oldest sons and heirs to the throne are rarely fostered, but Nikolas thought that getting Soren away from the Agrian court, even if it did not tame him, would prevent the poisoning of minds against him while he was so young. It was during this time that Soren got to know me, recognized my abilities, and asked for my services. I was sent to Agrius to serve the court here upon his return."

"What happened to Soren?"

Figor averted his gaze. "He died in a shipwreck, coming home from visiting your mother."

"And that's when my father became heir to the throne."

"Yes."

I thought back to that early morning in the Bibliotheca when I found the personal missive from my grandfather Nikolas to my grandfather Aleksandar. In it he had agreed to wed his son Bedic to Naria in exchange for his silence. But if my mother was first to wed Soren, why was it necessary for Aleksandar to bribe Nikolas regarding my father? It didn't make sense. Did I dare ask Figor about it? Did I risk exposing Figor in something in which he was complicit? Was this the root of the reason Figor remained so evasive regarding telling me more about my parents' past? I wasn't sure if any of it mattered except that Veris kept bringing it up as significant.

"Figor, what happened to Kassia in the Black Fortress?" With the question, Figor moved to standing as if to leave. I caught his hand. "Figor, please? She's my sister. I need to know."

He sighed and stayed put even if he did not sit again. "She endured things in prison."

"Things?" My heart sank as I thought about prisons.

"She was... ill-treated by guards, suffered broken bones and bruises. The wounds needed care, and when I learned of her fate I had her removed to a safe place before Veris found out. Once he found out she had escaped, he looked for her but turned his attention to finding you. Kassia was treated in Corium by a woman named Liri, a woman sympathetic to what happened to your father."

I took in the news. It shouldn't have surprised me. None of it. I knew she'd been in prison, knew she'd been injured, but perhaps I'd always chosen to believe her injuries were unrelated. I considered Grand Master Lito's grave and all the harm Ildor Veris had done to my family and to those I loved. I still didn't know how it connected to what he had implied about my mother and Kassia, but at the moment I didn't really care.

"What happened to her after we left Corium?"

"A small band of Agrian exiles took care of her."

"The ones Jahn knew?"

"Yes." And then as an afterthought, he added, "They actually stayed for a few days with Miarka before leaving the city."

It took me a moment to take in this news. So my sister had stayed with Miarka after my months in the same household? How many days could have been in between? "After staying with Miarka and Rolbert, they made their way to Elbra, to be with father?"

"For a time, yes. Until Prince Isary broke his agreement and turned his back on your father. Now they are both safe, living somewhere in Pania, though I'm unsure where. I have made inquiries but have yet to learn their exact location. It's probably for the best for her to stay anonymous."

"Figor, I am queen now. I can keep her safe, and I would love to see my sister again."

Figor nodded. "If I learn more, you will be the first to know." We fell again into silence, and I thought he might get on to the reason he'd come all this way to find me. Instead, he asked, "Why all these sudden questions about your mother, about Kassia?"

I couldn't read the expression that came over his face. Was there a hint of hope? As if he hoped I knew something more than what I'd yet told him, or was it that he hoped I didn't know more? My first reaction was to give him a scathing reminder that he hadn't been the most forthcoming source of information, but I held my tongue. Instead I considered his question seriously, wondering just how much I wanted to divulge.

"Ildor Veris told me that there is a secret about my mother. He has taunted me with it. I'm not sure I want to know it, but it must be relevant or else he wouldn't keep bringing it up."

Figor instantly paled. "Did he say more than that?"

"Only that it was a sad tale," I added.

Before I could press him further, he left me, the errand that had brought him outside the walls of the palace and to the temple's burial ground forgotten.

~*18*~

SOMETIMES I OVERHEARD THEM, *but they never knew that I did. Likely if they knew, they would never talk of the things they talked of. If they'd known their secrets weren't truly secrets, they would have stilled their tongues, and everything I overheard would never have been uttered.*

Today, however, was a day I never intended to eavesdrop. We were bound for the market, my mother, sister, Jeah, and I. Mother forgot to have me fetch my kerchief to cover my head before we left, so she sent me back. We had only gone as far as the corner when she'd remembered it. Kassia saw a friend she knew, so mother allowed her to talk to her friend while I returned home.

"Go quickly, Irisa, before the best selection is gone," she'd called after me.

I did as she bade, running as fast as I could back home, snatching the kerchief off its peg before running back to my mother. Rather than return back the same way I'd come, this time I returned by way of the back alley, coming around the corner from their right side rather than from behind them.

That's when I'd overheard my mother stifle a sob. My steps faltered, and I slowed, stopping completely when I saw a tear flow freely down her cheek. She brushed it quickly away, and as she did so,

Jeah put an arm around her shoulder.

How was it that her emotions had turned in such a short time? She had been so happy only moments ago. The day was bright and cool, and my father had brought home an unusually large sum of money the day before. We were going to the market now to buy some necessities, things we rarely had the money to purchase outright.

It was then I saw a young boy. He was older than me by several years, but his hair was the color of Kassia's, autumn brown with streaks of fire where the sun hit it. I had never seen the boy before, but he could have been my brother if I hadn't known otherwise. Moments later he ran up beside a woman who took his hand. Oblivious that anyone watched her, the woman checked to make sure that it was safe to cross the street and pulled the boy along with her.

My mother's eyes remained locked on the boy. It was because of him that the tear had broken free of her lashes and fell down her cheek. Jeah whispered some words into my mother's ear as I drew closer.

"Don't let the memory haunt you forever," she comforted.

I sidled around the rain barrel on the corner, and my mother straightened when she saw me, quickly wiping away another tear threatening at the corner of her eye.

"Ah, Irisa. Come, dear, and let's be quick."

We continued on to the market, but a shadow followed us the rest of the day.

Addis ticked off a list of names and ranks onto her fingers as we walked along a shaded arcade on the east side of the palace in the heat of the afternoon. The slave uprising in Dalery had prompted a flurry of correspondence from much of the nobility all over Agrius, and a large delegation had recently arrived in Prille to discuss it. Because of the high status of these individuals, a large feast had been planned, and many details

required careful attention. Far too many details for my
fledgling abilities. Most noble women had been raised to such
duties, but as I was still fairly new to my office, I relied heavily
on my women, primarily Addis, who gloried in her elevated role
within my household.

"Irisa, you have said no more than three words in all this
time. Have you no opinion?"

Addis had slowed her step to a complete halt, but I had
not even noticed. I had been matching my pace to hers
woodenly, without paying much mind to anything going on
around me.

"I'm sorry, Addis, I am a bit preoccupied." I alternated
between twisting the braided cord around my waist and flicking
at the bauble that weighted the ties. "You said one of these men
was from..."

"Haern," she prompted, doing her best to hide her
irritation at my lack of attention.

"That is where Veris is from," I added absently.

"Irisa..." Addis turned me by the shoulders to face her
directly. "Take your mind off the morrow. You will attend the
Council with confidence, honoring yourself and your father for
all his covert teachings, you will see. You have nothing to worry
about."

Thankful for her attempt to calm me, I gave her a half-
smile, still not convinced. She was right in that I had nothing to
worry about. As was my agreement with Casmir, I would attend
the Council meeting tomorrow and not speak. Until the
councilors became comfortable with my presence, I would
simply sit, watch, and listen. Casmir argued that this could only
benefit him, for I could be his eyes and ears. I could watch
closely, taking in the looks that passed among men, the
communications of those who had opinions yet did not voice

them. Sometimes what wasn't said was nearly as important, if not more important, than what was said. These were the things I would be able to decipher through observation.

"Thank you, my friend. You are, as always, most astute." We resumed our walking. "But I would be remiss not to inquire about your sister. How are things back home?"

She turned unusually quiet, and we continued to walk, the gravel from the path crunching underfoot as we went. "Iteya was born to rule. My brothers, while older, are inept." I let her words hang in the air so she could continue when she was ready. "When she is gone..."

"Addis, don't assume that she will die. She could still recover!" I interjected, more passionately than I'd intended.

She eyed me, her look dark. "No, she will not. Her physicians can do no more. They have seen her illness before and it never ends well. Likely I will only hear of her passing after the fact. Sometimes they forget me here, so far away from home."

Addis was a driven woman. She had a desire to be influential, and being the wife to a minor Agrian lord did not suit her. She'd had no say in the marriage, but when it came, it had removed her from an even more subservient role in the hierarchical order of her father's household with his multiple wives and children, and she had been happy at first. At least until the newness wore off. In fact she had seemed to grow more restless in the short time I had known her, and the illness of her sister only worked to invigorate that disquiet. The passing of any monarch can revive even the most obscure dreams, and the thought of her sister's impending death had been just the spark she needed.

"But your father is still Negus. He is not unwell, is he?"

"No, he is healthy as an ox," Addis admitted impatiently,

waving her hand in the air. "If Iteya passes on, he will need to look for a new heir. Aksum does not practice primogeniture like Agrius," she instructed me. "A decision will be made based on abilities, and it will not be immediate. So there is that in my favor."

"So what bothers you so much? You are very capable. Why should your name not be put forward?"

"Who would do that for me? If I do not put my own name forward, no one else will."

"Faulkner of Sayre... he is very young, and I think he might be just the voice we need to fill the shoes of Roger Moucel who saw too many ghosts of the past for my tastes. The only thing I worry over is his family's long history of feuding over the water rights to the Burce Estuary. His tendency toward surliness might hamper his ability to play nicely with others."

Casmir tapped his fingers on the tabletop, the oil lamp at his hand shining a feeble light and casting an eerie glow over his face.

"Cousin Ildor thinks that his inability to regularly supply levies might keep him attentive enough to be malleable when necessary. I wonder though, if his counsel will be flawed too much to make it worthwhile." He stood and paced then returned to sit in his chair again. "Arghhhh... there are no easy answers!" He leaned back, tenting his fingers behind his head and kicking the table legs as he did so.

After the coronation, it was traditional for the new king to rearrange the Council to suit his tastes, to appoint several new members, but not so many new faces that the old business and old wisdom was lost. It was a task that Casmir took seriously, and he had been staying up late the last few nights to finalize the decisions.

"And then there is Sidimund, who is quite wealthy, though I'm not sure how far off his manor lands he has ventured in the past ten years. And his wife has recently taken ill..."

I must have muttered something unintelligible, for Casmir's attention snapped to me. "My Adonia, something bothers you. What is it?"

"Addis wants to rule Aksum. Should we be concerned?"

He lay down the parchment in his hand, blew out the lamp, then came to bed. He slid in beside me and lay back, propping his hands behind his head. I curled into him with my head on his shoulder.

"What if she does?" If he had been standing, I could imagine he might shrug his shoulders. "I don't see why it should matter to us."

"Because matters of state, no matter which state, should matter to you, for one thing. But probably more importantly, because Wolf is your friend. What if she was successful somehow, and her father named her his heir? What would that do to Wolf?"

Casmir rolled to his side to look at me. "Irisa, I don't really see how it would impact Wolf one way or the other. They would remain married, and he would still have the control of her inheritance... at least the inheritance it was on the day of their wedding, not a new crown. That's truly all that matters to Wolf. If she got the crown of Aksum, they both win."

"But they would live apart!" I reminded him.

"And you know that neither of them finds much satisfaction in their marriage, so I don't see how that is a problem for either of them. Irisa, I have asked you to be my eyes and ears, to exert influence where and when you can. But I think in this you are seeing smoke where there is no fire."

I wanted to argue my case more, but he yawned and kissed me gently before rolling over to his other side. Soon his breathing fell into the deep rhythms of sleep. As I listened to his slumber, I told myself that it wouldn't matter. The ambitions of Addis were her own and likely had no impact on the sovereignty of Agrius. And with that self-prescribed assurance, I allowed sleep to take me.

"If the money is owed, it should be paid! Why are we even having this discussion?" Casmir's hand came down on the gleaming table with a reverberating slap, and all eyes snapped open in response.

Soon the councilors looked to one another for assurance, sheepish but firm in their resolve to keep trying. They obviously felt their case a strong one and would not be daunted or put off by any refusal to see reason, their reason, no matter who was doing the refusing, be it king or otherwise.

"He is right, we should pay them what they are owed. The dignity and sovereignty of our great land is reflected by our actions in this regard. Not to pay is akin to weakness."

All eyes turned to the newest speaker, and a hush fell over the room. The man was new to me, though as I considered him I recalled Addis mentioning a Taibel Rebane from Haern.

So he must be Ildor Veris' man, I thought to myself, the one Veris had put forward as his replacement once he was named Chancellor. I made a mental note to keep an eye on him in the future.

The quiet ended as soon as it had begun, replaced by murmurings which rose in increasing volume until a loud debate raged, silenced only with the exclamation: "Cousin Ildor!"

Ildor bowed at the waist in recognition of his acknowledgment. "Casmir, my boy, I wanted a brief word, if I may."

I hadn't seen the man enter, stiffened now that I had. "Irisa, my love, are you well?" Somehow Casmir noticed my rigidity and bent to whisper in my ear, his brows furrowed with concern. He picked up my hand and caressed it lovingly.

"Yes, I'm fine, my lord," I quickly assured him.

He accepted this, but I could tell he wasn't convinced. Straightening again he continued, saying more loudly this time so that everyone in the room could hear, "Cousin, we have just been discussing the latest in a long list of appeals for money. Would you care to join us?"

"No, thank you," Ildor replied as he strode across the room, stopping in front of me where I sat beside Casmir at the large table. "I will be departing soon. I merely wanted to pay my respects before I did."

He turned appraising eyes toward me, pretending not to be surprised by my presence in the Council meeting. With a smile, he raised my hand to his lips in greeting. I returned his smile and bobbed my chin in acknowledgment before removing my hand from his as politely as possible.

"I will take my leave then, if it pleases you." He spoke to Casmir, yet he kept his eyes on me as he did so. Casmir wasn't paying attention.

"Certainly...." Casmir waved his hand dismissively, returning to the discussion around the table.

Veris turned, taking several large strides, then paused momentarily, caught the eye of Taibel Rebane, and held it briefly before continuing on his way. Eventually the room descended more wildly into a cacophony of argument and counter-argument, and when he was certain he would not be missed, Rebane stood quietly and slipped out of the room.

Amalia, wife of Arnald of Dremesk, had been a petite woman. Strong of character and strong of opinion, she was a survivor. Like a cat, she always managed to land on her feet. Her first husband had been a wealthy man, and when he died young, leaving her with an infant son, she'd somehow managed to catch the eye of the heir to the throne, Nikolas Sajen. The things I had learned about her from her son, Eron of Dremesk, the man who had served as cup bearer at our wedding feast, reminded me of Kassia. Her feisty reactions to the world, her ability to land on her feet, her independent streak, and her inability to abide by the rules... It seemed as though some of these tendencies had stayed in the family. I wondered then if this was the reason our father had a special spot in his heart for Kassia. Did she remind him of his own mother?

"My mother had eyes like a hawk. As a young boy I could never get away with anything, no matter into whose care I happened to have been entrusted. Be it nursemaid or tutor, she would always hear news of me." The older man chuckled at the memory as we walked the upper garden behind the palace. Eron was older than my father by many years. As Amalia's first son, born to her in her first marriage, he knew both Soren, my father's elder brother, and my father. Despite their age difference, Eron and Bedic became close, being much more alike in temperament than Soren.

As happens with many men as they age, Eron carried a paunch about his girth, though his broad frame indicated he had been a powerful man in his youth, and he still stood tall and strong despite his age. His temperament was gentle, having more interest in animal husbandry and farming techniques than war. After his requisite years of education were complete in Prille, and because he wasn't needed or wanted at court, he'd returned to his father's lands, the prairies of Dremesk on the northern side of the island of Agrius, to raise his family. Despite his going, he'd managed to stay in close contact with my father.

"The death of Soren changed him."

"In what way? You have said they weren't terribly close."

"Oh, don't misunderstand. They got along well enough. They were just different." I thought of Kassia, and a smile curled the corners of my lips. "They were not confidants in the way that some brothers are. But they rarely quarreled. Until the later years." He held up a hand. "And before you ask, no, I don't know the reason for their quarrels. But whatever the reason, this was when your father... how would I describe it? He grew up."

"Someone who had reason to know told me that not many people knew about the change that came over him."

He looked sidelong at me, obviously curious who had told me this, yet perceptive enough not to ask. "That sounds about right. He began to take interest in governance then, I think. He had never been interested before." He paused as if remembering those long-past days. "And then the shipwreck happened, taking Soren's life. Things moved quickly after that. The surprise announcement came that he was to wed his brother's intended, Naria of Pania. And shortly after that... well, you know what happened."

He looked at his feet, uncomfortable at the idea of mentioning the arrival of Bellek and the events that turned the lives of my parents, my own life, upside down. "You need not be concerned for my feelings, Eron. I had a good life, even if we were poor. You speak of a history that I knew nothing about before coming here. You are maligning none of my memories."

I placed my hand gently on his arm and he smiled gratefully. "How is it that you remained safe after..."

Now it was my turn to be embarrassed.

He patted my hand in return. "I was on the far side of Agrius, in Dremesk. And my connection to the Sajens was not a blood tie. I posed no threat. It's only the blood ties that do, you know." Eron glanced overhead to gauge the time by the sun. "We should get you back to the palace before someone wonders if I kidnapped you. That might give them reason to finally dispose of me." He winked, and I laughed, happy to have found a new friend.

More and more nobles of Agrius trickled into Prille, and what once was simply the King's Council turned almost overnight into the Fiortha Court which wasn't meant to start for a few weeks yet. Each arrival brought news of more slave revolts. The problem had become more widespread than anyone in Prille first understood, and it seemed to me as though Agrius had reached a point of crisis. Action had to be taken one way or the other regarding the slave question. Reform was on the winds.

With my newfound position, I thought it best to press the advantage this momentum provided and spend one-on-one time with as many nobles as I could charm and cajole into meeting me. Most were delighted, even openly flattered, to meet intimately with the queen in her own audience chamber.

It was late into the night that I met with Milus from Berig, a region just west of the Fyrgdun range. After a long but pleasant conversation, I found that I was tired and thanked him for his time, urging him to retire. The man appeared happy to continue drinking my wine, relating more stories of his distant family, but I was eager to see Casmir after such a long day.

I damped down the charcoal brazier and blew out the candles. Most of the household was abed by now, and it seemed silly to wake them for such a trivial chore. Indeed I was queen, but I had been nothing above a manual street laborer not so long ago and likely would never forget my roots. At least I hoped I wouldn't.

I said goodnight to the duty guard outside in the corridor, dismissing his offer to accompany me, assuring him that the king's chamber was barely a stone's throw away. Life had been a frenzy of activity these last weeks, and Casmir and I had enjoyed few moments alone. I smiled a cat smile as I pondered the best way to wake him if he had already gone to bed.

So caught up in this daydream was I that I barely registered the movement from the shadows, a man stepping out to block my path. I uttered a small shriek before I realized who it was. "Oh, it's you, Cousin," I gasped, relieved despite myself. My heart beat wildly in my chest, and I looked over Veris' shoulder to see if anyone else was around or if we were alone. "How was your trip to the Panian court?"

"More fruitful than you could imagine. Thank you for asking."

His face hid in shadow, but a queer light burned in the depth of his eyes despite the darkness of the corridor. I'd have accused him of dabbling in the Occult of Rhazien if I hadn't known better.

"I am happy to hear it."

I inclined my head even as my heart skittered in my chest. I wanted to bypass him as gracefully as I could, but he seemed intent on something. Why else waylay me at such an hour?

"Have you heard how Evet fares in her new home?"

"Casmir received a letter only yesterday. She thrives. I am surprised you are concerned for her welfare?"

He laughed quietly. "Of course I am concerned. I have known her for many years. She is the mother of our king, is she not?" I didn't believe him for a minute, so kept quiet. "And I know you love Kathel. She is a sweet, innocent young girl."

Instantly a cold finger of dread poked my heart. "And I hope she stays that way for many a long year ahead," I said firmly.

"Of course, we all wish the same thing."

"I don't believe you."

He blinked heavily and inhaled a deep breath, his eyes turning steely, his smile distorting.

"Have you learned yet what happened to your sister when she proved useless to me?"

I shook my head, backing up a step and colliding with the wall at my back. I didn't like the man on the best of days, but he had never regarded me with more than a sly knowing. The look about him now was something out of a nightmare. He was capable of anything, queen or no queen, loyalty to Casmir or not. I cast about in the darkness for any signs of a night guard again, but still saw and heard nothing.

"I have been more than fair, Irisa. How many warnings have I given you?" I shook my head again, still not finding my voice. "Enough. I have given you enough." He slipped his finger under my chin and lifted my face toward his more directly. "I would have taken the honor myself, but there was much to do."

"Honor to do what?" I asked feebly, finding my voice, as tremulous as it was. I wasn't following where he was trying to lead me.

"Kassia. She is a stubborn little wench, do you know that? Thought she was tough, thought she could handle matters even though she knew nothing."

His hand gripped my jaw, holding it so I couldn't turn my head. He leaned into me, and I could feel the tautness of his body against me. With a single finger he traced a line down my cheek and throat. "It would have been fun, I admit, especially once she'd angered me. While she doesn't have your.... resemblance to the goddess..." His smile curled into a leer. "She is still remarkably beautiful in her own way. It would have been a pleasure." He let his finger trail down deeper down my neck and my fear took on sentience.

"What would have been?"

"It was a filthy little storeroom in the prison. Not really the sort of place I'm used to... taking my women. However, one of the guards was piteously lusty, so..."

"No...." My stomach churned, lurched, and I wanted to retch on him. "Why?"

"Irisa, I wanted to find your father, and I needed you two to get to him. He'd escaped my man Rebane, the one who'd imprisoned him, tortured him. I wanted him back." He searched my eyes, seeking and finding the intense pain he'd hoped to inflict.

And inflict it he had. I wanted to collapse. The news was akin to a physical blow. The horror couldn't have been more plain on my face, and as if pleased that his words had the effect he was after, he released me and stepped back, tucking his thumbs into his belt.

"I tell you this only so that you know I am serious with my warnings."

He wouldn't, couldn't touch me. Not like Kassia. Slowly the heat of anger rose in my chest with this resolve. He had no power over me, I decided. Not in the way he did with others at court. I was queen, I was married to Casmir, to the king. I was his queen.

Veris saw the war behind my eyes and laughed outright. "I'm done warning, Irisa. Next time comes a lesson that will never have to be repeated."

Spinning on his heel, he walked away, leaving me alone and breathless from the weight of all I'd just learned. Kassia violated, my father tortured.

Immediately I turned and retched into an urn behind me. Once done I cleaned off my face and found my way back to my room.

I entered the darkness on silent feet. Only the night candle burned, and no one waited up for me. Chloe stirred automatically when I came in and helped me undress, but she was half asleep and did not notice the tremble in my hands. For this I was grateful, for I dared not tell even her what had happened.

The chill of those memories pricked my skin, giving me gooseflesh, and I slipped under the coverlet finding Casmir already abed. He stirred at my arrival, and soon his hands turned exploratory.

When I made no move to return his caresses, he stopped, despite his drowsiness. "Irisa, what's the matter?"

I remembered the promise I'd made to honor his request not to discuss Ildor Veris, but as my husband he had a right to know.

"I just learned what happened to my sister in prison." He wasn't really paying attention, had resumed his explorations, but I would not be distracted from telling him. I stayed his hand with my own. "She was violated, Casmir."

At that, he stopped and sat up, fully awake. "What?" He

ran his hands over his eyes as if the motion would clear things up.

"The prison guards..."

"I'm sorry, Irisa." He didn't seem to know what more to say. "Prisons are not safe places for women. It's not fair, Irisa, but it's the way it is."

"It didn't just happen, Casmir."

"You know this for certain?"

I looked down at the sheet and wrung it between my hands, uncertain how to proceed.

"Yes."

His look darkened a bit, and he narrowed his eyes at me. "Who?"

I gave him a haunted, meaningful look. "You know," I said finally.

He fought with himself over how to react, the king warring with the husband for control. Matters of state, loyalty to family... Then there was the little matter of it being a man's world. How much did it really matter to most men that a woman was violated in prison? After some moments he contained the combating voices and asked simply, "Who told you this?"

"Your cousin."

"Irisa, this is a serious allegation. You are certain he admitted to it?"

I fought back my confusion and battered emotions to try to remember his exact words. "Not in so many words, no. But he implied it."

"It is late, and you are overworked. I will look into it, I promise. But I can promise no more."

I nodded, resolving to be content with it as being enough. For now.

~*19*~

"LORDS AND BARONS, MY friends, men of Agrius... thank you for your eager attendance upon the Crown this Fiortha Court, the first of my reign."

Casmir's opening words resounded loudly, strong and certain as they soared up into the heights of the great hall. Members of the full King's Council sat nearest the dais which held our thrones of state. I sat perfectly still, watching as my husband spoke his words then walked several paces to the left.

"As you know, it has long been the custom of the Crown to seek counsel from a group of advisers when making decisions of state. The King's Council is the body comprising these men, men from all over the land who have agreed to give up hearth and home to attend the king for what has been for most, many years of service. It is upon the advice of this Council that I call this Fiortha Court to session."

Thus began the yearly Fiortha Court, or fourth, quarterly court of the year. Despite being called the fourth, or quarterly court, this assembly was held only once a year. This year, because of the conditions in Agrius, attendance boiled over. Benches filled the great hall to such a great extent that there was barely enough room for a central aisle.

The idea of the Fiortha Court was not so much to let the assemblage make any actual decisions, but to give each person a sense of participation in the activities of the Crown. The historical purpose of the courts had indeed been to rule by consent, and thus the original need for quarterly courts. Yet over time, as the power and rule solidified under the sovereign, the necessity for the courts diminished. Now the Fiortha Court retained a more ceremonial purpose. The real power, the ultimate authority, rested with the sovereign who held the right to enact laws by mere proclamation, upon the advice of the sitting Council.

This wasn't to say the Fiortha Court didn't have its uses. In the best of times the Fiortha Court filled the vital role of garnering consensus amongst the leading men of the kingdom, even if it wasn't legally necessary. And consensus was something Casmir needed badly, for this year the question of slavery loomed large on everyone's mind.

Throughout the first day and much of the next several, matters of a more mundane nature would be covered. I spent much of the time listening and taking note of those who were more vocal and those who kept their peace. Men who felt passionate about the mundane were just as interesting as those whose tempers flared when heated discussions erupted.

By late afternoon of the third day, when all the routine matters had been raised, Casmir tackled the largest issue looming: the slave revolts. And so, with careful diplomacy and masterful discourse, Casmir raised the issue. It was why men had come in such great numbers, the reason Prille burst at the seams with retinues from all over Agrius. These discussions grew long, with debates raging long into the night, taking a break for a few hours of sleep before beginning again. All manner of proposals were raised, some involving diplomacy, while others took a more heavy-handed approach.

It was morning two days later, the day the Court was meant to come to a close, that Casmir played his last and most skilled hand.

"After listening closely to the thoughts and opinions expressed so eloquently these last many days, I will retire to make my decision and issue a proclamation on the subject first thing in the morning. Before I do, I would be remiss not to let another voice be heard, the voice of someone with a more unique perspective on this subject than anyone else in this room." Taking my hand, he lifted me to standing. "I present your Queen."

The room fell into utter silence, and groups of men eyed one another uneasily. Never before in the history of Agrius had a queen attended, much less actively participated in matters of state.

Casmir released my hand and sat, leaving all eyes on me alone. I took in the faces, some tired, others hopeful, many eager. I took a deep breath and began.

"I have a question for you, great men of Agrius, faithful men, strong men, men who love Agrius, your home. Your service to the Crown is renowned throughout the world. Few kings can claim the level of loyalty of you Agrian men and women." A murmur of approval rose from back to front as assent filtered over the throng. "Now I ask you: Am I of less value as your queen because I was born in poverty, in a small hovel on a back street of Corium?"

If Casmir's presentation of me had left them confused, my question left them astounded. The room fell deathly quiet. If a mouse had chosen to scurry from one side to the other, the scratching of its toes would have been deafening. How many men here knew my full story was hard to gauge. While the sport of idle speculation had been rife at the time of my wedding and coronation, Casmir had done a good job of keeping the details of my background secret. At least as much as possible. The wisdom in saving the telling of it to me for such a time as this he could not have foreseen, but it was proving to be a master stroke.

"It is not commonly known, good sirs, about my origins, or the place of my upbringing, is it?"

A murmur of confusion bubbled up, and heads leaned in to inquire of one another. I smiled to myself, realizing I rather enjoyed discomfiting these peers of the realm. Casmir seemed to know what I was doing, what I would do, so kept quiet, waiting for me to press the issue, his full approval evident in his straight back and raised chin. He gripped the arms of his throne, fully relaxed and enjoying himself. When no one came up with a response, I led them through a summary of my life up to the time Ildor Veris found me. I explained my education, but also the hunger, the dirt, the treatment from those who passed me on the street and who deemed themselves my betters. Yet I had the blood of kings in my veins, and now I sat the very throne of Agrius.

"I have met many of you in private audience. We have talked, have been honest with one another. You know me." I sought out as many pairs of eyes as I could, looking at them each directly, searchingly. "So I ask you again, am I of less value as your queen because I was born in poverty, in a small hovel on a back street of Corium?"

The more astute and diplomatic of the lords recovered first, murmuring their support of me followed by a more general proclamation of support from the body as a whole.

"I implore you then, good sirs, to consider the worth of flesh and blood, not in terms of the profit to be gained from buying and selling, but because each and every slave represents a human life, like you and me - flesh and blood, with hopes and dreams, and families. I realize that this may sound a mere fancy from a woman, but consider your wives and daughters." I let that thought sink in. "Abolish the barbaric practice of slavery. I can remain silent no more. What cost a human life?"

A low murmur rose, and discussion began, quietly at first. Then men spoke, voicing their opinions, some with disdain for the idea while others supported it with passion. It was apparent that the room was divided, though there were more in favor than opposed, and this both surprised and emboldened me.

The afternoon drew out, long and tiring. By the end of the day, few men appeared to want to continue the debate for much longer. A decision would have to be made.

"My lords," Casmir said, standing before the assembly then walking up the several steps to the top of the dais. "I am grateful to you all for your service to the kingdom. You hold your lands from tradition, that is certain. But you also hold them in pledge to me. You have made this clear by your vows of fealty the day I was crowned. The day we were crowned." Casmir held out his hand to me, and I rose to stand next to him, the appearance of solidarity not lost on anyone. "I have heard each and every one of you. I will take all of your thoughts under advisement. In the end, however, the decision is mine." A murmur rose, and Casmir held his hand palm out, toward them. "In truth, I do not yet know which way I will decide, but I promise that I will have a decision on the morrow."

The normal evening meal was served that night in the great hall, accommodating the large assemblage of guests, but despite our duties of hospitality, Casmir and I took our meal in the privacy of our chamber. A long line of men sought private audience with Casmir, but he instructed our steward to turn them all away. No one was to be given admittance. Not his pages, and not my maids.

I felt I had said my piece. Casmir knew my feelings. Now he had to search his own.

The evening grew long. Casmir sat before a cold hearth, searching the remnants of the ashes for an answer. From time to time he would stand, pace to the window, stare out, then return to his seat. I let him ponder, finding my contentment in a book which I read by the light of a lamp in a corner of the room where I could watch him without making him feel like I was.

I had intended to keep vigil with him for as long as he needed to make up his mind. Little did I know he would debate with himself long into the wee hours of the morning. At some point I moved to the bed, propping my back against a pile of pillows where I continued to pretend to read. In reality, I dozed.

Something made my eyes snap open. Perhaps it was a sense of closure that woke me. Casmir sat at his vast oak table, for once clear of papers. He watched me, and when he saw I had awoken, he came to stand at the foot of our bed.

"Irisa, I likely would not have come to this decision before knowing you. But your gracious ways, your inner beauty and outer strength show me a side to people that is not dependent on birth or place of residence. Our philosophers would have us believe that nobility is an inborn trait, that some are deserving while others are not. I have seen you with the people. They adore you, that is certain. But it's not because they adore your rank, your beauty, or that you give them alms and charity. They love you because you love them. You see them openly and directly. They know you value them as people first. I will never pretend to understand fully what your life was like before coming here. How could I? And I will never be jealous of it. But your coming has given me a rare opportunity to experience life away from all of this..."

He waved around the room, taking in all of our pampered existence. I nodded, uncertain how to reply. For the first time I fully comprehended the transformation he had made from the day I'd met him until now — from entitled lordling to ruler carrying the weight of concern for his people.

"The value of a human life...." His words trailed off. "While I may not go so far as you in removing the delineation of rank and title... for what kind of king would I be if I did that?" He smiled in good humor at his own remark. "I do agree with your point that the institution of slavery does not fit in Agrius any longer."

It was near enough to dawn, but his words energized me, and I flew up from my nest of pillows and into his arms, knocking him back several paces. He smiled and trailed his fingers through my hair. "While I didn't make this decision simply to please you, or to elicit such reaction from you, I will happily take it."

"We will progress across land, to the biggest cities first," Casmir told me in the privacy of our chambers one night after the evening meal. The last visiting noble had departed on the outgoing tide, and I could tell Casmir was exhausted.

"How long will we be gone?"

"It will take several months at least," he said, already losing interest in sharing the details with me, his mind moving on to the next matter he had to attend to. If we were to leave on progress, there was much he would have to do before then. "We need to be back before the deepest heart of winter sets in, of course."

Casmir had announced his decision regarding slavery the last morning of the Fiortha Court as promised. Days of discussion and deliberation occurred afterwards, prolonging the Court by necessity. To say "slavery is abolished" is one thing, but to actually enact the proclamation without utterly destroying the economy was another thing. There had been dissension, yes, and there would likely be years of trouble because of it. There were plenty who saw the justice in the decision and supported it, even if it seemed born of an excessively high philosophical ethos.

Casmir had made a decision based on ethical convictions, but he was also practically minded. Therefore it was agreed that the process would be a slow one. A detailed plan would have to be developed, giving merchants viable options once the heart of their trade had been taken from them. I was less than pleased by this concession, despite Casmir's assurances that he was committed to the long-term enactment. After mulling it over for a bit, I softened, seeing wisdom in it even if I struggled with my own impatience.

Out of compromise to those who felt they had a lot to lose, it was decided that the hardest hit towns would benefit from a personal visit from their king.

"People must see that this is a natural progression from what my father began," he explained, "but that I am willing to work with them rather than appear to be against them. I am not some distant overlord sent to crush their livelihoods."

"And I suppose Ildor Veris will rule in your place while we are gone?"

"Of course, he is Chancellor." Upon seeing my face, he came to me, taking my hands in his own. "Irisa, I know you don't care for the man. I know you believe he had something to do with your sister's violation, but he denies ordering it, says his men got out of control and that he punished them appropriately. Even you admitted that he didn't actually come out and say he ordered it." He saw the look of disappointment in my eyes. "My Adonia, it's not that I don't believe you, but how can I prove anything? Even if I found the men responsible, they could not counter him." He kissed me gently. "For now things must remain as they have always been. I trust him to do what's best for Agrius in my stead as he has always done. The time away will do you good, you'll see."

He could see the disappointment in my eyes, so turned to pace the room rather than push me. I stood motionless, taking in all he'd said, at a loss to know how to counter him.

"Once we reach the northern coast of Dremesk, the Árvök will be waiting for us. We will stop at the cities and towns of the western shores and then come home. It's late in the year, I admit, so we risk rough seas and the threat of early snow..."

He stopped as he pondered his last remark as if he'd not considered it already, so I cut in, "Why the Árvök? Why not the Sjórinn Mær?"

The Sjórinn Mær, or the Sea Maiden, was Casmir's own vessel. It was larger and more comfortable, and it would hold more of our attendants. Aboard the Árvök, we would only have one attendant apiece.

"Because the Árvök is built for speed, and at this time of year we will return home faster on the Árvök. And besides, with only Addis and Filip to attend us, I will need more personal attention from my wife." He smirked, and I shook my head. "It will be an adventure, you'll see!"

Agrius was an island nation, but it was a large island

nation. Our progress could not encompass all of it, so we would visit only the largest of the slave trade cities.

Leaving Prille via the north gate, we progressed first to Lyseby at the mouth of the Lyse River which fed the Lyse Inlet. A major trading port, this city was home to the largest slave market in all of Agrius. It was here Casmir expected the largest opposition.

To our great surprise, the Magistrate of Lyseby, a man named Ingólfer, had followed the advice of his lord in preparing the people ahead of time for what was to come. If there was opposition to their new king's decree, we saw and heard no sign of it from the people of Lyseby. Whether the decree would sit well once it was actually implemented was another matter, but there was time for implementation, and by then Casmir would have a good handle on how to navigate the dissent. So it was with success our processional moved from Lyseby heading north where we skirted the eastern end of the range of mountains that filled the heart of the island and made for the city Glenna.

Glenna was a more diverse city and had profited from a bustling trade beyond just slavery, for major trade routes connected here from all parts of Agrius as an obvious pass skirting the mountains at the heart of the island. Casmir voiced legitimate concern regarding our reception before we arrived, for the people of Glenna were fiercely independent. Past kings had faced uprisings in Glenna due to the free-spirited thinking of the people. Originally grown from a rogue camp of cutthroats looking to benefit at the expense of travelers taking the easiest route east around the mountains, the city today retained much of the same zeal from its early days. Despite Casmir's anxiety, our time in Glenna proceeded uneventfully.

On and on we went, staying for no more than a couple of

days in each location, stopping to make calls at the homes and manors of various landholders and barons, and to find shelter from the road rather than make camp. Eventually we arrived in the port city of Veria on the northern coast of Dremesk, a rich agricultural region, and home to Eron, son of Amalia, who had made the journey with us from Prille. After enjoying his hospitality at the castle nestled on a broad plain, we said our goodbyes.

"It has been my pleasure, Irisa, to meet you." He kissed my hand. "I would have enjoyed seeing your father again," he added quietly when he was certain no one was near enough to hear. "It is too late for me, but perhaps you will see him yet again."

"Perhaps. I thank you for your kindness, and for your friendship."

And with that, Casmir and I headed for the waterfront where the Árvök awaited us. Casmir noticed the bemused look on my face as we approached the ship, and he took my hand.

"The last time I saw this ship, she took me to my doom," I said, winking at Casmir.

"Doom? Is that your name for me now?"

I elbowed him gently in the ribs as we boarded then stepped onto the main deck. I immediately moved to the railing on the foredeck where I'd stood well over a year ago, watching the shoreline of Prille for the first time as it moved ever closer. Now rather than the soaring cliffs and stair step city of Prille, I saw a flat expanse of the Ain River Delta. Sands and silts built up over millennia to form this triangular region divided by seaward-distributing branches of the Ain River. The city of Veria stood proudly ensconced on one of the largest islands of these river branches, and controlled all trade coming and going in and out of Agrius from this strategic northern access.

"Winter appears to be coming sooner than anyone expected," the captain told us as he greeted us. "Likely we'll encounter fairly rough seas, so I advise that we cast off as soon as possible." Casmir agreed with the captain's wisdom, happy to ensconce himself below deck with his queen to get away from the snapping north wind.

The helmsman set a course for Balatyn on the northwest corner of Agrius across from the Luskka Islands. All we had to do now was huddle in the safety and warmth of our cabin.

I could never have predicted how miserable the next several days would become. The captain's prediction of stormy seas had been overly optimistic, for once out of the protection of the Ain Delta, the water grew increasingly choppy as winds picked up, blowing with powerful force as if driven by malevolent spirits. There were many times the sails had to come down completely.

"They'll be ripped to shreds in this otherwise," the captain explained.

But he didn't want to turn back. Casmir didn't want to turn back. And neither did I want to turn back. The sooner we returned to Prille, the sooner we would take back the power Casmir had lent to Ildor Veris.

I sat bundled in our cabin on the third day out, wearing an extra layer of skirts over thick woolen stockings. Because of the rough seas we had made poor progress, and we were behind schedule.

"The captain says a big storm is coming. Because of the speed of the storm and the difficulties in maintaining navigation, we'll just have to ride it out. There's no time to find safe harbor before it arrives."

Casmir knew little of ships and sailing, and I knew less than a quarter of that. Rather than question those more knowledgeable, I took the captain at his word and prepared for the coming onslaught.

And onslaught it was.

For three days the storm raged. We could do nothing but hide away, holding on to anything tied down while trying not to be sick. When the storms finally passed, we felt as if we'd been given a new lease on life.

Casmir immediately sought out the captain for a damage assessment. I stayed on the main deck taking in the scattered remains of what had once been a highly organized and efficient setting.

When Casmir returned with his report, he was grim-faced.

"There is damage both to the mizzen and main masts. A small crack in the main, but a more significant one on the mizzen."

"So what does that mean?"

"It means we need to find a safe harbor to make repairs before we can continue on. But that's not the worst of it," he grimaced. Casmir's lips thinned into a hard line. "See that smudge over there?" I followed his gaze and nodded that I did. "The captain thinks that is Pania."

"What??"

"Once he is able to determine where we are more precisely, we will make for the nearest port."

"Has there been any sign of the Arnborg?"

Casmir merely shook his head. While hopeful, I hadn't really expected a different answer. Storms made it difficult enough to keep one's own bearings. Keeping track of companion vessels at the same time was next to impossible. I thought of Chloe who was aboard and hoped for the best, pushing the worry from my thoughts.

It was later in the morning when our ailing vessel finally began to move, limping its way toward the shore. The sailors had placed rope bindings around the damaged masts, but the captain was unwilling to be under full sail in case the strain was too much. He hoped to fully repair rather than replace the masts once in port. If it meant we would get home sooner, his decision had my full support.

We anchored in a lagoon behind a barrier island. A tiny fishing village hugged the coastline here, and the captain felt certain that adequate repairs could be completed here. No one dared give voice to concerns about encountering additional storms on the remainder of the trip. It was best to stay hopeful.

Feeling at a loss to know how to help but having no desire to retreat back to the cabin that had been my prison these last several days, I found the most peripheral spot possible where I could cause the least inconvenience. The fresh air and sun felt good on my skin. Casmir pitched in, adding his hands to make the load of work that much lighter for everyone else.

"Perhaps it would be best if we waited on shore?" I had seen little of Addis during the foul weather. While she had done her best to attend to my needs, she had been noticeably absent the rest of the time. "These men can do their duty without distraction."

"You mean I'm in the way?" I interpreted.

She smirked. "Yes, if you put it that way. I think venturing out on solid ground would do us both good," she added coaxingly.

It didn't take much effort on her part to persuade me, and Addis seemed to need the escape as much as I did. The captain assured us that he could spare a couple of men to row us, instructing the pair to prepare the skiff to take us to shore, and Casmir insisted we take along two guardsmen for our protection.

Sadly the little fishing village had little to offer. With nothing else to do, we decided to walk the perimeter of the village. The solidity of ground was its own reward, and soon I reveled in the freedom.

The village was home to a dozen families whose homesteads spread along the shoreline. While there were clear signs of habitation, no faces peeked out of doorways or windows, no curious children hid behind hedges to watch us, and no dogs followed us hoping for scraps of bread. Likely the appearance of a strange ship in their peaceful lagoon had sent them all into hiding until we left.

Finding nothing more than a single alehouse, the village smithy, and a couple of unidentifiable shops, we reached the end of the village. When I turned to ask Addis a question, I found that she had dropped back, standing some distance behind the guards who now stood immediately behind me.

Before I could say anything, a queer look came over the face of one of the men who pressed himself up against my left shoulder. "Let's keep moving," he snarled.

My eyes sought out Addis, and when I caught her eye, a faint smile touched her lips. With a slight nod from her, the other guard took my arms from behind and held them tightly. I felt the press of a hard object into the small of my back as he pushed me forward.

"Keep your mouth shut," he hissed as he opened the door to a fishing hut. He tied a rough rag around my mouth, then bound my hands and locked me in.

What seemed like several hours passed before anyone returned for me, though the combination of surprise, anger, fear and discomfort might have made the passage of time difficult to track. When finally I thought they meant to leave me here indefinitely, I heard footfall on the trampled grass outside my prison. The door opened to reveal the same guardsman. He lifted me to standing and removed my gag, indicating I should go outside.

Addis was back, and she had returned with Figor. Casmir stood behind him, bound and gagged, his chin drooping onto his chest. He had obviously struggled, for an open cut bled at his temple, and hints of a purple bruise showed around it. Dirt caked his knees, elbows, and cheeks, and his hair hung loosely around his face.

I eyed Figor, wondering what his plan was. He did have a plan, didn't he? He couldn't have known about this, or he would have put a stop to it. And if he couldn't have stopped it, at least he could have warned us.

"Why?" I asked her. She had the decency to look away, a hint of embarrassment on her face. Her flowing woolen robe hung open at the neck, revealing the warmth of her kopi-colored skin, and I reminded myself that she had always been exotic to me. Somehow I'd missed her coming betrayal because of it. "What did Veris tell you he would give you, Addis, the throne of Aksum?"

She tossed her exotically oiled hair at the question, setting off a flash of glitter as she did so. "Irisa..."

Casmir's eyes widened in equal parts disbelief and confusion.

"Did he tell you how he would do it?" She didn't respond. "You know he can't be trusted."

Addis stepped toward me. Her fingers plucked a piece of debris from my hair, and she picked up my hands, examining my fingers as if she meant to trim my nails. "Salay, you remember it?" Intrigue. She had taught me the word. "I have been playing the game since I was a little girl. Your Cousin Ildor asked me to make sure you didn't return home. The storm was convenient, so I used it." She shrugged as if betrayal was a trivial thing.

"This is why the Árvök waited for us in Veria rather than the Sjórinn Mær, isn't it?" I accused. "So the crew would be loyal to Veris?" She didn't respond, but she didn't have to. I knew I was right. Casmir strained to get at Addis, but swords flew up, stopping him on the spot. "Trust no one, you once told me," I pressed her. "I was confused by the two princes I'd encountered when I should have been concerned about two versions of you."

"You should have listened more closely to me, Irisa." Now she didn't smile. She almost looked regretful.

"How is it that Ildor Veris can press your case any more strongly than the King of Agrius? There is still time to change your mind, Addis. Please, let us help you!"

"Le'elt Casmir? No, he wouldn't have taken my desires seriously. Why would he when I am a mere woman?" And then more quietly she added, "He's not going to be the king much longer, Irisa. Besides, even if he promised it to me now, do you really think he'd hold true to his word? You think he would let me live if I let you go? Hardly."

I looked at Casmir and found a furious fire of impotent rage in his eyes. Chloe had told me that everyone knew Casmir wouldn't ever exact summary judgment, but in Addis' case, I believed he would make an exception.

"I've chosen my path. Ildor Veris will put my name forward for the throne of Aksum. No one else would have done it for me. It's too late to change any of this now."

She turned to leave, but I called to her. "Addis, did Veris tell you to kill us?"

She met my eyes but didn't answer. "You will be happy to know that at least you needn't worry about your friends. You died in the storm along with any crew members who may have supported you. No one else needs to know what happened. The Council will know nothing of any of this." And then, as if reading my mind, she added, "Chloe will mourn you, but she is safe, Irisa."

"And Ildor Veris plans to take the throne himself?"

She studied me closely, as if considering her next words. "Irisa, did you know you have a brother?"

The blood drained from my face. "What? Of course I don't have a brother..."

"Veris didn't think you'd worked it out yet. You'd never mentioned it to me at least."

"This is about my mother, isn't it."

"Ethew is his name. Naria bore him before she wed your father, from what Veris said."

My mother's secret. It's what Veris had been teasing me with all this time.

"To Soren?"

"Yes, to your father's older brother. Brushed under the rug. No one knew."

"How..."

"I don't know Irisa, and I really don't much care. Does it matter?"

"Yes, to me it does," I replied quietly.

"Agrius will have a king beholden to the Kingmaker. That's all that matters. He blames you, you know. Your insistence on pushing against slavery was the last straw."

"Yes, I know," I breathed.

"You should have stayed out of it."

"I couldn't."

"I know." She picked up my hands again. "Goodbye, Irisa." She leaned in to kiss me softly on the cheek. "I'm sorry we couldn't have known each other longer." And then, in a whisper, she added, "It's nothing personal. I need Aksum, and this was the price I was willing to pay."

"But it's not your price to pay."

She paused momentarily, and a look of anguish hinted at the corner of her eyes. "You made a good queen." Then turning her attention to Figor, she said softly, "Figor, you know what to do."

Casmir tried to pull at his captors, but they held him fast.

My eyes darted over the backs of the buildings making up the tiny village, but I saw no one. Even if someone had happened upon us, likely they wouldn't do anything. A single villager, even several villagers, stood no chance against a handful of men-at-arms. We would think of something. We had to.

And Figor was with us. I trusted him. He hadn't been complicit in all of it from the beginning, had he? Had his involvement all been a ruse? If none of his effort had been about supporting my father, who had it been for?

Doubts nagged me as the men pressed us to walk away from the village, down a long track that led south, deeper into cultivated land, and then finally beyond it. On and on we walked until I thought my feet would wear through the soles of my boots. Though the storms had passed, wind lashed from the open water and across the treeless bluffs, whirling my hair out of its constraints and into my face. I couldn't brush it away to see where I walked, so many times I stumbled, tripping over the tangled grasses growing like strips of leather on the rock-hard turf. I was glad I'd worn extra layers of skirts and warm woolen stockings. Casmir had been hard at work aboard the Árvök when he had come to rescue me so wore only a light linen shirt.

He was without a cloak, and spasms of shivers coursed through his body. If they didn't kill us soon, he would freeze to death.

When finally we stopped, I looked back to see the fishing village far in the distance, like a speck along the shore. No one would see or hear anything. I turned my attention to Figor who still stood several paces behind the men-at-arms.

The men removed Casmir's gag and untied his hands, and immediately he made a move toward one of them, receiving a heavy blow to the jaw for his trouble. I cried out and made to move to Casmir's side, but the other man stepped into my path and whirled me around, holding a knife to my throat.

"Oh no, you just stand here and watch for a bit."

The punch to Casmir's jaw was only the start of it. Rather than get on with his grisly purpose, the man continued to rain down the blows. After one punch, another followed, then another and another. Whatever pent up aggression he'd had, he took out on Casmir. The intent wasn't just to kill. They intended Casmir to pay for whatever imagined crimes they held against him.

"If you mean to kill us anyway, why must you brutalize him too? Just get on with it!" I cried.

"He would fight back if we didn't, wouldn't he? Now stop struggling, or it will go worse for him," the man hissed in my ear, "much, much worse."

I flicked my gaze to Figor who still stood by placidly, taking it all in. Was he trying to make up his mind about something? His continued lack of willingness to make eye contact worried me. Perhaps he still worried for his own position. By helping us, he exposed himself. Or perhaps he participated in our betrayal.

Finally the rain of blows on Casmir stopped, and the man holding me began to move me toward the cliff's edge. If

Figor had any intention to help us, he had to do it soon, for our time had just run out.

~*20*~

TERROR IS A WORD best understood through a personal experience rather than in the abstract.

Specters or phantoms, darkness, the fear of inexplicable things lurking there; imagined things, things conjured in the light of a pale moon, or by a child hiding under a blanket in the night — this is terror for most people.

My terror became real because it became tangible, materializing as a piece of cold steel, sharpened and honed to a razor-like edge. It is true that a knife is only as fearsome as the man holding it, but in my case, the man holding it had been trained since youth to wield it, and he pressed the sharpened edge against the throbbing pulse of my warm, and still fully alive neck. His other hand clamped around my waist like a vice.

"Your miserable life isn't worth my spit," he hissed toward Casmir. "But your woman here…" He licked his lips and tightened his hold around my waist.

I felt a rush of horror as my imagination spun wildly out of control. Casmir lay face-first on the ground, heaving for air, blood and spit mingling then dripping in viscous streams to the grass. He could do nothing for me. Another savage kick connected with his stomach and he curled into himself. I screamed out and strained against the arm holding me.

The kick didn't have the desired effect. After a moment Casmir drew from a well deep within himself and pushed up onto all fours, slowly standing fully, making his way toward me. My captor sniffed and spun me, pushing me backwards, still holding the knife and grinning wickedly. I staggered backwards but caught myself, fighting for purchase on the crumbling edge of the cliff's face. While I dared not break my eyes from the man with the knife, I heard rather than saw pebbles and debris skitter over the edge behind me. Casmir stood at my side, took my hand in his. We would face our fate together.

"Alas, there is no time for sport, as much as I would have loved to make you watch."

The man with the knife sneered as he advanced forward a step, and his partner raised a sword, hefting it menacingly.

Death comes to us all, it is true; but for many death is seen coming from far off, and they are ready when it arrives, having already prepared for the flight into the unknown. I never imagined that I would die this way, and I never saw it coming. Murdered at the hands of those we should have trusted.

Ironic, since I'd always thought it would be my sister to be the death of me.

"If you are going to kill us, why don't you just kill us, you miserable sons of *Rækallin*," Casmir growled at the men. "Rather than push us off the edge like cowards!" His grip on my hand tightened, and his breathing quickened.

"Casmir, no," I cautioned him, knowing that he wanted to lunge out at the men. But he would be cut down in an instant if he did. We would have to think of another way.

"How much did Veris pay you to kill your Sovereigns? It must have been a tidy sum," Casmir continued.

"Oh, there was no payment necessary. We do it for pure pleasure, my king," the man with the sword said, offering a mock bow.

"Go to *Myrkra*, you *skingi*..." Casmir made to attack the man, but I pulled on his arm and held him back. He was too weak from his beating to resist me. How well did he think he'd fare against these men?

The sword man's mouth spread into a gap-toothed leer, and he hawked a laugh. Motioning Casmir toward him with a wave of his hand, he sneered, "If that's what you want then, fine, come fight me. *Myrkra's* exactly where you'll be soon either way!"

Waves pounded far below, splashing up sprays of icy water, and sea birds gathered overhead, shrieking their opinions far out of reach. My eyes flicked from our captors then to Figor who still stood still, watching. "Figor," I cried out. "Why are you just standing there? Do something!"

"Yes, loyal Figor... loyal like a dog," Casmir spat. A new stream of blood dribbled down the corner of his mouth, and he wiped it away with a filthy sleeve. "Another betrayal to add to the list. Everyone wins today, it seems."

Figor held out an arm to stay the men who pressed in on us, then moved close to Casmir so that the armed men couldn't see his face.

"He promised me nothing," he hissed, barely above a whisper, only loudly enough for us to hear. "My allegiances are not to Ildor Veris, the pig."

He moved his left hand slowly, slipping it inside the folds of his robe. I caught a glint of steel inside. My eyes widened in horror as he pulled a slender dagger from his belt. I had been horribly wrong about Addis. Had I been wrong about Figor too?

"I came along to ensure your safety," he murmured, and

pressed the hilt of the dagger into Casmir's hands. He flicked a glance at me to see if I had noticed then held Casmir's eyes for a long, somber moment. After a time, he turned to me, saying, "Kassia and her husband Jack live in Veithi, south of here on the coast, several days walk. Goodbye, Irisa."

And as simply as that, he turned his back and walked casually toward the man with the sword, reached out, and gripped his wrist, twisting savagely as he brought his knee up into the man's groin. It was such an unexpected move that the surprise of the act caught the man unaware, giving Casmir a chance to lunge at the other man who held the knife. Swinging the dagger Figor had given him high overhead, Casmir brought it down for a fatal blow, piercing the man's neck at the shoulder, downward toward his heart. The man dropped to his knees in the thick grass as blood gurgled from his throat, his scream silent.

By this time, the sword man recovered from the shock of Figor's assault. Gritting his teeth from the pain, he pulled the sword back and away from Figor, completing a quick half-arm draw-cut against Figor's belly.

But he had no time to do anything else, for in the very same heartbeat Casmir lunged at him from behind, bringing his arms around the man's neck, drawing his blade across the man's throat. A spray of crimson blood spread out in a fine mist, disappearing with the wind.

"I told you to go to *Myrkra*," Casmir spat, opening his hand and dropping the dagger. Staggering back a step, he collapsed from pain and exhaustion.

Seeing Figor's more immediate need, I stumbled over to him and dropped down beside him. He lay there with his eyes open, his breathing shallow. A large gash cut a swath across his midsection, oozing blood. I bunched up his robes and pressed them into the wound. Figor's face scrunched up with pain at the pressure of it.

"Figor, we'll get help. If we can get you back to the village, we can..."

Figor put his hands on mine and shook his head. "Irisa, no. No use."

I understood now that he was beyond my help. If I were to examine the wound, I knew I would see the glossy coils of his gut peeking out. Lifting his head gently with my hand, I propped it in my lap, and he gulped some air, closing his eyes in pain.

"Figor, is Ethew the secret no one would tell me about?"

Figor took in more deep breaths with his eyes closed before he would look at me again. He nodded. "Soren's son."

"Yes, Addis said that. Was he the reason Nikolas agreed to accept my mother as a wife for my father in exchange for silence? Was it to hide the truth of Ethew?"

He closed his eyes and nodded slightly. "Yes... but...more secrets..." And he paused, his breathing becoming labored.

"More secrets? Figor..." Tears started streaming down my face as I realized he was slipping away quickly. I wanted to know so much more, but there wasn't time. Why hadn't he ever shared more with me before now?

"My loyalty... not to your father but your mother..." The words slurred together so that it made it difficult to understand him.

"My mother? Why?" My tears blurred the image of the man dying in my arms.

"She knew about...my treason..." he breathed, the words as fragile as a bee's wings, though he got no further before what fragile flicker of life left in him flit away.

I turned my face toward the sky, searching out the

circling birds, spying them as they dropped lower and lower just waiting for the chance to feast on the carnage below.

After a time I closed Figor's eyes and lay his head down onto the ground as gently as I could. It was done. Casmir watched me from where he had collapsed, and I went to him, to see if there was anything I could do for him. He sat upright, but his breathing was labored.

"I think they cracked my ribs," he wheezed.

"I'd have been surprised if they hadn't. We'll need to find a way to bind you, so you can walk more easily." He nodded, and I ripped the bottom section from a petticoat and tied it around him as tightly as I could without hurting him too much.

Next I looked around to see how we would bury Figor. Tears streamed from my eyes, making it difficult to discern if there were even rocks we could cover over his body to keep the birds from their grisly work. I saw none, only a vast plateau of thick grass which broke away suddenly down to the sea far below.

"Irisa, we can't bury them. We must get out of here."

When no one returned to the ship as expected, a search party might be sent back to look for us. Even if they didn't come back to search, they would be on alert that we had possibly survived. We needed to get moving as soon as possible.

"We should go find Kassia, as Figor hinted. We'll need to find another way home to Prille."

His look turned forlorn, and I echoed his dismay in the look I returned.

"At least we have some practice at survival together," I offered as lightly as I could, reminding him of our flight after the ambush. He smiled wearily.

The truth of the matter was that our situation was worse

than after the ambush. This time we were stranded in a foreign land. Everything was unfamiliar, and we didn't even have a horse. I searched the men-at-arms and Figor, looking for anything of use. Figor had a money pouch on his belt, so I tucked that away. We deemed the sword impractical so left it, but took the knife and Figor's dagger then set out slowly, doing our best to maintain a straight path following the coast, through the thick grasses of the flatland above the ocean to our left.

The sun began its gradual descent over the western skies, would disappear fully in a couple of hours. The landscape had changed with the passage of time, and soon copses of trees dotted the landscape. At least now we would have fuel for a fire.

We made camp that night in a hollowed area cut into the side of a gully created by a stream running from the flatland down toward the ocean. It took some time to get a good fire lit without the proper tools, but eventually we had a warm blaze going.

Once I was certain we had a large enough pile of fuel to last the night, I sat down next to Casmir and laid his head in my lap. A swath of stars spread across the night sky like a cloud of fireflies in a summer meadow. Travel had kept us quiet all day. Now we had time to talk.

"How did they capture you?"

He took my hand in his, rubbing his thumb over my palm.

"You hadn't been gone long when the wherry returned. The men on board looked panic-stricken, told me that there was trouble in the village and that you were caught in the middle of it. They knew that was likely the only way to get me off the ship since I was so eager to oversee the repairs and help where I could. Of course I went with them immediately, cursing myself for not having sent more men along to watch over you.

"They hurried me through the village, pretending to look for the trouble. I wanted to bash in heads, was so furious I saw spots. Once we were off the main street and out of sight of anyone, one of them kicked me in the back of the knees, and while I was falling, the other slammed me to the ground. I struggled, but there were too many of them, and I hadn't been expecting it. They bound and gagged me, and brought me to you."

I worked to clean away the caked blood on his face. "Veris warned me he would do something. I just wasn't prepared for it to happen this way, at this time."

"Addis was opportunistic," Casmir added.

"Yes. It's her betrayal that hurts the most, Casmir. It just doesn't make sense to me why she thought this was her best option." Casmir didn't respond, so I continued. "I thought we would be safe for a while at least, until we got back to Prille. I didn't realize the viper's fangs reached so far, but I should have known better."

"I'm sorry, Irisa." He whispered the words so quietly that at first I wasn't sure he'd actually spoken. "You warned me about Cousin Ildor, but I wouldn't listen. I didn't want to believe it of the man who had been like a father."

It was true, but rather than confirm his statement, I let wisdom guide me by not adding to his guilt with accusations. "You loved him like family. It's understandable that you would be hesitant to throw away a lifetime's belief, to take my word against his."

"You had to throw away a lifetime's belief when you found out who you were though." He turned his face so he could look up at me.

I brushed his hair away from his face again. "Do you think the Council will go along with Ethew as the next king? If my grandfather was overthrown because he was of an illegitimate line, why would they accept Ethew?"

"What choice do they have?"

"What about Kathel, or one of your other sisters?"

"Kathel is a mere child. They would see the wisdom in accepting a grown man, even if he is unknown, over a child. Just like Sajen all those years ago. And my other sisters... they are married. The Council would not want their foreign husbands meddling in the business of Agrius. It won't matter though. We'll get back to Prille before they have time to do anything."

"But Veris was counting on this. Likely he sent away for Ethew the same day we left Prille. As soon as word gets back to the palace, he could hold a coronation."

"It's possible, but I don't see the Council moving so quickly."

"Except that you appointed new members of the Council, his recommendations, men loyal to him." I remembered the list of names, the long consideration Casmir had given, trying to make the best choices possible. All along Veris had been plotting, putting his men into place for exactly this reason. "Why didn't I try harder to do something about him when I could have? He killed Grand Master Lito, Casmir. I knew what he was capable of doing! And then he threatened me after telling me what he had done to Kassia..."

"He threatened you?" Casmir began to push himself up, growing more furious. "Why didn't you tell me?"

I gentled him down with my hands. "Would you have believed me?"

I asked it kindly, but the question seemed to deflate him, for he knew the truth of it. "No, probably not." He fell silent again for a moment before whispering, "I need you, Irisa. Out here, I am not a king. If we are to survive, you need to be Irisa

Monastero, the Irisa you were before leaving Corium."

It was a humbling thing for him to admit. I brushed his face with gentle fingers, and kissed him on the forehead. "Well, my sister would be much better at this survival business than me, but I will do all I can, if you will follow my lead."

"I will follow your lead, my queen," he replied soberly.

Night surrounded us as we talked, and eventually we both fell asleep tucked together against the hollow of ground behind us, and a gentle, warming fire before. Casmir and Irisa, castaways in a land not our own, king and queen of nothing.

Morning found us cold and uncomfortable. The fire had gone out because I hadn't woken up to tend it. We rose, and finding no reason to hide evidence of our fire, simply began walking, keeping the coast in sight as we sought the most direct path south. By late afternoon we came upon a small settlement of three homes huddled along a small creek. A little boy fishing in the creek saw our approach and ran to tell his elders. By the time we reached the settlement, we were greeted by a wary man who took in our appearance and offered us cautious greeting, realizing that even though our clothing was dirty and torn, it was finely made. We couldn't have been brigands. While hospitality would have been offered as a show of good manners anyway, I still offered to pay, a gesture which produced an immediate result. We were shown to a clean loft in a small barn which housed the settlement's animals. A young woman brought us clean water with which to wash ourselves, a pitcher of frothy ale, and a hearty meal. While we could not light a fire, the hay was warm, and just before darkness fell, a little girl brought us two thick wolf pelts to use as blankets.

In the morning, I awoke feeling much more refreshed than I had felt since before the storm hit at sea aboard the Árvök. Reflecting my physical improvement, my spirits also felt brighter. Casmir on the other hand, seemed to have taken greater weight onto his spirit in the night. His bruises had settled in, turning the side of his face a mottled purple and yellow running from his temple down nearly to his jaw line. He rose stiffly, and I suspected that if he wasn't trying to make such a good show of it, he'd have been limping too. His countenance however, had closed, and he said little. This worried me more than his physical ailments.

When it came time for us to leave, I spoke for us both, inquiring after Veithi, finding out that if we headed slightly west through a small grove of brushwood, we would come upon a road. If taken south, the road would reach Veithi late the second day if we traveled at a moderate pace. Because of Casmir's injuries, it was three more nights before we reached Veithi.

Larger than the fishing village where the Árvök had landed, Veithi looked to be a regional municipality with its own magistrate. This boded well for getting around unobserved. We made our careful way into the heart of the town, looking first for a market. Casmir's boot had developed a small hole in the toe, so we sought out a shoemaker to repair the leather before going in search of Kassia.

The man did not pretend to hide his scrutiny of us as we waited in his shop for a patch to be applied. Making a slow appraisal of clothing and manners, Casmir's speech and bearing, it was certain that he immediately determined we carried a certain rank. Fortunately he had no way of guessing our true identities. Or so I hoped.

"The maker of these shoes knew his business."

Before Casmir could open his mouth to speak, I answered vaguely, "Yes, indeed. The fair that year was full of many renowned craftsmen. We were lucky."

The man took this at face value and continued to work,

but I could see he was growing more inquisitive. Before he could ask more questions, I broke in. "We are looking for someone and wonder if maybe you know of them?"

"If I know of them, certainly, I would be happy to help. Who do you seek?"

"Kassia and..." I paused to remember the name Figor had spoken.

"Jack," Casmir supplied for me.

"Indeed, you have come to the right place."

And the man proceeded to give us directions to their house outside town toward the foothills to the west. I would soon see my sister.

"Casmir, stop holding me back."

"Irisa, you weren't the one to take the beating, remember? I cannot keep up your pace!"

"I wonder if she lives in a meadow, if she has sheep," I bubbled, oblivious of Casmir's apprehension. "She always wanted sheep, though I could never understand why. She had no skill with animals, or with people for that matter." I couldn't help the babbling. It had been nearly two years since I had seen my sister, and I was anxious and nervous and excited all at once. Kassia and I had both lived what seemed like several lifetimes in the time since we'd last been together, and I wondered how she had changed and how we would get on because of it. I stole a glance at Casmir, wondering most of all what she would make of him. His facial bruises were still very apparent, but they had begun to fade.

We rounded a bend, and just beyond it, a meadow opened up. A cottage nestled into the far side of the meadow dotted with wildflowers throughout. A small pen contained a flock of sheep, and there were chickens running loose in the yard.

"It's just how I imagined it," I breathed out loud. Casmir eyed me warily, but I couldn't bring my feet down to earth, so responded with a jaunty, "Come on, let's go."

Together we walked up the long path toward the house. A dog heard us coming and started barking, though he didn't leave the close proximity of the house. A man emerged from the door. Jack, I presumed. He didn't call out, simply watched as we got closer.

We were near enough to call out when Kassia stepped out. I wanted to run to her, but Casmir leaned too heavily on my arm, so I remained patient. Both Jack and Kassia watched us together, and as I got nearer I noticed her distinctly rounded abdomen. My sister was going to be a mother, it seemed.

Soon recognition registered on Kassia's face. "Casmir!" Her eyes widened, round orbs like the moon.

Jack reacted before anyone else moved, and hurled himself at my husband, throwing a strangle-hold around his neck. "I'm going to kill you!" he cried.

~*21*~

"JACK, STOP!" KASSIA CRIED as she ran toward the pair of men, trying to stop her husband from killing Casmir. "Jack, stop. Let's find out what's going on before you murder a man in our own yard." Jack hesitated but would not let go of Casmir.

"It's that rutting scut of a prince, the pox-marked clot pole himself," he shouted. "He owes a huge debt for what he did to you..."

"Jack... Stop," Kassia pled.

Jack was in a fury, but somehow, whether because of his wife's pleading and gentle hands on his arm, or because he found a grain of reason in the midst of his red-hot fury, he loosened his hold.

For Casmir's part, he was humiliated and shook off Jack's arms. He wanted to retaliate, but I put a hand on his arm to steady him. "Casmir, no."

"Kassia," Jack queried as his red-hot eyes bored into Casmir, "what possible excuse could he give to convince me not to kill him right here? The world would be a better place for getting rid of him, I would think."

"Look at my sister, Jack. She would not cling to him so if he was the monster we think him to be. The sister I know would not. I for one want to hear their story." Then turning to me, she said, "Because I know there is a story. Perhaps you had better come inside and explain why the king and queen of Agrius are at our door before my husband commits regicide."

Kassia held her arms out toward the door, indicating we should enter. Except for Jack. She steered him back out to the yard to collect more wood, giving him a chance to cool his temper. Once inside, I immediately forced Casmir to sit in a chair which he gratefully did. His wounds had been done no favors by Jack's ill-treatment. While Kassia retrieved something to offer us to drink, my head filled with a multitude of questions.

When Jack returned, we sat together, and Kassia began: "Now, sister, tell me everything." Her clear green eyes flicked back and forth between me and Casmir, her expression open and curious. The closed-off, guarded sister I remembered was nowhere to be found.

So I told my story, starting with the day I heard the news about Issak's death and the fire at the family's forge, continuing through the arrival of Figor, to my stays with both Miarka and Swine. Kassia uttered several black oaths under her breath at the talk of Swine, but something in her eyes shifted when I finished explaining about Orsilla's treatment of him and the loss of his daughter. Whether she was aware she did it or not, her hand caressed the mound of her unborn child as she likely connected now with the love bond between parent and child.

I explained my capture by Ildor Veris in more detail now than I'd ever told Casmir, explaining Figor's part in all of it. I did my best to describe my conflicted feelings upon meeting Casmir, and then of meeting more people at court, particularly those from whom I learned the truth of all that had happened to the Sajen family, of the truths about our grandfather Nikolas and the resulting effect on our father. I breezed through our wedding and coronation as well as life at court, focusing more time on the decree banning slavery and our subsequent progression through Agrius, leading to our betrayal on the coast. I described Figor's help in saving us, and the sacrifice he made in doing so. By the time I finished, with many questions peppered throughout by both Kassia and Jack, it was well into the wee hours of morning.

"So you see, Kassia, Jack," I said, eyeing them each in turn, "nothing is as it seems, at least not as you thought when we arrived here. Whatever evils you want to attribute to Casmir, or even to Bellek," I said, eyeing Casmir, "are more properly attributed to Ildor Veris. He is the puppet master behind the throne, the Kingmaker. He initiated the rebellion against our grandfather and put Bellek on the throne instead, simply out of a mind to control the throne. He couldn't have done it with our father, because father realized his position and power and vowed to change things. Casmir was unaware of these swirling undercurrents before, but he has tangible reasons to know all about dear Cousin Ildor now."

Jack studied Casmir as if to ascertain the truth of what I'd just said. He seemed to find the truth there, for his look softened. I felt as if we'd won him over.

"So we host a king and queen in our palace this night. I would offer the deepest obeisance, but I think you'll understand if I refrain." A twinkle lit Kassia's eyes as she spoke. Then turning to Casmir, she placed her hands over his, and offered, "My sister is better at treating wounds than me, though I have had reason to learn a thing or two..." she quirked a smile at Jack who returned it, indicating a shared secret between them. "But between us we will stitch up that cut above your eye first thing in the morning. You are welcome here for as long as you need refuge."

Kassia stood and stretched her back then placed her hands protectively over her swollen abdomen. Jack rose and stepped in behind her, placing his arms possessively around her as he did so. It was good to see her happy, for she glowed with it.

"We will have much more time to discuss this on the morrow. But now it is late. There is a small room off the hall," she said, studying Casmir as if to judge his ability to sleep in such poor accommodation. It seemed as though she considered a sardonic quip then thought better of it, saying instead, "It's not much, but you will be comfortable enough."

"We will be fine, sister." And then I hugged her, each of us clinging to the other. A single tear broke and rolled down my cheek. When we pulled apart, I saw that Kassia's eyes too were wet with tears.

"Oh how I have missed you," she whispered.

"And I you."

"I have much to tell you. Tomorrow. Sleep well."

Jack cracked a smile for me as he led Kassia to their bed.

I rose late the next morning, tired from the arduous days of travel and the late night before. I found Kassia already engaged in her morning chores, and when she saw me, she flashed a wicked smile, making a comment about the lazy noble class. She turned to finish instructing a young boy about work needing completion that day then took my arm. We strolled the yard for a tour of the life that she and Jack had created since moving here.

"The farmstead had recently become vacant, and since I left Elbra with a heavy purse of money, we bought it." Her mischievous smile was back, and it was infectious. "Jack works his trade in the town, but he is happy to walk there each morning since I like the peace and quiet living here rather than elbow to elbow with people as we did back in Corium."

"It has done you well, it appears," I said indicating the evidence of her impending motherhood.

"The babe is due in mid winter." She grinned widely, and I laughed with her. I never would have imagined my sister as a mother. "Jack is beside himself with anticipation. He says the boy will learn his trade and they will work together."

"Boy?"

"Men are nothing if not optimistic about their ability to produce male children, are they not?"

"It is very true," I laughed, and just then Casmir came outside. He had done his best to dust off the worst of the travel dirt from his clothing, but he still looked a rumpled wastrel. I smiled, and Kassia followed my gaze.

"Handsome rogue, that one. But he doesn't look very much like a king, does he? I mean, his clothes, they are in need of a wash. And yours as well. But never mind, he can borrow something from Jack while we wash those." I agreed that it would be a good idea. "You love him, don't you, sister?"

I couldn't hide the blush that rose to my cheeks. "I didn't expect to. But yes, despite my attempts to the contrary."

After finding spare clothing for Casmir then forcing him to endure the stitching of the cut over his eye, we sent the men to town together to inquire after a means of getting us back to Agrius. There was still need for caution sailing so late in the season, but what choice did we have? With heavy warnings that Jack not kill Casmir, and even more severe warnings that he not to let slip Casmir's identity, they set off.

"Do you think we'll see either of them alive again?"

Kassia quipped.

"The odds are equal either way, I'd say. I'm not sure Jack looks too forgiving."

"Irisa, it is hard to change one's opinions of a man when they have festered for so long. Considering all the atrocities we attributed to Casmir... It's not like flinging the spindle. It turns more like the miller's wheel: with effort."

"Come, sit with me and tell me," I invited.

We went back inside to escape the wind and enjoy the warmth of the hearth while she took her turn to tell her tale. When she had finished, the weight of all she experienced sat heavily on me. "It seems I have had an easy time of it, sister, compared to you."

"Irisa, we have both borne our own cares. But no matter. We are together again, for now at least."

We sat quietly for a very long time, each of us lost in our thoughts. There was so much we had gained in the last year and a half, but there was also much we had lost.

"What of Father?"

Kassia's face clouded over momentarily before she recovered. "I will take you to him when you are ready."

"I am ready now. Why would I not be?"

"He has changed since you last saw him."

I met her eyes. "Kassia, I heard what happened to him in the three years he was gone from us."

"How much of it?"

"Well, not much, really, but enough to know that he will not be the same man we knew."

She nodded. "Come then. But prepare yourself."

She led me outside and down a quiet path through the trees toward the town until we came to a small cottage beside a clearing in the woods. Pushing the door open, we entered a dimly-lit room.   A middle-aged woman sat in the corner, tending to her sewing. Kassia nodded to her, and we made our way to a small bed at the back of the room.

"Hello, Father," Kassia said to him. She leaned over him and kissed him on the forehead. He looked at her with rheumy eyes and patted her hand.

What Kassia had warned me about couldn't have been more true. The man in the bed could not have passed for my father if he'd tried. No longer the tall, stately figure he had been in my youth, he lay a frail figure, his hair wisps of wool on the wind. I shook my head and wanted to back away, but Kassia would not let me.

She pulled back and nodded toward the bed, indicating I should move closer to him. My eyes pleaded with her, but she remained steadfast. With a lurch in my stomach, I did as she bade.

"Father, it's me, Irisa." My voice sounded harsh in my ears, scratchy as if a rodent had jumped down my throat and clawed its way back out again.

"Irisa?" He squinted up at me with deep scrutiny.

"Yes, Father."

"Oh, Irisa! You are back, my daughter! You have come just in time. I must tell you what I've learned from the lands distant of the Romanii, of their *Curia Regis ad Scaccarium...*" He continued to speak as I looked to Kassia for help, not understanding a word my father was saying, but she had none to give. He continued on for some time, and when he finished, ended with, "My heart is happy now, my daughter. Now that you understand these things you will be the perfect queen." He misread my quizzical look. "Yes, Irisa, you will be queen some day, did they not tell you? I shall instruct Figor to tell you the details. And your son will be heir after you."

"But Father, I already am..." Kassia coughed meaningfully, cutting me off. "Yes, Father," I finished weakly instead.

"You are the daughter of a king! But now I must sleep..." and just like that he closed his eyes.

Kassia took my hand. "We should go now. He is rarely so lucid. I am happy you could see him this way. I wasn't sure how we would find him."

I looked back as we crossed the room, thinking as we went that it was probably the last time I would ever see him. He would never make it to Agrius, and it didn't seem likely I would ever be back here. At least not any time soon.

"The woman who tends him is the new wife of Rem, Jack's father." Kassia informed me, knowing I wondered about the woman. "She cares for him most days, and Rem is happy to let her. They were friends many long years ago. Perhaps you will meet him — Rem — though perhaps not. He has gone away to market in Wesnin and may not be back for many days yet."

We left Father to the care of Rem's wife and returned to Kassia's home. Once arrived, we set to work scrubbing the dirt and stains from our travel clothes. Kassia admired the quality and skill of the craftsmanship, the intricate embroidery, even down to the details of our underclothing.

"It suits you, Irisa. You deserve nice things." She smiled brilliantly at me as she said this.

I was too caught up in my memories to be infected by her lightness. "Why didn't you warn me about our father?"

"I told you he was greatly changed."

"I had no idea just how much. What was done to him?"

Kassia shook her head, glanced at the door in thought. Finally, she answered. "I don't know, honestly. He has never spoken of it. But when I found him again, we... connected... I don't have to imagine it to know it was awful. A living death."

She didn't have to say more. I knew she referred to her own abuse.

"He thinks he is king, and he is happy. Those few Agrian exiles who live here visit him regularly, just to please him, and he rules them as a king. In his world, he has aspired to his dream."

"He has found peace at last," I offered.

After we had finished with the washing, I left Kassia to empty the tubs and put everything away while I ventured inside to fetch us a light meal. When I returned, she stood up from her work to stretch her back again. Her face took on a look of understanding as I took only small bites of bread, nibbling like a bird.

"When is your babe due?"

"What??" Her question caught me so off guard that I nearly choked as I took a drink. "How did you know?"

She massaged her belly. "Let's just say I'm recently familiar with the signs." I wasn't certain what signs she meant, for I didn't think I had done or said anything different. "I suspected, but when father talked about your heir and your hand came up, covering your womb, I was certain."

"Kassia, Casmir doesn't know. I hadn't even been certain until we left Veria, and since then there just hasn't been a good time to tell him. Now if he knew, he might not let me continue on to Agrius, might want me to wait for him to take action and send for me later when he deems things safe for my return. I don't think I could bear that. I can't bear to be apart from my loved ones anymore."

"Is he a good man, sister, truly? You bear the child of a deserving man?"

"Yes, he is, and I do. And he will be a good king, like our

father would have been. And after all of this, he is not content to let Veris wield the power that is his. He doesn't fully realize his potential yet, but he is getting there. I will help him."

Kassia nodded, and just then the men returned. Casmir's shoulders slumped, his look sullen.

"We bring dismal news. There is no ship available at present, or at least none suitable to our needs. None are large enough to handle the weather this time of year, and no one expects one to arrive any time soon. We shall have to consider other options."

Kassia took Casmir in hand and spun him by the shoulders. "That's a problem for later. You look horrendous." He looked at me over his shoulder as she led him, his face a study in shock at the impudence with which my sister regarded him. I shrugged my shoulders and followed. "Let's get you inside to treat your wounds again."

Once she had him sitting down, she took his face in her hands. "So, is now an appropriate time to ask you why you bought me that horse in Corium?"

"I don't recall meeting you before. What am I missing?"

"The horse trader... the thieving lout who tried to swindle me? You hopped a fence, came to my rescue. I think you had just arrived in Corium."

Casmir's jaw dropped. "That was YOU?"

"Yes. I named her Rose, and she served me well, getting me out of Corium and all the way to Elbra, then safe here to Pania. You were too kind to give me such a gift." Kassia winked at him and Casmir continued to stare. "But I appreciated it. I honestly had no idea what I was doing that day."

When Kassia was satisfied that she had done everything she could for Casmir's wounds, we went out to the stable to meet Rose.

"You may need to borrow her." All eyes turned to Jack, who made the offer as he entered the stable behind us. When none of us followed his line of thought, he added, "Sometimes I think you two forget who you are." We continued to stare at Jack in confusion. "Your mother was a princess, the daughter of King Aleksandar of Pania. Her brother, your uncle, Alexio, now sits the throne. Why not go to him for help?"

Kassia's face darkened. Apparently she had come to terms with her relationship with our father, but not her royal heritage.

"No," Casmir interjected before even Kassia could protest. "We cannot go to Alexio. No one must know we are alive, especially not the Panian court. News travels on the breath of wind and we would lose the element of surprise with that hound Veris. No, there must be some other way."

I noticed that Casmir did not use his normal form of address, *Cousin Ildor*. He used his surname instead, something I often did. Casmir sensed the line of my thoughts. "He is attainted, Irisa — guilty. Or he will be once we return and I affix him with a bill of attainder. I don't intend to let him stand trial, for his actions have already condemned him. He is cousin of mine no longer."

His look darkened, and I put my hand on his arm. "Will the council support you, do you think? Now that Figor is gone... You don't know what he told them, what they think happened. And it's his supporters who fill it now. Will we even be received back?"

"They will have to. Their anointed king is still alive. No one will want to revisit the events that happened to... your grandfather." Turning back to Jack, he asked, "Do you know anyone else who might benefit from having the king of Agrius beholden to him?"

"He's a pirate??" My shriek was likely heard in Veithi itself.

Casmir had the decency to look ashamed. "He's a friendly pirate?" he added helpfully, as if that would change my opinion.

"Casmir, you want to owe the likes of him a favor?"

Casmir turned from me and paced the room. Kassia and Jack had discreetly disappeared when they noticed the tension between us. "Irisa, I don't see that we have much choice. We need to get back to Prille, and we need to do it now. There is no telling what Veris instigated while we were gone. Is Ethew in Prille yet? If not, he is on his way, expecting to arrive for the coronation he was promised. What about the matters the Council was left to discuss while we were away? What matters have they undone now that they've been given the chance?" He looked at me meaningfully, and I knew he referred to the slavery question.

"But a pirate?" My opposition was losing its force. He was right; there didn't appear to be much else we could do, and waiting was not the answer. Not only could Veris cause more damage the longer we were away, we also risked the rage of full winter seas. If we waited too long, they would be impassible.

Casmir closed the distance between us and took my hands. "Irisa, we will get home. We'll straighten this out." He pulled me toward him and I leaned my forehead against his chest. "Swain 'Golden Tooth' and the debt we might owe him is the least of our concerns right now."

"Casmir?"

"Hmmm....?"

"When you said we'd get home just now, do you know

what I thought?"

"What?"

"How natural it sounded. Home." I looked up at him. "Prille is home."

It took Swain "Golden Tooth" two more days to send for us, to tell us we could depart the following day and to meet him at the shoreline of a deep water bay about an hour's ride south of Veithi.

Kassia and I spent what remaining time we had together simply enjoying each other's company. For the first time in all my years, I truly appreciated my sister, and I sensed she felt the same way.

Night sat heavily over the little farmhouse, and Kassia and I relaxed on cushioned chairs near the warmth of the hearth. Casmir and Jack remained stoical, playing a game of dice across the room. Kassia worked on a small tunic for her baby while I plied my hand at spinning some newly washed and carded wool on the drop spindle. It had been a long time, and I was out of practice. Kassia eyed me with amusement.

"So queens don't spin often?"

I muttered a quiet curse under my breath as the fibers refused to carry the twist when the spindle rotated. I tried again. "You would be surprised how hard queens must work." I looked up to see if she believed me and found her smiling her quiet smile.

"Is it so very luxurious then, the palace?"

"You lived at Caelnor, didn't you?"

She looked down. I understood that her time there had been difficult. She thought she had lost everyone she loved, and the experience changed her nearly as much as her time in the

Black Fortress had done.

"Kassia, you have changed. You were once a wild, unpredictable young woman, and now you have grown into... well, an impressive woman."

"We have both changed, Irisa. How could we not have, after all we've experienced since our paths parted? My hardships taught me to restrain my impulses, that there is wisdom in foregoing one's more base inclinations in favor of full consideration."

"You grew more patient?"

She laughed at that. "Perhaps."

"And now you have sheep."

"If ever there was a good reason to have patience!" She grew serious again. "I felt so powerless most of the time, Irisa." I watched her work, her fingers flying as she stitched with precision. "And in the course of time I discovered a strength that I didn't know was possible. I had to. My survival depended upon it."

I swallowed deeply, realizing that my struggles had never been about life or death. Not really. Not like hers had been. She had suffered horrendously at the hands of evil men who had abused her terribly.

"Losing that babe..." Her hands jerked, as if the memory formed itself in a tangible way on the fabric of the cloth she worked for her new child. Tears welled up around her eyes, and I knew she recalled her old demons, no matter how happy she found her present life. "I was happy at first, Irisa. I welcomed it as the solution I thought would erase my memories. But now..." She wiped away her tears. "Now I just mourn."

I rose from my seat and knelt down next to her, taking her into my arms. Soon she straightened, glancing at the men to see if they had noticed.

"Irisa, I am happy for you." She smiled, indicating my still-flat abdomen with her eyes.

"Thank you," was all I could think to say.

We returned to our work again for some time, letting the balm of our companionship soothe us. After a time, Kassia spoke again. "What does it all mean, this game of kings and their thrones? Inside we are all human, not so different."

Just then the men broke into a mutual exclamation of equal parts triumph and defeat, one of them having beat the other at their game. "You owe me a purse of gold now, dear king..." They talked excitedly before starting a new game.

Kassia quirked a smile at them before turning back to me. "Princes and paupers play the game equally it seems."

"Kassia, you did not come away from Elbra a pauper..."

"Perhaps not." She smiled her mischievous smile again and I knew then that not everything about her had changed.

"You will come to Agrius someday to visit? Now that we have found one another again, I could not bear to lose you again."

She remained quiet for a long time before replying. "Irisa, I am happy to remain the daughter of a scribe. You... You were meant to be the daughter of a king."

"That doesn't mean you cannot visit me."

"Then everyone will know who I am. I prefer a quiet, anonymous life."

"We can tell them you are my maid."

My attempt at humor brought a sad smile to her face. "I will think on it."

The next morning we woke early in order to reach the bay before the tide went out. Swain's ship anchored there as promised, a skiff beached along the sandy strip of shore to take us out to it. Kassia rode her horse, Rose, in the lead, while I rode pillion with Casmir. Jack brought up the rear. Once we dismounted, Jack tied our horse to his saddle for the return trip.

Casmir gripped Jack by the arm. "Farewell, Jack, brother-in-law. You have been good to my wife's sister, and for that I am grateful."

Jack grinned widely in response. "A man is good to the wife he loves. I'm afraid it is no more than that, my friend."

Casmir slapped him on the shoulder. "Even so, I would repay you for all you have done. If you ever find that you develop an appetite for a barony, I may be able to help you out."

"My father would find irony in that, no doubt. It's a pity he could not meet you."

"Then you must bring him to meet me."

"I have learned that the impossible is possible. I would not have thought that a year ago."

They slapped each other's shoulders again, and Casmir turned to me. "My queen, our ship awaits."

I turned to Kassia, tears flowing freely down my cheeks.

She leaned in and kissed me, saying, "Farewell, sister. We will meet again, I think," she eyed Jack, "if my husband has anything to say about it." She pulled me into a fierce hug, adding in a whisper, "Send me news about your babe."

"And you yours."

We held each other for a long time, until finally Casmir pulled me away with gentle hands. We boarded the boat to ferry us to the waiting ship, and as we went I watched Kassia all the while. She stood straight and still with Jack behind her, her auburn hair blowing in the wind.

~*22*~

OUR SHIP SAT AT anchor just off the coast of Agrius, around the small headland protecting the entrance to Tohm Sound. As expected, rough winter seas had hampered our passage from Pania, though nothing that matched the anxiety-ridden storm that stranded us in Pania. Even so, it was with great anxiety that I waited out our time aboard ship. Casmir tried to be supportive, but his mood remained non-conciliatory. Any anxiety he might have felt only fueled his anger toward Ildor Veris, motivating him to make a plan for our arrival in Prille.

Much time was spent closeted with Swain Golden Tooth, though lately the pair debated how to get us into the heart of Prille. Casmir argued that the pirate must take us directly into port while the privateer, as he preferred to be called, favored leaving us on the headland to make our way on alone.

"It would take us a month to reach Prille on foot! And that's assuming the weather doesn't kill us first!"

"Better that than us captured as pirates. We're dead if recognized. Better your month long trek than us dead, I'd say."

"And if I don't make it back to Prille, no one else owes you anything," Casmir fumed. "Who's to reward your bravery then, huh?"

On and on the men discussed. Until a decision was reached, we would go nowhere.

"Excuse me, gentlemen," I interrupted late in the day. "Casmir, what about the sea gate? The one to the east of the city at the side of the palace?"

Casmir eyed me curiously. "How do you know about that? I don't think it's ever been used in my lifetime.

"You can thank Wolf. That's where he gave me my lessons. No one goes there, and we won't be there long enough for anyone to question why a ship is docked. Swain can simply drop us off and be on his way."

Casmir studied me, his mouth flopping open and shut like a fish out of water. He shook his head and turned to Swain who screwed up his face in thought, clearly intrigued by the suggestion. His golden tooth protruded out over his bottom lip, giving him the appearance of a wildcat. "Should work." He turned and signaled to his first mate and the navigator to follow him.

While the idea of accepting passage from Swain the pirate had not settled well with me at first, the man had proved himself a worthy sailor and a companionable enough man. I found his manners genteel and refined, and he was knowledgeable on a wide range of subjects. Perhaps he had been a younger son with no inheritance and without prospects, succumbing to the lure of easy wealth, though he remained close-lipped about his past.

Late in the evening, the ship pulled anchor, and we entered the bay at twilight. Navigating a wide arc along the eastern side of the sound, we avoided the busiest part of the port, slipping into the sea gate as I had suggested.

"When you have need of me, send word," Casmir whispered.

Swain simply nodded, then quirking a smile added, "Oh, that I will, you can be sure."

And with that, we stepped out onto the crumbling boards and scurried up to the gate itself, never once casting a glance behind us to see Swain's crew push off, leaving us on our own. Now there was nothing for it but to see who among the palace garrison was still loyal to their king, or if everyone had turned loyal to Ildor Veris.

"Here, take this."

I handed Casmir a sword from the niche in the crumbled wall where Wolf hid our practice swords. He had healed well enough to wield a sword now, though I briefly considered taking the other one along just in case.

I remembered the heft and weight of the steel length as I returned many times to practice, extending it in a reach, making circles with my hand. My outstretched fingers hovered near the grip momentarily. *You never want to pick up a sword in a moment of panic, thinking to defend yourself with it,* Wolf had said. No, I would rely on my knife.

By this time night had fully descended over the city. The sky was clear, the weather mild. Winter's grip would not fully tighten on the land for a few more weeks yet; even so, a light northern breeze brought with it enough of a bite to remind us the bitter season was not far off.

Casmir pulled me close to him, pressing a kiss onto my lips.

"What was that for?" I whispered.

He shrugged and raised his eyebrows. "It's just a habit I've formed, to kiss my queen before setting off to retake the capital single-handedly. That's all."

"Oh."

"Now that we're here, I'm not sure where to start."

"How about in the guard tower in the lower ward?"

"Why there?"

"Because I know someone who will help us. I can't imagine he has changed his loyalty in the last several weeks, though I have no idea if he is on duty. We'll only know if we check."

Casmir nodded agreement, then glancing over his shoulder, added, "I will have to remember to secure that water gate. We can't have any more rogue kings using it in the future."

We threaded our way around the out buildings and into the kitchen garden behind the great hall. Everything was silent here, as it should be. Unless someone used the garden for a secret tryst, it would be empty overnight.

While it would have been quicker to choose the route directly through the great hall, that was the last place we needed to be seen before we could ascertain the quality of our reception. Instead, we chose to skirt the inhabited areas, keeping our backs to walls as we came across them.

We stopped behind a thick courtyard hedge to allow a watchman to pass us unseen. Once safe to continue, we threaded a circuitous route along the edges of the final yard to reach the last crucial passage: a gate into the lower ward.

"This person who can help us, you're sure his help is worth it?" Casmir whispered. "If we commit to leaving this ward and go through that gate, we face whatever fate awaits us. If we are seen, there is no place to hide. This could be the fastest counter-coup in history."

Casmir's face appeared disembodied in the feeble light of the waxing crescent moon. How many nights had I seen that same face in the safety of our chambers? A pang of grief pierced me, and I wished, more than anything else in that moment, that we were back there now, that we had stopped Veris before any of this happened.

"His name is Luca, and I befriended him after Chloe's encounter in the guard tower."

"Of course you did," he said dryly. "You would."

He squeezed my hand and we turned our attention back to the gate. Each of us had processed through it countless times, though never had its formidable construction intimidated so much. Narrow and tall, its uppermost arch curved to a graceful point. Patterned and dressed with bright white stones, it reflected the dim moon making it glow.

"Casmir, do you think he knows we'll come?"

He remained quiet for some time. "I would think so, yes. When everyone failed to return to that ship, likely they sent someone back to check on what happened. They found the dead men."

I thought of poor Figor left there alone with the guards who had betrayed their king, and I shuddered.

"Possibly they did a quick perimeter search, but it was better for them to make a hasty retreat and return to Prille as soon as possible."

I eyed the sword strapped to his waist. "Will you have to fight him?"

He saw the direction of my gaze and softened. "I hope it doesn't come to that."

"But if it does? Casmir, your experience does not extend beyond the practice yard."

He cocked a smile. "Do you doubt my abilities, my love?"

"You know I never meant..."

"Irisa, I'm only teasing. It's true what you say, and one of the downsides to the peace Agrius knew during my father's reign, but remember that neither has he. I would never make him out to be a coward, but he is a man happier in the campaign tent than in the open field. And don't forget that he's got a good twenty years on me. That's got to count for something."

I felt less than reassured, but there was nothing for it.

We waited there for some time, watching and breathing. Finally Casmir rose, offering me his hand. "We go, now."

As it turned out, we had nothing to worry about. The gate and adjoining yards were empty. Our going became easier, for the lower yard provided more coverage as we made our way toward the tower on the outer wall, overlooking the city.

I dared not dwell on the weakness of my plan - that we had to find Luca who was likely tucked away snugly in the barracks, fast asleep. As it turned out, the night winds blew our way.

"That's him, descending the stairs from the wall," I whispered to Casmir. "Luca!" I called out, raising my voice to a speaking level without shouting. Luca instantly raised his weapon.

"Who is it?"

"Luca, it's me, Irisa."

"Irisa..." He sounded confused, his sword tip wavering in his uncertainty. "You mean the Queen?"

A look of utter horror crossed his face. Likely he thought me a malevolent spirit, for if Addis was to be believed, news would have spread that we'd perished in the storm. He began to slowly back away.

"Luca, wait, I'm alive, look! In the flesh..." I emerged from the shadow and walked toward him. I overheard Casmir inhale a sharp breath, worried for my sake that Luca might not be reassured and try to run me through with his weapon to test his specter theory.

"Indeed, it is you!" Relief flooded over his face, and he looked around him quickly to make sure we were alone. "Word came that you and the king had been washed overboard in the storm. I didn't believe it, but it is hard to dispute news of events when you didn't witness them firsthand."

"We were betrayed, Luca."

He nodded, as if this was no surprise to him. "Come, let's get inside before someone sees you."

He made to pull me along behind him, but I stopped him. "Wait, just a minute. Casmir!" I called back. Casmir came out from hiding and joined us. Taking this newest revelation in stride, Luca simply nodded, then turned and led us inside.

He directed us toward the stairs and the area just beyond it where a wicker screen hid a pallet. Sleeping soundly in the pallet was Chloe, and in that moment I knew we had a chance.

"Casmir," I whispered, "Look who it is!" I tugged at his sleeve, but Casmir only seemed confused. "Luca, why is Chloe here?"

His look turned sheepish. "When she returned on the Arnborg, what was she to do? Her mistress was dead, or so she thought. There was no place left for her. I couldn't leave her abandoned, could I?"

I offered him a knowing smile. "No, of course you couldn't. How gallant of you, Luca."

Our conversation disturbed Chloe, for we heard a deep intake of breath, and she rolled over, stretching. "Oh!" she startled, as if she too had seen a ghost.

A milky light washed over the predawn sky as sea birds called out to one another in the daily hunt for breakfast. I pulled my thin blanket close around my shoulders, fighting to stay warm in a cold room above the armory which was now our hideaway. Casmir still slept near me, having been up until only a few hours before, talking to Luca. Lines of concern tight around his eyes the night before smoothed out now as he slept, relaxed away by his stolen slumber.

I eyed the edge of his pallet, wondering if there was any way I could curl in next to him to stay warm. The chance that I would wake him wasn't worth his loss of sleep, so I remained where I was, shivering instead.

I turned my thoughts to the previous night. After we'd discovered Chloe, Luca called another duty guard to him, and after a few quiet words with a promise to explain the situation later, he ushered us away from the guard tower, up onto the curtain wall, and along it into the upper ward by a way known only to the patrols. After waiting for several sentries to change shifts, Luca led us into the armory and up a set of rickety stairs to the loft above.

"This is used for long-term storage only, and since there hasn't been a war in... well, since before our grandfathers' day... these things mostly rot." He motioned to the storage crates of plate mail and hauberks, sacks of arrows and other items. Unless the armorer decides to tally inventory for the first time in all the years he's had the post, you should be left alone up here."

We cleared space behind a sturdy stack of crates, making beds out of piles of quilted jerkins, then sat down to a council of war.

"Taibel Rebane is now Captain of the Guards, Veris' old position after you made him Chancellor. The Árvök only arrived a week ago, and the city has been scrambling to mourn you and the queen."

"Do you think they suspect we'd try to come back to

Prille?" I asked.

"Oh, they have to believe it. They can't imagine I would do anything else," Casmir replied.

Luca went on to explain that Veris had agreed to the city's request to prolong the usual mourning period by a week, and once that was done, it would be time for a new coronation.

"Ethew is here, only just arrived from Pania two days ago."

"Does no one find the timing a bit suspicious?"

Luca shrugged. "I can only tell you the rumors I've heard, nothing more. Rebane has his most loyal men in the posts that make them closest to those kinds of secrets, I'm afraid. We don't learn anything first hand down on the wall."

The men continued to talk about the King's Guard and its makeup, and while they did so, I whispered to Chloe. "How about my women, what of Raisa?"

"She is still there, my lady. Your household has not been dismissed. Not yet. No one knows what to do with your things, so until someone else wears the crown, she still looks after your apartments along with the maids and other pages. Shall I fetch you some new clothes? Something to make you look more... queenly?"

I spread my hands over my skirt, one lent me by Kassia before we left Veithi. It was plain and simple but had served me well enough.

"Not if you have to tell her why you need it, no. For now, the fewer people who know we are alive, the better."

"But what if I can do it without her knowing?" She curled a smile and I laughed despite myself.

"Well then, in that case, yes. Only so people don't think me a kitchen maid. Nothing extravagant. Just a day gown."

Chloe nodded.

I turned my attention back to the men who discussed rumors of the happenings in the Council chamber. A long debate had raged all week, with some men wanting much more time to plot the course ahead. Crisis gripped the Council, and while many of them were loyal to Veris, the rest had enough wisdom to advise caution. Ildor Veris needed to buy enough time to soothe ruffled nerves, for it would go better for him if they were on his side, and this worked in our favor.

"What of Wolf," Casmir asked Luca.

"And Addis," I added peevishly.

"Wolf is gone," Luca related. "He raged like a madman when he heard the news, threatening anyone he thought might be cowed. The Council didn't take well to it. To make it worse for him, Addis spoke against him, claiming he had swindled the exchequer and stolen funds meant to improve the king's highway. They sent him under guard back to Bauladu, and his lands have been placed under direct control of the Crown until he pays the heavy fines."

"They didn't take away his titles then?"

"No, not yet. For the time being he just has to pay the fines."

"And Addis?" I reminded him.

"Addis left for Aksum almost immediately after she indicted him."

Casmir took a moment to consider all we'd just learned and chewed on it, standing to pace. "We are in a better position than we could have been, though not as good as I'd hoped." He paced some more, and I watched him.

"What mean you to do?" I asked him, stifling a yawn.

It was well into the early hours of morning, past the darkest part of the night. We had been up at the break of dawn the previous morning, and it was all I could do to keep my eyes open.

"I am going to visit the Council."

Luca eyed him. "Are you certain that's the best move?" And then, as if he'd only just now remembered who it was he was talking to, he added, "sire," with respect.

"They can't kill me outright. You said yourself that some of the Council is still loyal and will welcome me back. They can't cover up my return that way. It's the safest place in all of Prille."

"And how will you get there undetected?"

"I can think of one or two ways," Casmir replied, but he would say no more. "First however, we have to consolidate our allies. There are other King's Guard who we can trust to help us, I assume? Not everyone has turned, have they?"

"No. It might take a few days to figure it out, but I think we should have a good number."

"Won't Rebane turn over the complement of guards to make sure the men are loyal to him?" I asked.

"That would be my first move if I were him," Casmir admitted. He looked to Luca as in question.

"As far as I know he hasn't done it yet."

"Then we'll get started first thing in the morning."

I yawned deeply again, and Casmir took my hand. "Irisa, why don't you get some sleep. Luca and I have a few more things to figure out, but there is no sense in you keeping vigil with us."

I nodded and curled up, asleep before they resumed talking.

"Here, put this on."

Luca handed Casmir a drab garb made of rough wool. Casmir took the garment, giving Luca a quizzical look.

"If you are dressed like me, you'll pass virtually unnoticed. Just act nervous, like it's a new post."

"Which in a sense it is," Casmir quipped. Luca shot him a return grin. They were having entirely too much fun.

Casmir slipped the tunic over his head then donned the surcoat with its crimson and yellow badge.

"How do I look?"

I straightened his belt. "Now if only you could shave." I ran my hand along the edge of his scruffy beard. "They would certainly never recognize you."

Casmir caught my hand and planted a kiss in my palm.

"Then let's just hope my menacing appearance alone will keep them at bay."

He winked and I laughed then scrunched up my eyes and searched his face. "Casmir, you're certain this will work? Why do you think no one will recognize you? You are their king, after all. You grew up here and men know you."

"Irisa, people see what they expect to see. They know for certain that I am dead. Why would I be here? They aren't looking for me, so they won't see me."

It made a certain amount of sense. I hoped he was right.

Luca handed him a kettle helmet, and they crept down the stairs and were gone. There was nothing left for me to do but trust to Luca's ability to keep my husband safe in his own home. Chloe had slipped away before I'd awoken, likely to retrieve some of my things. I hoped she would also bring food, for I found I was ravenous.

"I can cinch it more loosely, my lady," Chloe said eyeing me sidelong.

She had returned as expected, bearing gifts of clothing

and a hamper of food she'd stolen from the kitchens. For a woman of her talents, I'd harbored no doubts that she would. When she helped me slide the old shift off my head to be replaced with a fresh one, she took note of my changed body but said nothing.

I nodded. "Thank you, Chloe."

"Does Casmir know?"

"Not yet. We've not had many private moments these past few weeks."

It was her turn to nod. She knew better than to question my choice to keep the news secret from him. He would have to know soon, but for now it would only serve to distract him.

It was mid afternoon when Luca and Casmir returned. Both men were exhausted, but both wore grins suggesting the day had been a success.

"We started first with my closest friends, men I knew would want to know and would be the first in line to help."

Casmir clapped Luca on the shoulder.

"From there we hovered near conversations to see if we could gauge the mood. A few converts were made this way, after Luca approached them," Casmir added.

"So when will you act?"

The men looked at each other, and as if coming to a silent, mutual agreement, Casmir answered: "A few days. We want to reach several more yet."

"I must get back to my post now." Luca nodded to Chloe. "If you need me, or if anything else comes up in the meantime, tell Chloe. She knows how to find me."

I bet she does, I thought to myself, smiling.

Later that night Casmir and I sat together in the darkness, talking. Chloe had supplied us with ample woolen blankets, so at least we would stay warmer this night since we dared not light even a small oil pot lamp, never mind a charcoal brazier for warmth.

"Did you see Ethew?"

"Yes."

"And what did you think of him?"

He thought for a moment before responding. "He is older than you by several years, but somehow he looks much, much younger."

"I don't know how my mother came to be pregnant with Ethew. Did Soren force himself on her, or did she go willingly to his bed?" I shook my head in the darkness as if that would clear it up for me. "I might not ever know."

"Your uncle will know the story."

"Yes, it's possible."

Casmir spoke of Alexio, my mother's brother, the current King of Pania. Ethew had been raised and harbored there all his life, my mother sent off to marry Bedic of Agrius to hide her secret. How Veris had found out about him I had no idea. Perhaps he'd learned it from Grand Master Lito's stolen book. Evet implied that the Grand Master had known.

"And maybe once this is over, we can find the book of Master Lito's that went missing," Casmir added, reading my thoughts. When I remained quiet, he murmured, "We will clear this up, Irisa."

I nuzzled in against him, welcoming his familiar scent and the extra warmth his nearness provided, and he stroked my hair. I trusted Casmir's assessment. I only hoped we would be in time before anything else happened.

"What will you do if this fails?"

"No idea," Casmir admitted. "We'll just have to succeed."

Two more days of preparation had passed, and Luca and Casmir assembled their support. "The rest will be convinced once they are certain we're in control," Casmir had assured me, shrugging. Most people, be they peasant or minor noble, did not have the right to an opinion. And most people didn't care who ruled them as long as their lives remained peaceful.

Luca turned to me now, late in the morning on this day of reckoning. "My queen, we will proceed, together with a few other men who have agreed to help us, for the upper ward. More will meet us there, and once everyone has taken their positions, we will make our move."

"And you're certain everyone will be there? Veris, Ethew, everyone?"

"That's what we've been told. A decision has been made about Ethew's coronation."

"Irisa, I need you to stay here, do you understand? No matter what happens. If things go wrong, I don't want you in the middle of it. Someone will come back for you and get you out of Prille if it comes to that."

I opened my mouth to protest, but Casmir stopped me, squeezing my hands.

"I mean it, Irisa. Stay here. I could not live with myself if I knew you were in danger. If I don't make it, or if there are plans afoot we know nothing about, you must be safe. Get back to your sister and Jack. Do you understand?"

I pleaded with my eyes, but he pressed me.

"Do you understand?" he asked again.

"Yes," I said quietly, nodding my head and looking down at our clasped hands. I fought back the tears that threatened. It was time to be strong.

Luca handed him the rest of his disguise, the cloak and helmet of a King's Guard to enable them to get to the Council chambers without question, and they slipped away.

After they'd gone, I sat heavily on a stack of crates.

"I've come so far, Chloe. How can I just sit here in isolation, having no idea what is happening, how they fare, and more importantly, what will become of them?"

It was only as I said it that I realized how selfish I'd been. Of course Chloe felt the same way. It was clear that she and Luca had an attachment to one another. She didn't want to be here either, guarding me like a nursemaid.

"There is a back room," she offered, so quietly I almost didn't make out her words.

"What did you say?"

More loudly this time, she said again, "There is a back room. If we leave now I can get us there. No one knows about it."

"And how will we pass unnoticed?"

"People see what they want to see, remember?" she said. "It works for maids even more so than for guardsmen." She smiled the wicked smile I'd come to associate with her schemes and pulled me along behind her.

I tugged at the kerchief Chloe had fashioned over my golden locks. I'd become so used to wearing my hair freely exposed, no longer needing to hide the beauty the gods had given me, that I'd long forgotten how cumbersome the cloth covering could be. Even so, her idea had been a sound one. We were both dressed as ladies' maids, and since no one expected to see me, no one was looking for me. It was easy enough to pass along quickly and silently without much notice. Most people were too caught up in their own affairs to concern themselves with a couple of women.

We'd entered the great hall through the kitchens then skirted the dais and through a small storage area. Chloe pushed aside a rotting tapestry on the back wall, revealing a small door.

She opened it and stood aside for me to enter.

The narrow corridor beyond the door smelled musty and stale from decades of dust and mold. I fought back a sneeze as Chloe nudged me forward and closed the door behind us.

"You will need to feel your way along. The way should be clear, so just go straight."

"Chloe, how do you know about this place?"

She laughed faintly. If I could have seen her face in the gloom I'd have known she smiled knowingly. Instead she pressed me forward, and we set off. It wasn't far, and soon the corridor opened into a small antechamber. It was brighter here, for a tiny window set above a storage rack let in a single beam of sun, and I could make out the lines of scant furniture in the derelict room.

"This used to be the Council armory back when men came to court armed. They had to leave their weapons here before entering the Council chambers."

I just shook my head, not bothering to ask her how she knew the history of this room.

"Peek in there," Chloe said, pointing at the wall.

I did as she bade and was rewarded with a view through a small screen disguised within intricately carved stonework opening into the Council chamber. Immediately in front of the screen was the ornate seat in which the king would sit. Ildor Veris occupied it now. There was no sign of Casmir and the rest of the men.

After my brief survey, I gave Chloe a look. Soon she pulled away and turned back to me, her mouth turned down at the corners.

"Ethew is not here."

"Are you certain?"

She nodded. "We must warn Luca and Casmir before they arrive."

"How?"

"Leave it to me. You wait here. I'll be back."

And with that, she left as silently as if on cat's paws.

I turned back to the screen and watched for a time, but the men simply sat and engaged in casual conversation. No business had started yet, and thankfully Casmir hadn't arrived. I grew restless so turned away to examine the antechamber.

The passageway we'd followed from the Great Hall was cleverly designed, so much so that no casual observer would ever have known it was there from the outside. I certainly had never noticed it. The furniture in the room held layers of dust and clearly hadn't been used for generations. Cloak hooks hung bare and cabinetry empty, but scratches and gouges aplenty gave evidence of past use.

My scrutiny came to an abrupt end with the sounds of raised voices and the scrapings of chairs against the flagged floor of the Council chamber. Casmir had arrived. I rushed back to the screen and peered through. Everyone stood around the table, including Ildor Veris, though two of his personal guards had closed in directly behind him making it difficult to see exactly what was going on.

Everyone spoke at once, voices in upheaval, arms raised, accusations flying. I could not make out what Casmir said, but it didn't take long for him to press his case, for soon the soldiers with Casmir fanned out through the room to claim their territory.

This was the moment in which Veris chose to act. Once those closest to him moved to intercept the armed men and

Veris' personal guards engaged the newcomers, Veris turned and dashed directly for the tapestry hiding the door to the Council Armory, the room in which I was hidden.

I jumped back, away from the viewing screen, but there was no time to hide. As the door opened and he stepped into the room, we came face to face, his eyes finding my own instantly. Without skipping a beat, his long, broad arm lashed out, his fingers grasping my kerchief sure and strong. He swung us, dragging me behind.

I couldn't walk straight, and I nearly stumbled multiple times. A searing pain rippled across my scalp, and panic muted my tongue. He pushed us out and into the Great Hall then whirled me around before him with a shove. The momentum propelled me into a fall, but his reflexes were faster, and he swept me up by the elbows. I gulped a breath of sweet, fresh air.

"Walk, and don't say a single word," he hissed.

Few servants tended chores in the hall at this time of day, but there were one or two. Since Veris was not a man to be questioned, no one dared make eye contact. And since none of them had seen the drama play out in the Council chambers just now, none had reason to raise an alarm even had they been tempted otherwise.

We traversed the tiled hall then out a side door and into the kitchen gardens where we crossed into the sheltering shadows of the outbuildings, weaving our way around and behind, heading for the water gate. Once we reached the flagged pavement where Wolf had given me my lessons with the blade, Veris pushed me toward the parapet overlooking the sea dock below, yanking the kerchief off my head as he did so.

"I commend you, Irisa. I knew you would be back, but your speed has astonished even me," he fumed.

He came up behind me, pressing himself against me, and

wrapped his left arm around my ribs just under my breasts with a grip so tight I thought he might crack them. Then like a flick of a snake's tongue, he brought his blade up to my neck and pressed its finely honed edge against my pulse. I felt a sharp pain and knew he'd pierced the skin. A warm trickle of blood oozed, and I felt my heart beat wildly against my chest.

"Tell me why I shouldn't just slit your throat and push you over the edge this very moment?"

Figor wasn't here to save me this time. No one else knew I was here. My mind scrambled to think of a way out.

"Because I carry Casmir's child," I breathed. "We are worth more to you alive than dead."

~*23*~

HOW OFTEN CAN ONE face impending death before becoming accustomed to it? Perhaps the human mind is not capable of adjusting to such a state. The rise of panic in one's heart and soul is then, the mechanism to keep a person alive, to motivate one to action, to the doing of things not otherwise contemplated in order to survive. I knew in that moment that if I had a sword, I would use it, warning from Wolf or not.

Still I had impacted Ildor Veris with my news. That it had startled him was obvious. His tension softened somewhat, and his grip loosened, even if only slightly. I took a deep breath and tried to calm my breathing. Only a clear head would help me now.

"If you take me hostage, you will have more control over what happens. You'll have the power, and you and I both know you're all about the power," I reasoned. "Casmir doesn't know about the babe yet. The news will be a shock to him, and he will want us back. Do you have any idea what he would give in exchange for my safe return? I carry his child, the heir to the throne after him. He would give anything — at the very least a safe conduct for your passage out of here, if not more."

I knew no such thing. In fact after Addis' betrayal, I

believed any act of mercy on his part unlikely. But it didn't matter. Veris had to believe it, and I knew he was listening. Each shallow breath he took slowed, becoming deeper, more relaxed. With careful movement, I probed inside my sleeve for the small knife I kept hidden there. It was no sword, but I had used it successfully with the man who held me at the ambush; perhaps I could use the same move again, buying me enough time to cry for help even if I couldn't outrun Veris to get fully away.

"You know I speak true," I murmured as I continued to work. My nails scraped the bone handle.

"Perhaps," he conceded.

Finally I teased it close enough to my hand to grasp it. The grip fit securely in my palm as Wolf had taught me. Carefully I slid the blade out, holding it low enough so he wouldn't see. I was just about to raise it, to strike at him over my head, when distant sounds of our pursuers echoed in the small courtyard above the water gate.

Veris turned his head just as I lashed at him, slicing his cheek rather than anything more damaging. With a cry, he spun me, striking me hard with the back of his hand. His hand clamped down on the wrist of my knife hand and he wrenched it away, nearly breaking bones as he did so. I cried out in pain.

Before he could do me any more violence, echoes of running feet met our ears, and Veris spun me around once again, placing the blade of my knife against my neck once more. We turned toward the sound of the oncoming pursuer. The outlines of Casmir and Luca materialized out of the shadows.

"Let her go, Veris," Casmir called. He kept well enough back so as not to spook Veris into doing something stupid.

"Oh, I don't think so."

Casmir took a careful step toward us. "You know I could

call down dozens of guards now if I wanted? The palace is mine again. You can't get anywhere."

Veris barked a laugh. "Ah, but I have a very valuable prisoner. You and I both know I can leave here if I wish."

Casmir flicked a glance at me, and I met his eyes. I returned no look of pleading, only of ice and stone, hard and unyielding. I would not beg him to do anything for my sake. We were all in a tough spot, for Casmir would no more let him take me than Veris would give me back freely. This would not end well for at least one of us, and the longer the standoff lasted, the worse it would be.

Luca made a step toward us, nearer to Casmir's left shoulder, and Veris tightened his grip on me, bringing the blade just under my chin. Casmir didn't turn back to Luca, merely raised his arm, palm out, to stop him.

"Luca, find who you can, those who are not rounding up the betrayers," he ordered calmly.

Luca cast one more glance my way then nodded and ran off, the sound of his pounding feet diminishing with each heartbeat.

"How do you think this will end, Casmir?"

He was far enough away from me still, but even so I could see the vein at his neck pulsing with anger. The muscles of his jaw twitched as his teeth clenched.

"With you dead."

"You would do that to family, dear boy?"

"No, not to family. To traitors."

"Funny you should speak so ill of family, my king. Did you know your wife is breeding?"

At first no appearance of understanding crossed Casmir's features, but then slowly, like the sun at dawn just peeking over the edge of the horizon, a startled understanding crept over his face. The edge of the sword he carried wavered.

"I see you understand our position more clearly."

This did change things. Casmir would be less likely to do anything rash now. Since I wasn't sure what Veris would do next, I knew I needed to act, to force the confrontation. I turned my head and bit down hard on his wrist.

In a single jerking movement, he pulled his arm away and roared, then with the reaction of a wounded bear lashed out with his fist, catching me in the jaw and snapping my head to the side. I skittered across the pavement, my head whirling, black spots forming before my eyes. I landed hard against a wall and slipped down against its side, crumpled in a heap with little knowledge of what happened around me. My entire world had become flashes of pain and throbbing pulses, making my jaw feel like it had enlarged several times its size. I wanted to shake my head, but the motion made things worse. Vague voices echoed as if across a vast gulf, but I could make no sense of the words.

Ever so slowly awareness returned to me, and the sounds of clashing steel overcame my sense of confusion. I scratched at the wall behind me with grasping fingers, edging myself to standing. Casmir and Veris circled each other like savage vultures, swords raised and flashing. The struggle raged with ferocity, each attack brutal and fast with no *dance of lovers* Wolf had told me existed in such a contest.

Neither man appeared to have the advantage, and this despite Casmir's relative youth. Veris showed no signs of weakness. I could do little to help, so held firm near the wall, watching and waiting. Luca had yet to return with more men, and with each attack and block, each counter attack and reply, my heart beat out a pattern, hoping he would be back in time. No personal fear had ever come close to the fear I felt now for

Casmir as I watched the brutish display before me. Each man fought with the passion of one who knew that to lose would mean death.

Very quickly it became apparent that both men had grown weary. Veris' chest heaved with effort, his breathing labored, his motions slowed. Casmir leaned forward, giving up any advantage just as Wolf had warned me.

"Casmir, don't lean forward!"

My warning came too late. Veris caught Casmir's blade in a slide, stopping it on the cross guard then twisting and slamming the pommel back against Casmir's face. Something caught and tore at his skin, slicing a deep cut from jaw to cheek bone. Bright ruby droplets of blood bubbled up from the cut as Casmir fell back. With regained momentum, Veris let loose a savage kick, connecting with his stomach. I cried out and wanted to rush to Casmir's side, but Veris whipped around and shoved me, sending me headlong back at the wall. I twisted to avoid hitting it face first, but as I landed hard on my hip, my head knocked back against stone. Immediately a surge of nausea overwhelmed me, stars replacing what had been open air only moments before.

"You should have stayed away," Veris cried as he lunged to pierce Casmir through the heart.

Just then a blur with flowing dark hair streaked across my vision, launching itself at Veris, causing him to pierce Casmir's shoulder rather than his heart. Chloe. A knife flashed, and with a downward stroke it impaled Veris in the neck, a gush of bright crimson erupting before he could react.

I rose to lunge forward but didn't get far. The last thing to reach my consciousness as the pavement rose up to meet me was a shriek and sight of a crumpling pile of bodies.

Never before had a bath felt more luxurious than it did now. Not even my memory of using a public bath house for the first time as a child could compare. A bevy of maids kept it hot by refilling the tub with freshly heated water carried in buckets from the kitchens. For an hour I indulged before finally giving in. The hour had grown late and I still had hopes of being allowed a visit to Casmir's bedside.

I rose from the bath, water rolling off in rivulets. Chloe met me with a towel that had been heating near the fire over a bed of lavender, and I embraced it, inhaling the calming scent.

I'd awakened in my own bed none the wiser regarding what had happened at the water gate after my world had gone to black. I peered around, discovering a huddle of physicians at the foot of the bed, each scurrying to my side when they realized I had rejoined the land of the living and the awake. The lead physician bustled about to read my signs of wellness or ill health, but I ignored him, begging instead for information about Casmir. Upon hearing my voice, Chloe rushed to my side, glaring at a younger physician who tried to stop her.

"Yar Hátin, all is well. The King is resting, and the doctors are certain that with time the wound in his shoulder will heal well enough. It pierced muscle but did not break bones. They require him to remain abed for some time."

I thought it doubtful they would be successful keeping him there for too long.

"May I see him?"

"Yar Hátin," the lead physician broke in, "he has been given something to make him sleep. He will not wake for a very long time."

"And Veris? What of him?"

Chloe smiled her cat smile. "His fate is very

unfortunate."

"You mean…"

"Dead. Lung pierced. Choked on his own blood."

I shuddered. "Most unfortunate, yes."

She went on to explain how she had followed Luca when he returned with men to help, then circled around the tiny courtyard near the water gate to get closer to the fighting men. Luca held back the men he'd brought, not wanting to intervene too soon.

"Those two may have been intent on killing each other fairly, and Luca intended to honor that, but I wasn't about to let Casmir die. Stupid manly pride."

"You were none too early, I'd say," I replied, a smile playing at the corners of my mouth. "Thank you for intervening, Chloe."

My own head pounded, and though the doctors found nothing wrong with me beyond the sizable lump on the back of my head where I hit the wall and significant bruising at my hip and jaw, they still required me to stay abed for the rest of the day.

It was only by the end of the next day that I felt much better and insisted that I be allowed a bath. "And then I go see my husband," I argued.

I took one more deep breath, allowing the lavender to further the calm I felt. Chloe had only to help me dress and then I would go visit Casmir.

Except that he found me first. After Chloe dried my hair with another towel, I turned to see him leaning against the door frame, dressed in light linen breeches and a shirt open wide at the neck to allow room for the heavy bandages around his shoulder. He stood there and watched me for only a moment before crossing the room in several sweeping strides then dropping to his knees before me. Pushing aside the edges of my towel, he placed his open palms over my gently rounded abdomen.

"Why didn't you tell me?" He turned his eyes upwards to meet mine.

I smiled gently down at him, brushing his hair aside, smoothing it back with my palm. Dark circles smudged his eyes, and he looked pale. I imagined he'd lost a fair bit of blood between the deep gash on his cheek and the wound in his shoulder. The surgeon had done an excellent job stitching his face. The wound looked angry now, but the stitches were tiny and exquisitely done. While he would have a scar, it would be a neat one. His shoulder would require a fair bit more healing.

"I hardly knew myself before Pania," I replied. "There just wasn't time after."

"You should never have come back with me. You should have stayed with your sister."

I took his hands into my own and he rose to stand before me.

"And that's why I never told you. I couldn't stay there. I needed to be with you, to come home."

Chloe took the towel from me and eased a cotton shift over my head. She guided me to a cushioned stool near the fire and worked to comb out my tresses. Casmir began to pace, but fatigue quickly overcame him and he slumped down onto a stool. A maid brought him a flagon and he waved her away, pouring himself a measure into a cup at hand.

"When will my son arrive?"

"Late spring or early summer," I replied lightly. "Men are certainly confident of their ability to produce sons."

He smiled a cocksure smile but said nothing.

After swallowing down a good measure of wine, he set

his cup down and studied me from across the room. Chloe had finished her work braiding my hair into its night plait and draped a warm cloak across my shoulders. She slipped out the door, taking the rest of the maids with her as she went, leaving Casmir and me alone for the first time in our own apartments.

A swath of stars streaked across a velvet night sky, just visible through the panes of glass of the window. I rose from my stool gingerly and crossed to Casmir, taking his hands in my own and leading him to our bed. The hearth still sheltered a vivacious fire, the dancing flames casting shadows all the way across to the back of the room. I put out the rest of the lamps, leaving only a single night candle.

Once cocooned under the coverlets, I studied the bandages covering Casmir's shoulder.

"Is there any hope of retrieving Addis?" I asked.

"I have asked the Council to inquire of Aksum, but it's unlikely we'll ever see her again. We will pursue her, Irisa. I've sent for Wolf for reinstatement. Addis' charge won't stand."

I nodded. "Would they consider her as the new heir after her sister, do you think?"

"Who's to say. I certainly will not put in a good word for her." he stroked my cheek and kissed my forehead. "Irisa, I have been wondering...just before Veris struck me, you shouted out, don't lean forward. How did you know to warn me of that?"

"Wolf. He told me about it during one of our last training sessions. Says he's always known you did it and that he's warned you of it countless times."

"It's true, he has," Casmir admitted sheepishly. "What else did he teach you?"

"Oh, nothing. Only that swordplay is like the dance of lovers."

"Is it?"

"Yes. He taught me that as we danced a volta." I smirked at him in the shadowy light. The volta was a highly seductive dance rarely danced in polite company, and I knew that Wolf had chosen it on purpose, just to rile Casmir. "But that was only after he'd kirtled my skirts," I continued as I nuzzled more closely against him.

"That cockered malt-worm. I'll kill him." Casmir tried to sit up, wincing at the effort.

"That's what I told him too," I said, easing him back with a gentle hand. "But you can't kill him until your sword arm is healed."

"True. Until then, what shall we do instead?" He leaned in eagerly.

"Sleep," I replied, pushing him back.

It took only a few weeks for matters to settle in Agrius, to sort out those loyal to us from those who had turned. Many on the King's Council had to be stripped of lands and titles, sent away in disgrace, with new oaths of fealty taken from the rest. Casmir ordered an audit of the ranks of King's Guards, reassigning and replacing where fault was found.

The citizens of Prille too, required attention. While Casmir's personal physician seemed reluctant to allow him to be too active too soon, Casmir insisted that he must be seen by the people to reassure them that he truly did live. After multiple assemblies before the Seat of Kings, the mood of the city relaxed.

After being captured in the Council chambers immediately on the day Veris escaped with me as his hostage, Taibel Rebane now languished in the deepest depths of prison, awaiting his fate. Ethew had been captured quickly too, though he had been dealt with more lightly, sitting under heavy guard in the comfort of guest apartments rather than prison until we decided what to do with him.

Casmir ordered Ethew questioned closely, and only after listening to the findings called him to the Great Hall for an audience, to draw our own conclusions.

My first sight of Ethew could not have impressed even if I'd wanted it to. He stood tall, with narrow shoulders and a lanky frame, not like my father at all, and I wondered if he took after Soren, my father's brother. His round cheeks and bright hair, his open features and expression, put me in mind of a child, one with no experience of the world. Indeed it took me no more than those first moments to determine that he had been used for ill, had merely been a pawn. Veris would not have bothered with him otherwise.

Casmir clearly felt the same, for neither of us seemed inclined to prolong the audience.

"I don't believe he was complicit in Veris' scheme."

"No, I don't either," I agreed.

"Stupid maybe, but not complicit."

I nodded. "What are you inclined to do with him?"

He sat staring at the bustle of servants preparing the hall for the night meal. Ethew had long since been removed back to his quarters, the Council dismissed.

"I think I want to give him a barony."

I turned to stare at him, raising my eyebrows. His fingernails clicked against the polished ebony armrest as his fingers tapped down upon it in consecutive order. His back slumped, his face pained even though he tried not to show it. His shoulder still gave him trouble.

"Haern is in need of a baron, and I for one would prefer to have Ethew close at hand where we can keep an eye on him."

"Do you think we can trust him?"

Casmir shrugged his shoulders. "Only one way to find out."

"And Rebane?"

"Certainly no barony for him, or do you disagree?"

"He must pay for torturing my father," I replied quietly.

"Never fear it, Irisa. We will see justice done."

"Justice may not be enough in this case. I'd rather have my father back as he was before."

Casmir nodded. "Perhaps you will at least have the chance to see him again. I plan to send for Jack and Kassia once the spring thaw comes. They will want to meet our son, and they are welcome to bring your father along."

"Do you think it's wise? To allow him back here into the city again? Will it renew any remaining hostilities?"

He considered my question. "No. The people love you, and I don't see what good would come from a renewed rebellion to put him on the throne. You are his daughter. Besides, what would he do with a throne in his present state?" He paused and searched my eyes. "He will be safe enough here. In fact, no one needs to know who he is. All the exiles are welcome back if they so desire."

"I long to see my sister again, but I'm not sure if she will come."

"Not even if I create a new barony from a share of Haern and give it to her husband? It's a big place, Haern." Amusement smoothed out the lines of anxiety from around his eyes. He enjoyed this overmuch.

I laughed at that, imaging how Kassia would fare at court again. Still, I doubted if she would be happy about it.

"There is no one I'd rather have keep an eye on Ethew than your sister," he quipped. "He'd not dare defy the Crown again!"

It was a bright afternoon in late spring when we stood in a meadow bursting with wildflowers to the north of Prille. A priest of Zinon wrapped the hands of Luca and Chloe with a strip of cloth as they vowed to live with one another, creating a home together as husband and wife.

The small crowd burst into cheers when it was done. Luca beamed with pride as he presented his wife to the onlookers, a gathering made up mostly of Luca's friends and family, and a handful of ladies' maids who were curious enough about Chloe to come along. It wasn't often that the king and queen of Agrius attended the wedding of one so lowborn as Chloe, a former slave. Stories would abound hearthside this night, I was certain.

After bowing before his sovereigns, Luca kept his chin lowered. Casmir raised up the newlyweds, encasing Luca in a hug.

"Congratulations to the pair of you. I hope for nothing but happiness in your future. Each of you deserves it."

"Thank you, my king," Luca replied, barely daring to make eye contact with Casmir. The events we'd experienced together still had not taken away the awe he held for the man before him or his awareness of the disparity in station between them.

"I am proud to call you friend, but even that is not enough to repay you for all you've done," Casmir continued.

This caught Luca's attention, and finally he looked Casmir full in the face. Chloe watched eagerly, not sharing the same awe for royalty that her new husband did.

"I would try to make up a portion of what is owed you. A

wedding gift."

Casmir handed him a sealed scroll. Luca broke the seal and read the contents, discovering an endowment of land."

"My lord?"

"You will have much to learn, of course, and you may not thank me for that in time."

Luca stared open-mouthed at Casmir, looked to Chloe, then to me and back to Casmir again.

"It is too much!"

I laughed outright at his confusion. "Luca, we would have nothing, not the throne nor the power to grant you even a pittance if not for you," I assured him.

"But I can't... I am only a simple soldier," he stuttered.

"True, which is why you will have a title to go with it."

It was too much to take. Luca's knees went weak, and Chloe hoisted him up, grinning at him then back at Casmir.

"But I can't," he began again.

"You can and you will, Luca," I replied, laughing.

"Now stop arguing," Casmir added.

Later that night we received word of a change in the Bibliotheca. Master Orioc, the man who had taken Grand Master Lito's place, had been removed from his position by the other masters in the Bibliotheca.

"He was forced upon them by Ildor Veris as a reward to him for 'services rendered.' No one was overly pleased by the choice, but what could they do?"

I stared at Raisa as she murmured the gossip she'd overheard behind the screens in the servants' hall. I did not care for the man, but his tone and demeanor had subdued considerably since Casmir and I had returned from Pania, and he'd kept his distance from me. Even so, we had not been able to prove his complicity in the death of Grand Master Lito, nor had we found the missing book.

"Perhaps it's best if you never know the story of Soren and your mother, or of how matters came to be as they are," Raisa whispered, more kindly than was her usual inclination. I agreed that maybe she was right. Though perhaps salay would one day serve me well.

"My lord, a message."

The page dropped to a knee, holding up a rolled parchment sealed with wax.

Casmir and I sat together on a cushioned bench on the balcony outside our apartments overlooking the sea. The sun angled low in the sky, the retreating rays splashing a display of oranges and reds across the dome of the heavens. A light breeze blew off the water, stinging my nose with the tang of salt.

It had become our habit to stand here together this time of day, welcoming the coming night, but now I was too heavy with child to be comfortable, and the unpredictable pains of ever-nearing child birth had begun. Casmir ordered a bench be brought out for our ease, insisting I be as comfortable as possible for as long as may be.

Casmir accepted the message from the page, and I massaged the rounded bulge that was our son. Or so Casmir would have me believe.

I watched his face as he broke the seal and scanned the contents. His expression changed little, and as was usual, I could glean little of his thoughts. I flicked a glance at the page, but there was no help from that quarter. I had no notion as to who had even sent the missive.

Casmir walked the length of the balcony, from one end to the other then returned.

"Word has come from your sister."

"That should be good news, but your face says otherwise. Is it about her babe?"

Kassia had given birth to a son, and they'd named him Cai in honor of the friend who had helped them so much during their escape from Corium. This news had reached us two months ago. Now the mere suggestion that something could have happened made my heart threaten to seize.

"No, her babe is fine. At least she makes no mention of the lad."

The message had been too short. No, the news she sent could only be about one thing.

"It's my father, isn't it."

Casmir nodded then knelt beside me. He took up my hands.

"Irisa, your father..."

"Is dead."

"Yes. He died peacefully in his sleep a fortnight ago. He had never been happier, Kassia says. He didn't know what truly went on around him. He thought he was home in Prille. Do you want to read her letter?"

I shook my head. "No, I will read it later. For now I want to enjoy the peace of this moment."

Casmir returned to his seat beside me and took me in his arms. I laid my head on his shoulder.

"What shall we name our son?"

"Your confidence knows no bounds, does it?"

"What kind of king would I be otherwise?" I made no response, and each of us fell into silence. After a time, Casmir ventured a guess. "How about Bedic?"

"Yes, I think he would have liked that."

"Do you ever wonder what would have happened if Veris

had not found you in Corium the way he did?"

"Yes, I have often thought about that. As you have so kindly reminded me so often in the past, I would be wed now to Isary of Elbra. And we both know how disastrous that would have been. Never mind the fact that our families would likely be at war now. Countless lives would have been lost as a result."

"Oh, my queen... you underestimate the abilities of the Agrian forces somewhat, do you not?"

"Perhaps," I allowed, letting those thoughts drift away. "Even if the man was an evil conniver, I do remain grateful to Veris for one thing - his plan to unite our houses was brilliant, and we will both be forever in his debt because of it."

"I suppose so," Casmir conceded.

"And you are now the king I knew you could be. Had you not been pushed to it..."

"By my brash, presumptuous wife..."

I pinched his arm. "You would be the puppet ruler, and Veris would still wield the power he had for so long."

The evening sun pulled its last rays below the hungry horizon, flickering out like a lamp in the wind.

"Come, my lady. Let us get you to your rest."

Casmir stood and raised me up next to him. I rubbed at my lower back which had begun to spasm like a band of steel.

"You speak wisdom, dear husband. For tomorrow, I think, we shall have a son."

"Or daughter," he added, winking.

25 years ago
Prille, Agrius

THE MAN WAS UGLY. Yet however unfortunate his looks, he'd always carried himself with a quiet dignity. Coupled with his unassuming nature and fierce loyalty to his prince, I generally looked beyond the surface of things, seeing only what was underneath the trappings of his lamentable mortal guise.

The man as he was before me now was something altogether different.

He stooped now, groveling on both knees where he had collapsed after entering my chamber only moments before. Tears streamed down his face, and he clutched at my feet as if for his very life.

The day was warm and I sat on a padded bench near the doors leading out to a marbled terrace overlooking a lush courtyard. It was late morning, and as the sun slanted through the pillared balustrade, light played over his face, casting awkward shadows and giving him a pathetic look.

I set down my embroidery frame since I was loath to work on it anyway, and studied the man at my feet, at the woeful face pleading up at me.

"Figor, what is it?" I meant no unkindness, but my tone was sharper than I intended.

I was to be married in only a matter of days to Bedic, prince of House Sajen of Agrius, and there was much to do. Even so, I felt I owed the man a hearing. He had been a friend of sorts, though at a distance. My father, Aleksandar of Pania, had brought him to live at court, to be tutored and raised up to a life of service to the Crown after a courtier stumbled upon him as a young boy in the marketplace. Once trained, Figor had excelled far beyond anyone's imagination. This youngest son of

401

a minor merchant paid back my father a hundredfold for his kindness.

And then Soren of Agrius arrived at my father's court.

A breeze picked up through the garden, sending a thrill of goose bumps over my arms and neck. I withheld a shudder, though whether it was from the breeze or my memories I could not say.

"My lady... Naria..." Figor's voice shook, and he paused as a spasm wracked his body. "I have come to beg your forgiveness and to ask a boon."

I could fathom nothing which would require my forgiveness. Soren had been granted Figor's services by my father once asked, and had served House Sajen in Prille faithfully since. A more loyal servant I could not imagine.

I arched an eyebrow and inclined my head in invitation that he continue.

"My vain foolishness and bloated pride has started a war likely to bring death to your house, an end to the rule of the Sajens." He swallowed heavily. "Bellek Vitus comes at the head of an army to take the throne."

I sucked in a breath. I had no response for the man, could hardly believe what he'd just told me.

"I am a traitor, my lady," he continued. "No attempt of his would succeed except that I have allowed it. The plan has been set into motion, and nothing can stop it."

His admission hung thick in the air, like a blanket of heavy wool.

"Why have you done such a thing?"

He swallowed heavily, letting escape another sob. "My pride, lady. It would not dispel the competition I have long felt for that son of Inor, Ildor Veris. He taunted me mercilessly in my youth, and used a feeble promise of retribution to goad me into helping him."

"And this brings war upon our land? How could it possibly be so?"

"My lady, I do not have time to explain, for it is a long and winding tale."

My throat constricted. "And what boon would you ask of me?" I whispered finally, my voice steady and measured.

"You must not tell my prince that I had anything to do with it. Bedic must never know, I implore you!"

I removed myself from his grasp and stood, walking unsteadily to the fresher air near the door then out onto the balcony. Figor followed.

After several moments of silence, I managed to speak.

"It seems you have a story to tell me, sir, and I would hear it fully in time. Promise me this." He nodded miserably. "But first I must know why Bedic is never to be told?"

He didn't immediately answer, and I turned to meet his look. What I found on his face was unmistakable. The young man before me was ruthlessly brilliant, a scholar without compare. Yet even so, beneath the staggering intellect beat the heart of a man made of flesh and blood, full of desire and longing just like anyone else. Why had I never seen it before?

The realization stiffened me, and he looked away, ashamed at what I'd discerned so clearly.

"Because if I am to undo what I have started, he must trust me. It is the only way I can help him."

"And why should I trust you?"

The question wasn't overly fair. Figor was one of the select few that knew about Ethew. He'd protected my secret when he had no reason beyond loyalty to do so. He was perhaps the most trustworthy man I knew...had ever known.

Misery pooled behind his downcast eyes, collected in the

creases of his furrowed brow. After taking a shuddering breath, he rasped: "Because I am desperately in love with you."

My heart thudded in my chest, and I turned away from him, taking up the study of the garden. After all the months I'd lived in Prille, the outlines of the greenery, of the hedges and walls, of the paths and walkways, it had all become overly familiar. I saw it all now without really seeing it. My sight looked beyond it to the future, to the consequences of his admission. That my life would change because of what he had just told me was beyond doubt. Just how much that change would be I could not fathom.

After some time I turned back to him and he sank to his knees again in supplication.

My brow furrowed, my eyes cold and hard. "For the love that you say you have for me, you must promise me this: If this war is not stopped, and we are forced to flee, you must do everything within your power, not even stopping short of your own death, to help my husband regain his throne."

"I do swear, my lady. With everything that is in me, I will. You will have my life and my service from this day forward. To the death."

Thank you for reading The King's Daughter! I hope you enjoyed reading it as much as I enjoyed writing it.

Indie authors do best surrounded by the community of their readers for support. Without a publishing house to back me up, I have no "people," which means I have no promotional department working furiously behind the scenes to ensure that the largest number of people possible know about my books. If you enjoyed what you read, it would mean the world to me if you would go to your favorite review site (or your own blog if you have one) and write a review. Even a few simple sentences will do the trick. Once you've done that, tell a friend! I can't do this without you, and neither can I adequately express just how much your help means to me.

With all my heart, THANK YOU!

Stephanie Churchill, June 2017

Author's Notes

If you read *The Scribe's Daughter* and were left wondering what happened to Irisa, I hope your curiosities have been satisfied. Uniting the two sisters brought a sweet resolution to one of the largest remaining dangling threads. It was a reunion that had me waiting far too long to tell! While I would have loved to give their father, Bedic, a happier ending, it wasn't meant to be. Not everything can have a Walt Disney finale.

I wrote chapters two through four with a sense of nervous anxiety. Would these chapters flow into the rest of the book, or would they simply be perceived as an unnecessary dalliance? I am a fan of back story, and I find that the motivations behind the actions of people are mostly complex. Nothing is as simple as it seems at first. Take nothing at face value. For this reason, I decided that the back stories of Miarka and Swine were not only interesting, but also might shed some light on the actions and decisions they'd made in the first book, revealing the motivations behind them. Hopefully those earliest chapters were received in the spirit with which they were meant rather than as a pure indulgence on the part of the author.

Now for a few text notes:

The poem Casmir quotes to Irisa in chapter 11 comes from Edmund Spenser's *Faery Queene*, though I did delete a few lines here and there to reduce the length. It was from this passage that I derived the name "Adonia" from the original "Adonis" in the poem, thinking it a good goddess name.

Inspiration for Irisa's thoughts on her coronation came while watching "The Crown" on Netflix, specifically the episode where Elizabeth Windsor is preparing for her own coronation and contemplating the enormity of what was about to happen to her. Very few people alive can imagine the weight of such an event. If you've not seen this series, I recommend it.

For Casmir and Irisa's coronation, I studied the sequence of events as recorded for Queen Elizabeth I's coronation on January 15, 1559, using the primary material and adjusting it to my personal tastes. If my version of the coronation intrigued you, and you want to learn more about the real one, I recommend the History Today article entitled "The Coronation of Queen Elizabeth" (History Today,Volume 3, Issue 5, May 1953). It can easily be found by doing a Google search.

For anyone who might have been a little confused by the familial connections between House Vitus and House Sajen, I have provided a family tree on my website. Feel free to take a peek: http://www.stephaniechurchillauthor.com/the-kings-daughter/agrian-royal-family/

People are insatiably curious creatures, and I knew there would likely be many readers who wouldn't be able to handle not knowing the sex of Casmir and Irisa's baby (ahem... my mother and Marsha Lambert). If you fit this category, I have a surprise for you! But you are going to have to work for it. Visit my website: http://wp.me/P7hrUg-8p

And finally, a note about the story of Naria, Irisa and Kassia's mother: The book ended with some hints about Figor's secret as well as a significant dangling thread regarding Naria, Soren, and their son Ethew. Rest assured that these individuals will have a chance to tell their own story soon enough. A prequel is in the works!

Acknowledgments

No book is ever written in isolation. Ideas need feedback, prose needs impartial critique, and experts need to be consulted. The King's Daughter is no exception to any of these rules.

My instructions to Mr. David Blixt were simple: "Make it so I don't sound like an utter buffoon." That was a tall order, and I wouldn't ask anyone to do that for me if it was on too large a scale. In this case, I simply needed his help writing Irisa's sword lesson with Wolf near the water gate. Not only is David an author and a playwright, he is also an expert in swordsmanship. David is active as a Shakespearean actor, and teaches on the side. He was a presenter at the 2015 Historical Novel Society in Denver where he taught other authors how to sound believable while writing about swords and swordsmanship. From David I got the phrase "extension is stronger than tension," and specific ideas like having Wolf kirtle Irisa's skirts, and making them dance together. Thanks David.

A huge thank you goes out to my helpers in the trench: Amy Maroney and Linda Hein who volunteered to be early beta readers. There is a time when a manuscript is loose and sloppy and not very mature (painful, if I'm honest). It was through this format that these ladies slogged, and they lived to tell about it (kind of like cup bearers of old). For that I am truly grateful. If you are looking for more wonderful fiction, I would be remiss not to mention Amy's book, *The Girl from Oto*. You can find a book review on my website.

The final level of editing is a copy edit. After reading one's own manuscript 100, 200, even 300 times... (okay, so that may be a slight exaggeration)... an author can't see errors any more. The brain reads what it expects to see rather than what is actually on the page. So for this, I called in a pair of detail-lovers. Dayle Jacob and Linda Churchill (my mother) took on this role, and I can't thank them enough for their perfectionism and attention to detail. One final champion of copy editing was an unexpected but delightful surprise: Thank you, Nicky Galliers, for providing editorial feedback even as you read my ARC for review. I will promote your editorial services to anyone who will listen.

Thanks also to Nicole Benkert who gave me advice on period clothing and cloth. And I would be remiss not to say thank you to my long-suffering husband who rarely complained about a house constantly in disarray or a wife who wandered the house lost in thought for much of the last two years.

I still have to give my thanks to friend and author Sharon Kay Penman whose continual support and friendship started me down the road of authorship. "Have you ever thought about writing" will forever be the cornerstone of any book I write, because none of it would have happened had you not uttered that phrase.

Thank you also to Paula Mildenhall, Shelly Lovegren, Bethany Scuttinga, Rachel Kroll, Rhonda McConnell, and Sarah Strand. Except for Shelly, who inspired a certain character in the book, you didn't actually DO anything. It sure is cool to see your name in print though, isn't it?

And finally, thank you to my loyal readers. Your constant excitement and encouragement kept me smiling and kept me writing. Your support humbles me.

About the Author

I grew up in Lincoln, Nebraska, and after attending college in Iowa, moved to Washington, D.C. to work as an antitrust paralegal. When my husband and I got married, I moved to the Minneapolis metro area and found work as a corporate paralegal. While I enjoyed reading, writing was never anything that even crossed my mind. I enjoyed reading, but writing? That's what authors did, and I wasn't an author.

One day while on my lunch break, I visited the neighboring Barnes & Noble and happened upon a book by author Sharon Kay Penman. I'd never heard of her before, but the book looked interesting, so I bought it. Immediately I become a rabid fan of her work.

In 2007, when Facebook was very quickly becoming "a thing," I discovered that Ms. Penman had a fan club and that she happened to interact there frequently. As a result of a casual comment she made about how writers generally don't get detailed feedback from readers, I wrote her an embarrassingly long review of her latest book, *Lionheart*. As a result of that review, she asked me what would become the most life-changing question: "Have you ever thought about writing?" And *The Scribe's Daughter* was born.

When I'm not writing or taxiing my two children to school or other activities, I'm likely walking Cozmo, our dog, or reading. The rest of my time is spent trying to survive the murderous intentions of Minnesota's weather.

Follow Me

Website:
www.stephaniechurchillauthor.com

Facebook:
https://www.facebook.com/stephaniechurchill

Twitter:
https://twitter.com/WriterChurchill

Made in the USA
San Bernardino, CA
07 December 2017